Malcdm Johnson - No
Lond

Strindberg and Love

— To Derek —

Eivor Martinus

Strindberg and Love

*To Malcolm
with best wishes
Eivor Martinus*

Amber Lane Press

Published by Amber Lane Press Ltd
Church Street, Charlbury, Oxford OX7 3PR

First published in 2001
Copyright © Eivor Martinus, 2001
Photographs: 1-9, 11-18, 20-29 Copyright © The Strindberg Museum, Stockholm
Photographs: 10, 19 Copyright © The Royal Library, Stockholm
The moral right of the author has been asserted

ISBN: 1 872868 33 9

All rights reserved. No part of this book may be reproduced in any form or by any means without permission in writing from the publisher, except by a reviewer, who may quote brief passages in a review.

Printed and bound in Great Britain
by Creative Print and Design Group, Ebbw Vale, Wales

Contents

List of Illustrations 7
Acknowledgements 9
Introduction 11

Part 1   Siri von Essen (1850-1912)

1   The Friend of the Family 21
2   The Young Lioness 33
3   Omnia Vincit Amor 45
4   Happily Married 53
5   Productive Years 61
6   On the Move 71
7   Troubled Times 81
8   Reality Turned into Fiction 93
9   Time to Part 105
10 Siri's Legacy 115

Part 2   Frida Uhl (1872-1943)

11 A Well-Known Beauty 129
12 Friendship and Courtship 137
13 Jealousy 145
14 Not So Happily Married 153
15 Separation and Pregnancy 161
16 The Beautiful Jail-Keeper 173

Part 3   Harriet Bosse (1878-1961)

17 Waiting in the Wings 191
18 The Immortal Beloved 203
19 A Mother and an Artist 211
20 Strindberg as Childminder 221
21 After the Fire 235
22 Harriet's Legacy 249

Part 4   Fanny Falkner (1890–1962)

23 The Last Romantic Attachment 263
24 At the Last Gate 273

Conclusion

25 1912: The Final Curtain 285

Notes 293
Select Bibliography 303
Index 309

List of Illustrations

1. August Strindberg, 1875
2. Siri von Essen, c. 1881
3. Siri as Camille, 1877
4. Siri as Margit in *Sir Bengt's Wife*, 1882
5. Siri, Switzerland, 1886
6. Strindberg and Siri, Switzerland, 1886
7. Siri, 1891
8. Strindberg, Switzerland, 1886
9. Strindberg with his daughters Karin and Greta, Switzerland, 1886
10. Karin, Hans and Greta Strindberg, Helsingfors, mid-1890s
11. Frida Uhl, Vienna, 1892
12. Frida Uhl, London, 1890
13. Kerstin Strindberg, c. 1905
14. Strindberg, Värmdö in the Stockholm archipelago, 1891
15. Harriet Bosse as Puck in *A Midsummer Night's Dream*, 1900
16. Harriet as Eleonora in *Easter*, 1901
17. Harriet as the Lady in *To Damascus*, 1900
18. Harriet as Indra's Daughter in *A Dream Play*, 1907
19. Anne-Marie Strindberg, 1904
20. Fanny Falkner as Judith in *The Dance of Death (Part II)*, 1909
21. Fanny as Judith and Anna Flygare as Alice in *The Dance of Death (Part II)*, 1909
22. Fanny with Johan Ljungkvist in *Swanwhite*, 1908
23. Fanny, 1909
24. Fanny [undated]
25. Greta Strindberg as Kersti in *The Crown Bride*, 1909-10
26. Strindberg, Furusund in the Stockholm archipelago, 1907
27. Strindberg in the Blue Tower, 1908
28. Strindberg, Stockholm, 1912
29. Strindberg's funeral cortège, Stockholm, 19 May 1912

Acknowledgements

The idea for this book came to me when I was dining with some friends at the late Karin Jonzen's studio in Earl's Court in the early 1990s. Karin was a Swedish sculptor who, then well into her eighties, gave wonderful parties. On one particular evening she had invited a young actor who had just left drama school. The conversation naturally drifted into acting and playwriting and the young man aired some very firm opinions about Strindberg, 'the misogynist'. This sparked off a passionate tirade in defence of Strindberg on my part and Karin was delighted about the animated discussion that followed. As we were leaving, she said, 'Why don't you write a book about Strindberg and his women?'

The seed was sown and all I had to do was find a publisher and the time to research the subject. I was lucky to find Judith Scott of Amber Lane Press, who showed great enthusiasm and faith in the project from the beginning and whose searching questions have kept me on my toes throughout. Little did I realize that it would take me more than six years to complete, reading some ninety books on the subject along the way and extending the Strindberg collection on my shelves by at least two metres.

Many people have been extremely helpful in various ways in bringing this project to completion and it is hard to single out any individual in particular. However, during my visits to Stockholm I have enjoyed the kind and generous support of Margareta Brundin at the Royal Library and Agneta Lalander, Marianne Landkvist, Marie-Louise Jaenssen and Erik Höök at the Strindberg Museum. Helen Sigeland and Elisabeth Seth at the Swedish Institute have often helped me at very short notice, and my numerous trips to Stockholm would not have been possible without the International Writers' House on Drottninggatan, which offers subsidized or free accommodation (depending on availability) to visiting authors, translators and playwrights from other countries.

In addition, a bursary from the Swedish Society of Authors and a prize from the Swedish Academy were welcome boosts during this impecunious period and served as an encouragement when the task seemed almost insuperable.

A lot of my research around the world has been conducted by telephone and e-mail and I have had some illuminating conversations with

Carl Olof Johansson, the Secretary of the Strindberg Society, Lars Dahlbäck, Editor of the National Edition of Strindberg's Collected Works, and Sven Hugo Persson at Dramaten.

I am also grateful to Professor Michael Robinson, Docent Hans Göran Ekman and Erik Henriques Bing, and to Dr Karin Petherick, Reader Emerita in Swedish Literature at University College, London, and my old friend Inger Asker, Librarian at the Malmö Civic Library, who have all supplied me with valuable information, data and comments.

Special thanks too to the Cultural Department at the Embassy of Sweden in London and to His Excellency Mats Bergquist and his wife, Agneta, for their generous hospitality when hosting the Strindberg evening to mark the 150th anniversary of his birth in January 1999, where some extracts from this book were read to an invited audience.

I would also like to acknowledge the following for permission to use copyright material: Maj Dahlbäck (*Siri von Essen i verkligheten*), Professor Bo Bennich-Björkman and Mr Richard Cork (articles in the *Svenska Dagbladet* and *The Times* respectively), Thames & Hudson Ltd and J.P.Hodin (*Edvard Munch*), and the Royal Library, Stockholm for permission to quote from unpublished letters by Frida Uhl and Harriet Bosse.

I am also indebted to the Strindberg Museum and the Royal Library, Stockholm for the use of photographs.

During the last fifteen years or so I have had the good fortune to work with many talented directors on various Strindberg projects and each one has offered a unique interpretation of the plays. Most of the time these have been very fruitful collaborations, especially in the case of Ned Chaillet's version of *The Father* for BBC Radio 3 in 1999, and the eight productions that my husband, Derek, and my daughter Charlotta have directed between them. Working with one's own family means that one can use a kind of shorthand which is very rare in writer/director relationships; because of a greater understanding of the Swedish psyche we have been able to explore areas that are not always so obvious to English-born directors, and for this I am very grateful.

Last but not least, I would like to acknowledge the valuable work done by the late Michael Meyer, who made Strindberg accessible to a large English-speaking audience in the 1960s and published the first major biography in 1985. I don't always agree with his translations but he managed to bring Strindberg out of the stilted academic mode and gave him a voice in the wider world.

Eivor Martinus
London, April 2001

Introduction

It is hard to imagine an author who has been more accused of misogyny, at least in Britain and America, than August Strindberg. It is true, he did utter some outrageous things about women, but then he made some pretty offensive remarks about a lot of other things too, including fellow writers, politicians, the monarchy and the Church. He was a formidable *provocateur* and thrived on controversy. In *A New Blue Book* (1908) he wrote: 'The fact is – and this is something that every man in love knows – a woman, when she is attracted to a man, is able to penetrate him with her soul or parts of it, so that he loses himself and becomes obsessed by her.'

This, I believe, is the key to Strindberg's fascination with women. He fell deeply in love many times in his life and he clearly enjoyed the company of women and yet the label 'misogynist' has stuck. It is interesting to note that none of Strindberg's wives or close women friends ever called him a woman-hater, and he used to make fun of the epithet himself and was the first to protest against the veracity of it.

I think one of the reasons why Strindberg has this reputation in Britain and America is that only a very small, unrepresentative sample of his work is staged in English on a regular basis. Although several of his plays have been published in new translations and/or performed on the London fringe in the last fifteen years there are still others that deserve a decent production. None of the History plays, for instance, and hardly any of the Symbolist plays, have been given a major production yet. It may be that English-speaking audiences want to have their prejudices about Strindberg confirmed again and again, and that is why his harrowing marital dramas are preferred to the more intellectual or metaphysical work in his repertoire. But Strindberg wrote sixty-five plays and at least twenty of them are of sufficiently high quality to be reckoned with.

A few of these lesser known plays have been produced by the Gate Theatre in London in recent years. In the early spring of 1985 I was approached by Pauline Cadell, a young actress who was looking for 'Strindberg premières'. She had acted in *The Stronger* and *Creditors* and this had prompted her to find out more about Strindberg. She felt convinced that there must be some interesting but unknown plays waiting to be translated and presented to an English audience. The Gate Theatre had offered her a slot in September that year. After a long search we finally settled for three one-act plays – *The First Warning, Pariah* and *Motherly Love* – to be performed as one evening's entertainment with two short intervals. My translations of those plays were the first to be seen in Britain for about seventy years. The production was staged on a shoestring and was well received by the critics. It was even billed as 'Critic's choice' in both the *Sunday Times* and *Time Out* magazine. The three plays were subsequently published by Amber Lane Press in 1987 and although I did not realize it at the time that was the beginning of my serious relationship with August Strindberg. Four years later *Thunder in the Air*, Strindberg's first chamber play, was put on at the Gate Theatre and the Absolute Press asked me to translate five more works, including Strindberg's last play, *The Great Highway*. In the last ten years many of his more obscure dramas have been done on the fringe in other translations.

There is still a lot of uncharted territory waiting to be discovered and in order to whet the appetite I have introduced some unfamiliar women characters from his plays and short stories in this book. Most of the extracts are, by necessity, very short, but I hope that these will present a more complex and at the same time more sympathetic portrait of Strindberg than the traditional one.

Strindberg was especially enthralled by talented, artistic women and altogether he was married to three – two actresses, Siri von Essen and Harriet Bosse, and one writer, Frida Uhl – and he proposed to a fourth, Fanny Falkner, who was initially an actress and later became a professional painter. These four women are the subjects of this book.

Each time Strindberg fell in love he felt as though he had jumped over a precipice. He had great respect for science and he was used to looking at the world in a rational way so love, when it hit him, intensified his naturally passionate nature and made him lash out. Whenever he was in this state his raw emotions were like sensors and he over-reacted at the slightest hurt, whether real or imagined. But how seriously should one take these outbursts? To what extent were they the result of circumstances beyond his control?

The passion that ran away with his feelings often turned into the fuel that engendered some of his best plays. He also used it to explore the darker corners of the human psyche, and in his ruthless pursuit of truth he never shied away from exploiting himself or his lovers as raw material. He would take a personal experience or a feeling, heighten it and then highlight and magnify it to suit his own dramatic or, in his own opinion, 'scientific' purposes. His honesty may have been shocking and cruel at times but it was also redeemingly disarming and he was always conscious of what he was doing. As he wrote to the Norwegian writer Jonas Lie in 1884, 'In me there is a brutal, animal-like urge to tell the truth.'

Siri, Frida, Harriet and, to a much lesser extent, Fanny, were all clay to him and it is perhaps thanks to his relationships with them that he has left behind a series of unique portraits of some of the strongest and most intriguing women in world drama. But to draw a direct line from these real-life women to his fictitious heroines and label them 'distorted truth' would be a gross over-simplification of the whole creative process.

There is no doubt that Siri von Essen was his first great love and the first woman to combine all the qualities that he worshipped: intelligence, beauty, youth, sensitivity, spontaneity, a certain dignified aloofness. Like the others who came along later, she could also be vulnerable, unpredictable, capricious, stubborn and flirtatious, which he found unsettling.

As a young couple eager to make their mark in the world of the theatre, Siri and Strindberg were well matched, at least to begin with. The cracks in their marriage start to reveal themselves after Strindberg's trial on a charge of blasphemy in 1884. Before this, he had been an early pioneering spokesman for the rights of women, as is evident in his introduction to the short stories in the first volume of *Getting Married*. However, it was this very book that led to his prosecution in the first place and he blamed one particular woman, Queen Sofia, whom he believed was instrumental in getting the case to court. Even though he was acquitted of the charge, he felt he had been publicly humiliated, and it is in the second volume of *Getting Married*, written shortly afterwards, that we begin to see the first signs of the bitterness and hatred towards women that he was capable of expressing.

Things were not helped by the poverty that Siri and Strindberg endured while they were married. They were living abroad for most of the 1880s, travelling all over Europe, settling in one place for no more than a few months at a time, and with three young children, Strindberg was driven to the brink of a nervous breakdown on many occasions while trying to earn enough money to support them. Under these circumstances it is not surprising that their relationship ended in divorce. I strongly believe that it was poverty more than anything else that finally destroyed their relationship – and his second marriage, to Frida Uhl, as well, for that matter.

It was while he was struggling to keep his marriage to Siri alive in the late 1880s that Strindberg wrote *The Father, Lady Julie* and *Creditors* –

considered by many to be his three best plays. The women depicted in these dramas are driven by the same passion and fury as their male counterparts and their psychological make-up is just as complex.

Laura in *The Father*, for instance, is no submissive, conventional nineteenth-century heroine, even though, as a wife and mother, she has no legal or economic independence from her husband. What Strindberg gives her is a superior intelligence and the will to outwit the man who assumes he has the God-given right to control every aspect of her life just because she is his wife. It is her cunning and her intuitive knowledge of his weaknesses that gives her the power to emasculate him and drive him insane. It is every man's nightmare and it was Strindberg's too.

Many of us can identify with Lady Julie as a powerful character – intelligent, sensual, highly strung – constrained by social conventions that will not allow her to follow her own instincts. In spite of her high birth and privileged background, she is trapped. She has enough spirit to break the rules by seducing a servant in her father's household but has no way of coping when he subsequently rejects and humiliates her. Suicide is ultimately the only honourable course open to her.

In his foreword to the play Strindberg issues a warning to women who engage in this kind of battle of the sexes. He condemns the man-hating 'half-woman', that strange mixture of suppressed female sexuality and male ambitions that he felt he had identified in the lesbian artists that he had met (most notably Siri's friend Marie David, whom he claimed had tried to turn her against him), as a stunted and ultimately tragic type.

Tekla, the heroine of *Creditors*, is less easy to define. Like Lady Julie, she is seductive and intuitive but Strindberg turns her into a vampire. And though she is by no means a direct portrait of Siri, it was his way of expressing his fear of women as all-powerful, devouring creatures at a time when his marriage was falling apart.

But this is not the only image of women that Strindberg presents and in many of his plays he portrays them as tender, loving companions to men. This is certainly true of the loyal Kristina in *Master Olof*, Margit in *Sir Bengt's Wife* and Lisa in *Lucky Per's Journey*. And elsewhere his heroines are more mythic and have something almost holy about them, for example Eleonora in *Easter*, Indra's Daughter in *A Dream Play* and the Hyacinth Girl in *The Ghost Sonata*. These are women who represent an almost platonic form of love, based on equality and mutual respect, and maybe they reveal more about Strindberg's attitudes overall than Laura, Lady Julie and Tekla.

It is, of course, important to remember that Strindberg was not alone in feeling threatened by the growth of feminism. His attitude was common among men at the time and in many ways he was more progressive than most of his contemporaries. His vitriolic attacks on women were, largely, 'theoretical', according to him. In practice, he was unusually tolerant and supportive of his wives and their desire for independence through their own careers. But some of his statements still have the capacity to shock, and however puzzling and untypical they may seem, we have to accept that they are a part of the paradoxical man that was Strindberg. His worst excesses cannot be excused but we should be careful not to place too much emphasis on them.

In *Strindberg and Love* it has been my intention, as far as possible, to let Siri, Frida, Harriet and Fanny speak for themselves, through their letters, interviews and autobiographical writing, about their relationship with Strindberg. One thing emerges clearly from this material: for each of them he was the most important influence in their lives.

Siri, as the only one of the four women to die before Strindberg, did not write an account of her life with him but we have the fascinating letters that they exchanged when they first met while she was still married to her first husband, Carl Gustaf Wrangel. Strindberg collected this correspondence together into an epistolary novel called *He and She*, which was published posthumously.

Strindberg's second marriage was the briefest – he and Frida Uhl effectively lived together for just eighteen months – but because they were often apart they wrote a large number of letters, many of which have survived. Young and vivacious, and with a generous and loving nature, she arrived like a whirlwind in his life and swept away the depression he was in after a messy divorce from Siri and a lost battle for custody of their children. Frida produced a highly entertaining if not altogether reliable book about their short time together, entitled *Marriage With Genius*.

When Strindberg's third wife, Harriet Bosse, announced that she planned to marry again in 1908, he returned all the letters that she had written to him. She destroyed most of them but Strindberg carefully kept the letters of his that she returned to him, intending to use them as the basis for a work of fiction; the bundle that was handed back to her after he died was labelled *Inferno 2*. After keeping the letters private for many years, Harriet allowed them to be published, together with an introduction and commentary that she supplied, in 1932. A second batch of letters that Strindberg had written to Harriet in 1901, and just eleven that she had sent to him at the same time, surfaced many years later.

These letters show a man who was much more forgiving and humble than he had been with his first two wives. While Harriet was young and headstrong, Strindberg, with a store of professional failures and personal disappointments behind him, had mellowed somewhat by the time he married her in 1901, though he was still a romantic, was still capable of feeling intensely jealous and had not lost his capacity for passion.

There is one writer, Adolf Paul, who knew Strindberg well and met all three of his wives, and he gives a short description of each of them in his book *Min Strindbergsbok*. He dismisses Frida as manipulative and coquettish, and while he is respectful about Harriet, it is clearly Siri who evokes the greatest sympathy:

> It wasn't easy to meet Mrs von Essen, but in the end I was lucky and I stood before a tall, slender woman with slightly greyish hair and a lined face. Her resemblance to Strindberg was striking! The same facial expression, the same hairstyle and a lot of other things which showed how much the two had absorbed of each other during their long marriage. One had the definite feeling that they belonged together and that they were inseparably united despite the divorce.

The last significant woman in Strindberg's life, Fanny Falkner, inevitably failed to occupy such a key role as any of his three wives. They met just four years before he died and developed a close friendship but never married. She wrote one book about their relationship, *August Strindberg i Blå Tornet*, which was published in 1921.

Apart from the sources mentioned above, I have also turned to accounts written by Strindberg's close friends and relatives, as well as drawing from his own *Occult Diary* and his semi-autobiographical novels *A Madman's Defence*, *Inferno* and *The Cloister*. But, above all, I have let Strindberg speak for himself through his letters. We have to bear in mind that he was aware that everything he wrote was destined for publication at some stage so one cannot take even his personal correspondence at face value. So this material does not always constitute a reliable primary source – he was capable of some surprising contradictions at times – but that is the essence of his mercurial personality.

The more you delve into his world the harder it is to define Strindberg, the man. There are no ready answers. He was always open to new ideas and always prepared to revise his opinion about things. His mind moved at breathtaking speed and it is very hard to give a fair portrait of this intellectual giant without taking sides or without lifting certain sentiments out of their context. To me, this statement from *A New Blue Book* sums up his true feelings about women and love:

> In my visions of something really beautiful I always include a walk by the seashore with the person I love. There is no need to talk, we just walk beside each other and feel in tune; and you can feel every vibration, sense every wavelength in the other person.

Part 1
Siri von Essen (1850–1912)

— Chapter 1 —

The Friend of the Family

The Baroness in particular perplexed me. When I tried to conjure up her picture, I was confused by the wealth of contradictory characteristics I had discovered in her and from which I could choose. Kind-hearted, charming, brusque, enthusiastic, communicative, reserved, cold, spontaneous – she seemed to be subject to melancholy moods and brooding over-ambitious dreams. She was in no way commonplace; and without being clever, she made a strong impression on people. Of Byzantine slenderness, which allowed her dress to fall in simple, elegant folds, like the dress of a St Cecilia, her body was of bewitching proportions, her arms and legs of extraordinary beauty. Every now and then the pale, rigid features of her small face lit up momentarily and displayed immense gaiety.

A Madman's Defence

Strindberg's novel *A Madman's Defence* is a fictionalized account of his relationship with his first wife, Siri von Essen. With echoes of Maupassant and Musset, it is a shockingly intimate story of a passionate affair that develops into a troubled and stormy marriage. By the time Strindberg started writing the book, in 1887, he and Siri had known each other for twelve years and had been married for nearly ten. Now, after countless quarrels, their relationship was finally breaking down. Lack of money and Siri's poor health had put great pressure on the marriage.

Although Strindberg used Siri as a role model in many different ways during the time that they were together, and in spite of the bitter feelings he had about her towards the end of their marriage, the archetype he always returned to was the early one of her as a 'child-woman'. It was an image that went very deep and one that he could never quite eradicate.

The character of the Baroness in *A Madman's Defence* is a highly exaggerated version of Siri, and Strindberg's portrait of her as a faithless wife is acerbic and cruel but there are places in the novel where his lyrical descriptions of her just shine through and seem to capture her essence:

> What struck me about the Baroness was her girlish appearance. Her body was almost that of a child, even though she must have been at least twenty-five years of age. She looked like a schoolgirl, with a pretty little face framed by roguish curls, golden as corn. She had the shoulders of a princess and a supple, willowy figure. The way she

bowed her head expressed at the same time candour, respect and superiority. And this delicious little girl/mother was still hale and hearty after having read my tragedy!

With her complex personality, Siri was the sort of woman that Strindberg would often be drawn to: aristocratic but somewhat unconventional, impulsive, strong-willed and unpredictable, a natural flirt, and capable at times of displaying a shocking lack of inhibition – a real-life Lady Julie, in fact. For the first twenty-eight chapters of *A Madman's Defence* he refers to her simply as 'the Baroness' as if her title alone embodied all that he finds irresistible and powerful. She is unattainable and he worships her. And then the transition, so imperceptible to the casual reader: 'the Baroness', Madonna figure and goddess, turns into a fallible woman called Maria. It happens at the same time as her magical aura begins to disappear and she is reduced to the same mortal level as her lover.

When Strindberg first met Siri in 1875 she was twenty-four and married with a two-year-old daughter, and he was twenty-six and working as an assistant librarian at the Royal Library in Stockholm. They were introduced by a mutual friend, a young professional pianist called Ina Forstén, who, like Siri, came from a Swedish-speaking Finnish family.

By the time he took up his post at the Royal Library in December 1874 Strindberg had been a student, an elementary schoolteacher, a private tutor and an actor. He had also worked for a while as an apprentice to a doctor, who encouraged him to study medicine; he had abandoned this idea when he failed a preliminary exam in chemistry. In 1867 he had enrolled at the University of Uppsala and his main subjects in the Department of Humanities were Aesthetics and Modern Languages; he completed only six of the eight courses that were required for a degree and so he never officially graduated. With his impatient nature and rather unorthodox attitude to learning he found it difficult to keep within the framework laid down by academia and preferred to spend his time writing discourses in the form of fiction. He also needed to earn some money to support himself. His father had started him off with a small allowance but was unable to continue. Strindberg was the only one in his family to go to university and there were younger brothers and sisters still at home. Like many students, he turned to teaching in his spare time and private tutoring in the vacations to supplement his income.

Strindberg's acting career lasted for barely four months and was totally undistinguished. He joined Dramaten (the Royal Dramatic Theatre) in Stockholm as a trainee in September 1869 and by Christmas he had left.

He was offered only walk-on and minor speaking roles and at the students' end-of-term production found himself ignominiously relegated to the role of prompter. Frans Hedberg, a popular playwright, and the dramaturge at the theatre and head of the school of acting there at the time, told him that he would never make it as a performer but should persevere with his writing. Strindberg took this advice and decided that he would go back to Uppsala for another year to study the classics. He felt he needed more education if he was going to make a career for himself as a playwright. And so it was under these circumstances that he wrote his first plays, which he circulated among his fellow undergraduates to be read aloud and discussed.

Two disrupted years at university produced passes in Aesthetics, German, French, English, Italian and Latin but Strindberg's greatest achievement from this period was undoubtedly the completion of four plays. He sent the manuscripts to Hedberg at Dramaten and two of them – *In Rome* and *The Outlaw* – were accepted for production. *In Rome* was staged in 1870 and was also published anonymously for a library that provided middle-class families with plays for amateurs to perform. When *The Outlaw* was produced a year later King Karl XV, who attended the première, was so impressed that he summoned Strindberg to the palace and gave him 200 kronor from his private purse in order to encourage him to go on writing. Although Strindberg later rejected these early youthful works and refused to allow them to be revived they set him on the road to becoming a serious dramatist.

Over the next four years he continued writing plays and tried to scratch a living from journalism, submitting articles to the daily newspapers, most notably the *Dagens Nyheter* and the *Stockholms Aftonpost*, on a whole range of subjects from theatre and art to nature and politics. His windfall from the King was quickly spent and he was disappointed to discover that the money had been an ex gratia payment only and there was no more to be had from that source.

The salary of 140 kronor a year that he was earning from his job at the Royal Library when he first met Siri von Essen was not much but he had been lucky to secure the post without a degree and at least it gave him a regular income for the first time in his life. He was used to living in spartan conditions and it did not stop him enjoying the camaraderie of the young artists – all of whom were just as impecunious as he was – who frequented the inns and restaurants in the city. These friends and the bohemian life they led together later provided him with rich material for his novel *The Red Room*.

The Royal Library was an environment that suited Strindberg for he had access to all the books he needed and was able to use the facilities for his own research. He was a natural linguist and when he was asked to compile a catalogue for the Chinese collection he studied the written language and taught himself enough to complete the job. It was his most important contribution to the Library's work. He stayed in this post for eight years altogether and it was the only salaried position he ever held.

Before he met Siri, Strindberg had never really been in love. He had had the usual student friendships with barmaids and waitresses and he sometimes visited prostitutes. His only serious affair until then had been with Ida Charlotta Olsson, a young waitress, who, according to one of Strindberg's biographers, Olof Lagercrantz, belonged to a circle of women who were available to gentlemen without any obligation of marriage. When Strindberg wrote about this relationship in his autobiographical novel *The Son of a Servant* he described Ida as a married woman but there is no record of her having a husband at this time. Strindberg had already broken with her (some time in the early spring of 1875) when she informed him that she was pregnant. It is impossible to say whether or not Strindberg was the father of her baby but he certainly denied all responsibility and told Ida that as she now had a new lover she should look to him for support.

It was around this time that Siri's friend Ina Forstén first entered Strindberg's life. She had come to Stockholm to give some piano recitals at the Royal Opera House. Her fiancé, Algot Lange, a singer at the Svenska Teatern in Helsingfors [now Helsinki], had known Strindberg from their days together at university and he had written to him asking him to look after Ina while she was away from home. Strindberg had no trouble complying with this request for Ina was a lively young woman, if a trifle too forthright for his liking. Ina certainly found him attractive and she spoke of him all the time whenever she and Siri met.

Sigrid ('Siri') von Essen was born in Stockholm on 17 August 1850. An only child, she grew up at Jackarby, a large country estate near the seaport of Borgå [now Porvoo] in southern Finland, some 30 miles from Helsingfors. At this time Finland was part of the Russian Empire, having been ceded by Sweden in the 1808-09 war.

Siri's father, Baron Carl Reinhold von Essen, belonged to the old Finland-Swedish nobility and, like many of his forebears, had had a distinguished military career. By the time Siri was born, however, he had

The effect that Siri von Essen had on Strindberg the first time he saw her on Drottninggatan, the most fashionable shopping street in Stockholm, was strong and immediate. He was instantly enchanted. Some years later he wrote a romantic poem about their first encounter.

Sailing

It was in Drottninggatan
A flaming day in June
On the narrow pavement
That we met, you and I

Then you disappeared in the crowd
Past the shop windows
And the sound of your small boots
Died away with the rustle of your skirt.

Above hats and parasols
Your blue veil floated at first
Then it was submerged in the human river
Which slowly absorbed it.

But I went in search of it;
Like a pennant at the top of the mast,
And whenever I brave the storm
I always hoist it.

retired from the army and the family lived off their investments and the income from his land and properties.

The Baron enjoyed all the traditional pursuits of a country landowner, such as riding and hunting, but he had no head for business and managed his estate inefficiently, preferring to spend his time reading classical literature. He had a well-stocked library, situated in a separate wing of the manor house, and he would often send Siri across the courtyard after dark on some errand or pretext. Siri always protested – the place was believed to be haunted because a relative had committed suicide there – but it was the Baron's way of toughening her up.

Siri's mother, Elisabeth ('Betty') Charlotta In de Bétou, was a cultured and sociable woman who came from an upper-class Swedish family with Dutch connections. She found country life frustratingly dull and was always much happier when the family moved to their town residence in Helsingfors for the winter season. The Finnish capital was something of a cultural backwater – St Petersburg was the main metropolitan centre at this time – but Betty could at least find congenial and entertaining company there. She was a talented violin-player and singer and she enjoyed making music and painting, and liked to spend her time conversing with friends, dancing – and flirting – a social skill that she passed on to her daughter.

Siri inherited her love of music and a facility for languages from her mother and she spent hours practising the piano. She had a Swiss governess to give her a basic education, including French conversation, and the Baron taught her a little history and literature. He also encouraged her interest in gymnastics and horse-riding, which she tackled enthusiastically, ignoring her mother's hysterical claims that such tomboyish activities were unhealthy and ruined the complexion.

At home Siri spoke Swedish with her father and French with her mother, a practice that reflected the contrasting strands in their different characters and outlook. It was a conventional upbringing for a girl of her class and by all accounts she was a sweet-natured and pretty child. She was still very young when she announced that she had decided she wanted to be an actress when she grew up. Her parents disapproved, of course, and they never expected that a daughter of theirs would ever want or need to earn her own living, especially by doing something that they considered to be disreputable.

In 1863, when Siri was thirteen, her parents decided to spend a leisurely winter in Paris, where they had relatives and friends. On the first leg of the journey the family took a horse and carriage from Jackarby to St Petersburg, a distance of some 150 miles. From there they travelled by train to France. Siri's first experience of Paris was miserable. She was sent to a convent school for girls as a weekly boarder in order to brush up her French and although her knowledge of the language improved considerably she resented the fact that she was underfed. The nuns believed that their pupils needed to be kept on a near-starvation diet for the sake of their figures but Siri defied the strict regime by persuading her maid to smuggle in some extra food for her. To make up for this there were compensations in the form of treats such as trips to the opera, and Siri was thrilled when she was taken to see hot-air balloons floating in the sky above the city. She and her mother also had their portraits painted by her uncle, the Danish artist Lorenz Fröhlich.

By the time she was about eighteen Siri's father had lost so much money through risky investments and poor management of the estate at Jackarby that Betty felt that the family should cut their losses and sell up. The Baron was naturally reluctant to do this but Betty, always the stronger of Siri's two parents, insisted that it was the only sensible thing to do. The Baron left for Stockholm, leaving his wife with power of attorney to take care of all the financial arrangements. The manor house and most of its contents, the land and the livestock, the forests, the sawmill and the distillery were all put up for auction. Siri stayed behind to help her mother. It was a painful time for everyone. Although the Baron was spared the humiliation of actually seeing the estate and most of the family heirlooms (including his beloved library) going under the hammer he never recovered from the sense of failure he experienced at being forced to break with the family tradition. Betty was devastated too and for Siri it marked the end of a childhood that had been largely happy and carefree.

For Siri and her mother the one good thing to emerge from this change in their lives was that they would be living in Stockholm again. In 1868, when they arrived to join the Baron, it was a large, modern city with a population of around 150,000. Compared to Helsingfors, with its 28,000 inhabitants, the Swedish capital was a cosmopolitan and sophisticated place. And the important thing about Stockholm for Siri was that it had many theatres and was home to some of the best actors and writers in Scandinavia. She had reluctantly accepted her father's veto on her becoming an actress but as soon as the family had settled in to an apartment on Grev Turegatan she managed to persuade him to let her train as a singer. Aunt Mathilde In de Bétou, her mother's sister, who was a professional soprano, supported Siri in her ambition and coached her privately for a year. Siri then applied to the Academy of Music in Stockholm and was accepted. She had only been studying there a few months, however, when she contracted a serious throat infection that affected her vocal cords. On the advice of her doctors she reluctantly gave up her voice training. It was a serious blow, though she continued to nurse the hope that one day she would appear on stage in front of an audience in one way or another.

Betty compensated for the shock of being uprooted and losing status as the wife of a wealthy landowner by making plans to launch Siri into

Swedish society, making sure they were on the guest list for all the important functions in Stockholm's social calendar. Siri had grown into a confident, vivacious young woman and, with her blonde hair, dark eyes, slim figure and long, slender neck (a feature so striking that one sculptor friend of hers declared that he wanted to 'cut her head off and keep the neck'), she had no trouble attracting admirers. At one ball, to her mother's delight, Crown Prince Oscar (later Oscar II) asked Siri for a dance.

Siri's prospects improved dramatically when her father died early in 1870, leaving her a legacy of 25,000 kronor. She was due to inherit this money when she reached the age of majority, which for unmarried women at that time in Sweden was twenty-five. She was now an heiress of some substance with a sizeable dowry to offer. Furthermore, if she married before she was twenty-five any husband of hers would be entitled by law to take over the management of her financial affairs or would at least be able to negotiate a favourable marriage settlement.

That summer Betty took Siri on holiday to stay with relatives at Södertälje, then a fashionable spa resort south of Stockholm. Siri discovered that some of her friends had become involved with amateur dramatics and she joined in with enthusiasm. It was in this group that she met Baron Carl Gustaf Wrangel, a young captain from the Svea Liv Garde [the Swedish Life Guards], the most distinguished of the infantry regiments, whose Commander was the King himself. Wrangel was a respected name in Sweden, with an escutcheon in the House of Nobility, and although Carl Gustaf had very little capital and his family had no country house, Siri's mother thought him a thoroughly eligible suitor. Siri thought so too, for he was handsome and courteous and was passionate about the theatre. He had even started his own amateur group at the regimental headquarters.

The couple were married in Stockholm on Siri's twenty-second birthday in August 1872 and their daughter, Sigrid, was born ten months later. They lived fairly modestly in an apartment on Norrtullsgatan in the northern part of the city, about a mile from Siri's former home, and employed two servants. Their shared interest in amateur dramatics continued and they amused themselves with drawing-room recitals and play-readings with friends. As an upper-class wife and mother Siri had to put aside all thoughts of a career outside the home but she kept up to date with developments in the theatre by reading all the new plays that were published. And so it was that she came across the work of a young dramatist named Strindberg, who was acquainted with her friend Ina Forstén.

Siri and Carl Gustaf were both keen to meet Strindberg, especially after Ina had told them about his new play, *Master Olof*. He, on the other hand, had no particular interest in meeting an aristocratic army captain and his wife and resisted all attempts to bring them together – until he and Ina bumped into Siri by chance one day. And then he was as eager to make her acquaintance as she was to make his. Siri lost no time in inviting him to visit her and her husband at home and this time he accepted willingly. By coincidence, the Wrangels' apartment on Norrtullsgatan turned out to be one where he himself had lived as a child.

Strindberg's arrival into Siri's somewhat sheltered life triggered all her old longings and made her realize how much she still yearned to do something more creative than running a household and dabbling in amateur dramatics. She told him of her dreams of becoming an actress and he listened to her sympathetically, knowing that it was an unrealistic ambition for a woman in her position. He was careful not to raise her hopes, bringing her books to read instead and encouraging her to express herself through writing. Siri protested that she was not qualified to be a writer because she had had no formal education to speak of and was not widely read. In a letter that he wrote to her on 27 June 1875 Strindberg dismisses her fears:

> God preserve us from writers who regurgitate what they have learnt from books. It is people's secrets we want to know – it is the natural history of the human heart that we have been trying to put down for a thousand years and everyone must and can leave their contribution.

He goes on to explain about the craft of writing, telling her how to capitalize on her emotions:

> Anger is the most powerful emotion, so if you can recall something with anger or sadness the words will become more potent. [. . .]
> Think of an insult – you feel angry – include the dreams you had of becoming an actress while you were at the convent school – let the abbess or whatever she is called surprise you while you are acting out a part – rage about the fact that they have sent you there to squash your most beautiful dream – let a young gentleman who thinks he has all the worldly experience tell you that it is just nonsense and beat him to the ground with your conviction – Note that you have the freedom to cheat – yourself and everybody else! Bring out invisible enemies, make up antagonists – say what you like – be mad – There is something known as sinning against the Holy Spirit. I think what is meant by that is – that you resist your vocation. That sin is said to be the only unforgivable sin. Remember that! Qui est fort est Dieu!

And so Siri started to record her childhood memories, especially the time she had spent at the convent school in Paris. As the couple got to know each better and started meeting and corresponding regularly, Strindberg adopted the role of mentor, going into more and more detail about how to write. He set Siri specific tasks and exercises, such as recalling particular past experiences – always urging her to add some spice to it.

Siri's writing style was lively and original, and when the critic Erik Hedén reviewed *He and She*, the collection of letters between her and Strindberg that was published in 1919, he was no less fulsome in his praise for her as he was for him:

> It would have been difficult to distinguish between Strindberg's and Siri's letters if circumstances had not revealed who the writer was. Both of them have the same powerful temperament, both have the same great sense of insecurity. Both a sensuousness which tends to end in a burning idealism, a yearning for purity. In both there is a need for religion, coupled with doubt. In both – not least her – a clear sign of misogyny. In both a mixture of supernatural lyricism with a strong predilection for powerful expressions. In both the same impressionistic style, the same inability to write calmly and evenly. Their letters are full of dots and dashes.
>
> *Social-Demokraten, 3 July 1920*

As well as encouraging Siri to write her own material, Strindberg also urged her to try translating foreign novels into Swedish as a way of sharpening up her literary skills. Significantly she rejected his choice of *Madame Bovary* as she disapproved of the book on moral grounds and she was later to have the same reaction to Ibsen's *A Doll's House*, maybe because both stories came a little too close to mirroring her own life for comfort.

Strindberg's relationship with Siri, and indeed her whole family, was one of affectionate friendship to start with. He became very fond of little Sigrid and would bring her expensive presents and once, when Siri left Stockholm to visit relatives in the country, he and Carl Gustaf found comfort in each other's company.

Neither Strindberg nor Siri admitted, even to themselves at first, that they were falling in love. Strindberg distracted himself by pretending to develop a more serious relationship with Ina. It was a strategy that backfired. Ina was led to believe that Strindberg's intentions were serious and before long her father called on him to interview him as a prospective son-in-law. Somehow Strindberg managed to persuade them both that there would be no marriage.

By this time rumours about the affair had reached Algot Lange in Finland, probably via Constance Mellin, who was friendly with both Ina and Siri. Lange responded with a letter in which he advised Strindberg to shoot himself – 'since duels are not fashionable any more'. The tone of his message was jocular but there was no disguising the underlying anger and jealousy that he was really expressing at the thought of another man taking advantage of his fiancée.

This whole episode completely unnerved Strindberg and plunged him into a state of extreme emotional turmoil. In *A Madman's Defence,* when recalling this period of his life, he claims that it was like 'dancing on the edge of a volcano'.

In one of the letters that he wrote to Siri and published in *He and She* he acknowledges that he had not been entirely honest with Ina, though he professes not to have known how she felt about him:

> Then she left and wanted me to promise to write. I was unwise enough to do that but won't repeat it and I haven't written for six weeks now. What shall I do? Nothing! I am not in love with Miss F. and I don't know what kind of feelings she has for me. I am very fond of her and would like to keep up a correspondence with someone like her but I shall forsake that pleasure!

By the autumn of 1875 things had become so stressful that Strindberg decided he would have to leave Stockholm for a while in order to try and sort himself out. He had persuaded Rudolf Wall at the *Dagens Nyheter* to finance a trip to Paris and had promised to write a series of articles for him. So on 5 October Strindberg invited Siri and Carl Gustaf to a farewell dinner at his lodgings. After the meal Siri became so distressed that she threw her arms around him and, with tears in her eyes, kissed him on the mouth and made a sign of the cross on his forehead. Strindberg was upset but Carl Gustaf reacted calmly to his wife's outburst.

Strindberg set off the next day but he never made it to Paris. When the boat bound for Le Havre reached the Dalarö peninsula, south of Stockholm, he asked the captain to let him disembark. He knew the place as he had once spent the summer holidays there when he was a child. It is impossible to say whether he intended to commit suicide but he was clearly in a highly disturbed state for he stripped off and plunged into the cold sea and then ran, naked, through the forest. He recovered enough composure to get dressed and book into a boarding house, where he asked the landlord to find a priest to come and talk to him. A local minister duly arrived and when Strindberg had calmed down he sent a telegram to Siri and Carl Gustaf telling them where he was. He followed this up with a letter to Carl Gustaf in which he hints at an unhappy love affair with Ina. The Wrangels immediately took the first boat to Dalarö to fetch him home. Carl Gustaf was so concerned that he invited Strindberg to come and stay with him and Siri. Strindberg refused and told them that he intended to stay on Dalarö for a while. Siri and Carl Gustaf returned to Stockholm and Strindberg followed a few days later.

Strindberg's involvement with Ina was finally resolved when she married Algot Lange on 3 January 1876. In a letter that Siri sent to Ina on that day she wrote:

> Why was I not allowed to take the path that was meant for me, why has pride and pettiness governed the world and steered people away from the goal which God had decided for us, and why can I not pull myself together, since I was not allowed to do what I wanted, and make myself useful in some other way instead? A bad wife, a bad mother, a bad housewife – a wretched woman. My God, my God, why was I not allowed to become a good actress. That is what I was born for – that is what I was made for – and yet I can love for *real*. Nothing else is real – I sometimes wonder whether I myself am real. [. . .]
>
> Yes, you are quite right in saying that I am very lucky to be fond of and be near the kind-hearted person who is a friend to both of us. You don't realize how dear to us he has become – he is like a brother to me. It is as if I had known him from childhood, he is very precious to me – I don't mind telling him that to his face, to God and the whole world because that feeling is not something that is locked up in a box to be given away as a Christmas present to one single person and the person who is and always will be my number one in the world need not feel hurt by my loving a *friend*. [. . .]
>
> He was here on Christmas Eve, for dinner (we always start the festivities then, at five o'clock). In the evening he went to his father's. On Christmas Day we were together at mother's place; it is always as if something were missing when he is not with us – he has become like a member of the family.

Though the clues were there, Ina did not suspect at this time that Siri's feelings for Strindberg were developing into something more than a platonic relationship. The two women remained friends and Ina went on to enjoy a successful and distinguished career, eventually becoming the court pianist at the Royal Palace in Denmark.

As 1875 drew to a close Strindberg wrote a letter to Siri and Carl Gustaf saying how much he valued their friendship. 'The past year was the most beautiful year in my whole boring loveless life,' he said, and with this simple statement he was both speaking the truth and denying it. He and Siri had known each other for a little over six months and neither of them had yet dared to acknowledge their feelings for each other for fear of the consequences. Siri was a faithful wife who loved her husband and Strindberg was a loyal friend to them both. This tangled situation continued until March 1876, when Carl Gustaf revealed that he had a secret of his own to confess.

— Chapter 2 —

The Young Lioness

Rise, young lioness, shake your golden mane and send thunderbolts from your lovely eyes to make the idiots tremble.

He and She

It is debatable whether Strindberg would ever have revealed his true feelings for Siri — except in his fictional writing — if her eighteen-year-old cousin, Sofia In de Bétou, had not come to stay at the Wrangels' apartment on Norrtullsgatan, the first time in November 1875 and the second time in February 1876.

On the occasion of Sofia's first visit Strindberg had noticed that Carl Gustaf seemed to be paying her a lot of attention, and when she returned in the new year it was obvious to him that there was more going on than a mere flirtation. Sofia, self-assured and secure in the knowledge that Siri's husband was attracted to her, turned her attention to Strindberg but although he described her in a letter to Carl Gustaf as 'a younger and even more beautiful version of Siri' he was not tempted. Later on, in *A Madman's Defence*, he proclaimed Sofia to be 'cute and pleasant, but vulgar'.

Confirmation of an affair came when Siri found a letter that Carl Gustaf had written to Sofia telling her how much he loved her. Shocked as she was by this revelation, Siri confided in Strindberg rather than confronting her husband. When he saw how distressed she was, Strindberg was righteously indignant on her behalf and prepared to play the role of Knight in Shining Armour.

Carl Gustaf himself brought things to a head when he approached Siri one evening in early March and asked her permission to spend the night with Sofia. The reason he gave was that he was so in love that he could not stay away from her. His frankness at putting this request to Siri in such simple and direct terms was so totally disarming that she consented. Once again she confided in Strindberg and once again he declared himself appalled and disgusted by what was going on.

When Siri first told Strindberg about her husband's proposal to commit adultery with her young cousin Sofia he wrote her a long passionate letter pouring out his feelings for her and telling her that she must turn her back on her marriage and find happiness with him and fulfilment in a new career as an actress.

He and She

Forgive me!!!!!

Soon after 13 March 1876
Sunday morning!

I want to, I want to be mad!

Now I have told you everything! To whom? to the spring, to the sun, to the oaks, to the pussy willow blooms, to the spring flowers and the bells rang the message and the skylark said: 'do it!' What have I told them? – I love you!!!! And I walk down the streets as proud as a king and I look at the mob with compassion – why don't you fall down on your dirty faces before me! Don't you know that she loves me? Who? – The princess, my princess, the most beautiful woman in Sweden, the one with the bluest eyes, the smallest feet, the most golden hair, the loveliest forehead, the finest hands. – You are not worthy of hearing it!!!! The one with the noblest heart, the proudest mind, the finest feelings, the most beautiful thoughts! Mine, my beloved – and she loves me, wretched me. – If she does not desert me soon I shall go mad with hubris! [. . .]

You let him stoke himself up at her side and then extinguish his flame in your arms, while thinking of her! You condescend to sharing him with her! I am going mad! And your husband allows himself to insult you by asking your permission – under the same roof as your innocent child! My God, it is too much! [. . .]

I must fall down on my knees, put my head on your lap and kiss your hands and a thousand million times I must tell you that I love you so you believe me and become happy. You don't believe me – oh, but I love your soul – and have done so for a whole year! Don't be afraid of me, dearest! But I love your beauty as well, I must hold your hand, look into your eyes, I must kiss your forehead or I feel that I will die!! [. . .] – How I thank the slut who holds him while I kiss you! [. . .] – Rise, young lioness, shake your golden mane and send thunderbolts from your lovely eyes to make the idiots tremble. Break away from this detestable menagerie – out into the forest, into nature where a heart, a head and two open arms await you, and a love that can never die, unlike the last one. Do you know why it died? You continued to grow and develop. He did not change – now you are ahead of him and he will be behind forever.

Our love cannot die – because we are both growing, we have both been given wings, we can never get bored with each other, because we are resuscitated every day. [. . .]

Do you think the world will collapse because the Swedish Life Guards are stained by one officer who has behaved disgracefully towards his wife? Are you going to sit at table with an officer's mistress? Are you going to be your husband's procuress? God in heaven, can you forgive me for the sake of my great love? Yes, you must forgive everything.

Remember that Carl has compromised himself and the girl. He has ruined your reputation through his! The law is on your side! Run away from him! To your mother!

Dearest creature, you don't believe that you have genius – you think that genius means a sharp brain – not at all – I have not the sharpest brain – but the fire; my fire is the greatest in Sweden, and I shall, *if you wish*, set fire to the whole wretched nest! – You have the fire, it is this strange flame that worries you, torments you, upsets you and which has been lying dormant for so many years and which so many bloody fools have tried to stifle. Come! Fulfil your high aims! Become an actress – I shall give you a theatre of your own – I shall act with you and write and – love you. You have a great crime on your conscience! You have desired the reward of genius without being prepared for its martyrdom – oh, it is a pleasurable martyrdom! Fulfil your vocation, become the greatest actress or writer in this country! [. . .]

Are you afraid of becoming my wife, are you afraid of the prose? – Oh, don't you know that I have the magic wand that can bring water out of a rock – that I can bring out the poetry in dirt if needs be. – I shall work a coffee-grinder and make it sound like music – I shall go to the market and buy potatoes but I shall always put a flower on top of the pile – I shall lay a table and make it look as if van Huysum has painted a still life and how I shall work – and then – when I have found peace in my unsettled and unhappy existence, re-read all my letters – can't you hear how they tremble with love for you, my queen. [. . .]

You who can give this country its greatest writer – and that is what I shall become – you don't know who and what I am – I am a – well, I haven't met my peer yet – yes, in you, in you Siri, you with the most beautiful name I know. [. . .]

Forgive me all this, you must, you must – because I love you!!

The letters that Strindberg and Siri exchanged at this time are included in a collection of correspondence between the couple, running from 1875–76, that he later used as the basis for an epistolary novel called *He and She*. Written in 1886, Strindberg gave this fourth volume of his autobiography an air of fiction by changing the names – he and Siri become Johan and Maria (the same name that he gave to the Baroness in *A Madman's Defence*) and Carl Gustaf and Sofia are called Gustav and Mathilde. Compared to *A Madman's Defence*, which sees events solely from the author's point of view and then only after the passion has diminished, *He and She* reveals both sides of an ongoing story without the dampening effect of hindsight. The characters in *He and She* were so thinly disguised that Strindberg's publisher, Albert Bonnier, refused to accept the manuscript for fear of libel.

From the middle of March 1876, following Carl Gustaf's admission that he was in love with Sofia, the letters between Strindberg and Siri take on a new urgency. On hearing the news of a *ménage à trois* at Norrtullsgatan, Strindberg enters the arena like an angry bull, calling Carl Gustaf a 'filthy whoremonger' and Sofia a 'slut'. More significantly, he now feels he has been given licence to release the floodgates and pour out his love for Siri with a vehemence that he has suppressed for so long.

Strindberg told Siri that if she chose to stay at Norrtullsgatan it would only prolong the humiliation she was suffering; he reminded her that she had a duty to herself as an artist and should seek her own fulfilment. He urged her to leave her husband before her wings lost their power, before she herself sank irrevocably into the dirt. In order to add weight to his argument he told her that he had heard that Carl Gustaf had acquired a quantity of saffron (believed at the time to be an abortifacient), thus hinting that Sofia might be pregnant. Strindberg was to discover that jealousy was never one of Siri's afflictions, however. Her reaction to her husband's behaviour was not an explosive anger like his own – and she treated his outbursts with measured caution – but wounded pride and anxiety at the prospect of public disclosure and scandal. She had told Carl Gustaf about her feelings for Strindberg and was unexpectedly moved when he broke down and cried. How could she leave him? She loved both men equally. But she did remember Strindberg's advice about the potential for turning all experience and emotion into art:

> The roles are reversed! One should write a novel about this – if I had the courage to stir it up I would do it, but a novel must have an end, otherwise the readers are not happy. They don't know that the best, the truest novels do not have an end. Yes,

death of course – if you can't solve the riddle the heroine dies. But I don't want to die and you must stay alive and he must stay alive – our novel must not have an end, that would be dangerous – it must just die slowly, like it started. Just think when you tell me one day that you love someone else – because I think you are honourable enough to tell me that . . . and your wedding will take place – I shall be present – I hope you will invite me – and we shall see each other – and forget – nothing has existed – nothing.

He and She

She still feared that her husband's career would be ruined if the news of his affair got out but if she expected any sympathy from Strindberg in that quarter she was swiftly disabused.

Maybe the affair would have stayed behind closed doors if Strindberg hadn't wilfully forced things along. Siri had shown him the compromising letter that Carl Gustaf had written to Sofia and he was so incensed that he told Siri's mother about it. She immediately told her brother, Sofia's father, and then asked Siri what was going on. Siri denied that anything was going on, saying that she had reacted hastily because Carl Gustaf had accused her and Strindberg of having an affair.

> Mother! There is one thing I want to ask you. Please don't make a scene with Uncle. Forget the accusation I made against Carl Gustaf. I am now convinced that he is innocent. When he accused August I retaliated by accusing the girl. It was revenge but also my stupid imagination. She is more beautiful than I and I became jealous . . .
>
> *He and She*

Siri was furious with Strindberg for interfering, so to make amends for upsetting her he reluctantly agreed to confirm her denial. By this time, however, her mother's suspicions had been sufficiently aroused and before long she was aware of the full extent of Carl Gustaf's involvement with Sofia. Once the secret was out in the open things moved very quickly. It seemed that there was nothing that either Siri or Carl Gustaf could do to save their marriage and that a divorce was inevitable.

Carl Gustaf insisted that his feelings for Sofia were not serious, that it was an infatuation. He told Siri that he bore no grudge against Strindberg and said that he did not want to stop him visiting them. Strindberg felt that Carl Gustaf was being hypocritical and he wrote him a passionate letter in which he said that he was in love with Siri and offering to take the blame in order to protect her reputation in the event of a divorce.

It was an especially traumatic time for Siri. On 23 March, when she and Strindberg visited his sister Anna, she was in such an agitated and nervous state that she fainted. She knew that she could not hope to please everyone, least of all her mother, who was horrified at the prospect of a divorce in the family. A few days later Siri wrote an anguished letter to Strindberg, telling him about Betty's reaction:

> She is against this divorce completely (for instance, she wants me to promise never to marry you) but she knows that is the only way out, financially for us. The reason she does not approve is that it will reflect badly on her – people will avoid her and some of her acquaintances will show their disapproval at her daughter being an actress and a divorcée.

Betty did indeed have strong motives for trying to prevent the divorce between her daughter and son-in-law. Not only was she fearful of the scandal it would create but she also stood to lose a substantial part of her regular income because this was directly linked to the capital and assets from Siri's inheritance.

The financial arrangements between Siri, her husband and her mother were extremely complicated. Betty had always managed Siri's money and she had persuaded Carl Gustaf that she should go on doing so, taking a certain percentage of the income from the investments for her own living expenses. He had agreed to this at the time of his marriage to Siri but the prospect of a divorce now sharpened up his wits considerably. Looking for ways to safeguard his own future, he started pressing Betty to relinquish her role as Siri's financial guardian. He had his regular army pay but no private income and he does not seem to have been a particularly ambitious or dedicated soldier so his promotion prospects were probably not good. Betty agreed on condition that she received an annual income of 1700 kronor and Carl Gustaf accepted this even though that sum represented around 75 per cent of the yield from Siri's main capital fund with the merchant bankers Guillemot and Weilandt.

Siri's response to these backstage negotiations was swift and calculating: she denounced Carl Gustaf and exposed him to the entire family as her cousin's seducer. She then instructed her lawyers to draw up a deed of gift, formally transferring the bulk of her capital assets to Sigrid, to be managed by Carl Gustaf until the child came of age.

With the financial arrangements resolved, at least temporarily, and in spite of Betty's continuing protestations, the divorce proceedings went ahead.

Sofia, meanwhile, with the cool arrogance of youth, seemed oblivious to the central role that she was playing in the affair. While Siri, Carl Gustaf and Strindberg were locked in a dramatic conflict with her father and aunt, Sofia's main concern was how she was going to manage to attend two balls in one weekend, one in Uppsala and one in Stockholm.

Strindberg later saw the dramatic value of this situation and was even able to see the humour in it when he wrote his comedy *Playing With Fire,* where a young woman flirts both with the main character's father and his wife's lover with no concern for the trouble she is causing. He returned to the same theme with another one-act play, *The First Warning,* where a fifteen-year-old girl plays havoc with the lives of a married couple.

Once it became clear that there was nothing to be done to stop the divorce, Siri's family had to work out how best to limit the damage to their reputation when the news became public. Their aim was to avoid a scandal at all costs and to make sure that Carl Gustaf's military career was not harmed. It was quite common, of course, for army officers to have mistresses, but such liaisons did not usually involve one's own wife's young cousin. The best solution, it was felt, would be for Siri to leave the marital home – giving her desire to become an actress as the reason – so that Carl Gustaf could sue her for desertion. In this event she would lose custody of her daughter. She was persuaded not to sue him on the grounds of his adultery because, it was argued, everyone would lose out. If he was named as the guilty party his career and earnings would be jeopardized and he would be ordered by the court to pay alimony to Siri as well as maintenance for Sigrid and would probably not be granted custody. In addition, Sofia's name would be dragged into the proceedings and the divorce would take longer to resolve and attract more public attention.

The biographer Harry Jacobsen suggests that it was Siri's pride that led her to take the blame for the break-up of her marriage. She was hurt by her husband's behaviour but that did not mean that she was happy to be cast into the pitiable role of the wronged wife. On a more pragmatic level she knew that if she seriously wanted to be an actress then she would not be able to take care of Sigrid on her own. She was therefore willing to allow Carl Gustaf to divorce her on his terms and was prepared to reward him well financially and grant him custody so the child would be properly cared for. Unable to accept the possibility of Sigrid being brought up with Sofia as a stepmother, Siri laid down just one condition: he would relinquish his custody rights if he remarried. Carl Gustaf agreed.

In a letter that Siri wrote to Strindberg on 4 April she seems in remarkably good spirits, having appreciated that she was not entirely powerless as far as her marriage and the impending divorce were concerned:

The situation is superb – he is getting more infatuated with her – she with him – and bang! and there is an explosion – that is to say – he will have to ask for his liberty, in a perfectly civilized way, and I'll agree – we'll part as friends – and all that remains in order to carry the whole thing off in style is to have a double wedding, all amicably, the same evening – and then we'll go on seeing each other as a loving family. I should think that is quite a novel idea. – Ha! There you are, you see. I can be a devil as well if I want to. – Oh yes, a real devil.

From this point on Siri is looking forward to being an actress and to devoting her life to Strindberg. 'August has never been my lover,' she declared to her mother just a week later, 'but it is my firm intention to become his wife as soon as the law permits.'

If Strindberg did not quite share her exuberance at this time it is because once the rumours of the divorce started circulating he was put squarely in the frame as the co-respondent – the man who had abused a friend's hospitality by cuckolding him. When his boss came into the office at the Royal Library one day and asked: 'Which one of you is having an affair with a baroness?' Strindberg kept his head buried in his books and said nothing. Siri had extracted a grudging promise from him to keep quiet about Carl Gustaf's relationship with Sofia so he had to listen to the gossip without being able to defend himself with the truth. It was a bitter lesson – that an aristocrat's reputation is worth more than a humble artist's honour – and a classic example of the type of upper-class hypocrisy that would always both infuriate and confuse him.

The weeks leading up to the divorce were stressful for all concerned. Betty was still trying to salvage the situation by insisting that Siri stay married and keep quiet for the sake of appearances. She wrote to Strindberg on 13 April and appealed to him to give Siri up:

13 April 5 am
Herr Strindberg!
After a sleepless night I am now sitting here. Yesterday I heard things which I would not have believed before. I appeal to your honour, your friendship, your common sense and your sense of justice – return my poor child to her duties as a wife, mother, and daughter. You, only you can do this because she believes you to be above other people and of noble mind and I believe that too. Be merciful! Tell her, implore her, beg her to do the right thing and to remain calm. She can still be happy in her home because her husband loves her, I know, and I think that an immense unhappiness in the future could be prevented if you influence her in this. [. . .]

My head is reeling and I know I could not survive such a misfortune. I beg you, in God's name and in the name of those you hold dear in the world and your mother in heaven – prevent these awful things happening! – Perhaps you will not say anything about this letter to her, but hear my plea, be noble, be magnanimous and earn my respect and my eternal gratitude.

In haste
E. –
Give me a word of comfort!
Today they are going to make up their minds – please hurry!!
Think of her fragile health and her lack of money, and what a scandal!
We cannot endure it.

The 'fragile health' that Betty refers to in this letter relates to a nervous disorder of some kind, possibly a stomach ulcer, that Siri was prone to; it was a condition that was to recur several times in her life whenever she was under emotional strain.

It is not known how Strindberg responded to Betty's appeal to his sense of honour but the letter that Siri sent to her mother at the end of April can have left her in no doubt that the divorce would go ahead and that she *would* have to 'endure it'. In a declaration of independence that could almost have come from Nora herself as she walks defiantly out of the Doll's House, Siri tells Betty what she has decided to do and why. She has thought deeply about her position as a daughter, a wife and a mother and has come to the conclusion that it is not enough:

> I am not made for a quiet, peaceful home-life with the scent of roses – I need struggle to find my happiness. I have tried it: I have had a beloved and loving husband, a pleasant home, good friends – a lovable child – in one word, everything to make a woman happy. I have also been happy in a fashion, I have sincerely thanked God for his goodness, I have tried to adapt to my circumstances and tried to be completely contented – but I have never succeeded. Battle and progress is my motto – peace is not for me – I was not born to be a housewife – God wanted me to be an artist. [. . .]
>
> As Carl's wife I could never have become an actress – there was something that restrained me, his name, his reputation, above all his position – which I had no right to destroy since we could not afford to live without it, and my child's future had to be secured – I could have died before I became anything great – and then he would not have had any means with which to support the child. As August's wife I can live in obscurity and carry on training until the day when my beautiful goddess takes me in her arms and I am worthy to be her daughter.

Siri took the first, irrevocable steps towards divorce on 3 May. She booked a seat on the night train to Malmö and travelled on to Copenhagen to stay with her Aunt Augusta for two weeks. All Carl Gustaf had to do was to go to a lawyer and ask for a petition to be drawn up, claiming that his wife had deserted him.

While she was away Siri agonized over her decision. Her mother and her aunt were urging her to go back to her husband while Strindberg was sending her daily love letters addressing her as 'Ophelia', 'Cleopatra' and

'Juliet' and signing himself as 'Hamlet', 'Antonius' and 'Romeo'. Betty, still hoping for a last-minute reconciliation, asked Strindberg once more to leave Siri alone and ordered Carl Gustaf to go and fetch her back. Both men ignored her pleas. Strindberg continued to write to Siri, though he judged it wiser not to join her in Copenhagen as she had begged him to do. Carl Gustaf stayed resolutely at home. The case went to court on 16 May and Siri returned to her mother's apartment in Stockholm three days later. On 20 June the marriage was officially dissolved.

During the summer Siri rented a cottage in Upplands-Väsby, about 50 miles north of Stockholm. Sigrid, who was ill with what turned out to be tubercular meningitis, spent some time with her there and Strindberg came at the weekends. The child's health was a source of great anxiety and Siri started to have doubts about the decision to leave her with Carl Gustaf and felt that she should find a way to care for her herself. The obvious solution as she saw it would be to get married to Strindberg straight away and establish a new home for the three of them. When she broached the subject Strindberg was adamant: it was too soon and it was not what they had agreed. He reminded her of what they had decided before the divorce: he would be busy writing plays for her to star in and she would be devoting all her time and energy to becoming a great actress. And when they did get married they would live together in equal partnership with separate finances – and separate bedrooms. Fond as he was of Sigrid, he could see no place for a dependent child in this arrangement.

Siri had to accept that Strindberg was not to be pushed into premature bourgeois domesticity so she sent Sigrid back to live with Carl Gustaf and prepared to embark on her new career. At the end of the summer she rented her own apartment in Stockholm and Strindberg found her the best drama teachers to help her learn her craft.

With the small amount of capital and investment income that she had salvaged from the divorce settlement, and with her modest earnings from the occasional journalism and translation work that Strindberg was able to pass on to her, Siri calculated that she could raise around 3000 kronor, which was enough to support herself for about a year. She was determined to make it onto the stage before the twelve months were up.

As the autumn progressed, Siri and Strindberg were still living separately but they corresponded regularly and saw each other often, usually meeting in cafés or at his sister Anna's house. Strindberg went to the Royal Library every day and was working on a new draft of *Master Olof*. In October he took three weeks' leave and went to Paris to do some research for some articles he was preparing on modern art and the theatre. It was an invigorating trip and when he returned he told Siri all about it – the work of the Impressionists, including the new paintings by Monet, Manet and Sisley that he had viewed, and the refreshingly simple and natural acting style that he had seen on stage.

Meanwhile, Carl Gustaf had moved out of the marital home and was now living on his own in a cheaper apartment with Sigrid and a couple of servants. The divorce had soured his relationship with Siri's family, and Betty, perhaps in response to the shame and dishonour that she felt had been brought upon her, had become ill. Depressed and suffering from heart trouble, she took increasingly to her sick-bed. She was never able to forgive Carl Gustaf for what he had done and was to die a bitter woman.

Siri applied herself diligently to her acting lessons and she also helped Strindberg to plan and publish the first and, as it turned out, the only issue of a magazine called *Gazetten* to which she contributed the first part of a novel about a Finnish girl at a convent school in Paris. It is a lively piece of prose and even if it is safe to assume that Strindberg helped her to polish up her style, the tone is distinctly hers. At around this time she was also working on the outline for another novel, about her relationship with Strindberg.

Sigrid's health was still a worry and Siri was also anxious about her mother but her single-minded ambition kept her going. She was on good terms with Carl Gustaf and was busier and happier than she had been for a long time.

— Chapter 3 —

Omnia Vincit Amor

Her tiny body, more fragile than thin, is lying half veiled by her batiste chemise (reminiscent of a Greek chiton) gathered at the waist in a thousand folds, hiding her thighs but exposing her knees where those beautiful muscles and ligaments meet in a confusion of lines reminding me of an oyster shell. And the lacework reaches the edge of the chemise like a grid through which two young animals push their pink noses, and her shoulders appear inviting like handles carved in ivory to fit snugly in my hands.

She is reclining on my sofa, like a goddess, watching me worship her, stretching out her arms, rubbing her eyes, and casting furtive glances at me, half bashful and half provocative.

A Madman's Defence

Strindberg's love-hate relationship with the aristocracy found a perfect target in Siri von Essen and her family. By the time he met her he had already acquired a taste for good food, wine and clothes and he was to some extent seduced by the charm and fine manners of the social elite. He knew, however, that he would never be fully accepted as one of them, a point that was brought home to him during his student days when he was engaged to coach the children of a wealthy family with a large country estate south of Stockholm. Like many a tutor or governess before him he found himself in a kind of social limbo; his education and upbringing placed him well above the servants of the household but in the eyes of his employers he was still a hired hand, treated with civility but kept at a distance. He was also able to observe for himself how the aristocracy related to the *statare* – the tied agricultural workers. The conditions under which they lived and laboured had changed little since the seventeenth century.

His involvement with Siri brought him face to face with the aspects of upper-class behaviour that he had always despised: arrogance and ignorance. And the events surrounding the break-up of Siri's marriage to Carl Gustaf reinforced his view that these people were capable of gross hypocrisy, especially where sexual relationships were concerned.

While Strindberg's background was undoubtedly not as privileged as Siri's, his childhood, though hard at times, had been far from poor. He always liked to call himself 'the son of a servant' and while this is true up to a point – his mother, the daughter of a tailor, had worked as a housekeeper for his father, Carl Oscar Strindberg, before they married in 1847 – his upbringing was generally more comfortable, not to say bourgeois, than he sometimes admitted. Most of the time the family was able to afford to employ one or two domestic servants of their own.

Ulrika Eleonora, Strindberg's mother, was deeply religious, with Pietist leanings. She and Carl Oscar were betrothed in 1842 and lived together for five years, producing three children out of wedlock, before deciding to legalize their union. Strindberg, who was born on 22 January 1849, was therefore their first legitimate child. This this was not particularly significant: a betrothal was considered a sufficient moral obligation in Sweden in those days and it is estimated that around 46 per cent of all couples cohabited without being married. This practice extended to the better off, especially in Stockholm, but many people considered themselves too poor to marry and some were deterred by the prospect of taking the test on the Bible and catechism that was obligatory before the banns could be read.

Altogether Ulrika Eleonora gave birth to eleven children, seven of whom survived infancy: Axel, Oscar, August, Olle, Nora, Anna and Elisabeth. Some time between 1855 and 1858, during which period she went through four pregnancies, she contracted tuberculosis. Strindberg was just thirteen when she died, in 1862, at the age of thirty-nine, and he found it hard to cope when his father remarried within a year. His new stepmother, Emilia Pettersson, was another young housekeeper, whom Carl Oscar had employed to look after the children when Ulrika Eleonora was ill. Strindberg hated her from the very beginning and never accepted her.

Maybe it was the loss of his mother at such a crucial age that led him to exaggerate the physical rather than the emotional hardships he had to endure as a child. In his first autobiographical volume, *The Son of a Servant*, he complains that the family's accommodation was often cramped and uncomfortable but then goes on to describe one apartment where they lived that consisted of five rooms plus a kitchen, with two further attic rooms at their disposal. Considering that more than half the country's population of around 4.5 million in the middle of the nineteenth century had to make do with one room and a kitchen, regardless of family size, the Strindbergs did not fare too badly. Housing in Sweden for the working classes did not markedly improve until the 1940s.

The family moved around Stockholm quite a lot as Strindberg was growing up and the various homes they occupied – five in all – were all spacious by Swedish standards. These frequent moves, which were prompted by a fluctuating standard of living and an ever-growing family, were made easier by the ready availability of rented accommodation. Each move usually meant that Strindberg and his brothers and sisters had to change schools. He went to two different primary schools, Klara and Jacob, where he mixed with other children from the middle- to lower-middle classes. The difference in background among his classmates was not quite so great as he claims for although free education had been extended by law in 1842 to all children, the poorest tended to gravitate towards their own district schools and some never got more than a basic, sporadic schooling. All the Strindberg children attended private schools from the age of eleven.

Strindberg remembers his father as a strict, patriarchal figure with fixed ideas about his children's abilities and prospects. They all received a good education, including the girls, who would have been able to support themselves if necessary. They were introduced to art and music from an early age and all took part in musical evenings at home when everyone in the family played an instrument. Anna and Axel both attended the Academy of Music and Axel later combined his job as an insurance clerk with that of Musical Director at the Royal Opera House.

Carl Oscar was a solid burgher who started out in the family business as a spice merchant and trader in luxury goods and later became a steamship agent. In 1853 he suffered a setback when both he and his brother Ludvig, who had lent him money, were separately declared bankrupt. Strindberg was only four at the time but he was aware of the devastating effect this had on the whole family and it was a childhood experience that would later come back to haunt him. Carl Oscar managed to rebuild his business, however, and within a comparatively short time he had regained his financial stability.

Though conventional in many ways, Carl Oscar broke with tradition by employing his daughters as clerks in the firm for a while before they married. He would not have thought of giving them any real responsibility though, and it was Oscar, his second son, who was sent to Paris to acquire the necessary business skills to allow him to take over the running of the business one day. This apparent favouritism was to cause a family rift in 1876 when the time came for Carl Oscar to hand over the reins. The true background to this schism is obscure but it is generally believed that Strindberg and his sister Anna both felt disadvantaged when their brother Oscar was offered sole control of the family firm. Carl Oscar was not prepared to change his mind or to consider that his other children might have any rightful claims. Anna finally made her peace with him before he died in 1883 but he and Strindberg were never reconciled.

Strindberg's background, so much more worldly than Siri's, must have seemed exotic to her, representing a totally different realm of experience from her own. And in addition, though prone to overdramatization and exaggeration, even offstage, Strindberg had two overwhelmingly redeeming features: his good looks and the power of his imagination. Siri clearly found him impossible to resist. Strindberg also introduced her to an earthy form of language, full of expletives, which she was quick to adopt; her not altogether ladylike speech apparently sounded rather quaint when delivered in her lilting Finnish accent.

Siri has often been seen as some kind of Lady Julie in the making: her union with Strindberg was an explosive partnership which needed the trappings of wealth to survive. Neither of them was equipped to deal with the financial hardship that lay ahead as they were both big spenders who enjoyed good living. Siri had little idea of how to run a house and had never had to get by on a small budget. But money worries, of course, were never anticipated. They simply assumed that they would be successful, he as a writer and she as an actress.

With two plays produced by the country's most prestigious theatre company before the age of twenty-two, Strindberg had no doubt that he would be able to earn a good living as a writer. As soon as the practical obstacles surrounding Siri's divorce were removed he would create great roles for her and she would be the toast of the Stockholm stage. The bulk of Siri's capital would remain under the control of her former husband but she had set aside enough to cover her expenses while she trained and had an additional small investment income from her remaining stocks and shares in Guillemot and Weilandt to fall back on. With Strindberg's salary from the Royal Library they reckoned that between them they had some useful starting capital.

Contrary to popular gossip, Strindberg and Siri did not consummate their relationship while she was still living under the same roof as her first husband. And even when she was living on her own after the divorce they only met to begin with away from home. Strindberg writes in *A Madman's Defence* about how frustrating it was to be in love with Siri and to have the opportunity at last to make love to her but to have to abstain because they did not want to risk her getting pregnant.

> Her constant fear of pregnancy and my lack of experience with the secret means of avoiding this danger combines to make a prolonged torture of our love, which should have been a source of strength and vitality to help us put up with these oppressive circumstances. Joy, no sooner born than it is killed; her fear affected me too; and we part, dissatisfied, frustrated, robbed of the greatest bliss which is denied us. What a caricature of real love!
>
> There are moments when I miss the whores, but my monogamous nature hates a change of partners. Anyway, however unsatisfactory our embraces may be, they provide a spiritual joy of a higher calibre perhaps, and my unextinguished passion serves as a guarantee for the continuance of our love.

Towards the end of spring in 1876, after Carl Gustaf had told Siri about his relationship with Sofia, things changed and Siri began to visit Strindberg at his lodgings. On one occasion he was so aroused by the sight of her beautiful black-stockinged legs that he felt he could wait no longer. He told her that he suffered from a physiological defect that meant that he was more or less sterile. Siri was reassured and agreed that they should have sex – provided he took the responsibility for any consequences.

Strindberg recorded, again in *A Madman's Defence*, how he felt the first time he made love to Siri:

> She was radiant with happiness, blissful and grateful. Her beauty shone. Her eyes sparkled with happiness. My poor attic had become a temple, a sumptuous palace. I lit the broken chandelier, my reading lamp, all the candles, to illuminate our happiness, our 'joie de vivre', the only thing, which makes our miserable lives endurable.
>
> It is these intoxicating moments of satisfied love that accompany us on our thorny pilgrimage through life; it is the memory of these fleeting pleasures – condemned only by those who are envious – that give us the strength to live and to outlive our former lives! These moments constitute real love!

During the summer Siri started training privately for the stage with drama teachers and voice coaches that Strindberg had engaged for her and after a few months she had made sufficient progress to persuade Dramaten to take her on for a year's trial without the usual qualifications from a resident drama school that they normally required. She had to prepare three quite different roles to demonstrate her versatility and she set about learning her lines with great energy and focus. She was to make her debut as the tragic heroine Camille in a play by the French dramatist Leroy, which was due to open on 27 January 1877. Three weeks before the first night

Carl Gustaf offered to go through the play with her and sent her an invitation to dinner. Siri accepted and went alone, a decision that ignited the first spark of jealousy between her and Strindberg.

On 13 January, with just a fortnight to go before the all-important opening performance, Sigrid died. Siri's feelings of guilt at having seen so little of her daughter in the final days of her illness because of her own preoccupation with a tight rehearsal schedule were exacerbated by her mother's suggestion that the child's death was a punishment from God. This remark caused such bad feeling between them that Siri refused to speak to her mother for several weeks.

Siri went ahead with her performance as Camille and her reviews were consistently good, with only minor criticisms. She found it very hard to summon the same enthusiasm for her next part, the title role in *Jane Eyre*, adapted by Charlotte Birch-Pfeiffer, due to open on 13 April. Still grieving for her daughter, she now learned that her mother was very ill. She did nothing about it until her Aunt Mathilde, who was living with Betty at 7 Norrmalmsgatan, sent a letter begging her to come before it was too late. In spite of an implied accusation in her aunt's letter that she was somehow to blame for Betty's illness, Siri made the visit and mother and daughter were reconciled. Betty died on 29 May and Siri bought a burial plot and disposed of her mother's things. She inherited some money and a few pieces of valuable old furniture and decided to go and live with her aunt for a while.

While all this turmoil was going on in Siri's life, Strindberg had been busy acting as her unofficial publicity agent. He wrote an article about her, which was published in the *Dagens Nyheter*, the country's largest and most influential newspaper. He described a young aristocratic woman who had gone against the wishes of her family and broken through the prejudices of her class to become an actress. By way of explanation he gave the 'official' reason for Siri's divorce and praised her understanding ex-husband who had realized the importance of her calling. If only more people of noble birth were to take up acting, he argued, then the profession's reputation might be improved. 'She has a pale, sympathetic face,' he concluded, 'and she moves with the kind of elegance rarely seen outside her class.'

Shortly after her mother's death Siri was offered a contract at Dramaten to run for one year from 1 July. She was to receive a salary of 2100 kronor a year plus 3 kronor per performance. This was more than Strindberg was earning at the Royal Library and well in excess of Carl

Gustaf's army pay of around 570 kronor. It seemed like a vindication for all the hard work she had done and the sacrifices she had made during what had been an exceptionally difficult time. She had defied convention, confronted the stigma of divorce and had risked ostracism from society for the sake of art and love. She had successfully completed her period of training for the stage and was now an independent woman with a good salary and a promising career. Strindberg was delighted with her success and outlined his plans to write a series of plays especially for her. They would live and work together as equals, as artists.

It was during the summer break, before she was due to start rehearsing for the third and final role of her probation year – a Baroness in a play by Sardou – that Siri discovered that she was pregnant. Strindberg's assurances that he was unlikely ever to father a child had given them barely a year of carefree lovemaking. They faced up to the situation by deciding to get married and became officially engaged on 6 December.

Just before she got married Siri expressed her views on women and the position in society in one of her notebooks:

> Women have just as much right as men to property, work and wages;
> It is wrong to bring up women simply as men's companions, they should, just like men, be citizens first and then wives and mothers.

At about the same time Strindberg announced: 'I shall be a spokesman for you, for women!' This statement might be viewed as patronizing today but it can hardly be called misogynistic.

Siri and Strindberg's wedding on 30 December was a happy event. Strindberg's sister Anna knew Siri well and she and her husband, Hugo von Philp, were among the guests. Anna describes the occasion in a book that she and her sister Nora wrote:

> An enchanting woman, beautiful, ethereal, like a supernatural creature, intelligent, elegant – yes, it was not strange that August fell in love with her, she was just the sort of woman he liked. Their wedding took place in their future home and Siri von Essen's ex-husband was among the wedding guests. – The parties concerned took it quite naturally so I kept my countenance.
> *Strindbergs systrar berättar om barndomshemmet och bror August Strindberg*

Ina Forstén and Algot Lange also attended the wedding and Siri's Aunt Rosa Amalia (Sofia's mother) sent a letter of congratulation. It seemed that the tangled relationships of the past had been forgiven if not forgotten.

The newly-weds did not have a honeymoon as Siri was playing a small role in Ibsen's *The Pillars of Society* at Dramaten. By now very noticeably pregnant, she appeared on stage for all five scheduled performances between 8 and 16 January.

Barely a week later, on 24 January, Siri's daughter was born. The baby, whom she named Kerstin, was premature and was handed over to a midwife straight after the birth. There has been some speculation about this infant as she died the next day. According to the doctor's certificate the cause of death was 'general weakness', which is a vague and non-medical description. It is possible that Siri and Strindberg intended to have their child fostered until they felt ready to take her back, and that she died of natural causes – the infant mortality rate was then about 13 per cent – but it is also possible that they were following a practice, not uncommon in the days when contraception and abortion were not freely available, of allowing a baby to die by not feeding it.

Siri does not appear to have mentioned this child ever again but the death of a baby is a theme that can be found in some of Strindberg's works, for instance in the novel *The Red Room* that he started writing in 1879 and in his play *Crimes and Crimes* of 1899, so one can assume that it was something that affected him quite deeply.

The past couple of years had been tough for Siri, who had been through a difficult divorce and had then suffered the loss of two children and her mother. Her new-found freedom and career had been bought at an extremely high price. But she and Strindberg were in love, with each other, with the theatre, with music, with Victor Hugo, with noisy parties and with life itself.

— Chapter 4 —

Happily Married

> We have fulfilled our dream of a free marriage. No double bed, no shared bedroom, no shared lavatory. All the ugly details of married life have been removed. What a splendid institution marriage is when conceived like this, supervised and adjusted by us.
>
> *A Madman's Defence*

Separate bedrooms and bathrooms in the marital home gave Strindberg and Siri a sense of privacy and allowed them each to blossom as an individual. The fact that they had to knock at each other's doors for intimacy and sexual favours heightened their sense of excitement and anticipation and helped them to retain an aura of mystique in their relationship. They had moved into a new apartment on Norrmalmsgatan and had created a beautiful home furnished with Siri's family heirlooms.

A financial crisis was looming, however, and the first serious blow came just after their first wedding anniversary. Strindberg had agreed to act as guarantor for a friend of his, Ernst Lundgren, who had borrowed a large sum of money. When Lundgren was unable to repay the loan Strindberg was held responsible for the debt.

In the marriage settlement that Siri and Strindberg signed in December 1877, three days before they got married, her assets are stated as being 13,000 kronor, all invested in Guillemot and Weilandt. A year later she had only 3500 kronor left and this small sum was wiped out completely when Guillemot and Weilandt suddenly went bankrupt. Siri had used some of the money to pay for her drama training and there is also some evidence that Carl Gustaf had, unbeknown to her and Strindberg, squandered a large proportion of the funds held in trust for Sigrid.

With debts outstanding that they could not pay, on 9 January 1879 Strindberg had no other choice but to declare himself bankrupt. The creditors accepted 60 per cent of the debt but that still left them with a deficit of around 3000 kronor. He was due to start repayments in April and the gravity of the predicament galvanized him into looking for ways that he and Siri could both start earning some money straight away. He wrote to his friend the actor-manager August Lindberg, who was playing Hamlet in Malmö at the time, asking if he had anything for Siri. By this time Siri had played Jane Eyre, Ophelia, Blanche in *La Sphinx* and Geneviève in *The Useless Ones* and was eager to do more. Lindberg, unfortunately, was unable to offer her anything.

Determined to pay off his debts as soon as he could, Strindberg established a rigorous routine. He devoted the mornings to his own writing, went to his job at the Royal Library in the afternoons and spent the evenings doing translation work. On the morning of 15 February he sat down at his desk and began *The Red Room*, a contemporary novel set in Stockholm. Drawing on his own experiences in the 1870s he delivered a punching satire on public life in Sweden and took a swipe at most of the capital's public institutions. He dissected the political parties, the civil service, the business world (especially the insurance companies) and the theatre, and drew his characters from the intellectual and bohemian set who used to gather regularly in one of the rooms at Berns' restaurant.

Strindberg finished *The Red Room* in August and sent the manuscript to a new friend in the publishing world, Joseph Seligmann, a well-educated Swedish Jew, who competed with Albert Bonnier for the best young writers. 'Seligmann,' wrote Strindberg, 'is the most enlightened person I know. I almost admire him and that is something.'

Seligmann duly published *The Red Room* and it was such an immediate success that it ran to four editions totalling 6000 copies within the first few months. Altogether the novel netted Strindberg a respectable 2200 kronor, which was enough to pay off the remaining debt to his creditors. *The Red Room* became what could be called Sweden's first real bestseller and it made Strindberg a famous author. Ibsen admired it very much and singled it out as the only Swedish novel worthy of mention.

Siri was now starting to earn about the same as Strindberg and they were solvent again. The worst was over for the time being but the shock waves of this humiliating bankruptcy, which brought back fearful memories of Strindberg's childhood when his own father had been placed in the same situation, lasted for decades to come.

By the autumn of 1879 Siri was pregnant again. She was still working at Dramaten and because her by now fuller figure did not lend itself to the aristocrats she usually played she agreed to take the part of a police officer's wife in a play by Frans Hedberg. Her talent for comedy was praised by the critics but when her Aunt Mathilde read the reviews in Copenhagen she was shocked to learn that Siri was playing such a common character.

Their daughter Karin was born on 26 February 1880 and Siri returned to the stage two months later, playing the small role of Margaretha in Strindberg's new play, *The Secret of the Guild*. This was billed as 'a comedy in four acts', though the themes of the play are pride, punishment and redemption. The action centres on the completion of the Cathedral in medieval Uppsala. Two stonemasons, Jacques and Sten, are both eager to work on the project. Sten is the better craftsman of the two and, more importantly, he is privy to the secret of the guild – the original plans and drawings of the cathedral – which Jacques is not. Nevertheless, Jacques convinces the authorities that he is qualified to oversee the work and is duly appointed. His downfall comes when the cathedral tower collapses in a storm. He is saved by the love of his wife, Margaretha, who supports and comforts him in his humiliation. Like many of Strindberg's female characters in the early historical plays, Margaretha is the archetypal redeemer, who dispels evil spirits and washes away the human sins of pride and ambition. *The Secret of the Guild* is often compared to Ibsen's *The Master Builder*, which, though written twelve years later (as Strindberg was always quick to point out) has emerged as the stronger and more enduring work.

That summer Strindberg, Siri and baby Karin spent the first of four family holidays on the island of Kymmendö in the Stockholm archipelago. Strindberg later came to look back on these times as the happiest of his life, and the simple cottage, with its green shutters and the little garden by the shore, became a symbol of married bliss and harmony. He built himself a hut to write in while Siri, who loved the sea, would go sailing alone for hours. He cultivated his garden and lived the Rousseauan idyll. They would invite friends to stay – the painter Carl Larsson was a favoured guest – and ordered fine wine and food from the city at great expense. In the long, light summer evenings they would sit on the open porch and Siri would sing and Strindberg would accompany her on the guitar.

Siri was back on stage at Dramaten in the autumn, again playing the aristocratic roles that she was perhaps best suited to. It was around this time that she and Strindberg started thinking about forming a club or salon for artists and writers. They organized their first soirée in November and the stated purpose of these social evenings was simply – 'Pleasure'. The members of 'the Club' as it was known would meet in a restaurant in town or at the Strindbergs' apartment, where they often had a puppet theatre for entertainment. Siri made clothes for the puppets and Strindberg and the other members wrote the plays that they performed.

The opera singer Pelle Janzon was a regular visitor at these gatherings, as were the painter Julia Beck and the actress Gurli Åberg. Strindberg was a genial host and he and Siri both loved to be with like-minded friends, especially when there was singing and music as well. The stuffy upper-class surroundings where Siri had felt so restrained in her youth were now a thing of the past and she enjoyed her new freedom and the unconventional set-up of the artistic circles where she fitted in perfectly.

In the spring of 1881 Dramaten terminated Siri's contract when she told them she was expecting another baby. Several other actors had been laid off since Christmas as the theatre was going through a bad patch but Strindberg was still furious on Siri's behalf. He urged her to write to Ludvig Josephson, who had just accepted his play *Master Olof* for production at the Nya Teatern or, failing that, to try the Svenska Teatern in Finland. There were no offers so she helped Strindberg by taking on his commission to translate two plays by the Norwegian dramatist Alexander Kielland. She also took over his regular column for the Danish newspaper *Morgenbladet* for a while. Altogether she had three articles published, which earned her 15 kronor apiece. In the first she wrote about the need for universal education and recommended higher salaries for teachers; in the second she reported on a strike and championed workers' rights; and in the third she looked at working-class attitudes to the monarchy, revealing herself to be a strong anti-royalist.

Having lightened his workload somewhat, Strindberg had more time to devote to his next project. For a long time he had wanted to write a comprehensive cultural history from the point of view of the ordinary Swedish people. This extremely ambitious work, which owes some debt to the English philosopher Henry Thomas Buckle and the French philosopher Taine, was a huge undertaking. Initially published as a series of separate booklets, it took Strindberg eighteen months to complete and when it later came out in book form it ran to 1000 pages and was published in two volumes. Carl Larsson was commissioned to do the illustrations.

In *The Swedish People* Strindberg devotes a whole chapter to the position of women throughout the ages. He points out that Swedish women were held in high regard even before Christianity reached Scandinavia in the eleventh century. He praises the capable women of the Middle Ages who ran nunneries and excelled in politics, singling out the Danish Queen Margareta, who ruled over all the Nordic countries in the fifteenth century. Although he is ambivalent towards St Birgitta, the Swedish noblewoman who founded the Bridgettine order (which still has about forty religious houses around the world) in 1370, Strindberg recognizes her influence. He also admires the women of the seventeenth century who successfully ran their own businesses, like Sophia De La Gardie, who owned a paper mill and several coal mines. This reminds us that the various guilds did not discriminate against women: an artisan's widow, for example, was allowed to carry on her husband's trade after his death. And so, Strindberg claims, a kind of equality between the sexes reigned even then. Women were allowed to inherit property and were protected by law.

Adultery was a capital offence in Sweden in the early Middle Ages but the right to punish an adulterous spouse was extended to wives as well as husbands. Women also had the right to kill another woman if she found her in her husband's bed. Strindberg nods approval at this kind of equality, brutal though it may have been for both sexes.

It was not until the eighteenth century that women became 'sex objects' in court circles, gradually ceasing to take their share of responsibility in working life. Strindberg condemns the courtly excesses of Gustav III's time and blames this decline in mores on the indolence of the aristocracy. He makes it clear that he abhors coquettish, flirtatious and superficial women and admires those who are enterprising, hard-working and inventive.

In a poignant way this chapter on the role of women in *The Swedish People* reveals Strindberg's own personal taste. He always preferred naturalness and unaffected behaviour and he was, by his own admission, monogamous by nature. The kind of woman he looked up to throughout his life was the mother figure, the housewife, the healer. He detested the 'parasitical' women, those from the upper classes who employed domestic servants: a nanny to look after the children, maids to do the cleaning, cooks to run the kitchen. These were women who exploited other women simply in order to indulge themselves. Strindberg ends his chapter by saying that he hopes that a new kind of woman will emerge, one who is independent and who pursues her own career while fulfilling at the same time her duties as a housewife and mother.

It is not clear how much Strindberg expected a husband to contribute to the ideal household that he portrays. Though he speaks out against the employment of women as domestics by the upper classes he was never without a servant or two himself. He was interested in cooking and gardening – he created his own kitchen garden at the house on Kymmendö – and took care of the children some of the time but on the whole he followed the traditional role of the man as breadwinner. What was unusual for the nineteenth century, of course, was for a married woman to have a career and it is significant that each of his three wives – Siri von Essen, Frida Uhl and Harriet Bosse – worked for a living. This was something that Strindberg always supported and actively encouraged. He also believed that girls should be educated in the same way as boys. He never threw off the bourgeois trappings that he became accustomed to, especially in later life, but he was more progressive in his attitudes to women than most men of the time. Because a woman was gainfully employed outside the home and therefore not what he would have called a 'parasite' he presumably felt that hiring cleaners, cooks and nannies to replace them at home was wholly justified. As it happened, none of his wives was cut out to be a model housewife. None of them had much interest in doing their own cleaning, cooking or childminding, at least not full time, though they could not escape the responsibilities of running a household altogether. The domestic staff still had to be supervised and told what to do. Siri especially appears to have had very few homemaking skills when she was married to Strindberg, being an indifferent cook and a poor manager of the household expenses, and the shock of bankruptcy had failed to make her any more prudent than he was. Even after the birth of their next daughter, Greta, on 9 June 1881, they both continued to live and entertain beyond their means.

In December of that year, and after a long wait, what was to become Strindberg's first major dramatic work, *Master Olof*, was performed for the first time. He had started it nine years earlier and had reworked the text many times, producing three completely different versions, the first one (now generally considered his best) in prose in 1872, the second – also in prose but with some passages in verse – in 1874, and the last, in verse, in 1876. 'I don't mind saying that it must have been an extremely short-sighted, unartistic, lazy, unpatriotic management who could refuse to produce this play,' said Ludvig Josephson, who decided on the first prose version for the première at the Nya Teatern. This was a criticism aimed directly at Dramaten, who had, he believed, insulted Strindberg by turning him down at every stage of the play's development.

Master Olof is the most famous and the most accomplished of Strindberg's early plays, all of which have a historical setting. The central character, Olof, is a rebellious priest who has been studying under Martin Luther in Germany. He returns to Sweden in 1518 and introduces new anti-Catholic practices into the Church. With the support of King Gustav Vasa he is instrumental in making the break from Rome and bringing about the Reformation.

Master Olof

This extract is taken from Act Three, Scene Two, where Kristina begs her husband to reach out to her and acknowledge her feelings:

KRISTINA: I know that you've got an important struggle on your hands and I know that bold thoughts are taking root in your mind. I also know that I shall never be able to take part in that struggle, I shall never be able to advise you or defend you against your enemies, but I shall stay by your side and I'll live in my own little world and busy myself with those things that you may not appreciate but I'm sure you'd miss them if they weren't done, Olof.

Please come down from your great height where I can't reach you. Forgive me if I speak like a child. You're a man sent by God, I know that, and I have sensed the holiness in your words, but you're more than that, you're a husband too, or at least you ought to be. You won't fall down from your great heights if you put away your solemn speech for once and let the cloud lift from your forehead.

Are you too important to look at a flower or listen to a bird? I put flowers on the table to please you. But you ask the maid to take them out again because you say that they give you a headache. I wanted to break your lonely silence with some birdsong but you call it 'screeching'. I asked you to come and have dinner just now but you said you didn't have time. Since you despise my little world so much I will remove everything that might disturb your thinking process. I'll leave you and I'll take all my rubbish with me.

> (*She throws the flowers out of the window, takes the birdcage and is about to leave.*)

OLOF: Kristina, my child, forgive me! You don't understand.

Olof is a fiery idealist who ruthlessly pursues his cause. He falls in love with a young nun, Kristina, and persuades her that they no longer need to observe their vows of celibacy. She is happy to leave the claustrophobic atmosphere of the convent and, against the wishes of her father, agrees to marry Olof.

At the beginning of the play Kristina is portrayed as a Madonna-like creature, warm, gentle and obedient. She accepts her role as a loyal helpmeet and a good housewife but soon feels that Olof is neglecting her as he is too busy struggling with God's work and his own lofty ideals to appreciate her needs or even notice her. It is quite clear that Strindberg is issuing a warning to men here: they should not let their masculine values and uncompromising idealism blind them to the feminine virtues of loyalty and companionship. Maybe the situation was reminiscent of his own changed circumstances.

Kristina gradually gains in confidence and when Olof's mother comes to visit she dares to stand up to her. In her relationship with Olof she demands to be treated as an equal but displays a naivety that is a result of her restricted convent education. Olof is more concerned with public battles though in the end he is forced to recant and compromise his principles in order to save his life. Kristina supports him in his struggle and waits until he is ready to resume their relationship on a more equitable basis.

Master Olof is an extremely long play, with the full text lasting almost six hours in performance, but there was a full house at the première and the reviews were good. The critic of the *Ny Illustrerad Tidning* called it 'one of the foremost works in our dramatic literature' and the *Dagens Nyheter* proclaimed that 'at last Sweden has a playwright who can be compared with Ibsen and Bjørnson'. The production at the Nya Teatern earned Strindberg 750 kronor and gave his reputation an enormous boost. No longer would Norway be able to claim that it had produced the best modern dramatists in Scandinavia. It took Dramaten another nine years to rectify its indifference to *Master Olof*, when it staged the play in verse form (Strindberg's third and final version) in 1890.

By the beginning of 1882 Siri had two babies to look after and a somewhat faltering career. Strindberg, on the other hand, was starting to enjoy the benefits of his perseverance. His novel *The Red Room* and two plays – *The Secret of the Guild* and *Master Olof* – had all been successful, in critical terms as well as financially, and he was now clear of debt. He still intended to write great roles for Siri that would make her into a celebrated actress and the couple's optimism and belief in each other's capabilities made it possible for them always to look ahead.

— Chapter 5 —

Productive Years

> My interest in the theatre, and I am being honest now, centres around one single point and I have only one aim – my wife's acting career.
> *Letter to Ludvig Josephson, 22 March 1882*

Strindberg's five 'pilgrimage' plays, also known as 'station dramas' – *Lucky Per's Journey* (1882), *The Keys of Heaven* (1892), *To Damascus* (1898–1901), *A Dream Play* (1901) and *The Great Highway* (1909) – are often grouped together because of their picaresque structure and common themes. In each one the main character undertakes a journey of discovery and resolves a number of conflicts, both with other people and with God, in a sequence of unrelated scenes that represent the various stages of human life.

In 1882 Ludvig Josephson was looking for a Christmas play that would be suitable for family audiences. Strindberg, enticed by the fact that with 1230 seats the Nya Teatern was almost twice the size of Dramaten, offered him *Lucky Per's Journey*, a fable loosely based Ibsen's *Peer Gynt*.

Strindberg was still angry about the way that Siri had been dismissed from Dramaten and was concerned that no other producers had offered her anything since. He wanted her to play the role of Lisa in *Lucky Per's Journey* and he pressed Josephson very hard on the matter. Siri, at thirty-two, was perhaps too old for the part and Josephson did not commit himself. In the event the production was postponed until December 1883, by which time Siri and Strindberg were living abroad. However, Strindberg did have the satisfaction of seeing his daughter Greta playing the role in Stockholm in 1907 when she was twenty-five.

Lucky Per's Journey became Strindberg's most successful play to date, though he was later to find fault with it, believing it to be too slight and 'bourgeois'. George Bernard Shaw admired it very much and was prepared to promote the play in Britain but Strindberg declined the offer of a production even though none of his work had ever been staged there before.

Lucky Per's Journey

Per sets off on a journey with a companion, Lisa, a wise and tolerant young woman who stands for the cause of love and reason. Per is granted a number of wishes and experiences wealth, power, fame and genius, but nothing satisfies him. He doesn't realize that Lisa, who has been at his side all along, is the potential source of love and happiness until she shows him the true way.

LISA: You sought fame and glory.

PER: Doesn't everyone?

LISA: No, not everyone. But you've got the common people on your side at least.

PER: The common people have no voice, no power.

LISA: So you wanted the establishment on your side? Then you deserve to be disgraced. You didn't even believe in what you were doing?

PER: To be honest with you, it's all one to me whether I walk on sharp or smooth stones.

LISA: When you wear calf-skin boots, yes, then I suppose it doesn't matter much. But when you walk barefoot it is a different matter, believe me.

PER: This society is not worth fighting for. Everything is built on lies anyway. They never talk of anything but the common good, the common good. What's the common good then? It seems to be that it's the sum of a handful of private interests.

LISA: If you want society to change you have to do something about it yourself. But someone like you can never do anything about it.

PER: I want to! I want to do it, but I have no power.

LISA: Then make sure you get some power!

Siri finally managed to find work in the spring of 1882, when she once again played the title role in *Jane Eyre,* at the Nya Teatern in Helsingfors. She got excellent reviews, including one from Wilhelm Bolin (who later became Professor of Literature at the University of Helsingfors) in the *Finsk Tidskrift*: 'Mrs Siri Strindberg, in her excellent rendering of Jane, displayed not only the intelligence and thorough grounding which has been praised before by several people, but also a true artistry, the only thing that can bring such a character to life . . .' The production toured Finland for two weeks and Siri was well paid and stayed in first-class accommodation. She met up with some of her old childhood friends in Helsingfors but decided not to revisit Jackarby where she had grown up.

While Siri was away Strindberg took the children to the summer cottage on Kymmendö. He was lonely without her but he plunged enthusiastically into the management of the domestic chores. He took his role as a new father very seriously and his close involvement in his children's daily lives was quite uncharacteristic for a man of this period. He was always proud of his daughters' progress, following their development with genuine curiosity and joy, and his letters to Siri are full of news about them. On 14 May, just after she had returned to Stockholm, he wrote:

My dear Siri,
You have been away so long now!
    We are on Kymmendö! Everything is fine! The children are well! Greta is so clever. She crawls and stands up, supporting herself on the furniture!
    Everything is lovely here. The only thing missing is you! Don't stay on in town. We can always send someone in later to fetch the things you have not had time to get.
    But if you stay on a few more hours then please bring:
        The dining-table and some
        Rugs
        The sugar basin, salt basin, a jug, egg cups.
    And please send someone to buy
        A cream bowl – of glass (25 öre)
        A folding-knife with a corkscrew (strong)
        Four books, yellow beehive
        of the yellowest kind
        never mind how

He also suggests that Siri should let him take over the housekeeping duties, though only if she agreed, as he had no wish to interfere with her traditional role. Presumably he thought that he would be less extravagant than she was.

Your honour as a housewife, since you have returned to the artistic life, is not compromised by this and next autumn when you are working in the theatre it may be necessary for me to look after the finances.

All debts in town are paid off and we are now quite well supplied with groceries, paid for in cash!

Siri's role as housewife, it should be noted, was not especially onerous at this time as she and Strindberg hired a charwoman to help with the washing and cleaning (the laundry was sent out for ironing) and they had a nursemaid for the children.

While waiting for Siri to join the family on Kymmendö for the rest of the summer Strindberg had been getting on with a new play. He had always promised Siri that he would create challenging parts for her and so with the role of Margit in his latest work, *Sir Bengt's Wife*, he intended to establish her as a major leading lady. And if the play was put on at Dramaten in Stockholm as he hoped, she would be able to stay with him and the children while she was working instead of leaving them behind to go abroad on tour.

Sir Bengt's Wife is Strindberg's answer to Ibsen's *A Doll's House*, which was written just three years before, and had been produced in Sweden, at Dramaten, in 1880. The character of Nora and her decision to slam the door and not come back to her husband and children had caused quite a stir in Stockholm. Everyone was talking about it and 'the woman question' was a subject of intense debate. With *Sir Bengt's Wife*, however, Strindberg denied that he was addressing this issue directly, and in a letter to Karl Warburg, a literary critic and later Professor of Literature at the University of Stockholm, he said, 'I never intended to solve the woman question with this play.'

Though they had themselves been close to the reality depicted in Ibsen's play and knew about the pain of financial hardship and bankruptcy, Strindberg and Siri both disliked *A Doll's House* intensely and felt that the ending was totally unrealistic. What could Nora do once she left the marital home without a husband to protect her? She would have no status or means of earning a living and the only path open to her would be prostitution. Siri, of course, had had first-hand experience of what it was like to leave a husband and child in order to 'fulfil' herself but she had no sympathy for Nora.

In a way *Sir Bengt's Wife* carries on where *A Doll's House* leaves off, though Strindberg chose to set his play in the Middle Ages. His view is that love – illogical, sensual love – is stronger than the abstract notion of self-fulfilment and he underlines the irrational element that is always present in human emotions, a notion that he found lacking in Ibsen's work.

Strindberg and Ibsen both start off with a harmonious domestic setting and a couple who seem to be contented in their marriage until they get into debt. Then the real balance of the relationship between them is exposed. In each case the wife decides that she cannot stay with her husband any longer. The main difference between the two plays, apart from the fact that one has a modern setting with a middle-class heroine and the other a period setting with an aristocratic heroine, is that in *A Doll's House* Nora is first and foremost a woman who needs to fulfil herself; her duties as a wife and mother come second. She does not believe her husband is either willing or capable of adapting to her needs and so she has to break free of him in order to function fully as a woman. In *Sir Bengt's Wife* Margit also leaves home but unlike Nora she agrees to come back because her husband is willing to change the way he treats her and so the couple are able to reach a new understanding about their respective roles within the marriage. Strindberg's message is that women have to be educated and are entitled to equality with men. Husbands should not take their wives' loyalty for granted and should allow them to take an equal share of the responsibilities of married life. He described *Sir Bengt's Wife* as a play that is:

1/ An attack on the romantic upbringing of women
2/ An apologia for love as a natural force that survives all whims and stifles free will
3/ An appreciation of women's love as being of a higher kind than men's love
4/ A defence of women's right to be in charge of themselves

Introduction to Getting Married, Vol. I

In *Sir Bengt's Wife* Margit spends some time in a convent before she marries, a custom that was quite common among young noblewomen in the Middle Ages. She is highly emotional, with romantic ideas about love and courtship. When she becomes Sir Bengt's wife she finds the romance is beginning to fade. Bengt fails to communicate with her, keeping all his worries to himself, especially the fact that he is facing financial problems that threaten to ruin them.

The relationship between husband and wife is similar to that depicted in *Master Olof* but with *Sir Bengt's Wife* Strindberg puts the dilemma of the conflict between love and marriage at the heart of the play. There is an obvious parallel between Margit, with her aristocratic background and her convent education, and Siri, but there is no reason to believe that Strindberg was hinting at problems in his own relationship at this time.

Sir Bengt's Wife

In Act Four, Scene Ten Margit asks her husband for a separation. She has become infatuated with a local sheriff and has made a confession to her priest.

BENGT: (*on his knees*) Margit, Margit, don't go. You're tearing my life out of my body, you're condemning me. I love you, I love you!

MARGIT: You love me like one of your possessions. You love me about as much as you loved your corn when you were about to lose it.

BENGT: I worship you like one worships the Holy Virgin, because you are stronger than me and gentler than me. Look, I'm lying at your feet, begging you to take me back because I am so unhappy, let me be your servant. I'll do anything you want.

MARGIT: Do you think my soul could ever love a servant? I liked you better when you hit me.

BENGT: Margit, you who always had a tender heart, you who could be so good, how can you make me so unhappy?

MARGIT: (*gently*) Poor knight, I'm sorry I hurt you so much. Why can't I make you happy and merry again? I want to stay, but I have to go now. At once!

BENGT: You're leaving me now when I'm poor and unhappy?

MARGIT: Who stayed put when the bad times came? And who went into hiding then? I'm leaving for quite a different reason this time.

BENGT: Because you love somebody else?

MARGIT: Yes, it's your fault and the law has granted me my liberty.

Siri clearly relished the role of Margit and it brought her the recognition she had craved. At the end of the first night on 25 November she and Strindberg stood side by side on the stage to enjoy the enthusiastic applause of the audience. She was later singled out by one critic, who wrote: 'We have never before seen her display so much power in her acting, give such a nicely nuanced performance and such a strong impression of real emotion.' The reviewers were generally less complimentary about the play itself. Most of them didn't care for the medieval setting and many thought that the tone of the piece was too moralistic. So while he was delighted that Siri had made a breakthrough, Strindberg was dismayed by the critical response to his work and disappointed that the play earned him only 166 kronor when *Master Olof* had yielded over four times as much.

Strindberg felt that *Sir Bengt's Wife* was a significant failure (although he asked his publisher to send a copy to Ibsen, who was then living in Rome) and it was to be four years before he wrote another play. As it turned out, it stood the test of time and his third wife, Harriet Bosse, played Margit in an acclaimed production some thirty-five years later.

The year 1882 had been a busy and stimulating time for both Siri and Strindberg. His creativity was unsurpassed and he wrote book after book: prose, poetry and drama poured out of his pen with equal speed and inspiration. Before writing *Sir Bengt's Wife* for Siri he had completed a series of satirical essays about Swedish society. Sharply radical and republican in tone, this collection, published as *The New Kingdom*, exposed the hypocrisy and cant of the reign of Oscar II. Strindberg tackled his subject with characteristic venom and the conservative press, backed up by the establishment, responded in kind with scathing reviews.

He followed this up with *Swedish Destinies and Adventures*, a collection of short stories, all of them set in the past. They are full of dramatic action and good, strong characters and offer fine descriptions of milieu. Strindberg used these stories to continue his criticism of Swedish society and it was his purpose to stir up feelings, which he certainly managed to do. Of all his fiction, this is the book that Siri always said she liked the best.

Although he was extremely productive in 1882, Strindberg became somewhat withdrawn, a condition not helped by the fact that his daughter Greta contracted pneumonia that year and his sister Elisabeth suffered her first serious bout of mental illness. He continued working as hard as ever and responded to the pressure by drinking more heavily than usual and taking tranquillizers to help him relax.

Strindberg's depression may also have been due in part to his anxiety about Siri's behaviour now that she had had her first taste of celebrity. She embraced the theatre and all it offered with wholehearted enthusiasm, spending her money on expensive clothes – with the perfect excuse that an actress had to supply her own wardrobe – and often staying out with her new friends at late-night parties. All of this drew her away from Strindberg and he began to feel increasingly resentful. Though he was drinking more himself he did not like it when Siri did the same, as it made her, in his eyes, loud and vulgar, as a friend of theirs, Nils Selander, noted when he wrote about them in 1927:

> I remember Maundy Thursday in 1882, when after an Easter party celebrated at 'the Club', we were standing at Norrmalmstorg early in the morning. The rest of us wanted to go to bed but Siri was stubborn and tried to persuade us to carry on partying. Our resistance was not too great so she won us over. The Strindbergs were living at Östermalmsgatan at the time. August and I spent some hours after the late meal in his study with our cigars. Siri stayed with Pelle Janzon and Frithiof Kjellberg at the table where they were drinking into the small hours. ---It was impossible to break up the Bacchanalian feast because of Siri's obstinate resistance, and in the morning the crowd was even jollier, and the young wife and Frithiof Kjellberg were totally intoxicated.
>
> Later, when I talked to August about this unfortunate situation he told me that it did not help to speak to her about it, he could not stop her because then she would just drink in secret and that would be even worse.
>
> *Carl XVs glada dagar*

The biographer Harry Jacobsen reproaches Siri for not appreciating the effect her rather wild behaviour was having on her husband:

> Her character was not strong enough to avoid situations which inevitably had a disillusioning effect on the person who had made her into an idol. Jealousy was a feeling that she herself did not suffer from.
>
> *Strindberg och hans första hustru*

And Strindberg's sisters Anna and Nora make much the same point in their book, though they apportion the blame more equally:

> For thirteen years they stayed together, in happiness and sorrow and neither of them could be exclusively blamed for the break-up. Siri von Essen was an impractical person, nervous and strong-willed. August was unreasonably suspicious and jealous . . .
>
> *Strindbergs systrar berättar om barndomshemmet och om bror August Strindberg*

It would appear that Strindberg's outbursts of jealousy were not always unreasonable for there was one occasion when his suspicions about Siri might have had some foundation. When she came back from her Finnish tour she told him about a man she had met and mentioning him more than once. According to the critic Bo Bennich-Björkman, Strindberg seems to have been remarkably clear about the details of this mysterious liaison, including the name of the hotel in Helsingfors where Siri had met this man and the restaurant where they had dined together.

Over the following year Strindberg felt with increasing urgency that it was time to leave Sweden for a while. He had many reasons, among them a desire to get Siri away from her theatrical milieu perhaps, and the fact that the outspoken articles that he was writing for Hjalmar Branting's left-wing newspaper *Tiden* were bringing him a certain notoriety. The Swedish establishment had made it clear that they did not care for his views and they had the power to make things uncomfortable for him. As a result of all this he was beginning to feel claustrophobic. He was in touch with many friends and fellow artists who were enjoying more tolerant climes – in the political as well as the literal sense – in France or Germany, and he was tempted to join them.

The two deciding factors were a small legacy of around 2000 kronor that Strindberg's father left him when he died in 1883, and Siri's announcement at the end of the summer that she was pregnant again. She knew that she would have to give up work, at least temporarily, so it seemed to be the right time to go abroad. They planned to be away for about six months, returning in time to take their usual summer holiday at the cottage on Kymmendö.

At the beginning of September they sold most of their possessions, packed their trunks and left Stockholm with their two children and a maid. Neither of them dreamt that they would be away for the next six years, living in a succession of cheap hotels, boarding houses and rented rooms in more than twenty different places in France, Switzerland, Germany and Denmark. Nor did Siri realize that her career as a professional actress in Sweden was over.

— Chapter 6 —

On the Move

The children have given us great pleasure because they have scared all the passengers away from the compartment; we are displaying them regularly through the window at all the station platforms.

Letter to Pehr Staaff, 18 September 1883

The first place that Strindberg and Siri went to when they left Sweden was Grèz-sur-Loing (also known as Grèz par Nemours), a small village near Fontainebleau about 50 miles south of Paris. Carl Larsson had told them what a delightful place it was – it was fast developing as the centre of an artists' colony that attracted many Scandinavian painters – and it was he who came to meet them at the nearest railway station at Barron when they arrived. On this occasion the Strindbergs stayed just ten days but they were to return many times over the next four years.

Grèz was a relaxed and friendly place and Siri and Strindberg were made welcome straight away. A Finnish sculptor, Ville Vallgren, describes his first meeting with them in his book *ABC*:

> When Strindberg came down from his rooms into the big dining room for lunch he looked very earnest, dressed in a tight-fitting frock coat. Calle [Carl] Larsson introduced us. And Mrs Strindberg said: 'Dear God, Mr Vallgren, are you from Borgå? And I'm from Jackarby!' Strindberg scrutinized me. He was a bit glum and quiet, maybe because he did not know anyone else at the table, apart from Larsson. At dinner he was equally earnest, but later in the evening when we were having coffee and brandy he became more talkative.

Strindberg used his time on this holiday to write a piece on Carl Larsson for the Swedish journal *SVEA* while Siri produced an amusing article, 'The Artists' Colony in Grèz par Nemours', about the daily goings-on at the resort, which was published in February 1884 in the Swedish magazine *Ny Illustrerad Tidning*.

The company at Grèz was lively and stimulating and Strindberg later described some of the drinking parties as 'orgies', though his recollection of events tends to be inconsistent. In the letters that he wrote at the time he stresses the general bonhomie but in *A Madman's Defence* the activities

The Artists' Colony in Grèz par Nemours

Facing you in the best road in the village you will find Hôtel Chevillon, and a little further down the road, Hôtel Beauséjour, with a large garden stretching down to the river. [. . .]

At about seven o'clock in the morning people start moving in the hotel. That is when the servants begin their morning tasks. Maybe the odd guest can be seen as well before half past seven, when coffee is served. [. . .]

During your walk in the garden you will see strange creatures pass by. Ladies and gentlemen walk amicably side by side in their bathing costumes and bathrobes towards the river where a jetty provides the swimmers with opportunity for jumping into clear deep water. [. . .]

After lunch the real work begins in Grèz. It is a very convenient hour because you then have six hours left before dinner.

The painters take their canvases out into the open, often into the garden, which is already depicted from all corners, sometimes even further afield, to roads and meadows. Some take their motifs from the river bank and work standing up in their boats. One American has built himself a real Noah's Ark, without a roof, in order to harbour a canvas of larger than normal dimensions.

In rainy weather, when the artists prefer not to take cover under their large umbrellas, it is possible to work indoors. The billiard room is then transformed into a studio in a jiffy. The one big window in there seems to indicate that this is what it was originally intended for. On the walls there are masses of paintings: sketches and mad fancies to commemorate every artist who has left the area. [. . .]

Before dinner you can take walks in several directions. The small Swedish community usually keeps together and they set off on pilgrimages to nearby villages. Preferably to Moncourt to eat grapes. The walk there is of average length, the purpose pleasant enough and the little village, which still lacks Grèz's increasingly upper-class tone and remains rustic in a picturesque way, has become one of their favourite haunts.

At seven o'clock dinner is served . . . sometimes the odd bottle of akvavit manages to find its way there from Paris. Then there is great joy among the Scandinavians. Drinking songs are sung to the surprise of the Americans who find this custom strange but nice and let the tunes affect them in a favourable and uplifting way.

become more boisterous. Carl Larsson's wife, Karin, wrote a letter from Grèz to her parents where she describes an incident where the revelry certainly got out of hand:

> Last Friday the Strindbergs left. The evening before they left they invited us to coffee, brandy and liqueur in the dining-room where people were singing and playing the guitar. An American who had arrived that evening sat down with us. He had rather too much to drink, which made him utter some ambiguous remarks to us ladies so Carl took me upstairs. After that the American treated the company to some arrack, which resulted in him having to be carried upstairs to his room. He had resorted to rather violent embraces with a poor old lady at the hotel and since her room was adjacent to his she had demanded that his door be locked from the outside.
>
> In the middle of the night we all woke up from a gunshot – and then another one – the American is shooting himself!
>
> It was a terrible moment. Everybody rushed into the corridor, calling 'Garçon!' and 'garde champêtre', saying that we should force open the door etc. Finally, people realized, by listening at his door, that he was shooting at some invisible enemies. He was drunk and furious at finding his door locked.
>
> Madame West, stiff with fear, was rescued into our room and put on our sofa. You should have seen our gathering, the old lady in a raincoat and galoshes, Carl and I in our nightshirts, Spada in his Spanish coat. Then another couple of shots followed and after he had tried in vain to break the door, everything was quiet.
>
> The day after the poor man – who then looked like the meekest person you could imagine – had to beg forgiveness and solemnly hand over his gun.

Their brief holiday went some way to easing the stress that Strindberg and Siri had been under since leaving Sweden, though the mood does not seem to have lasted long. When the weather turned colder they found that their hotel was not quite so comfortable so they went to Paris. The city turned out to be something of a rude shock, however, as Strindberg wrote to his friend Claes Looström on 15 October:

> It is abominably expensive here. Our maid does not speak a word of French and my wife goes out in a serge coat and brings back the paraffin and the bread-basket herself. The fireplaces are just holes in the wall which inhale the smoke and exhale what little warmth there is. It is a bloody awful country and the whole nation is full of crooks.

In these rather squalid conditions Siri managed as best she could and Strindberg worked on some short stories for his book, *Swedish Destinies and Adventures*. He cheered himself up by writing a long narrative poem called 'Second Night', which is a light-hearted portrait of the writer abroad; it captures the contentment that he found with Siri during their visit to Grèz.

The Strindbergs stayed in Paris for the next four or five months, living in a series of draughty rented rooms in Passy and Neuilly. During this time Strindberg met two well-known Norwegian writers, Bjørnstjerne Bjørnson (who was a future Nobel Laureate) and Jonas Lie. Strindberg wrote a flattering article about Bjørnson for the French literary journal *Le Monde poétique* and their friendship flourished for a while but Bjørnson, with his well-meaning but passionate nature, tended to interfere too much in other people's lives. He did not care much for Siri. 'She ought to be content with just being August's wife,' he told Strindberg's publisher Albert Bonnier on one occasion, 'that is "the vocation" she should devote herself to – and as an outspoken friend I have told him so – with the risk of losing his friendship.' And lose it he nearly did for Strindberg would not stand by and see his wife criticized. 'Bjørnson is a spiritual cannibal who wants to eat up all souls that come within his reach,' he wrote to his friend Isidor Kjellberg on 1 November 1884. 'I fled from Paris for that reason. He wanted to eat up my wife too but then I hit back.'

Bjørnson thought that Strindberg would do better as a writer if he stayed away from Sweden but he realized that this would be frustrating for Siri, whom he knew was 'mad about the theatre'. She had no hope of finding work as an actress outside Scandinavia but she had made it clear that she was not prepared to give up her career just yet. Bjørnson had been told by various Swedish expatriates living in Paris that Siri's acting talent was nothing special and so he took it on himself to write to Ludvig Josephson in Stockholm asking him to persuade Siri to sacrifice her ambitions so that Strindberg would not be held back. Josephson did not do as he was asked, though this was not because he had any particular interest in Siri's prospects. What he wanted was to see Strindberg back in Stockholm, for *Lucky Per's Journey* had done well, running to 50 performances, and he was looking for more successful plays from the same source.

Lucky Per's Journey had earned Strindberg a respectable 2000 kronor and so, depressed by the gloomy Parisian winter, he decided to move on and go to Switzerland. In January 1884 the family rented a chalet in Ouchy, a village on Lake Geneva near Lausanne. When Siri saw the Alps for the first time she was so overcome by the grandeur of the landscape that she wept at the sheer beauty of it all.

Writing to Bjørnson a month later, Strindberg tells him how supportive Siri is:

> I can't live without my wife. She is a good wife, she is my only friend and I have often cried myself healthy and strong again with my head in her lap. Even if she

Strindberg's 'Second Night' was included in a collection of prose poems, Sleepless Nights on Waking Days, *which was published in 1884.*

Second Night

Sunny pictures from the day before
Pass before the tired eye:
Le déjeuner is already finished
By our little artists' colony of
Swedes, Yankees, Finns, negresses
Who sought peace in Beauséjour,
Left Paris, models, excesses
And settled down in Grèz par Nemours.

Diverse groups stroll in the garden
The sun is midday warm
Swedes and Norwegians
Frenchmen and Germans link arms,
The sun is shining on white walls
Blue grapes on a green trellis
A golden pear lurks among the foliage
Only to end up dead at the next *diner*.
Fiery red tomatoes glow like embers
Between forests of artichokes
Diaphanous lettuces shiver with anaemia
Cauliflowers which will never beget any
young.
[. . .]

Young couples joke and laugh
Children swarm in rollicking teams.
Now the wine is being passed around,
The flute is tuned to a Spanish guitar.
[. . .]

People dance on verdant ground
Without full evening dress.
Summer clothes in the light park —
Fête champêtre, an idyll by Watteau!

doesn't understand fully what I want and doesn't encourage me to do battle she will always comfort me when I go to her, defeated and wretched, because she has such an immense well of goodness . . .

On 3 April their son Hans was born. They had planned to spend the summer months on Kymmendö as usual but at the last minute they decided not to go. As Strindberg had already paid the rent on the cottage with the green shutters he offered it to his brother Axel.

In May Strindberg started work on the first volume of a collection of twelve short stories, *Getting Married*, completing the manuscript in six weeks. He was familiar with a play that Bjørnson had written about marriage called *A Gauntlet* and he thought it would be interesting to explore the same subject. Bjørnson's argument was that men and women should remain chaste before marriage and he believed that the same rules of conduct should apply to both sexes equally. In his play he exposes the hypocrisy of a society that allowed men to have pre-marital sexual relationships while women were condemned for doing the same thing, which he argued was both unfair and unethical. *A Gauntlet* fuelled the ongoing debate about 'the woman question' in Scandinavia. A large number of novels, plays, short stories and articles addressed this subject in the 1880s and the period saw several writers emerging who put the arguments in favour of women's emancipation at the core of their work, including, for example, Victoria Benedictsson, who published her work under a male pseudonym, Ernst Ahlgren.

Strindberg was certainly not against women at this point. A few years earlier he had planned to publish a radical journal with several prominent writers, including Anne Charlotte Leffler-Edgren, Anna Whitlock and Amalia Fahlstedt, as collaborators. In January 1882 he had written to the writer Helena Nyblom:

> Don't you agree with me that politics will become more humane and much simpler when, one day, women want to get involved. Nowadays, politics are as repulsive to me, as a poet, as the tavern because I can never meet my wife or my loved ones there; and all politics have to be conducted in basements. One can't bring it into the home. Why not? On the whole, it is the women's own fault. Women have themselves to blame.

In *Getting Married* Strindberg speaks very strongly in favour of equality between the sexes but rather than advocating enforced celibacy like Bjørnson he argues in favour of sexual relationships before marriage for both men and women. This was a revolutionary idea since at that time a girl of 'good family' was expected to keep her virginity intact until her wedding night. It was her most valuable asset as it gave the husband the reassurance he demanded that any children born of the marriage were his own. Even so, as Strindberg demonstrates in his play *The Father*, a woman could still tantalize a man by planting doubts in his mind about the paternity of his children if she chose. On the other hand, a man could always deny paternity if it suited him, a point that Strindberg also makes in *The Father*. Men had always had recourse to prostitutes (though invariably with the attendant risk of contracting a venereal disease), and there were certain categories of working-class women, such as waitresses and servants, who were regarded as fair game. These were the women who were usually abandoned or paid off by a man if they became pregnant.

Strindberg was not in favour of promiscuity or free love. What he did condemn was what he saw as the coyness of conventional courtship; he wanted the relationship between the sexes to be more natural. The recurring theme in the stories in *Getting Married* is that people should enjoy what nature – or God – offers and should learn to make fewer demands on life and greater demands on themselves.

In the foreword to the first volume of *Getting Married* he writes: 'The woman question as it now stands . . . only applies to the cultivated woman, maybe 10% of the population and is consequently a question for a small coterie.' In one of the stories he describes the old agricultural society where women were treated equally and shared the work and burdens with their menfolk. A farmer's wife was seldom unfaithful, he argued, because she simply did not have the time or energy for extra-marital affairs. Here Strindberg reveals that he was not ready to challenge the prevailing belief in patriarchy: he still expected a woman to return to her traditional role as a wife and mother after her daily work outside the home was done.

In many other respects, however, Strindberg was revolutionary in his support for women in an age when they had so few statutory rights. He listed a number of things which he believed wholeheartedly in, for example a woman's right to equal educational opportunities. He proposed that schools should be co-educational and was convinced that many problems in relationships between men and women were caused by single-sex schools. Girls and boys should be taught exactly the same things. In Paragraph 4.0 of 'Woman's Rights' he writes:

> Complete equality between the sexes would get rid of the awful hypocrisy called chivalry, or politeness towards the ladies. Consequently, a girl should not demand that a boy gets up and offers his place to her, because that is a sign of slavish submission, and a brother must not insist that his sisters make his bed or sew on his shirt buttons; he can do that himself.

Karin Strindberg confirms that her parents lived by these principles themselves and they wanted a good education for all three of their children. They treated them all the same and Hans was brought up alongside his sisters to learn how to sew, to make his own bed and to help with all the other domestic chores. He was even given his own dolls to play with.

Strindberg was ahead of his time in thinking that women should have the vote – this was not achieved in Sweden until 1921 – and that they should have equal job opportunities, although this did not extend to military service:

> Women should be exempt from military service. To those who think this is unjust I would like to point out that nature demands its own compensation in the form of pregnancies. Anyway, in future it will not be such a glorious thing to do military service. It will be just a duty.
>
> *Paragraph 8.0 'Woman's Rights'*

He foresaw a time when every citizen would be guaranteed a basic education and there would be a fairer distribution of wealth so that women would not be tempted to get married merely for financial security:

> Man and wife make a contract, orally or written, about a union, to run as long as they like, and which they, without the help of the law or the Bible have the right to dissolve whenever they please. Obviously, two males cannot want to possess the same female, but the battle will not be so cruel and the female will be the one who decides, which is not the case now, because no one should need to get married for the sake of money or rank; that will be abolished. So selection will be natural and the race consequently improved.
>
> *Paragraph 9.0 'Woman's Rights'*

Strindberg recognized the value of housework and child-rearing as equal work within the family structure and when it came to managing joint finances he proves himself to be more radical than many men are more than a hundred years later:

> If the woman earns money during her marriage and does not look after her household, she is obliged to leave as much towards the housekeeping as the husband. If she works in the house as well, she should keep her salary because her work in the home should then be considered a bonus and not a slave's job.
>
> *Paragraph 15.0 'Woman's Rights'*

He believed that a husband and wife should have separate bedrooms and that even if the woman depended on the man for an allowance this should not be regarded as a price she has to pay for sexual favours. He also thought that a man had a special responsibility to ensure that his wife and children would be properly cared for if anything happened to him.

The man should, when entering into marriage, be obliged to buy a life insurance so as not to leave his wife and children in need when he dies, especially if his wife used to have a lucrative profession.

Paragraph 11.0 'Woman's Rights'

Considering how many times Strindberg was forced to sell his insurance policies so that the family could eat, this was perhaps rather too much of an idealistic proposal, as was another of his more radical ideas – that a married woman should keep her maiden name. When Harriet Bosse proposed to do exactly this and, perhaps more importantly, pass her surname rather than Strindberg's on to their daughter some twenty years later, he was very put out.

Siri had always held strong views on the rights of women herself and when she read the manuscript of *Getting Married* she endorsed most of Strindberg's opinions and proposals. One of her earliest childhood friends, Constance Mellin, went on to become a well-known feminist in Finland, and Siri had met other women who were independent professionals, like the pianist Ina Forstén and the writer Emilie Björksten. Her brand of feminism was not totally radical for she agreed with Strindberg in much of his criticism of the emancipated woman who had no time for family values; she wanted to combine motherhood and a fulfilling career and had no desire to abandon her family completely, like Nora in *A Doll's House*. Maybe the death of her first child, Sigrid, so soon after she had left Carl Gustaf, and the loss of her next baby just a few months later softened her views, though she was certainly in no position to criticize women who wanted to have a career of their own, even at the expense of motherhood.

In the summer of 1884 Strindberg moved his family away from the heat of Lausanne to the town of Chexbres in the Swiss Alps. Ludvig Josephson travelled to see him in July and offered him a generous advance for a new play. Strindberg was not currently working on anything for the stage and did not have anything specific in mind so he shelved the project for the time being. But he was still writing prolifically. He produced a few more stories with historical settings for the *Swedish Destinies* collection and completed a light-hearted tale called 'The Island of the Blissfully Happy'.

It was while they were in Chexbres that Siri and Strindberg met Hélène Welinder. She was a Swiss, married to a Swede, and she was visiting her brother, who owned the small hotel where the Strindbergs were staying. She got to know the family well and she remembers Strindberg as a calm and considerate man, always careful about his appearance and polite towards the ladies but in an easy and effortless way. She found him absent-minded and a little withdrawn and sad at times but never sullen. He rarely went to the drawing-room after dinner but he would sit on the stone steps outside and listen to Siri singing and playing the piano and reading his poetry aloud for the entertainment of the other guests.

When Strindberg died in 1912 Hélène Welinder wrote a long article about him that was published in the Swedish literary journal *Ord & Bild:*

> My brother introduced me and the ladies uttered some polite phrases. In the end a slim gentleman dressed in a light grey suit and wearing a straw hat appeared; he carried a tin box attached to a strap across his shoulder. 'Monsieur Strindberg! – ma soeur!' A penetrating gaze, quick as lightning from the blue-grey eyes, a look which seemed to ask: 'friend or foe?' and his hand met mine in a firm grip.

Hélène had been living in Sweden for six years and she knew Strindberg by reputation. Her image of him had come largely from the right-wing press, who invariably portrayed him as a coarse, cynical and vulgar writer and a ruthless troublemaker who was a bad influence on the young. She also remembered all the fuss there had been when his controversial novel *The Red Room* was published, though she had not read it. When she met him in person she surrendered completely to his charm:

> All my prejudices about August Strindberg were dissolved like the morning mist and I was seized by an immense and as it seemed quite unmotivated feeling of compassion. It was inexplicable because he looked neither ill nor melancholy since he was revitalized after his walk.

Siri she found much more outgoing and sociable:

> She was, if I remember rightly, thirty-two, but looked younger, especially at a distance. Sometimes she let her blonde hair hang down her back in two plaits and with her slim figure, her fine little head and her pale complexion she looked quite a Gretchen.

The first volume of *Getting Married* was published in Stockholm on 27 September 1884 in an edition of 4000 copies and Strindberg received 3750 kronor for it. On the surface there did not appear to be anything really inflammable about the stories but within a week of publication Strindberg was to find himself at the centre of a huge public row.

— Chapter 7 —

Troubled Times

... the outrageous deceit which took place with Högstedt's Piccadon and Lennström's wafers of maize at 1 kr a lb, which, according to the clergyman, was the flesh and blood of Jesus from Nazareth, the rebel who had been executed 1800 years ago.
'The Reward of Virtue', Getting Married, Vol. I

On 3 October 1884, six days after the publication of the first volume of *Getting Married*, the Sheriff appeared at the offices of Bonnier's publishing house in Stockholm with a warrant to search the premises. He confiscated 320 copies of the book on the spot. At the same time the police were mounting a raid on the city's bookshops and managed to seize a further 140 copies. It is a measure of Strindberg's popularity that over 3000 copies had already been distributed and sold.

On 7 October an order for Strindberg's arrest was issued. The initiative for all this seemed to come from the King, Oscar II, and his German-born wife, Queen Sofia (who was widely regarded as even more conservative than he was), backed up by his ministers and certain proprietors of the right-wing press. The charge was 'Blasphemy against God or mockery against God's holy words and sacraments', in relation to a passage from the first story in *Getting Married*, entitled 'The Reward of Virtue'.

King Oscar II hated the radical press and he had tried more than once to get the old laws granting freedom of expression repealed. He perceived Strindberg, an ardent republican who had criticized the establishment and the monarchy on several occasions, most notably in his book *The New Kingdom*, to be a personal threat.

As a constitutional monarch, Oscar II's position on the throne was by no means secure. When he succeeded in 1872 Sweden had been through almost a century of turmoil that had begun with the assassination of Gustav III in 1792. Gustav III's son, Gustav IV, had been deposed in 1809 after taking the country into a series of disastrous wars that culminated in the loss of Finland and other territories to Russia. This marked the end of the Holstein-Gottorp dynasty. The next king, Jean Bernadotte, who became

Karl XIV Johan of Sweden in 1818, was a Frenchman who had served as a General under Napoleon. Oscar II, who came to the throne in 1872, was Bernadotte's grandson and was Sweden's third constitutional monarch. His position depended very much on public consensus and he had every reason to be wary of republicans like Strindberg.

Albert Bonnier urged Strindberg to return to Stockholm to face the blasphemy charge in person. As a prominent Swedish Jew, Bonnier was in a difficult position; he too faced the possibility of prosecution as the publisher and distributor of alleged anti-Christian material. Strindberg promised to sign a declaration exonerating his publisher and taking sole responsibility for his own work but Bonnier was not satisfied with such an undertaking. He sent his son, Karl Otto, to persuade Strindberg to come back and defend himself, with an inducement of 1000 francs to cover his expenses.

It was not an easy decision for Strindberg. Siri and their son Hans were both ill and he was reluctant to leave them, and Bjørnson, who had initially advised him to stay away, was now urging him to fight the charge. Either way, it was likely that Strindberg would be given a sentence of up to two years in prison or a heavy fine if found guilty. Accepting that he really had no choice, he set off on the long journey from Switzerland by train. When he arrived at the Central Station in Stockholm on 20 October he was surprised to see a crowd of some 500 people waiting there to greet him. He made an impromptu speech on the platform and thanked everyone for their support. He assured them that he believed in God and explained that his criticisms were directed specifically at the Lutheran Church, whose doctrine regarding the sacraments he believed were illogical and unreasonable.

To show his support, Ludvig Josephson put on a special gala performance of *Lucky Per's Journey* at the Nya Teatern on the day that Strindberg arrived back in Stockholm. The evening was a sell-out and the atmosphere in the auditorium was electric. After the third and fourth acts, which satirize the cant in society and refer to 'the true faith' as the only option, the applause was deafening. At the end Strindberg was called onto the stage, where he was decorated with a laurel wreath and showered with bouquets. Further crowds greeted him outside the theatre afterwards. It was one of the proudest moments of his life.

Strindberg made his first appearance in court the next day, having elected to conduct his own defence. Albert Bonnier was spared prosecution himself and he had instructed his lawyers to give Strindberg all the help and legal advice he needed. The trial lasted for two weeks, during which time experts in law and theology were brought in as witnesses for both sides.

The whole affair became something of a *cause célèbre* and as there had not been a similar case in Sweden for over fifty years the newspapers were writing about the trial every day. Strindberg received more than 300 letters of support, his champions coming mainly from the student population and the intelligentsia as was to be expected. He was backed by the left-wing and liberal press and he found an ally in the socialist politician Hjalmar Branting (later to become Prime Minister), who wrote a stirring piece in the radical newspaper *Tiden;* Rudolf Wall, editor of Sweden's largest newspaper, *Dagens Nyheter*, also defended him. His most vociferous opponents were the right-wing press and the Lutheran Church, together with members of various ultra-conservative women's organizations.

On 17 November the jury returned a verdict of 'Not Guilty' (by a majority of just one) and Strindberg was acquitted. He addressed his supporters in the crowd outside the courtroom before making his way to the Grand Hotel for a celebration dinner with several of his friends, including Gustaf af Geijerstam and Pehr Staaff

Altogether, Strindberg was away from Siri and the children for five weeks and in spite of his relief at the outcome of the trial the whole business had been an enormous strain. He had found the legal proceedings and their aftermath totally humiliating and felt that he had been publicly pilloried. The establishment had used all its force to try and destroy his reputation, and the knowledge that he had hundreds of supporters did not console him. He left Stockholm hating the country that had tried to silence him in such a brutal way. When he returned to Chexbres he found that Siri was still not well and was suffering with respiratory problems.

Hélène Welinder recalled how Siri and Strindberg celebrated their seventh wedding anniversary at her brother's hotel in December 1884: after the meal Strindberg proposed a toast to Siri, who rose to her feet and raised her glass to him with a graceful gesture, saying in a tone that was so genuinely affectionate that Hélène never forgot her words: 'Thank you for seven happy years!'

It is possible that they would have gone on to enjoy another seven years of happiness if Strindberg had not had such a harsh encounter with Swedish justice that autumn. The distasteful episode began a process that was eventually to turn his whole marriage sour. Siri's health was adversely affected by the stress of the court case and Strindberg's absence and, being of a nervous disposition, she seemed to collapse just when he needed her most.

The blasphemy trial therefore marked two important turning points in Strindberg's life: the beginning of the end of his relationship with Siri and his dramatic loss of sympathy towards women in general. From this moment he sharpened his claws and went into battle in almost everything that he wrote. Up until then he had always been a strong defender of women's rights but he had lost patience with the cause during the trial because of the upper-class bias of the feminist organizations that had attacked him. (When he returned to Switzerland he discovered that Siri had received a letter from Sophie Adlersparre, who was in the process of setting up the first official Swedish women's group, the Fredrika Bremer Association. Strindberg was both suspicious and offended by this approach and he urged Siri to have nothing to do with it.) His rigid response at this point meant, unfortunately, that the more politically radical women's groups that sprang up later failed to enlist his sympathy.

Strindberg's specific response to the blasphemy trial was to sit down and write a second volume of *Getting Married*, which he began in the spring of 1885 when he and Siri were staying in France, first in Paris and then in Luc-sur-Mer on the Normandy coast. He used the book to launch an outright attack on all those women – including Queen Sofia – who had called for his prosecution. His bitterness and desire for revenge permeate almost every page. He starts by marshalling a series of quotes from world literature by writers such as Aristotle, Rousseau, Schopenhauer and Herbert Spencer to support his opinions about the real power that women hold and their capacity for cunning and goes on to deliver a number of scathing statements that fly like bullets: 'Woman loves her man only because of the advantages he offers.' 'Why isn't there one single hymn to Man, written by a woman in our whole National literature? Because she despises the person she has subjugated.' Volume II of *Getting Married* is the book that first gained him his reputation as a misogynist.

Siri, who until then had been totally supportive of everything Strindberg wrote, made it clear that she did not approve of these latest stories. She thought that they were negative about women, hateful in places even, and she found the tone offensive. She would have preferred him to stick to drama and historical fiction. Victoria Benedictsson, on the other hand, found a lot to admire in the new collection. She was the only contemporary Swedish woman writer that Strindberg respected and took seriously and she shared his distrust of the upper-class feminist clique in Stockholm, having refused to align herself with the new women's association that had tried and failed to recruit Siri to their cause. When Sophie Adlersparre warned her against the radical intelligentsia, Benedictsson responded sharply by telling her that she was already a part of it.

As soon as she had got hold of a copy of *Getting Married II* Benedictsson immediately told everyone how good it was. She wrote enthusiastically about it to her friend Axel Lundegård on 9 October 1886 before she had even finished it:

> It is the truth that he tells us. He can be prejudiced, I don't deny that, but it is great, healthy truth that he speaks. I feel in a way more honourable and better as a person after having read them; ---- He is torn asunder and nervous, he is on the edge of madness, where you see enemies everywhere, ---- but the basic idea is true: it is against the indolence of the well-to-do women that the fight should be aimed. It is the husbands who are unfairly treated in such middle-class marriages, where women are too refined to work, so he is a slave. I have seen that happen long before Strindberg started to talk about it. So the basic idea in the book I agree with. That is why I have been so fascinated [. . .]
>
> I have read it ['It Is Not Enough'] twice. It is short. It is about nothing in particular. It is a masterpiece.---- It is so simple, so warm, so fine in feeling. To think that he could write something like that! It is just about an old woman. I am so fond of it that it brings tears to my eyes, and I would like to sleep with it under my pillow so that I could touch it with my thin old hand when I wake up. It is so artless, without any adornments, any stab; it is a slice of life, lifted up by the most tender hand and put inside an unadorned frame, the smallest little frame. Just the head of an old woman – but that is what I call art.

In a letter to another male friend, written a few weeks later, on 2 November, she is more critical:

> Strindberg is right when he insists that women have obligations too, he is wrong when he says that she is bad and evil all the way through. He has completely forgotten how much women's vanity is due to men's superficiality. And he forgets that lack of freedom always engenders deceit, that refers to unfree men as much as unfree women. The law has been against women, that is why women have had to claim their rights with cunning.

Strindberg had attacked Ibsen's ideas about women in *Getting Married I*, even going so far as to call one of his own stories 'A Doll's House' so that there could be no doubt who and what his target was. He returned to the subject in his foreword to *Getting Married II* but on the advice of his publisher, Isidor Bonnier, he had the sensitivity to cut the references to Ibsen before it was published:

> Ibsen has committed an ugly self-violation in *A Doll's House* where he preaches female tyranny inside marriage. She lies and cheats on her husband, but he puts his trust in her completely. And yet, he is the one who is portrayed as the bad person.

The story in Getting Married II *that Victoria Benedictsson liked best was 'It Is Not Enough', which describes self-sacrificing motherly love as something noble but ultimately ungratifying.*

It Is Not Enough

Madame St. Brie owns a small family hotel in Passy. She is a widow of forty-eight and has three sons. One is twenty-eight and married, one is twenty-six and also married, one is twenty-four, unmarried and an artist. Her husband was a doctor but died, after having been honoured with a decoration two years previously.

She runs a small hotel, which is enough to live on, but her son, who is a painter, needs models, paints, brushes, canvases, a studio and his absinthe. That is the reason why she is running a hotel, but she also loves having people around her.

Her two elder sons never come and see her. The daughters-in-law have wrenched them away from their mother. During her whole married life she has lived only for her children and she has no other interests. Now they are gone and she is alone with the youngest who is never at home. She may live another thirty years but she has no one to live for any more and she can't live just for herself because she was born and brought up to be a mother, or to live for others. Charles, the artist, has squeezed a lot of money out of her this April because he is going to exhibit at the Salon for the first time, and they are now waiting for a reply from the jury. This morning Charles came down to breakfast. He was pale-faced with some dark colour under his eyes. His eyes looked as if they had been smeared with green engine oil. A dewy cold sweat had settled around the hairline and a less than fresh breath emanated from his mouth.

'Where were you yesterday, my dear?' asked the mother, while putting six oysters on his plate.

'That's none of your business,' answered Charles, smelling the oysters. 'Portuguese! Ugh!'

'I wanted to give you something nice,' said the mother.

'Don't fuss,' said Charles. 'You're killing me with your fussing around and I'll bloody well move out if you carry on like this.'

The mother turned to one of her hotel guests, a young wife with two little boys at her side.

'These children of ours are a source of joy, aren't they? Two of mine have flown the nest and this is the last one. Isn't he charming towards his mother?'

'Certainly not,' answered the guest.

Charles rose, red-faced, as red as he could be with his thin blood. He shouted: 'Goodbye – I'll send for my things after breakfast.'

The double doors slammed shut and Charles left. His mother burst into tears.

After breakfast a messenger came to fetch his things.

The mother gathered Charles's drawing materials together and wept.

She emptied the drawers and put his clothes in his suitcase. She took the pictures down from the wall and let the maid beat the dust out of his suits and overcoat, and then the room was empty. All her children had flown the nest and now the nest was deserted. What is she going to live for now, for whom is she going to sacrifice her heart for the next thirty years, or perhaps a whole lifetime?

'The laws of nature, my dear Madame St. Brie,' says the guest. 'And we must not bring up our children for our own benefit. We left our parents once and our children will leave us. We demand too much from life and life gives us so little in return.'

'But what am I supposed to do now that everyone has left?' objects the deserted mother.

'Work for us, I suppose,' answered the guest.

'It is not enough. I cannot live alone. I must have someone. I must have someone.'

And now the widow sits there alone, grieving. But she devotes all her attention to the guest's little boys. She plays with them, plays dominoes with them and takes care of them when they are ill. So she has someone to live for for a whole month. But when the month is over they depart. She stands on the steps when they get into their carriage and when the cab moves away towards the highway she follows them with her eyes for so long that one might even think that they took another piece of her heart with them.

But her heart is like Prometheus's liver. It heals up again, even though the vulture keeps pecking at it. And so a new guest arrives, one who travels around, indulging his great sorrow. And he meets the pecked mother's heart. So he gets his share of it and does his own pecking. And then he orders a cab and finally leaves, giving the maids a louis d'or each for their hearts, which he has taken a bit out of. But he doesn't give the widow anything because that would not have seemed right. It is true, he opened his heart and gave her a piece of his sorrow as a souvenir, and she received it and added it to her collection.

But it is silly to live for others. It is not enough, it is not enough.

Ibsen is reported to have been furious when he read Strindberg's story in the first volume of *Getting Married*, so angry in fact that in 1884 he refused to sign a petition calling for money to support the Danish writer J P Jacobsen when he saw Strindberg's name on the list of supporters. Three years later, however, he read *The Father* and was impressed by its dramatic power.

Ibsen and Strindberg never met, though they would have had plenty of opportunities to do so. Instead they circled around one another in print, each of them always fully aware of the other's progress. Ibsen once admitted that he could only work effectively when he sat beneath Christian Krogh's portrait of Strindberg that hung on the wall behind his desk: '. . . not because I am Strindberg's friend,' he said, 'I am his enemy. Nor is it because I am Christian Krogh's friend. I hardly know him. But I can't write a line unless that madman stands there, staring at me with his crazy eyes.' He was always fascinated by Strindberg because he found him 'so subtly, delicately mad'.

The critic Sten Linder points to several direct influences from Strindberg in the later Ibsen plays. For example, Strindberg's nihilistic hero, Doctor Borg, in his novel *The Red Room* (1879), can be compared to Ibsen's Doctor Relling in *The Wild Duck* (1884). Both men are pragmatic and cynical physicians and they serve to throw into relief the human need to maintain illusions. And in *Hedda Gabler* (1890), for instance, Ibsen created a character very closely related to Lady Julie. Strindberg would probably have denied this – he despised Hedda as a wilful, self-seeking sensualist, whereas he sympathized with Lady Julie as a beautiful caged bird who had no defences against the cruelty of men and society. (Strindberg, for his part, was convinced that Ibsen had used him as the model for Hedda's lover, Eilert Lövborg.)

There is no doubt that Strindberg and Ibsen were both interested in strong-minded women. Linder argues that there is an even more striking similarity between Hedda and Hélène, the main character in 'Against Payment', one of the short stories in Strindberg's *Getting Married II*. Each woman is the daughter of an army general and they both enjoy a social position based on the status of their fathers; they are both keen horsewomen and have an aversion to motherhood. They are proud and beautiful, coldly sensual, with a ruthless streak. When they do finally decide to get married, having struggled for independence in a society bound by conservative conventions, each woman makes the mistake of choosing a weak and ineffectual academic for a husband.

Autumn

'Autumn' is one of the most popular stories in Getting Married II *and it illustrates Strindberg's belief in motherhood and the power women have as the life-givers. In the following extract, which is the end of the story, a couple who have been married for ten years return to their familiar domestic routine after failing to recapture the passionate feelings they once had for each other.*

His wife came into the room when she had finished with the children.
—It is no weather for picking wild strawberries she said.
—No, my dear, summer is over and it is autumn.
—Yes, it is autumn, she answered, but that doesn't mean that it is winter, which is always a comfort.
—A comfort! Not much of a comfort when you only live once!
—Twice if you have children, three times if you live to see your grandchildren!
—But after that it is definitely finished.
—Unless there is a life after this.
—There is no guarantee of that! But who knows? I believe in it, but my belief is no proof!
—Yes, but it is nice to believe, let us believe so, let us believe that there can be another spring for us! Let us believe that!
—Yes, we shall believe that, he said and put his arm round her waist!

The End

Strindberg and Ibsen both saw the role of women in society as an important subject for debate and analysis and on occasion it turned out that their opinions were not so very different after all. Ibsen gave a lecture to the Norwegian Women's Association in 1898 and said that he 'was not quite clear what the woman question was all about. To me it has been more of a human issue . . . It is women who are going to solve the human problem but as mothers. And it is only in that capacity that they can they do it.' This is a statement that could have been taken directly from Strindberg's second volume of *Getting Married* for it echoes his sentiments entirely.

Towards the end of the summer of 1885 Strindberg and his family returned to Grèz-sur-Loing, where they stayed for nine months. As usual they had trouble paying their bills and Strindberg raised some money by getting his brother Axel to sell off what remained of their books, furniture and other household effects in Stockholm.

At Grèz Siri and Strindberg made the acquaintance of two young Danish women, Marie David and Sophie Holten, who were to have a long-lasting effect on their marriage. Marie was twenty years old, intelligent and wealthy. She came from a well-known Jewish family but declared herself a confirmed Protestant and said that her mother, who had recently died, had converted to Catholicism. It was rumoured that Marie was illegitimate – her mother had had several notorious love affairs during her marriage – and her real father could have been either the family's one-time tutor or the writer Georg Brandes. Marie had originally wanted to become a doctor but now, encouraged by her companion, Sophie, who was seven years older and an artist, she had ambitions to be a writer. Sophie had studied painting in Paris and had lodged at the apartment of Siri's Aunt Caroline Fröhlich and Cousin Edma.

Back in Grèz once more Siri was in her element and she had no difficulty slipping back into the old bohemian lifestyle. She joined forces with Marie and Sophie to perform *tableaux vivants* that she and Strindberg had devised for the entertainment of the other guests at the *pension*. Strindberg enjoyed himself too. In November he wrote to his friend the Swedish poet Verner von Heidenstam, describing the fun:

> ... a decent orgy ... with singing, guitar-playing, tambourines, pipes and wild joie de vivre, cabaret, dancing, late supper with the girls (a couple of Danes), dinner with our own café-chantant and then dancing at Chevillon's. It was almost Decameron-like.'

To begin with Strindberg enjoyed the stimulating company of Marie David and Sophie Holten, who, even in the relaxed and liberal atmosphere at Grèz, had caused something of a sensation, and he would have animated discussions with them. He suggested to Sophie that they should go on a cycling tour together, travelling through France and writing a series of articles for the newspapers in Scandinavia. This idea came to nothing but Sophie did become a regular contributor to the Danish newspaper *Politiken*, writing about art in France and her impressions of the artists' colony at Grèz.

Strindberg's amicable relationship with Marie and Sophie did not last and it was Karl Nordström, a Swedish painter who was staying in Grèz at the time, who insinuated that there was maybe something unhealthy about Siri's relationship with the Danish women, especially Marie. Nordström was the only person at Grèz to make such remarks so it is difficult to know whether there was any truth in the suggestion that Siri was having a lesbian relationship with Marie as he had alleged. It was known that Nordström was envious of Strindberg's reputation, and was reckoned to be something of a woman-hater himself. Whatever the truth of the matter, his comments fell on fertile ground. Strindberg believed the allegations and became almost paranoid.

Strindberg writes about this period in *A Madman's Defence* and gives his imagination full rein, producing a grossly exaggerated account of *fin-de-siècle* decadence. The people he describes are loud and grotesque and the 'decent orgy' that he had written to Heidenstam about is no longer a jolly feast but an ugly and debauched event. The whole thing is a gross deviation from the truth. The central female character, who is based on Siri, is depicted as a hedonistic slut who allows both men and women to kiss her in public and he uses Marie David and Sophie Holten as thinly disguised models for a couple of outrageous Danish lesbians.

Once Strindberg had allowed himself to be influenced by Nordström's malicious suggestions about the nature of the relationship between Siri and Marie he became obsessed with the idea. He began to interrogate Siri about her relationships, past and present, convinced that she was being unfaithful to him, not only with Marie but also with an unknown man as well. Siri protested her innocence. Marie told Siri that she ought to leave Strindberg and go back to Sweden to try and rebuild her career.

Strindberg reacted by drinking heavily and his consumption of alcohol, especially absinthe, acted as a distorting mirror on his relationship with Siri. He applied more and more pressure on her to 'confess'. He even wrote to several friends asking them to tell him the truth. Had they heard anything about Siri's lover? Did they know who it was? His suspicions and accusations became more and more bizarre. In the end Siri admitted that she had once been involved with a man, an engineer, whom she had met on the boat while travelling back from Finland in 1882. She told Strindberg that this man had forced himself on her and she had not resisted but swore that she had not had an affair with him.

It is strange that Strindberg's obsessive jealousy should have come at a time in Siri's life when she was least likely to have had an affair. Hans, their youngest child, was not yet a year old and Siri had not been well since the birth. After suffering from post-partum bleeding she had gone on to have respiratory trouble. She had also had serious dental problems and had had a steel plate inserted into her upper jaw, which had fractured during earlier treatment at the dentist's. Forced to manage on her own while Strindberg was on trial in Stockholm, she was now physically weak and exhausted by the nomadic lifestyle they were leading. They never had enough money and she had had to come to terms with the fact that she would never have the acting career she had dreamed of. She was desperate to put down roots somewhere, even if they could not go back to Sweden, and had often thought about finding a place to settle and running a boarding house. Strindberg refers to this idea in a letter he wrote on 20 January 1886 to his friend and fellow writer Gustaf af Geijerstam:

> ... I have a drawer full of outlines and finished manuscripts which are impossible to get published. Half a year's work, and my present projects are lunatic. I am either finished as a writer or I am going through a crisis – but it is not worth spending anything on me. If, on the other hand, you want to rescue my family, then make a quick and energetic effort. Siri wants to go to Neufchâtel and open a boarding house for all the Scandinavian men who are learning French there, because everything is so cheap there. I'll go with her and become head gardener, because my doctor has stressed that if I don't take exercise or work with my body the fire in my brain will never be extinguished. On his suggestion I have started drinking and I'm now playing billiards and cards and seeking company. It helps momentarily but feels seven times worse afterwards.
>
> Projects chase projects; I have two briefcases full of outlines for plays and a travelling itinerary, plans for a new Swedish constitution and new school books. My head is spinning and never stops.

It is impossible to say whether Strindberg's increasingly neurotic and unreasonable behaviour led to his excessive drinking and taking of stimulants on top of the bromide potassium and phosphate that his doctor had prescribed or vice versa. Whatever the root cause, it is clear that this, coupled with his anxieties about money, had added fuel to his already overwrought state of mind. Like Siri, he was exhausted with life.

— Chapter 8 —

Reality Turned Into Fiction

> Well, now I have sold everything that can be sold, the only thing that remains is my corpse (and above all the cranium) to the Karolinska Institutet (for medical research).
> Letter to Axel Strindberg, 28 June 1887

Siri was eventually granted her wish to return to Switzerland but her idea of settling down and running a *pension* there remained a pipedream. The family stayed on in Grèz for the winter of 1885–86 as they did not have enough money to pay off their debts and move on. This was a familiar pattern: Strindberg's freedom to travel was usually curtailed by lack of funds. Some relief came in March 1886, however, when he received a gift of 3500 francs. The Swedish actor Emil Hillberg, who had appeared in the production of *Master Olof* at the Nya Teatern in Stockholm, had heard that Strindberg was struggling and had organized a collection for him. This sum helped to pay off some of his debts (the monthly bill at the *pension* in Grèz was 1000 francs) and, encouraged by this slight improvement in the family's fortunes, he started work on his autobiographical novel *The Son of a Servant*. He also completed a second version of his play *Marauders*, which was a forerunner to his great naturalist dramas *The Father* and *Lady Julie*. *Marauders* was the first play that Strindberg had written since *Sir Bengt's Wife* and, inspired by the artistic atmosphere at Grèz, he had decided to tackle a modern subject with modern characters.

Known in English as *Comrades* or *The Companions*, this new version of *Marauders* provides an interesting insight into his view of the playful battle of the sexes before the subject became a rather more deadly theme in his dramatic work. The English title *Comrades*, which is a literal translation of the Swedish *Kamraterna*, is rather misleading as the word has associations with communism, which was certainly not Strindberg's intention. *The Companions* is a more appropriate title as it refers to a couple who are equal partners in a marriage.

The leading female character in the play is Bertha, who is supposed to be the same Bertha who later appears as the fourteen-year-old daughter in *The Father*. Strindberg originally planned to write a trilogy about this woman and in *The Companions* she is a practising artist though not a particularly talented one. In *The Father* she is just a young girl who enjoys painting. Her mother wants her to train to be a proper artist but her father insists that she should have a broader education. As it turns out, it would appear that the father's assessment of Bertha's talent — or lack of it — was the more perceptive.

In *The Companions* Bertha is married to Axel, who is also a painter, and they are living in Paris. They both enter a painting for exhibition at the annual Salon. Bertha's picture is accepted but Axel's is rejected. Bertha delights in her success and gloats over Axel's failure. He retaliates by sending her away and inviting his mistress to come and stay. It is later revealed that Axel had switched the labels on the pictures and it was in fact his painting that was chosen and not Bertha's. The play is written in a light satirical tone and is a gentle send-up of the emancipated women that Strindberg had met on his travels. Bertha and Axel had wanted an equal partnership but this is threatened by professional jealousy. In the first version of the play Strindberg decided that the couple should be reconciled at the end; in the later, reworked version he changed the ending and they remain estranged.

Strindberg sent *The Companions* to Ludvig Josephson at the Nya Teatern, who rejected it, as did Dramaten, the Svenska Teatern in Helsingfors and the Folketeatret in Copenhagen. Albert Bonnier did not dare to publish it. The author of *Getting Married* was *persona non grata*. Even some of Strindberg's radical friends, like Hjalmar Branting, did not approve of his new 'anti-feminist' tendencies. Later on *The Companions* was to prove one of his most popular plays in Germany where it was performed more than a thousand times between 1905 and 1927.

During their winter stay in Grèz, Karin and Greta, who were then six and four, started their formal education. They went to a new secular school with very strict discipline and they wore clogs like all the other local children. Their French schooling did not last long, though, because in May Strindberg sent off the finished manuscript of *The Son of a Servant* to Albert Bonnier, who accepted it with the promise of a first print run of 4000 copies. This was Strindberg's cue to move on and in May 1886 they went to Othmarsingen in the Aargau canton. They stayed there for a couple of days before finding accommodation in Weggis and later Gersau, two beautiful little villages on Lake Lucerne.

It must have been difficult for the children to be constantly on the move with no permanent home and no chance to make friends but Karin

The Companions

In this extract, from Act Two, Scene Three, Strindberg is rewriting history in a way. He may be referring to the period when Siri was training to be an actress while he was still working full-time at the Royal Library and writing in the evenings. Like the couple in the play, he and Siri were newly married, initially supportive of one another, and both trying to build a career from their art at a time when a wife was not expected to earn her own living.

BERTHA: Axel, let's be friends. And listen to me for a moment. Do you think that my position in your house – because it is yours – is comfortable? You give me my board and lodging, you pay for my lessons at Julian's, while you can't afford any lessons yourself. Do you think I can accept that you waste your talent with all those draughtsman's drawings and only manage to paint in your spare time? You haven't been able to afford models even, but you pay for mine, five francs an hour. You don't know how good, how noble, how self-sacrificing you are, but neither do you know how much I suffer to see you struggle like that for me. Oh, Axel, you don't know how I feel in my position. What am I to you? In what capacity am I in your house? Oh, I'm ashamed when I think of it.

AXEL: What, aren't you my wife?

BERTHA: Yes, but . . .

AXEL: Well, then?

BERTHA: But you are supporting me.

AXEL: Isn't that a man's duty then?

BERTHA: Yes, it was in the past, in marriages of the past it used to be like that, but we were not going to be like that.

AXEL: What nonsense! Shouldn't the husband support his wife?

BERTHA: *I* don't want you to.

remembers her early childhood with affection, with some happy times filled with gaiety and laughter. Her mother undoubtedly had a sunnier nature than her father, always able to see the funny side of some minor upset, like the time Strindberg paid six months' advance rental on a house, hiring curtains and furniture, only to decide after a few weeks that the place didn't suit him. Siri's main task during these episodes was to oversee the constant packing and unpacking of their dwindling possessions. She usually sent Strindberg on ahead to get him out of the way and to spare him the trouble of helping her.

Strindberg always took these upheavals in his stride and within three months of arriving in Switzerland he had completed parts two and three of his autobiographical novel *The Son of a Servant*. He finished the fourth and final part before the year was out (though this was not published until 1909). Albert Bonnier's enthusiasm did not always match his own, unfortunately, and the pile of unpublished manuscripts was growing.

Money troubles loomed yet again and they were not the only problems the family had to face in 1886. They had not been in Switzerland for long when Siri started having abdominal pains. After consulting several doctors she was sent to Geneva for an operation, staying away for three weeks to recover. Health worries automatically turned into financial worries: her medical bills on this occasion amounted to 700 francs.

As he had done before when he was short of money, Strindberg cashed in his life assurance policies. He also asked his brother Axel to sell the original manuscript of *Master Olof*. And, never averse to turning his life into art, he managed to squeeze 200 kronor out of Albert Bonnier as an advance for a book based on some old love letters that he and Siri had written to each other ten years before. Strindberg honoured his contract with Bonnier and he completed the manuscript, calling it *He and She*, but the material was deemed too personal and intimate to be published in his lifetime.

The difficulties that Siri and Strindberg, the once so perfect lovers, faced at this time were a drain on them both, though it was to be another five years of exhausting separations and reconciliations before they finally broke up for good. During one period of relative tranquillity in 1886 Siri used Strindberg's newly purchased camera to take some pictures of him and the children. Strindberg thought that they were good enough for publication so he added some humorous captions and on 15 November he sent them off to Albert Bonnier with a note: 'With today's post I send a parcel containing 18 impressionistic photographs with text, made by my wife who asks me to negotiate the terms if it is possible. The photographs represent the terrible Woman Hater August Strindberg...' Bonnier replied that the pictures would be too expensive to reproduce. Strindberg never saw them in book form but an album was eventually published by the Bonnier firm in 1997.

In January 1887 Strindberg moved the family yet again, to Lindau in Bavaria, where he was to write two of his most famous works: his play *The Father,* and *The People of Hemsö*, a comic novel set in the Stockholm archipelago. He and Siri seem to have called a temporary truce and Karin remembers this interlude in her life as an idyllic time. They lived in a charming house surrounded by beautiful countryside, and she and Greta went to a Catholic school in the village.

Strindberg sent *The Father* to Dramaten in February and to his great disappointment they turned it down. Apparently the actors had found it embarrassing and distasteful. Their response may have been affected by a rather vicious pamphlet that was circulating around Stockholm at the time. Penned by John Personne, a teacher and writer, it condemned Strindberg as an immoral influence on the young. It was a pernicious personal attack that was fuelled by the growing reactionary mood in Sweden.

Understandably, Strindberg felt betrayed by the radical Left, who had not supported him sufficiently in his view, and he was disillusioned with religion and the Church, which had always been an important part of his life. He gradually came to favour Nietzsche, espousing the concept of the *Übermensch,* and announced that he was now an atheist. Siri found this very upsetting. She had never been overtly religious but she was nevertheless a believer and found comfort in prayer. To her, Strindberg's loss of faith represented a rejection of old values and was symptomatic of an ever-widening chasm between them.

In *A Madman's Defence* Strindberg identifies this period as a time when he begins to fear for his own sanity. He loathed the world, he loathed Siri and above all he loathed himself:

> I hate her now with a hatred more fatal than indifference because it is the reverse side of love. It grows there in hiding to such an extent that I am tempted to formulate an axiom: 'I hate her because I love her.' During a Sunday lunch, while we were sitting in the summer arbour, the electric current that had accumulated during the last ten years discharged itself. I don't know what caused it. No matter. I struck her, for the first time in my life, I slapped her face repeatedly, and when she tried to defend herself I seized her wrists violently and forced her onto her knees. She uttered a terrified scream. But the temporary satisfaction I felt at my action soon gave way to dismay when I heard the children, frightened to death, cry out with fear. It was the worst moment of my miserable life! It is a heinous crime, a most unnatural crime, to

strike a woman, a mother! And in the presence of her children . . . I felt the sun in the heavens should not shine on such a scene . . . I felt sick to death.

Karin remembers this incident, which she witnessed – her mother lying on the floor, with her blonde hair spread out around her. Strindberg bitterly regretted losing control and referred to his physical attack on Siri as one of the most shameful acts he had ever committed in his life.

In June 1887 Axel sent him the proceeds of the sale of the manuscript of *Master Olof* – 500 kronor – and Strindberg wrote to him in tones of desperate jocularity: 'Well, now I have sold everything that can be sold, the only thing that remains is my corpse (and above all the cranium) to the Karolinska Institutet (for medical research).' Having saved the family from ruin with *The Red Room* eight years before, he was confident he could do so again, telling Axel that 'Albert [Bonnier] is going to get a Swedish novel in August which will make him happy again.'

The People of Hemsö is about a young man who leaves his home in a rural area in central Sweden and takes a job as the manager of a farm in the archipelago. He does not know very much and he bluffs his way through. He falls in love with a servant girl then decides that he would be better off marrying the rich widow who has shown an interest him. The rich widow drowns and the young man is caught in a snowstorm on his way to fetch the priest, and then he too drowns while trying to cross the ice floes. The widow's son takes over the farm and life returns to normal. Despite its somewhat melodramatic ending, the novel is a humorous account of life in the archipelago and it satirizes the 'new man' who tries to revolutionize traditional farming methods.

Although Strindberg did not rate *The People of Hemsö* as highly as *The Red Room* it was to prove the more popular novel, constantly reprinted, dramatized and filmed in new versions. In October Albert Bonnier sent him an advance of 2000 kronor and Strindberg was able to settle his bills in Eichbühl where they were living at this time and move north. He had managed to find a theatre in Copenhagen that was prepared to put on a production of *The Father*.

On first arriving in the Danish capital the family stayed at a hotel called Leopold's, which was a favourite haunt of Scandinavian artists and writers, and found themselves in the company of Gustaf af Geijerstam and Victoria Benedictsson. *The Father* opened on 14 November at the Casinoteatret and the first night was completely sold out. The reviews were on the whole positive though some critics found the ending too strong. The theatre management must have thought so too for they put on a farce immediately afterwards as if to lighten the tone of the evening and send the audience out into the cold night laughing rather than weeping.

Strindberg's publisher Hans Österling had sent a copy of *The Father* to Ibsen, who responded positively to it:

> Strindberg's observations and experience in the areas that *The Father* deals with do not correspond to mine, but this does not stop me from admitting that his new play has moved me in its violently forceful way. *The Father* is soon to be produced in Copenhagen. Play it as it should be played, with an uncompromisingly realistic language and it will have a powerful effect.

Ibsen saw the play in 1891, when a Danish company took it on tour in Norway. The performance he went to was very poorly attended and he sat alone in the front stalls. When the curtain came down everyone left and the farce that was scheduled to follow after the interval was abandoned.

Cheered by the success of *The Father* in Copenhagen, Strindberg decided to stay on and start a theatre there. He was pretty well destitute again so the family moved out of Leopold's and rented a summer cottage that had been abandoned by its owners for the winter. Siri wrote to several publishing houses in Sweden asking if they had any translation work for her but had no luck. By this time she and Strindberg had definitely decided to divorce though they had not yet started the legal proceedings.

It was during his stay in Denmark that Strindberg had a brief affair with the half-sister of the landlord in one of the run-down manor houses where they were lodging. She was sixteen and, according to him, kept coming to his bedroom last thing at night and early in the mornings. He considered that it was she who had seduced him. He wrote about her to Heidenstam, saying that nothing would come of it because he had used a condom. 'I had her once but got the itch!' he said. 'Scandal.' He told Siri too but she seems not to have minded.

Strindberg later turned this episode into a one-act play, *The First Warning*, which forms part of a series of nine short dramas that he completed between 1888 and 1892 in which women are portrayed either as strong females who fight against their nature or as calculating seducers against whom men have no defences.

The most accessible of the short plays from this period is undoubtedly *Playing With Fire*, which takes a light-hearted look at marriage and jealousy. A young woman, Kerstin, and her husband, Kurt, a mediocre painter, are staying with his rich parents at their summer residence on the Swedish

The First Warning

Rosa, the young girl in The First Warning, *is a seductress. Strindberg significantly gives her age as fifteen and makes her the daughter of a baroness (like Siri) rather than a working-class girl, in order to render her uninhibited behaviour all the more shocking.*

(*The* HUSBAND *walks up to her and is about to kiss her forehead but* ROSA *throws her head back and kisses him on the mouth. The* WIFE *watches from the porch then leaves.*)

HUSBAND: Rosa, my child, I only meant to give you an innocent kiss on the forehead.

ROSA: Innocent, ha! Was that innocent? And you believed mother's fables about father? He died several years ago. But there was a real man! He knew how to make love, and he was not afraid of it. He didn't tremble when he was kissed and he didn't wait until he was asked either. If you don't believe me, come up to the attic and I'll show you his love letters to various women. Come!

(*She opens the door on the left and we glimpse the stairs leading up to the attic.*)

Ha! Are you afraid that I might seduce you? You look surprised. Are you surprised that I, a girl of fifteen, know about love already? Did you think that I believed children were born through the ear? I can see that you despise me now, but you must not do that because I am no worse or better for that matter than any of the others . . . It's just the way I am.

west coast. She flirts with Axel, a family friend, who has been infatuated with her for a long time and is now divorced, and contemplates starting an affair with him.

> KERSTIN: You're playing your cat and mouse game with me. You can see how I'm caught in your trap. You can see how I'm suffering and how I'm struggling to get free. Have pity on me. Just give me one friendly look and don't sit there like a lifeless statue, expecting adoration and sacrifice. (*She kneels*.) You're so strong and you're so good at keeping your passionate feelings under control . . . so proud, so honourable, but it's because you've never been in love, you've never loved anyone like I've loved you.

Later in the play Axel declares his love for her:

> AXEL: I love you, body and soul. I love your beautiful, slender feet which I can glimpse beneath the hem of your dress. I love your pretty white teeth and your soft, sensual mouth, your ears and your hungry, welcoming eyes. I love your whole supple body which I'd like to pick up and run away with, into the forest. Once when I was young I grabbed a girl in the street, lifted her up and ran up four flights of stairs with her in my arms. I was just a young man then. Think what I could do now!
>
> KERSTIN: Love my soul as well!
>
> AXEL: I love your soul because it's weaker than mine, it's fiery like mine, unfaithful like mine . . .

Strindberg used this play to explore the indolent existence of the 'parasitical upper-class women' that he though so little of. Though he may not have intended it, he created one of his most erotic pieces of writing in the process. He tried several different endings. In one early version, which he later discarded, Axel flees in panic when he finds out that Kerstin is pregnant; in another version (the first to be translated into German), Axel receives a letter that reveals that he has not been granted a divorce and he and Kerstin talk sensibly about their infatuation and part as friends; in a third version, which Strindberg authorized for publication and which is the one that is normally performed, Kurt tells Kerstin that he will not stand in her way as long as Axel promises to marry her. At one time Siri would have been amused by a piece like this but now that the passion in her marriage had given way to more mundane worries and anxieties she had grown tired of the flirtations and the 'cat and mouse games' that he depicted.

The winter of 1887 was a miserable time for Strindberg and the family. Their rented summer cottage was isolated – their only neighbour was an abandoned cat – and they were desperately cold because the stove did not work. More importantly, they could not afford to pay the rent.

Siri wrote to Strindberg on 17 December while he was away in Copenhagen on business, telling him that the local tradesmen were pressing her for payment.

> It has been a difficult day here.
>
> The butcher has asked for his 17 kronor in a rather impertinent way. The washerwoman has asked for her money – and the restaurant for their last three dinners – they have told Eva [the maid] that they will only hand out food for cash – and that they do not know us ...
>
> I calmed the bears by telling them that you had gone into town to get money. Now the 200 kronor have arrived. You tell me that I should pay the grocer. But it is not enough, because we owe 220 kronor.
>
> So I will go down and tell them that you have gone into town to take out some money and you will not be back until tomorrow morning, but if they want to accept some of the money I have at home, they can.
>
> I must pay the restaurant 9 kronor this evening or we will not get any dinner tomorrow.
>
> The butcher was also going to come back this evening.
>
> I have not heard from the baker but I expect he will be here tomorrow morning.
>
> So I cannot give the grocer more than 100 or 125 kronor as part payment.
>
> I hope you will be home tomorrow when Holenberg arrives.
>
> Talk to Leopold's and see if you can get a reduction – I don't think it will be possible to stay on here.
>
> What a damned bad bunch! I much prefer the mean Germans!

They moved back to Leopold's briefly over Christmas and then rented a villa in Taarbaek, a small seaside resort outside Copenhagen.

Throughout the following spring, while Strindberg was writing *A Madman's Defence*, he and Siri discussed getting divorced and quarrelled a great deal about it. Siri said that she wanted a settlement of 2500 kronor a year, which, Strindberg noted acidly, was equivalent to a full captain's salary. Since they could not afford to maintain two separate households the plans were postponed.

It was around this time that Siri told Strindberg about the man she had met while on tour in Finland in 1882. He was not an engineer as she had claimed but an actor called Erik Dahlström, who was a member of the company at the Nya Teatern in Helsingfors. He had been staying at the same hotel and she had not been forced to have sex but had enjoyed a brief affair, which had ended when she returned to Stockholm. This confession proved too much for Strindberg, coming as it did on top of his financial and health problems. He owed Bonnier 8000 kronor and the second volume of *Getting Married* was not selling well. He poured all his hurt and disappointment into *A Madman's Defence*. There is no evidence that Siri was ever unfaithful on any other occasion while she was married to Strindberg and even her relationship with Erik Dahlström cannot be proved beyond her own account of the episode.

In July 1888 the artistic community in Copenhagen was shocked by the news of the suicide of Victoria Benedictsson, who had killed herself in her room at Leopold's hotel. One of Georg Brandes' many mistresses, she had been feeling increasingly neglected and ill-used by him. When he spoke disparagingly about her latest novel, *Fru Marianne*, she felt that she had failed as a writer as well as a woman. It was not the first time she had attempted to take her own life – she had overdosed on morphine six months earlier.

A few days after her death Strindberg started a new play, *Lady Julie*, in which his heroine commits suicide by cutting her throat with a razor – the same method that Victoria had chosen in her final, successful bid to end her own life. He completed *Lady Julie* in a record two weeks and immediately started work on another play, *Creditors*. He was back in the fold of drama and his old idea of starting a theatre, modelled on André Antoine's experimental Théâtre Libre in Paris, was rekindled.

In November he put an advertisement in the paper inviting dramatists to send him their new plays. He also tried to borrow some money for his new venture but nobody was keen to lend him any. Nathalie Larsen, a talented young Danish actress and writer, offered to translate *Lady Julie* and *Creditors* and told Strindberg that she was keen to act in them, and this in turn led to other actors in Copenhagen expressing an interest in joining her. Siri recognized this moment as a real opportunity to re-launch her career and it was she who got the project going. With 1000 kronor borrowed from her Uncle Lorenz she hired the largest private theatre in the city, the Dagmarteatret, and prepared to make a comeback as Lady Julie.

The old divorce plans were shelved once more and Siri and Strindberg were now back in a professional partnership. Strindberg appointed her *directrice*, a job that combined everything from producing and directing to managing the accounts, publicity and finding the props. Siri, who had not been on stage for more than five years, summoned up enough strength and energy to oversee the whole project as well as rehearsing for her demanding new role. One of her aunts moved into the rented house where the family was staying to look after the children while Siri went to live with another aunt in the city. In the meantime Strindberg wrote two more plays in quick succession, *The Stronger* and *Samum*, with Siri in mind. He also adapted a short story by his friend Ola Hansson, called *Pariah*. They were going to develop a great repertoire for their new theatre with lots of good parts for Siri, exactly as Strindberg had promised before they were married.

The première of *Lady Julie* was scheduled for 2 March 1889. They had a splendid theatre, a first-class play and a strong cast. What they had not bargained for was the censor. He considered that the play was obscene and refused to give it a licence so the first night had to be cancelled at the last minute. Disappointed though undeterred, Strindberg decided to open a week later with *Creditors*, *Pariah* and *The Stronger*. Nathalie Larsen played the heroine, Tekla, in *Creditors*, and Siri, deprived of the role of Lady Julie, sacked the actress who had been engaged to play the speaking role in *The Stronger*, and took it over herself. They got good reviews and Siri was praised for her light touch and quick dialogue, though some critics had difficulty in understanding her Swedish. The plays brought in enough money for Siri to repay the 1000 kronor loan to her uncle.

Lady Julie was still unperformed but then someone had the bright idea of presenting it as a private performance, which would not require the censor's permission. So, a week or so later, on 14 March, the play opened at a students' hall that seated 150 people. It was sold out well in advance. Overall the reviews were consistently good. The critic on the *Social-Demokraten* found it hard to believe in Lady Julie's hysterical state, which would later lead to suicide, but praised Siri's great assurance and experience in the role. Others said her performance was too restrained. Strindberg, who was convinced that Siri was having an affair with the actor playing Jean, could not have made it easy for her to act 'without restraint'. Lady Julie was Siri's triumph and marked the pinnacle of her acting career. It was a role that would have suited Harriet Bosse years later but she promised Strindberg never to play it and she stuck to her word.

In April, barely four months after the foundation of their daring new theatre company, the venture collapsed for lack of money, and many of the actors went unpaid. Strindberg left for Malmö, leaving Siri behind to wind everything up.

— Chapter 9 —

Time to Part

We are enemies for the short part that is left of my life!
A Madman's Defence

Once he was back in Sweden, Strindberg slipped easily back into his old pattern of working and decided to spend the summer on the island of Runmarö in the Stockholm archipelago; he was writing a new novel, *By the Open Sea*. He wrote often to Siri and the children, who were still in Copenhagen, sometimes sending two letters a day. They had still not taken any formal steps towards a divorce, the children being a significant factor in their reluctance to formalize their separation. In the early summer Strindberg made a last attempt at reconciliation.

> 8th May, in the evening, 1889
> I have two cottages on an island more beautiful than the green island of our youth and one is as pretty as a castle and that is where you, Karin, Greta and Putte are going to live and I shall live in the other one . . .
> It is so lovely here that I feel quite emotional. It is so incredibly wonderful to be in one's own country again, and for you this area ought to be particularly attractive, because it looks like the part of Kymmendö that we used to call Finland . . .
> I have been soul-sick for a fortnight. I have tormented you, poor Siri, forgive me! Come here and bring the children! Do you agree that I am a good father to your children – then chain me with a little kindness. And if you want me to bend, then just be feminine, and I'll come to you without humiliation, like a man will and should do for a woman. As a human being you are not superior to me, but as a woman you are, because, happily, there are two genders, which are very different from each other.
> Farewell then and welcome here.

In the end Siri agreed to join him and she brought the children to Runmarö. It turned out to be a difficult summer for her. Strindberg, wrapped up in his work, did not live up to his promises and hardly communicated with her, and her oldest childhood friend, Constance Mellin, died.

Back in Stockholm for the winter, Siri and Strindberg turned their attention to the girls' education. Thanks to Siri's excellent tuition while they had been abroad, Karin and Greta were if anything more advanced in their learning than other children of their age. Strindberg had encouraged them both to write and had taught them some science, including botany, though his lessons had been more sporadic than Siri's. Given that their schooling had been so disrupted during their travels it is quite remarkable that they did so well.

By 1890 Strindberg was enjoying some moderate success in Sweden and Finland at last. *The Father* had had its Swedish première at the Nya Teatern in 1888 and in 1889 *Creditors* was produced at the Svenska Teatern in Helsingfors together with the newly written one-act play *Samum*. In the spring of 1890 Dramaten produced *Master Olof* in the second version. It was a huge success and the whole family attended the première, proudly adding to the tumultuous applause as Strindberg stepped on stage after the performance to be crowned with a laurel wreath.

For most of that year Siri and Strindberg lived apart and by the beginning of December they had given up any hope of reconciliation. Strindberg went to see the vicar at Värmdö where he was staying, who explained the procedure for divorce to him. The Church Council would first of all caution the couple and if they decided to go ahead the matter would automatically be dealt with at the next local hearing. The marriage would be formally dissolved after they had been separated for one year. If either party admitted adultery then a divorce could be granted straight away. Strindberg wrote to Siri on 11 December explaining all this and told her that it would be easier if they could agree beforehand on how much money she needed:

> Discord in general is enough and the court does not care whose 'fault' it is. So, no accusations and no defence. The children will go to you. But if you don't want to go to the vicarage then the vicar is happy to come to your home (although he has the right to come and fetch you!) That is the way it stands. Let me hear your thoughts.

They decided to separate and wait for a year as neither of them wanted to face the stigma of claiming adultery as the reason for their marital breakdown. They were summoned to see the vicar on 19 December for the official caution but Siri was ill with chronic bronchitis and did not attend. A second appointment was made for 2 January. At the official hearing before the Parish and School Councils they were asked to explain why they wanted a divorce. Strindberg said that they were incompatible, both in temperament and religious beliefs – he was by this time a confirmed atheist – and Siri replied that she had not initially wished to be divorced but had now resigned herself to it because that is what her husband wanted.

At this stage they seemed to agree on the details and Strindberg did not contest Siri's demand for custody of the children plus an allowance of 100 kronor a month for them. She did not ask for any money for herself.

Shortly before this hearing Siri had written to her aunts in Copenhagen asking them to forward a letter to her old friend Marie David, whom she had not seen for four years. Siri told Marie that she was going to get a divorce and invited her to visit her in Stockholm. Marie arrived on 24 January 1891 and she stayed with Siri and the children on and off until 1896.

Karin remembers Marie as a somewhat flamboyant woman who wore expensive clothes and smoked cigars. What she probably wouldn't have realized was that Marie was an alcoholic. Strindberg certainly knew and was furious when it became obvious that she had moved in with Siri on what looked like a permanent basis. All his old suspicions about the two women having a lesbian relationship flared up again and he accused them of 'unnatural behaviour towards one's own sex', a crime then punishable by law that could lead to two years in prison. He told Siri that he had changed his mind about her having custody of the children if Marie was intending to stay. She was an unsuitable companion and would be a bad influence on the whole family. He also claimed that Siri was no longer fit to be a mother because she herself was often drunk.

When Marie got wind of what Strindberg was saying about her she decided to pay him a visit at his cottage on Runmarö. He had no wish to talk to her and he pushed her down the steps, telling her to leave. He later sued Marie for violation of the privacy of his home and she countersued him for slander and physical assault. The court found in Marie's favour and Strindberg was fined a total of 500 kronor on both charges. All the time this was going on, Siri, to her credit, stayed on the sidelines.

Marie clearly appreciated the opportunity that Siri gave her to be part of a family unit and the stability and support she received eventually helped her to control her drinking. It is hard to imagine how Siri would have coped on her own in the long term and Marie helped her out financially. Karin claims that her mother did not have a sexual relationship with Marie but acknowledges that the two women were extremely close. A friend who had known them in France reported that he had seen them kissing passionately and these rumours fuelled Strindberg's jealousy yet again. Whatever the true facts of the matter he always felt threatened by their relationship. His hostility hardened when, after a long drawn-out battle, Siri was finally granted custody of the children. Siri's attitude had changed too. Something had now died in her and she closed the door on Strindberg forever. From this point nothing that he could do by way of conciliatory gestures would ever win her back.

Karin claims that she found it surprising that her mother stayed in the marriage for as long as she did, given all of Strindberg's shortcomings – his tempers, his suspicious nature and his nervous disposition. As a daughter, on the other hand, she saw things that were genuinely good in him. He had a big heart, a great capacity for affection and felt compassion for anyone who suffered.

After the separation Strindberg soon transformed reality into fiction and the boundaries were blurred forever in his mind. A vital period – probably the most important in his entire life – ended with his divorce from Siri on 9 September 1892. The creative influences that this fascinating woman had exercised on him were immense.

Siri and Strindberg both remained in the Stockholm archipelago for the summer before the divorce came through. He then announced that he intended to leave Sweden again. His fictionalized version of his departure on this occasion, written in 1887, points forward in an uncanny way to the time when he would leave his second wife, Frida, taking the boat across the Danube on his way to France:

> One beautiful Sunday at noon I went on board a steamer bound for Konstanz, having made up my mind to visit friends in France, where I would immediately write down the story of this woman, the true representative of the unsexed.
> At the last moment Maria turned up with tears in her eyes, agitated and nervous, and, alas, incredibly beautiful. I remained cool, however, silent and uncommunicative and I received her faithless kisses without responding to them.
> –Tell me that we're friends at least.
> –We are enemies for the short part that is left of my life!
>
> *A Madman's Defence*

In his reference to 'the true representative of the unsexed' he expresses his worries about a future when men will be emasculated by a new type of independent woman – like Marie David and Sophie Holten.

When Siri learned that Strindberg was intending to go abroad again she decided she would go back to Finland, taking the children and Marie with her. Without Strindberg there would be nothing left for her in Sweden. She was twice divorced, her inheritance was long since dissipated, and without his financial and practical support she would never be able to resume her acting career.

Strindberg left for Berlin at the end of September 1892 and Siri went to Helsingfors in May 1893. If she had expected to find friends in Finland who would welcome her back to her home country and help her to establish a new life for herself she was to be disappointed. Helsingfors, she discovered, was as provincial and small-minded as it had always been and the 'foreign' habits she had picked up did not go down at all well with her old acquaintances. She smoked and drank in public and she often went to the theatre alone. She did not care a damn about *comme-il-faut* and this was just too much for the bourgeois sensibilities of the place.

Gradually, however, she managed to carve out a niche for herself in this reactionary backwater. She started by giving lessons in elocution, acting and dancing and soon gained a reputation as an excellent teacher. She became a very popular drama coach and one of her students, Märtha Hedman, who later became an actress in America, remembered her with affection when she wrote her memoirs in 1949:

> It was arranged that I should study with Madame Siri von Essen-Strindberg, the first wife of August Strindberg. She was the foremost dramatic teacher in Finland. She had herself been a fine actress before she married the great dramatist . . .
>
> Young people adored Siri von Essen. How could we help it? Was there ever such an inspiring person? With such understanding of youth, with such generosity, highmindedness, with such a delightful sense of humour? Was there ever anyone so valiant and with a courage so gaily expressed?

Siri gave public recitals and poetry readings and, with occasional translation work, she was able to offer her children a reasonably stable upbringing. She worked extremely hard but in spite of this her financial situation was always precarious. She faced extreme poverty in 1893 when Marie became very ill with tuberculosis and had to spend eighteen months in a sanatorium. Siri was reduced to accepting second-hand clothes and anonymous gifts. It was all very humiliating but she always coped somehow with these indignities, always willing to find new ways to support her family. At one time she earned some extra money playing the organ at a Catholic church.

In 1896 Marie left Siri and the children and went to Breslau in Poland where she entered a nunnery. She died there, aged thirty-one, just before she was due to take her final vows.

Siri never saw Strindberg again. To begin with she kept in touch with him by letter but during the last twelve years or so of her life they communicated only via the children. Most of the correspondence between them centres around the issue of money, with Siri always asking for financial help and Strindberg, more often than not, pleading poverty. She was once so desperate that she wrote a begging letter to his father-in-law, Friedrich Uhl. Strindberg was furious. His letters to the children vacillate between deep affection and frustrated anger. 'How long am I going to have to support you?' he wails, on learning that they were still not contributing anything to their upkeep even though they were now in their late teens. However, he sent money whenever he had any to spare.

In 1896, for example, he asked for the entire proceeds from a benefit performance of *Lucky Per's Journey* at the Vasateatern in Stockholm to be sent to Siri and the children in Finland. Siri, who had been juggling her debts with no hope of paying them all off, could not understand why the promised money never arrived and it was not until she read a newspaper report that she learned what had happened. The theatre producer in Stockholm, Albert Ranft, had apparently sent the donation to Helsingfors care of Dr Waldemar Ekelund and Miss Adelaide Ehrnrooth, who had already started a collection for Siri in Finland. They then decided, without consulting Strindberg or Siri, to keep the money from Stockholm (which amounted to 1664.34 Finnish Marks) in trust and pay her an allowance in monthly instalments. Siri felt angry and humiliated. 'You have a father, a mother and a legal guardian [Strindberg's brother Oscar],' she told her children. 'And yet Waldemar confiscates our money!'

During his last few years Strindberg was in a better position to help out financially. When Albert Bonnier published his collected works in 1911 he gave Siri and all three children 6000 kronor each, a sum that was the equivalent to a middle-class man's annual salary at the time. Siri could not bring herself to thank him personally and asked Karin to write to him on her behalf. The following year he sent the children a further 10,000 kronor each and promised more if they ever needed it.

By this time their daughter Greta had established herself as an actress, having started her career at the Svenska Teatern in Helsingfors in 1904. Strindberg proved to be extremely supportive and advised her to come to Stockholm where there were, just as there had been for Siri, greater opportunities than in Finland. He managed to negotiate her release from her contract with Rönnblad's Provincial Touring Company and persuaded Albert Ranft, then the most important theatre producer in Sweden, to take her on. He also paid for her to have lessons with a voice coach to get rid of her Finnish accent.

Strindberg and Greta developed a warm relationship after this and they became very close. She acted in several of his plays, most notably in *Lucky Per's Journey* in 1907 and *The Crown Bride* in 1909–10, and appeared on stage with his third wife, Harriet Bosse, on a few occasions.

In 1907 Greta married her cousin Henry von Philp (the son of Strindberg's sister Anna), who was studying to be a doctor. Their only baby – Siri and Strindberg's first grandchild – died on the day that it was born, a sad reminder of their own daughter Kerstin, who had lived for just two days. When she was interviewed for an article that appeared in a Gothenburg newspaper on what was to be Strindberg's last birthday in 1912, Greta spoke with great fondness about him: 'I can only say that he has always been the most affectionate and considerate father you could ever imagine.'

If Greta was Strindberg's favourite, he was still fond of his first daughter, Karin, who had shown early promise as a writer, something that he had always encouraged. She married a Russian university lecturer, Vladimir Smirnoff, in 1911, and before the wedding Strindberg wrote to her, offering to play host for the occasion:

> My dear child
> I am very happy that you too Karin are going to enjoy happiness like Greta wished.
> But why postpone the wedding – which could take place here – a civil ceremony . . .
> But you do as you wish, of course!
> But my dear child! Seize the moment; it is still summer; come here and get married and I shall celebrate the wedding for my first-born who once came with the first joy in my life. (Mother won't mind.) And as soon as you are married you can return to Finland!
> I shall be happy for you because I have no happiness myself and ask for nothing.
> Give my warmest regards to my future son-in-law whom I shall soon hope to be able to call son-in-law and friend!
> Your friend for life
> Daddy

Vladimir Smirnoff belonged to the Russian Orthodox Church and Karin was a Lutheran but had not been confirmed so they settled on a civil ceremony in Stockholm, followed by a reception at Strindberg's apartment on Drottninggatan. They chose to marry in Sweden because Karin wanted to retain her Swedish citizenship in case they needed to return if the authorities found out about Vladimir's political activities in Finland, which was still under Russian rule. He was actively involved in the Socialist movement in Russia and he helped to smuggle political pamphlets out of the country via Finland, often with Greta's help when she was on tour. Strindberg knew about these activities but never spoke to anyone about them.

Siri and Strindberg's son, Hans, also got married in 1911 and he too chose a Russian partner, Olga Leväinen. Strindberg had not seen his son for eighteen years and the relationship between them was always awkward. Hans did not tell him that Olga had been expecting a baby by another man when he had first met her a year before. Greta had considered adopting this child, a boy named Erik, after she had lost her own baby, but she was to die before any arrangements could be made. Erik was placed in an orphanage, then in 1915 Hans officially adopted him and gave him the surname Strindberg. Hans survived his parents and sister Greta, who all died in 1912, for just five years – he collapsed with heart failure at the age of thirty-three. Erik later married Karin's only daughter, his cousin, who was also called Karin.

There were so many conflicting reports and so much libel published in the wake of Strindberg's death in 1912 that his daughter Karin wanted to put things straight with her own version of her parents' life together. She wrote two biographies, one in 1925 and the second in 1956, and while they give some insight into the marriage, especially in the later years, it was impossible for her to convey the intensity of the relationship that Siri and Strindberg had had at the beginning.

It is accepted that Strindberg's own accounts of his relationship with Siri emerged as highly dramatized. His autobiographical novels have never posed as the undiluted truth although posterity has always had a tendency to treat them as such. It is worth remembering that Strindberg deliberately changed people's names and stressed repeatedly that the works were works of fiction rather than authentic memoirs even if a lot of the descriptive details were drawn from his own life. *A Madman's Defence*, for example, was a deliberate attempt to rid himself of the feelings he had once had for Siri, and by creating this dramatic myth and giving it a coherent shape he managed to 'write her out of my blood'. This was something he was totally conscious of at the time, as he acknowledged in a letter that he wrote to Edvard Brandes on 18 March 1888:

> After I had made my decision [to write *A Madman's Defence*] I allocated one year to the surgical operation, the Caesarian which will remove the foetuses from my life. It may end by my bleeding to death! Then so be it!

Later, in his novel *Inferno* he describes the process of writing as a way of 'flaying myself and selling the skins to the highest bidder'. The physical act of writing was a form of catharsis and it was something that he recommended others to do, including Siri. The last line of *A Madman's Defence* is: 'That's the end of the story, my Beloved. I have got my revenge. Now we're quits.' With this he felt able to bring that chapter of his life to a close.

For Siri, however, the resolution was not so easy. She saw his methods as an elaborate game that she wanted no part of and although she had laughed when she first read the novel in the autumn of 1893, she later understood that posterity would judge her by the main character of *A Madman's Defence*. Strindberg had definitely gone too far and he realized this, though only after the damage was done. It is significant that he never wanted Frida Uhl or Harriet Bosse to read it. Was he ashamed of it afterwards? Did he feel guilty that he had been dishonest and disloyal to Siri? The word he uses in his foreword to the book in 1887 is 'horrible'. And yet there are many warm and passionate passages in the text. Having worked through the humiliation and pain of his wife's adultery the narrator in the novel decides to go back to her and give the marriage another chance:

> And for the sixth time I returned to the fold; this time determined to use the respite to finish my story and equip myself with detailed information about this mysterious affair.

Of course, in reality it was not such a neat ending to their relationship. Unlike Strindberg, Siri never found another partner. She had loved him 'immeasurably' and he had been the greatest, and the only, love of her life. 'You ask me if I was in love with Strindberg! My God, how I loved him!' she told her daughter Karin. 'I could have done anything, however mad, for him.'

Siri died of a stroke in Helsingfors on 21 April 1912, aged sixty-one. Karin and her husband took her ashes to Stockholm four days later and her remains were interred in the von Essen family vault. Barely three weeks after this, Strindberg himself was dead, and in June of the same year Greta was killed in a train crash in Sweden.

— Chapter 10 —

Siri's Legacy – Two Naturalist Tragedies

The Father (1887)

Laura, the leading female character in *The Father*, has a will of iron and refuses to accept the subordinate role that robs her of all rights to decide about her daughter's education and upbringing. Her obstinacy is a result of years of being suppressed and denied freedom of movement. As a substitute for her own lack of career she now has ambitious plans for her only daughter, Bertha. She wants her to have a more interesting life than she herself has had. In order to bring that about she wants Bertha to study art and become a painter, one of the few professions where she may succeed on an equal footing with men.

Laura heads a large household but she has no control over the family finances. Her husband, the Captain, whose rights are protected by law, is the guardian of all the women in the house, an onerous responsibility that he refers to repeatedly in the play. In addition, he has to sort out the problems below stairs. It is he who interrogates Nöjd, the orderly, about the pregnant maid, for instance. The Captain's duties do not end there: he has to support an ever-increasing number of dependants. He also has ambitions to explore his scientific hobby further with a view to pursuing a career in that field at a later date.

As a wife and mother, Laura is locked into her traditional role, caring for an ageing mother who never appears on stage but who keeps crying out for services from her bed, as well as humouring her husband's old nurse, who is still living with them. In addition to this she is concerned for her daughter, an only child, who at fourteen is getting too old to stay at home without any youthful company around.

Whenever she needs any money Laura has to ask her husband for it, a humiliation that she does not accept easily. Besides, the Captain has a short temper and as an army officer he is obviously used to being obeyed. He does not consider it necessary or proper to enter into discussions on important matters with his wife any more than he would do with the men under his command – he simply gives orders. Strindberg underscores the relationship of this married couple by giving the wife a name, Laura, while presenting the husband only by his role, the Captain. (The only character who addresses him by his name, Adolf, is the Nurse.)

Laura's pent-up frustrations come to a head when her husband first claims that one can never know who a child's father is. This statement is uttered innocently enough in connection with the orderly, Nöjd, who denies that he is the father of the baby that the maid is expecting. With this intellectual argument on the subject of paternity Laura sees an opening that could free her from the trap that she is in. Men who made women pregnant out of wedlock had always been able to use the comforting excuse that no one could prove that they were the father (at least in the days before DNA tests) and so extricate themselves from all sorts of trouble. Laura's plan is to use that fact to cast doubt in her husband's mind about his own daughter. Is he her real father or not? It is a dangerous accusation and what starts out on a playful, teasing note develops into a bitter battle of life and death.

Strindberg puts Laura in an explosive position: a woman without the means to support herself or even occupy herself in a satisfactory way is suddenly presented with a way out. What will she do? Like Ibsen's Nora, Laura is unfulfilled as a woman but Strindberg makes his heroine more intelligent and therefore more dangerous. Unlike Nora, however, Laura realizes that there can be no life outside marriage for her as long as she has no money of her own. The only way she could survive is with her husband's income – whether he's dead or alive. And then the obsession takes hold of her: as a widow she would be free and financially secure.

CAPTAIN: Put the bills down here and I'll have a look at them.

LAURA: The bills?

CAPTAIN: Yes.

LAURA: You want to see the bills now?

CAPTAIN: Of course I want to see the bills. Our situation is precarious at the moment and if it comes to a head we must be able to produce bills, otherwise we could be sued for mismanagement of the accounts.

LAURA: If our situation is as precarious as you say, it certainly isn't my fault.

CAPTAIN: That's exactly what we shall find out by looking at the bills.

LAURA: It isn't my fault if the tenant doesn't pay us.

CAPTAIN: Who recommended the tenant? You! And why did you recommend a . . . how shall I put it . . . good-for-nothing?

LAURA: Why did you take on a good-for-nothing then?

CAPTAIN: Because you didn't let me eat in peace, or sleep in peace, or work in peace until I'd agreed to take him on. You wanted him because your brother wanted to get rid of him, mother-in-law wanted him because I didn't want him, the governess wanted him because he was a Baptist and old Margaret because she had known his grandmother from childhood. That's why we took him in. And if I hadn't agreed to have him here I would either be in a madhouse or the family vault by now. However, here is the household money and some pocket money. You can give me the bills later.

LAURA: [*curtseys*] Thank you very much. Do you also keep account of the money you spend outside the household expenses?

CAPTAIN: That's none of your business.

LAURA: No, that's true. Nor is the education of my child, apparently. Have you two gentlemen come to a decision regarding that this afternoon?

CAPTAIN: I had already made my decision beforehand and all that remained for me to do was to pass on my resolution to the only friend we have in common in this family. Bertha is going to lodge in town and she is leaving in a fortnight's time.

LAURA: With whom is she going to lodge if I may ask?

CAPTAIN: Mr. Sävberg, the lawyer.

LAURA: That atheist?

CAPTAIN: Children are to be brought up in the faith of their fathers, as stipulated in law.

LAURA: And the mother has nothing to say in the matter?

CAPTAIN: Nothing at all. She sold her birthright and surrendered her rights when she agreed to accept her husband's offer to provide for her and her children.

LAURA: So she has no rights over her children?

CAPTAIN: None at all. Once you've sold something you can't ask for it back. You can't both have your cake and eat it.

Act One, Scene Four

There it is, in black and white. It is a man's world and women have no rights. The conflict is set up, and from now on it is perfectly clear that Laura is powerless. But she has a way with words and it is the power of the word over physical and economic power that finally triumphs. The discussion about paternity is first introduced later on in the same scene.

LAURA: What did Nöjd want in here?

CAPTAIN: That is my military secret.

LAURA: Which the whole kitchen knows, yes.

CAPTAIN: Good, then you must know it as well.

LAURA: I do.

CAPTAIN: And you have your verdict ready?

LAURA: The law is quite clear about it.

CAPTAIN: The law cannot prove who the father of the child is.

LAURA: No, but that is something you usually know anyway.

CAPTAIN: Wise people claim that you can never know.

LAURA: That is strange. You mean to say that you can't know who the father of a child is?

CAPTAIN: That is what they say.

LAURA: That is strange. How come the father has such rights over his child then?

CAPTAIN: Only in cases where he shoulders the responsibilities or is forced to do so. And inside marriage there are no doubts about the paternity, of course.

LAURA: No doubts?

CAPTAIN: No, I hope not.

LAURA: What if the wife has been unfaithful to him?

CAPTAIN: That is not relevant in this case. Have you got anything further to say in the matter?

LAURA: Not at all.

Act One, Scene Four

The Captain is so sure of his wife that there is not even the slightest doubt in his mind that she might have been unfaithful. This overconfidence has to be challenged and Laura's provocation is a natural reaction to her husband's cockiness. By the end of Act One the power struggle has moved on. Bertha confides in her father that she wants to get away from home and go and live in town but when her future is about to be discussed he sends her out of the room. In his eyes she is still a child, and a female one at that, and he believes that it is his right alone to decide what is to be done.

LAURA: You were afraid of what she might say, because you thought she was going to agree with me.

CAPTAIN: I happen to know that she wants to leave home but I also happen to know that you're quite capable of putting the pressure on her and get her over to your side.

LAURA: Really! Am I that powerful?

CAPTAIN: Yes, you have a devilish power when it comes to getting what you want – in common with other single-minded people you think the end justifies the means.

Act One, Scene Nine

He overrules her and announces that Bertha will leave home and live in the nearby town as he originally planned. With this he expects there to be no further debate on the subject.

> CAPTAIN: Do you think a father will allow ignorant, conceited women to teach his daughter that he's a charlatan?
>
> LAURA: It doesn't matter so much about the father.
>
> CAPTAIN: How's that?
>
> LAURA: Because the mother is closer to her child than the father, especially as it has now been discovered that you can't tell who the father is.
>
> CAPTAIN: That doesn't apply in our case.
>
> LAURA: You don't know if you're Bertha's father, do you?
>
> CAPTAIN: Don't I?
>
> LAURA: No, how can you tell, if no one else can?
>
> CAPTAIN: Is that supposed to be a joke?
>
> LAURA: No, I'm just putting your theories into practice. Besides, how do you know that I haven't been unfaithful to you?
>
> CAPTAIN: I believe you're capable of a lot of things, but not that, and even if it was true, I don't think you would tell me about it.
>
> LAURA: Just suppose that I'd prefer anything, being thrown out, despised, anything, as long as I could keep my child and decide over it, and just suppose that I'm telling you the truth now when I say: Bertha is my daughter, but she isn't yours! Just suppose . . .

Act One, Scene Nine

It is still only word-play at this point. Laura is trying her wings; she is using his own argument against him and she is surprised to discover how effective it is. This is an awakening for her and she is soon intoxicated by the potential of her new-found power.

> LAURA: I'd only need to name the real father, the time and place . . . for instance . . . when was Bertha born? Three years after we got married . . .
>
> CAPTAIN: Stop it now! Or else . . .
>
> LAURA: Else what? Yes, we shall stop it now. But think carefully about what you do and what you decide. And above all, don't make yourself ridiculous.
>
> CAPTAIN: I think this is a sad spectacle.
>
> LAURA: That makes you even more ridiculous.
>
> CAPTAIN: But not you.
>
> LAURA: No, nature has organized it wisely for us.
>
> CAPTAIN: That's why we can't fight with you.

LAURA: Why do you want to fight a superior enemy then?

CAPTAIN: Superior?

LAURA: Yes, it is strange, but I've never been able to look at a man without feeling superior.

CAPTAIN: You'll meet your superior one day, mark my words, and when you do you'll never forget it.

LAURA: I'm looking forward to that.

NURSE: (*enters*) Dinner is served.

Act One, Scene Nine

Laura's sense of victory makes her strong and now she is hungry for battle. This is an aspect of her character that the Captain has not seen before and he is taken off guard. In Act Two he really does begin to doubt that he is Bertha's father. At first Laura does not realize to what extent he is already weakened.

CAPTAIN: Remove my suspicions and I'll surrender.

LAURA: Which suspicions?

CAPTAIN: About Bertha's birth.

LAURA: Are there any suspicions about that?

CAPTAIN: Yes, I have many suspicions about it and it was you who planted them.

LAURA: Me?

CAPTAIN: Yes, you poured poison in my ear and now it has spread because of what's happened. Take away the uncertainty, tell me the truth and I promise to forgive you.

LAURA: You want me to plead guilty to something I haven't done?

CAPTAIN: What does it matter to you, I won't tell anyone about it. Do you think a man would cry out his own shame?

LAURA: If I say it isn't true, you won't be convinced but if I say that it is true then you will be sure at least. So you obviously want it to be true.

Act Two, Scene Five

After this the Captain throws a burning lamp at her in a fit of extreme jealousy. Laura then manages to lock him up and takes over the running of the house, including the finances. Towards the end she seems perplexed about the way events have worked out.

LAURA: I don't know that I ever planned or intended any of the things you accuse me of. Maybe I had some vague desire of wanting you out of the way, when you were being obstructive, but if you think you can detect a plan in the way I acted it's possible that there was one although I couldn't see it myself. My actions weren't premeditated, they just glided forward on rails which you laid down yourself, and

I swear by God and my conscience that I feel innocent, even if I'm not. Your presence has been like a stone pressing on my heart; it's pressed me down until my heart tried to rid itself of this cumbersome weight. That's probably how it is and if I've hurt you, then it wasn't my intention and I'm sorry.

CAPTAIN: It sounds sincere enough. But what good is that to me? And whose fault is it? Maybe the fault lies with the institution of marriage itself. In the past one married a wife, today one sets up a company with a woman who goes out to work, or one moves in with a friend. And then one either goes to bed with one's working partner or desecrates one's friend. What happened to love – healthy, sensual love? It died in the process. And what issue comes from this limited company of love shares? Who is the main bearer when the crash comes? Who is the biological father of the spiritual child?

LAURA: As far as your suspicions regarding the child are concerned, they are completely unfounded.

Act Three, Scene Seven

Thus Laura deals the final blow and emerges the victor. It is unlikely that Strindberg intended it as a feminist tract – in fact most people would claim that the opposite is true – but Laura acts in the true spirit of someone who is fighting for her rights and who does not balk at the means to achieve them. She is strong and intelligent and she is a worthy opponent in this fierce battle of brains. She has defeated her husband against all odds. What could she put up against his financial, physical and moral power? Words! There may be a hidden message of 'Beware women!' in the play. Her intelligence is certainly never underestimated.

Lady Julie (1888)

In *Lady Julie* Strindberg reverses the roles of his male and female protagonists. Julie has all the advantages of high social position and money while Jean has neither of these. But he does have intelligence and the sexual power to seduce her. Her naivety about what the lower classes really think of the aristocracy contributes to her downfall although her desire to mix with ordinary working people – she dances and celebrates midsummer with the servants – is genuine.

Midsummer celebrations, which usher in the sun and the warmth of the short summer season, have always been synonymous with sexual freedom and drunkenness in the Nordic countries and so Julie has the perfect pretext to shed a few inhibitions. She is drawn to the servants' quarters not only because of Jean but also because she recognizes a vitality there that is lacking 'upstairs'.

Julie believes in equality between men and women more than Jean does and so it comes as a shock when he reveals the brutal attitude he has towards people like her. For him the difference between the social classes is much more powerful than the difference between the sexes. She is neurotic, that's true, but she is seeking a salvation beyond her own inner circle. She chooses to do this by taking the sexual lead, an audacious act that Strindberg admired – he liked his women to be strong and assertive – but one that polite nineteenth-century Swedish society certainly didn't approve of. Making that leap and stepping out of her class proves to be fatal for her.

Her dream is about letting go, leaving her position on top of the pedestal. She wants to belong to the people. There is also a self-destructive element in her dream: once she has let go and reached the ground she wants the earth to swallow her up. It is a kind of death-wish, in other words. Jean, on the other hand, dreams of climbing. He wants to reach the top of the tree and help himself to the riches up there. To do this he needs to find a foothold and Julie is offering herself as the first branch.

Jean and Julie get drunk and make love and afterwards she realizes the enormity of what she has done: she has lost her virginity and so has given away her greatest asset. In Sweden at that time a man could return his bride to her parents if he discovered that she was not a virgin on the wedding night, and that would mean public shame and humiliation for the girl and ruin her marriage chances in the future. With this one impulsive and reckless act Julie has not only committed a sin in the religious sense – she has also disgraced her father and the family name. Her only way out is to marry Jean.

In her innocence Julie imagines that Jean will agree to her plan to elope without question. He does not, of course. If he is going to marry her then there are conditions, the most important of which is money, and a substantial amount at that, so that they can go abroad and set themselves up in business running a hotel. When Julie explains to him that she has no money of her own he loses interest immediately. His cold matter-of-factness is devastating and in desperation she is driven to stealing from her father.

Strindberg makes it clear that their relationship is doomed from the start. Julie prepares to leave her father's house with Jean and when she comes downstairs in her travelling clothes she is carrying a greenfinch in a cage. Jean is contemptuous that she could be so sentimental about a bird and kills it without ceremony. It is his answer to everything that Julie, and all the women like her, stands for. This unleashes a tirade of hatred and venom from Julie and she employs the greatest weapon she possesses – the superiority of her aristocratic background. It is her only advantage over him and though effective enough at the time, in the end it is not enough.

With Julie's suicide Strindberg is making the point that she has no future, neither as an individual nor as a representative of her class, for the aristocracy is a rotten anachronism. The future belongs to people like Jean, who, with education, will recognize their oppression and shake off the traditions that threaten to keep them tied to the past.

In the following scene, Lady Julie and Jean have been dancing and though he is wary of her motives in singling him out he is flattered. She flirts openly with him and asks him to kiss her shoe, ignoring his warning to be more discreet in front of the servants.

> JEAN: You're a strange creature, Lady Julie.
>
> JULIE: Maybe. But so are you. Everything is strange, really. Life, people, everything is a seething mess that's carried on top of the waves until it sinks, sinks. I have a dream that keeps recurring. I'm perched on top of a pillar and I can't see a way of getting down. I feel giddy when I look down, but I know I must get down. But I haven't got the courage to throw myself down. I can't hang on and I long to fall. But I don't fall. And yet I won't find peace until I've come down, I can't rest until I've come down, down on the ground. And once I hit the ground I want to get swallowed up by the earth . . . Have you ever had that feeling?

Towards the end of the play, after Jean has killed her greenfinch, Lady Julie flares up for the last time and displays a furious contempt for him and his class; she has to acknowledge what she has done and knows how her actions will affect her life from now on. Jean has humiliated her and the backlash takes the form of 'eloquent' hatred.

> JULIE: Don't you think I can stand the sight of blood? Do you think I'm so weak? . . . Oh, I would like to see your blood, your brains on the block . . . I would like to see your balls swimming in a sea like that . . . I think I could drink from your skull, I'd like to wash my feet in your ribcage and I'd like to eat your heart fried. You think I'm weak, you think I love you because my womb lusted after your sperm, you think I want to carry your brood under my heart and nourish it with my blood, bear your child and take your name . . . what is your name, by the way? I've never heard your surname, I suppose you haven't got one. I was to be Mrs. or Madam Pigsty . . . You . . . dog, who's wearing my collar, you lackey, who's got my family crest on your buttons . . . I was to share with my kitchen maid, I was to have a maid for a rival – oh, oh, oh. You think I'm a coward and want to run away. No, I'll stay now . . . and wait for the thunder to break. My father will come home . . . and find his bureau broken into . . . his money gone . . . and then he'll ring . . . that bell . . . twice for the servant . . . and then he'll send for the police . . . and then I'll tell him everything. Everything!

Strindberg's Works: 1879-92

Strindberg wrote the following works during the period when he was married to Siri von Essen:

Master Olof [*Mäster Olof*] play (later revisions), 1876, 1878

The Red Room [*Röda rummet*] novel, 1879

The Secret of the Guild [*Gillets hemlighet*] play, 1880

Lucky Per's Journey [*Lycko-Pers resa*] play, 1882

Sir Bengt's Wife [*Herr Bengts hustru*] play, 1882

Studies in Cultural History [*Kulturhistoriska studier*] essays, 1880–82

The Swedish Nation [*Svenska folket*] essays, 1880–82

The New Kingdom [*Det nya riket*] essays, 1882

Poems [*Dikter*] poems, 1883

Sleepless Nights on Waking Days [*Sömngångarnätter på vakna dagar*] poems, 1884

Swedish Destinies and Adventures [*Svenska öden och äventyr*] short stories, 1882–83

Getting Married, Vol. I [*Giftas*] short stories, 1884

Utopias in Reality [*Utopier i verkligheten*] essays, 1885

Getting Married, Vol. II [*Giftas*] short stories, 1885

The Son of a Servant [*Tjänstekvinnans son*] novel, 1886

A Madman's Defence [*Le Plaidoyer d'un fou*] novel, 1887–88

The Companions [*Kamraterna*] play, 1886

The Father [*Fadren*] play, 1887

The People of Hemsö [*Hemsöborna*] novel, 1887

Vivisections [*Vivisektioner*] essays, 1887

Lady Julie [*Fröken Julie*] play, 1888

Life in the Skerries [*Skärkarlsliv*] short stories, 1888

The Romantic Organist of Rånö [*Den romantiske klockaren på Rånö*] novella, 1888

Tschandala novella, 1888

Pictures of Flowers and Pieces on Animals [*Blomstermålningar och djurstycken*] essays, 1888

Among French Peasants [*Bland franska bönder*] essays, 1889

Creditors [*Fordringsägare*] play, 1889

Pariah [*Paria*] play, 1888–89

Samum play, 1889

The Stronger [*Den starkare*] play, 1889

By the Open Sea [*I havsbandet*] novel, 1890

The Keys of Heaven [*Himmelrikets nycklar*] play, 1892

Debit and Credit [*Debet och kredit*] play 1892

The First Warning [*Första varningen*] play, 1892

Before Death [*Inför döden*] play, 1892

Motherly Love [*Moderskärlek*] play, 1892

Playing With Fire [*Leka med elden*] play, 1892

Part 2
Frida Uhl (1872–1943)

— Chapter 11 —

A Well-Known Beauty

A completely new type in my life – gentle, full figure, dark-haired! And a real rogue!
Adolf Paul: Min Strindbergsbok

Strindberg's second wife, Frida Uhl, is never given much space in Swedish accounts of his life and work. They were officially married for four years but spent no more than eighteen months actually living together. The most flattering thing that has been said about her is that she was the most intelligent of his three wives. She showed great resourcefulness and maturity in dealing with Strindberg's affairs and did all she could to promote his work and to introduce him to the influential people she knew in the literary and theatrical world.

Her autobiographical book, *Marriage With Genius*, written forty years after she first met Strindberg and published in two volumes in 1933–34 in Sweden, is the fullest account of the relationship. In her foreword Frida stresses that 'This book is neither a novel nor a biography, nor a memoir. It is simply the story of my marriage to August Strindberg.' Given her great capacity for freely mixing fact and fiction, however, critics generally agree that hers is not altogether a reliable account. She created a myth about herself and her marriage and her book is a mish-mash of bits of dialogue and passages from Strindberg's writings interspersed with her own observations and recollections. Embellishment and exaggeration are of course traits that one finds in Strindberg too, especially in connection with his marriage to Siri.

Frida's *Marriage With Genius* and Strindberg's semi-autobiographical novel *The Cloister*, together with the letters that they wrote to each other, form the core of material about their short but intense relationship. Because they did not stay together very long, and because she was not an actress, Frida had less impact on Strindberg's work than his first and third wives, but *To Damascus*, his drama in three parts about his struggle back to Christianity, was undoubtedly influenced by the Uhl family, in particular Frida's mother, who was deeply religious. Frida herself was convent-educated but remained completely hostile to religion throughout her life.

When Strindberg first met Frida, less than six months after his divorce from Siri was finalized, the prospect of re-marriage was the last thing on his mind. He was bitter about losing custody of his children and disillusioned with Sweden, with the theatre and the world of publishing. He was also, as usual, desperately short of money. From a letter that he wrote just before leaving Stockholm to his friend Ola Hansson in Berlin it is clear that he had reached a crisis in his life:

> Dalarö, 13th September 1892
> In order to keep alive I have been doing some painting and I've sold some pictures – at Norrbro street-art prices, of course.
> Have been toying with the idea of becoming a photographer in order to preserve my talent as a writer.
> If you can see any way of getting me away from here in order to preserve my mental state – because I can't hope to play a role in Germany, maybe some sideline, something to keep myself afloat, for the time being . . .

Ola Hansson sent him 100 kronor and other friends in Berlin managed to persuade the Freie Bühne, a small independent theatre that had put on productions of *Lady Julie* and *The Father* earlier that year, to send him a further 400 kronor by way of royalties. It was enough to pay for his escape.

Strindberg arrived in Berlin on 1 October 1892 and rented a furnished apartment consisting of a kitchen, which he turned into a dark room for his photography, a study and a bedroom. Ola Hansson and his wife, Laura Marholm, who were both writers, helped him to settle in and introduced him to everyone they knew. He soon found himself at the centre of one of the most sparkling artistic and intellectual circles in northern Europe. Berlin was a magnet for writers and painters – especially those who came from artistically conservative cultures like Scandinavia – and the more outrageous they were the more they were feted. Strindberg entered this milieu as a radical young writer of some standing – some of his admirers addressed him as 'Maestro' – and he was immediately made welcome. He took to the cosmopolitan life straight away and there was no shortage of invitations to parties, theatre premières and exhibitions.

One of the most popular meeting places in the centre of Berlin at the time was a wine cellar called 'Türkes', better known as 'Zum Schwarzen Ferkel' ('At the Sign of the Black Piglet'), a name that Strindberg invented in reference to the sign above the door. The 'Ferkel' functioned as a delicatessen and off-licence, with a couple of rooms set aside for customers who wanted to drink on the premises. The landlord, Gustav

Türke, was said to have kept 900 varieties of liquor in stock. Strindberg was a frequent visitor and quickly gained a reputation as a prodigious drinker. He would also entertain the company by playing the guitar and singing songs that he had composed himself.

The 'Ferkel's' popularity may have had something to do with the fact that Herr Türke offered his customers generous credit and would sometimes take a work of art in lieu of payment. He accepted one of Strindberg's paintings and proudly displayed it on the wall of the bar for many years.

The bohemian set who gathered at the 'Ferkel' was headed by the temperamental Polish writer Stanislaw Przybyszewski and the German poet Richard Dehmel, known as 'the wild man'. Other writers in the circle included Adolf Paul and Karl August Tavaststjerna from Finland and Holger Drachmann from Denmark. It was here that Strindberg first met the Norwegian painters Edvard Munch and Christian Krohg. Munch was another 'wild man' and just before he met Strindberg he had had an exhibition in Kristiania that had been forced to close because his avant-garde paintings had so shocked the critics. Berliners were similarly shocked when the exhibition opened in their city but at least the authorities were tolerant enough to keep it open. Munch encouraged Strindberg to paint and became an important influence on him.

Both Krohg and Munch painted portraits of Strindberg during this period. Ibsen bought Krohg's painting at an exhibition in 1895. 'It is really a portrait of Strindberg,' he wrote to his wife, Suzannah, 'but Sigurd [Ibsen's son] calls it "The Revolution" and I call it "Madness Breaking Out".'

When Strindberg died Munch gave his portrait, which he had never sold, to the Swedish National Museum. 'To be honest,' he wrote to them at the time, 'it feels empty in the room where Strindberg has been hanging for twenty years. To me, the picture is the incarnation of those two remarkable years in Berlin.'

A few months after Strindberg arrived in Berlin the Residenztheater offered to stage a production of his play *Creditors*. It opened on 21 January 1893, the day before his forty-fourth birthday, and ran for 71 performances, becoming one of his greatest successes to date. There was a hunger for the avant-garde across Europe, especially in Germany and France, and his reputation outside his conservative homeland was in the ascendant.

It was shortly before this that Strindberg first met Frida Uhl. They spoke briefly when they were introduced at a reception on the opening night, 7 January, of the play *Heimat* by the German dramatist Hermann

Marriage With Genius

In Marriage With Genius *Frida records her response at meeting Strindberg, in the company of Edvard Munch and the German painter Hermann Schlittgen, for the first time:*

I only need to close my eyes and I can experience that evening again. I can hear every voice, image after image recurring, one of them . . . dream-like . . . another quite clearly, many of them . . . in a moment's flash.

Eleven o'clock. I have left the theatre. The snow is white and thick in the moonless and starless night. [. . .]

A long, well-illuminated vestibule on the first floor. Right at the end of it, in the shadow of a door three men about to say goodbye to the hostess, a bit early. [. . .]

. . . a slim, blond man transfused by spirit. A thin, pale face with marvellous blue eyes, a person who is shy in life but risks everything in his art: Edvard Munch, the painter, whom I had wanted to meet for a long time.

But I look past Edvard Munch even. Behind him, in the shadow, a tall grim creature appears. He wears a dark grey raincoat over his shoulders. Like a rugged grey rock he grows out of the floor. Stone-grey is the colour of his coat, stone-grey his hair. Like stone, his mighty head. Grey his roving eyes, grey his hollow cheeks.

'The flying Dutchman!' I can't take my eyes off him.

The hostess comes up to me, greets me cordially, looks enchanting, young and maternal in her white dress. She introduces the gentlemen in a friendly way to me, first the two painters.

And then 'Mr. August Strindberg.'

'Mr. August Strindberg,' repeats our hostess – 'Miss Uhl from Vienna.'

He emerges from the shadow into the light.

Miss Uhl from Vienna has, despite her aristocratic convent upbringing, a very poor idea of dignity. She looks like an abandoned foundling who has suddenly discovered the key to the gates of Life amid the tinsel.

And Mr. Strindberg regards her in the same unconventionally surprised way and gives her a long and serious look, without a trace of curiosity or desire. Simply like one who immediately perceives his subject correctly and takes an interest in it.

In the sobering light from the lamp he does not look at all ghost-like any more, but quite normal and earthly.

Sudermann. Frida's name had been linked with Sudermann's and their relationship had caused something of a scandal because he was married. He based one of the characters in *Heimat*, a seductive young woman, on Frida.

Frida Uhl was born in Austria on 4 April 1872 and was the youngest of two children. She was a premature baby and her mother gave birth to her at an inn near Mondsee, where the family had a summer home. Her father, Friedrich, was a friend of Emperor Franz Josef and occupied a position in court of *Hafrath* – a Court Counsellor. He was also Editor-in-Chief of Vienna's prestigious newspaper, the *Wiener Zeitung,* and so was a man of some influence.

Frida's parents separated not long after she was born, though they remained officially married, and she lived with her mother and maternal grandparents and several single female relatives in a large villa overlooking the Danube in Dornach, 50 miles west of Vienna. Friedrich spent most of his time in the capital, where he kept a mistress, but he would join the family for part of the summer at Mondsee, at the country house overlooking the lake that he had had built to house his art collection.

After an education at various different boarding schools in France, Italy and England, Frida decided that she wanted to be a journalist like her older sister, Marie, who was a theatre critic in Vienna. Her father secured her a position as an arts critic for the *Wiener Zeitung* and the *Wiener Abendpost*, based in Berlin, where she wrote about literature, painting and the theatre. Given the circumstances of her family background it is perhaps not so surprising that her father allowed her to live and work abroad, alone and unchaperoned, at the age of eighteen, though such personal freedom was certainly not the norm amongst young women of her class. She was used to living away from home and Friedrich made sure that she would not starve – he installed her in a grand four-room apartment and gave her an allowance.

When she arrived in Berlin Frida found, as Strindberg was to find some two years later, a city that was buzzing with new ideas, both politically and artistically. Berlin's place at the centre of the art world ensured that exciting things were always happening and she found plenty to write about.

The novelist Adolf Paul wrote about Strindberg and Frida in his memoir, *Min Strindbergsbok* [*My Book About Strindberg*], and he describes the impact that she made right from the beginning:

> Once after a dinner at a Berlin critic's he [Strindberg] came home quite besotted with a young lady whom he had got to know there, and who had challenged his fighting spirit courageously. 'A completely new type in my life – gentle, full figure, dark-haired! And a real rogue!'

Paul considered that Strindberg had found an intellectual sparring partner in Frida. Like Siri, she was to prove strong-willed and unpredictable and not half as gentle as Strindberg had supposed. Frida was well aware of his reputation as a 'woman-hater' and this made him all the more of a challenge. There were many women in Berlin competing to tame him and she was determined to be the one to succeed.

The Cloister

In his novel The Cloister *Strindberg describes his second encounter with Frida, which took place on 5 February, at the house of the critic Otto Neuman-Hofer:*

One of the three ladies nodded, as if she knew him, and held out her hand. He immediately asked his hostess in a whisper who she was.

–Who? Miss X of course, whom you talked with at Doctor E's supper party.

–Really? How odd that I, who have such a good memory should be quite unable to remember what Miss X looks like. The other evening I walked past her in a theatre foyer which was fully lit, without saying hello to her.

–Well, I suppose that as a woman-hater you are unable to see that she is beautiful.

–Is she? he said, leaning forward to scrutinize the young lady who had sat down at the far end of the table. –Yes, she is not bad-looking.

–For shame. She's a well-known beauty of the most attractive Viennese type. . . .

Whereupon their conversation drifted into other subjects. After supper the guests assembled in the drawing room and very soon these two people, the beautiful Viennese woman and the woman-hater were so deep in conversation that a group of ladies and gentlemen, looking roguish, gathered round in a circle to watch. But the couple noticed nothing, they only talked and talked, until their hostess interrupted them by offering them some tea.

When the party finally broke up, he and she inexplicably found themselves again in each other's vicinity so he helped her on with her coat. And when she asked who was going to see her home he answered: 'I am of course,' and was accepted.

— Chapter 12 —

Friendship and Courtship

> . . . and I love you because your mouth is so beautiful and your little teeth so wonderfully white; when you are angry I love you, because your deep eyes give off sparks; I love you because you are so terribly wise and greedy, because you write those awful business letters for my sake.
>
> *Letter to Frida Uhl, 1 March 1893*

On the surface Frida had a lot in common with Siri von Essen. Both women were from the upper classes but were unconventional and independently minded. They were both artistic, sociable and flirtatious and were drawn to Strindberg by a fascination with his character and an admiration and respect for his creative talent. But whereas Siri always retained an innate dignity and pride – despite some of the worst excesses of her behaviour in the 1880s – Frida seemed to grow more brash and pushy as the years went by.

Like Siri, Frida appears to have made the first move to get to know Strindberg better after their first two meetings. She wrote letters to him that were delivered by hand on the same day, arranged their rendezvous and suggested walks and excursions. As is clear from a letter that Strindberg wrote to her on 20 February 1893, he wants to treat her as a friend rather than a potential lover but he cannot help expressing the strong attraction that he already feels for her:

> Dear Fräulein and Friend
> I can't tell you how our walk in the park tamed the evil spirits that haunt me . . .
> But I must see you every day, even with the risk of compromising you. Were I to compromise you – I assure you – then I am prepared to give you an honourable redress such as can be expected of a man of honour. Is that enough?
> Your old young friend
> August Strindberg

For Frida mere friendship was never going to be enough and she did not care that Strindberg was twenty-three years older than she was and only five years younger than her mother. One evening, after they had been out together, she kissed him on the mouth through her veil and fled into her apartment before he had time to respond with an embrace. It was a provocative act that obviously surprised and delighted him. How audacious of her to take the initiative and kiss him first and how seductive to lower her veil in a contradictory gesture of modesty. He recreated the mood when he described the episode in *The Cloister*:

> He stood there utterly dumbfounded, unable to grasp how it had happened. Then he thought: She loves me, she hasn't been playing with me! But how bold! True, she let down her veil, that was a sign of modesty, and she fled, surprised at her own action. That was original, but not modest. Other countries, other customs! [. . .]
>
> She loved him! To be loved was like being able to say to oneself: 'I'm not so bad after all since someone can look up to me, can think well of me.' And thereby self-esteem, hope and trust were revived. He felt young again and ready to begin a new spring. It was true that he had only shown her his good sides, but the habit of temporarily suppressing the bad ones had made him seek out those that were good. And that was the secret of the ennobling effects of love.

Frida's relationship with Strindberg developed quickly and most of the time it was she who took the initiative, inviting him to visit her at her apartment alone and taking him out to dine. She was not interested in playing the helpless female and when she realized how poor he was she was quite prepared to pick up the bills. Strindberg still had his male pride, though, and on one occasion he made a scene in a restaurant when Frida insisted on paying for their meal. He called the waiter back and refused to leave until the bill was split and he was allowed to pay his half at least. Money was always a sensitive issue for him and he hated being under an obligation to anyone, least of all a woman. He always made a point of paying back his debts to the last öre.

As he and Frida continued to write to each other and to meet regularly in and around Berlin, he began to appreciate and admire more and more about her – her looks, the way she walked, her intelligence and her quick wit. Her deep voice, which had a rather sad cadence to it, 'awakened memories of forests and lakes'. In *Min Strindbergsbok* Adolf Paul describes Frida as self-confident and impulsive but found her also possessive and immodest:

> A perfect upbringing, educated in a convent school in France; an affected, childish, half surprised, half apologetic expression in her voice, when she asked or answered a question in her correct way; – her gaze invited confidences and did not betray anything except a heart of gold when she looked at you, and yet she knew how to be coquettish, but with great charm . . .

Frida was more mature and better informed than Siri had been at the same age but both were keenly interested in people, books, the arts – all subjects that Strindberg enjoyed discussing too. Of the two women, he confessed to having found Siri more alluring physically but Frida was certainly attractive and intriguing; she aroused his curiosity and he wanted to get to know her better. He declared that he had never before met anyone capable of changing their shape the way Frida could. Her face, he remarked, 'seemed to change its mind as it grew up, for it took a sudden turn on the bridge of the nose and in an instant became Roman. This unexpected little bit of mischief on its part lent charm to her profile.' When she walked, he noticed, she seemed to stoop slightly, which gave her a 'witch-like' appearance when seen from a distance. And there was no denying the capacity she had to create a dramatic impact wherever she went:

> When they entered the brightly lit premises and she removed her fur and her scarf, she was suddenly transformed into a youthful beauty. A simple, close-fitting moss-green dress revealed the figure of an eighteen-year-old, and her hair, which she wore brushed back, made her look like a grown-up schoolgirl. He could not conceal the effect this magic had on him, but let his eyes sweep over her whole figure, as if he were looking for some hidden enemy with a searchlight.
> (Eros! Now I am lost! he thought and from that moment he was!)
> She saw perfectly well the effect she had produced and she phosphoresced, sat as if enveloped in light, sure of victory, with a triumphant look, for she saw that the woman-hater was conquered.

This passage from *The Cloister* is matched in Frida's *Marriage With Genius*, where she describes the same event and reveals how aware she was of the effect she had on men and how artfully she presented herself to Strindberg in a carefully prepared act of seduction:

> I had not had time to dress elaborately. I had only tied a lace scarf around my head and put the leopard stole over my shoulders. When I slid out of the stole I stood there in my dark green princess-style dress which I was wearing that afternoon. I noticed that Strindberg's eyes caressed my whole body. It gave me a lovely feeling of power. I know that I look good in that dress.
> 'Little Miss Uhl has a trim little figure,' said old Franz Lenbach to me once, when I was wearing that dress.
> Thanks to the dress! It hugged my body like a snake skin and wriggled into a tapering train behind me. 'Swish,' hissed the silk lining at the slightest movement.
> 'Green leaf . . . yellow sunshine . . . love . . . joie de vivre . . . spring on your doorstep . . . swish.'
> He is blushing. His eyes are smiling at me. There is something strangely humble and imploring about his person.
> Is that how little is needed to bridge the unsurpassable gap between the male genius and the young girl – who is nobody?
> Just a green dress and a tapering train and a little swishing sound.

Strindberg's growing infatuation with Frida was coupled with anxiety. In *The Cloister* he observes that four men in his circle were divorced and some of them, like himself, had been married to women who themselves had been married before. Why was it, he wondered, that some of the most remarkable men from the Nordic countries picked their wives from other people's marriages? Frida had never been married, but was she the right companion for an intellectual who was more than twice her age? A more mature, more worldly woman might have complemented him better. He felt that love and hate were interchangeable, the one simply being the reverse of the other. In *Marriage With Genius* Frida records her puzzlement at this axiom: 'Can one hate when one loves?' she asked. 'He looked at me with surprise: Can one love without hate?'

His recorded reservations read like a cautionary note to himself, uttered too late. Frida already had his soul in her pocket. His only salvation lay in tying her as securely to himself as she had managed to tie him. He appealed to her maternal instincts, made himself small, aroused her compassion. She was a good listener and stayed calm and dignified, majestic even, he thought.

He surprised himself by growing steadily more dependent on her. In a jocular letter written on 24 February he said that he would be the first person to warn her against August Strindberg. He was no suitable companion for a lady like Frida Uhl, 'unless she aims at the artistic heights which demand cruel sacrifices'. In another letter, written on the same day, he describes love as 'the divine lie', calling it 'the loveliest illusion that life can offer':

My dear Fräulein
Is it really true that you intend to leave on Wednesday? And without saying goodbye?

What will become of me? Or should I prepare to follow on next Saturday?

I am feeling sad today and I am sorry about the lost evening yesterday. Do you permit me to meet you tomorrow, at the museum, under the arcades or in the park? I am burning with longing to talk to you properly à deux. I feel I owe you so many answers, so many interrupted explanations, a number of excuses! I would like to walk by your side forever, endlessly under the trees, along the beach, across mountains and valleys. Is that madness? Have I tired you out? Are you afraid that your soul might blend into mine? Do you think I want to swallow you like a cannibal? Are you so self-confident that you can no longer abandon yourself to the loveliest illusion that life can offer, the divine lie which makes us happier than the most sublime truth? Do I care about all that? Maybe!

Send me a word, I beg you!
Yours already too sincerely,
August Strindberg

A week or so later he was urging her to come and see him, and his greeting – 'My dear precious friend' – betrays his desire for greater intimacy with her:

> Berlin 3rd March 1893
> My dear precious friend,
> Where are you? I have left my soul with you and you have run away with it so now I am walking around like a ghost. Seriously speaking though, and upon my life: have you been playing with me? In that case I want to die. But no reproaches. You have avenged yourself and you're justified. I'll die and bless you, my good woman.
>
> I never demanded that you should love me, only that you'd allow me to love you. Is that too much?
>
> Let me see you before evening or I'll go mad.
>
> Preferably at your place or at our own little Ferkel far off in the West.
>
> I am at home, waiting, waiting, waiting!
> Yours
> August Strindberg
> P.S. The money has arrived, the bill is paid and everything is in order!

Later on the same day, after he had spent the evening at the 'Ferkel', he wrote her another note, which was maudlin and full of remorse, confessing to having indulged in a few drinks in his loneliness.

The next day he wrote to Frida again, asking her to marry him. He reminded her of their first unforgettable evening together at her apartment when she had offered him roses and wine. He told her that he had been madly in love with her from that moment. Frida responded immediately in a letter that she delivered to him personally. Fearing his reaction she left before he could open it:

> Berlin 4. 3. 1893
> My dear Friend
> I have only two minutes to answer your letter or I shall be late for our rendezvous so that answer will be short. You asked me once what had made me so mature in looks and character. Nothing special. Except an event that took place in March '92. Tomorrow we shall celebrate the first anniversary, maybe together.
>
> You see, my dear friend, one does not die just because a few dreams come to an end, if one is in good health.
>
> I am feeling quite well today. [. . .]
>
> I am very fond of you as a friend and am prepared to do anything to help you or make you happy. Firstly, because I admire your genius and secondly because I am personally fond of you.
>
> But I am unable to feel anything that bears the slightest resemblance to passionate love. I think that is for the best as far as you are concerned. When you assure me that you love me I believe you. I think you are too noble to play with the feelings of a girl who could not possibly interest you as an object of study and who has not done you any harm. But I am convinced that your love is only an illusion. You are

in love with love, you love the dream in your own heart, you are seeking the materialization of your dream and when you don't find it, then you deceive yourself.

But the day will come for you – I hope – when your dream becomes true, when you find a woman who is worthy of you, and who loves you, and then you will be happy. Let me remain your friend until that day, your most sincere, devoted, dearest friend. It is the only alternative we have and the best one, believe me.

Give me your hand, if you agree with me!

Frida

Strindberg was puzzled by her claim that she was the sort of woman who would never be able to feel real love. 'What kind of creature is that?' he wrote in *The Cloister*. 'It sounds to me like a literary invention.' However, in spite of Frida's protestations, only a couple of days later she and Strindberg agreed to consider themselves secretly engaged. This event may well have been precipitated by the fact that speculation about them had already appeared in the press, no doubt as a result of Strindberg's own indiscretion. He had spoken openly to his friends at the 'Ferkel' about his feelings for Frida and, according to Adolf Paul, he had revealed quite intimate details about his relationship with her.

By now Frida's reputation was at stake. She had not yet come of age and she still needed her father's consent to marry so it was a gross *faux pas* on Strindberg's part to have said anything about a possible engagement before the family had been consulted. The rumours that reached Friedrich Uhl in Vienna were that Frida was involved with a penniless Swedish writer, a man much older than she was, a Protestant and a radical freethinker. She had only known him for six weeks and now, it seemed, they intended to get married. Friedrich ordered his daughter to go to Munich to stay with friends to reflect on what she was doing and to allow time for the gossip to die down.

Frida heeded her father's advice and told Strindberg that she would be leaving Berlin for a while. He wanted to go with her but she protested that she needed to be away from him in order to think things over. Her departure for Munich on 7 March left a sudden vacuum and although he had promised her that he would stay away from the 'Ferkel' loneliness drove him back to the familiar haunt in search of company. His friends had offered him so much support and companionship since his arrival in Berlin, depressed and bereft, that he was not prepared to give up his drinking sessions and reform completely – even for the sake of an exciting new love affair. Despite his anguish whenever she went away, Frida's influence over him always weakened considerably when she was out of sight. He knew that the emancipated women he met at the 'Ferkel' posed more of a threat to his peace of mind than Frida, who had hung on to her bourgeois attitudes about many things, but he could not keep away.

While Frida was in Munich she became more circumspect about their relationship while her absence made Strindberg all the more passionate about her. He begged her to return to Berlin so that they could become officially betrothed and exchange rings. In a letter that he wrote to her on 11 March he assured her that he loved her and that he would remain faithful to her. He loved her youth, her beauty, her wisdom and all the crazy things she did:

> . . . and I love you because your mouth is so beautiful and your little teeth so wonderfully white; when you are angry I love you, because your deep eyes give off sparks; I love you because you are so terribly wise and greedy, because you write those awful business letters for my sake.
>
> So come and live here in West Berlin and I shall want to live here too and I want to work and I want to love you until I drive you mad.
>
> Now you know everything!
>
> Goodnight, my child!
>
> Yours
>
> August Strindberg

Maybe Frida's father was right. She was used to money and an extravagant lifestyle and Strindberg would not be able to provide that. But the more guarded she became in response to his letters the more he pursued her.

— Chapter 13 —

Jealousy

> A smile that made you long for kisses, but at the same time inspired fear of the two rows of pearly sharp teeth that lurked behind her thin lips, waiting for a chance to bite.
>
> *Adolf Paul: Min Strindbergsbok*

'Your fiancé has the finest cosmic vibrations,' one of Frida's friends told her before she officially announced her engagement to Strindberg in April 1893. It is true, he was always in touch with his own feelings and claimed to have developed extrasensory perception. After he met Frida and her family he became increasingly interested in occultism and mysticism. Whether he really was a hypersensitive person who experienced and gave off 'cosmic vibrations' is a matter of interpretation but he was certainly charismatic and many people have confirmed that there was definitely something 'otherworldly' about him. Adolf Paul always insisted that he had seen Strindberg's ghost at the 'Ferkel'.

Whatever the fascination between Frida and Strindberg it is hard to understand his motives for embarking on a second marriage so soon after his divorce from Siri. She was struggling to keep herself and the children in Finland and at this stage in his life he was rarely able to help her out. Having virtually stopped writing – it would be another six years before he completed his next play – his main source of income had dried up. He was planning a book, *Antibarbarus*, based on the scientific experiments that he was conducting, and was also painting, but these projects were not lucrative. He was hardly able to support himself, let alone a second wife, and was largely dependent on his friends in Berlin to pay his boarding house bills and subsidize his drinking. It was a fairly dissolute life and he knew that this would not be compatible with marriage. Frida disapproved of him spending so much time in bars and he made an effort to be more moderate:

> [Undated] March 1893
> Last night I only drank two glasses of red wine with soda water. Strange, isn't it, but I don't like the taste of alcohol any more. You have set light to me so I don't need the fire from wine any more.

His good intentions were short-lived. If Frida was not around he invariably slipped back into his old ways with the motley crowd at the 'Ferkel'.

The month of March 1893 was a turbulent period for them both. Frida stayed in Munich for about three weeks and during that time Strindberg's letters reveal that he vacillated violently between infatuation and indifference. He was longing for a close sexual relationship with her and that was clearly going to be impossible unless he promised to marry her. And so they talked about marriage and Frida generously offered to use the money she had set aside for her trousseau to pay off all his outstanding debts. Though embarrassed and humiliated at the thought of financial dependence on a woman, Strindberg reluctantly accepted her help. He still had to write to her father asking for permission to marry and kept putting it off, knowing only too well that he would appear to be a very poor prospect as a husband. He was hoping for a windfall or a change of fortune but Frida was becoming impatient.

The correspondence between them while Frida was away is full of contradictory messages on both sides, showing how uncertain they both were about making a commitment to each other. They both made frequent declarations of love – one day Frida impulsively sent Strindberg some flowers from Munich and he was moved by this reversal of the conventional roles in their courtship – but also expressions of real doubt. Being the more organized and businesslike of the two, Frida had helped him up to now in his dealings with producers and publishers. When he thought about this side of her character Strindberg became quite disenchanted with her. He remembered one occasion when she had accompanied him to a meeting with an editor: she had been carelessly dressed and had ink on her fingers and it irritated him that she appeared not to have noticed how she looked. He already sensed how dangerous it would be to allow his fate to become too closely entwined with hers.

Just when he had managed to convince himself that marriage to Frida would be a mistake, Strindberg added a further complication to his life by getting involved with another woman: Dagny Juel. She was twenty-five, Norwegian, and a friend of Munch's. They met at the 'Ferkel' and she told him that she had already heard a lot about him. She flirted with him, he was flattered, and within a few days they were lovers. Like Frida, Dagny was young, beautiful and intelligent but unlike Frida she was totally uninhibited sexually and Strindberg became obsessed with her immediately. He and his friends at the 'Ferkel' called her 'Aspasia', after Pericles' second wife, who was famed for her beauty and intelligence. He also sometimes referred to her as 'Laïs', after two courtesans in ancient Greece who were renowned for wheedling large sums of money out of their lovers. Adolf Paul was not immune to her predatory charms either:

> A classically pure profile, her forehead concealed by a wreath of curls, so that you could estimate its height and its intelligence as you liked. A smile that made you long for kisses, but at the same time inspired fear of the two rows of pearly sharp teeth that lurked behind her thin lips, waiting for a chance to bite. There was also a snake-like, affected languor in all her movements, which nevertheless did not exclude the possibility of a lightning attack.
>
> *Min Strindbergsbok*

Dagny moved freely from lover to lover, becoming a confidante and friend to each in turn, always careful to retain an aura of mystery. All who came into contact with her saw her as an enigma and she guarded the secret of her attraction well. She had come to Berlin in 1892 to study music and she later wrote poetry and plays and translated works from Norwegian into German. To begin with she modelled for several Scandinavian artists and acted as Munch's impresario, helping him with his exhibition in Berlin in December 1892. Before long she was the most lusted after woman in Berlin. Poets, novelists and painters — she was a muse to them all. Munch immortalized her in several of his paintings, most notably 'Jealousy'. They maintained a warm friendship that outlasted all other relationships throughout her life and Munch always defended her, however badly she behaved, and spoke well of her after her death in 1901.

The Polish critic Ewa Kossak exonerates Dagny Juel from some of the worst excesses attributed to her, though it is evident from numerous other accounts that she was an exceptional woman. The German art historian Julius Meier-Graefe, for example, records a typical scene with his description of Dagny entertaining a group of admirers that included Strindberg, Munch and the Polish novelist Stanislaw Przybyszewski in her room in north Berlin:

> He was a Pole, known to his friends as Staczu (short for Stanislaw), who wrote his bold, ecstatic works in German and who suffered from hallucinations. She was a Norwegian, very slender, with the lines of a thirteenth-century Madonna and a smile that drove men to distraction. Her nickname was Ducha (which means soul) and she drank absinthe by the litre without ever getting tipsy . . . Against the wall by the door stood an upright piano, a peculiar instrument. It could be toned down by means of a lever so that the other inmates of the house were not disturbed even when Staczu hammered on it with his fists . . . One of us would dance with Ducha while the other two looked on from the table: one spectator was Munch, the other was generally Strindberg. The four men in the room were all in love with Ducha,

each in his own way, but they never showed it. Most subdued of them all was Munch. He called Ducha 'the Lady', talked drily to her and was always very polite and discreet even when drunk . . . The Paris of Huysmans and Rops provided the background of the conversation about pathological eroticism carried on by Staczu . . . Strindberg would talk about chemical analysis while Munch remained silent . . . It was in that room in 1893 that the journal *Pan* was born. Ducha gave it that name, which is probably the reason why Munch was against it. Some time later Ducha went to Tiflis and there she became involved with a strange character, a barbaric young Russian who held a revolver to her forehead, and as she went on laughing, he pulled the trigger, shooting first her and then himself . . .

Przybyszewski left his two children and common-law wife, Martha Foerder, to marry Dagny in the autumn of 1893. This marriage, which produced two more children, was brief and tempestuous. Przybyszewski was a drunk and a womanizer and even after he had married Dagny he continued his relationship with Martha and had another child with her. He was unable to support either of his families adequately and it was not long before he and Dagny separated. It is clear from his novels, most of which are autobiographical, that his relationship with her had had a profound effect on him. Of the woman he had once called 'Ducha' or 'soul', he wrote in his novel *The Sons of the Earth*: '. . . her soul was an empty soiled canvas. He didn't love her, but he wanted her to love him. She could not, she lacked the ability to love.'

When Martha was found dead at her home in 1896, Przybyszewski was arrested on suspicion of her murder; he was later released when it was confirmed that she had died of carbon monoxide poisoning and had almost certainly committed suicide. Dagny showed no compassion for the three motherless children and wanted nothing to do with them. They were split up and allocated to different foster homes and one of them later ended up in a lunatic asylum. One should not assume, however, that Martha's suicide had had no effect on Dagny: her surviving fragmentary writings show that she often returned to the theme of two lovers causing the death of a third.

It has been suggested that Przybyszewski 'sold' Dagny to Wladyslav Emeryk, the young Pole who had become her lover, and that the two men deliberately planned her murder. The evidence reveals that Emeryk certainly threatened to kill Dagny – he had written letters to various people beforehand outlining what he was going to do – but Przybyszewski's involvement remains unclear.

The events leading up to Dagny's death were complicated and messy. Przybyszewski was drinking heavily and was involved with two other women in Poland, both of whom soon became devoted to him, while

Dagny was living in Paris and was having affairs with at least three other men simultaneously, including Emeryk. Emeryk invited Dagny on a trip to visit his family home in the Caucasus and while they were staying in a hotel in Tiflis, on 5 June 1901, he shot her and then turned the gun on himself.

With Przybyszewski significantly absent from the funeral, Dagny was buried in Tiflis three days later, on her thirty-fourth birthday. Tributes poured in from all quarters. One of her Paris lovers, the Polish writer Wincent Brzozowski, who had immortalized her in his poetry, was devastated: 'Dagny was killed because she was seen to be a goddess, or a demon, a metaphysical absolute,' he said, 'not a woman, not a human being.'

An unattributed obituary that appeared in the *Svenska Dagbladet* on 21 June confirmed that Dagny Juel had been a remarkable woman with an extraordinary power over men:

> She was definitely not beautiful and yet she was seductive like few. Tall, slim, supple with a dark forehead and light eyes under constantly half-closed, tired eyelids. She had very dry frizzy reddish brown hair which made a crunchy noise when you touched it like ripe rye in a storm. Far too large a mouth with thin lips, which shone bright red over her pointed, white genuinely Nordic weasel teeth so that people who did not know Aspasia swore that they were artificially coloured. That was not the case, however. How and on what she lived no one knew, but no one cared either, to be honest. People assumed that she slept through the days and to judge by the late parties at Zum Schwarzen Ferkel this was probably the most likely scenario. There was a soulfulness in her gaze, in her smile, in every movement of her supple being and everyone became soulful when they spoke with her. She only needed to look at a man, put her hand on his arm and he soon found an expression for something that he had long been mulling over without being able to give it a coherent shape. She was the one who released the fettered thoughts in these slowly creating poets. But one never felt calm or cosy in her presence, not even the people who desired her company most eagerly.

Dagny Juel owes her place in history, unfortunately, not for her superior intellect nor for her musical and literary talents, which were considerable, but for the number of famous men her name was linked with in the 1890s. She was the archetypal siren or *femme fatale*: exotic, sensual and mysterious, part vamp and part Madonna, a she-devil, a 'Belle Dame Sans Merci'. With her sexual appetite and nonchalant manner she drove men wild with lust. It wasn't so remarkable then that Strindberg had been drawn into her magic circle and had fallen under her spell like virtually every other man who met her, nor that she, the friend and muse of geniuses, should have been attracted to an already celebrated and charismatic writer.

With Frida away, Strindberg had found someone he could confide in and for the three weeks that their relationship lasted he and Dagny were inseparable. Not that Strindberg could forget about Frida altogether. On one occasion he had woken up to find Dagny in bed beside him. In a panic he pushed her out of the room and left her naked (or, as some sources claim, wearing only a flimsy chemise) on the communal staircase, where she remained for the rest of the night. Having locked her out, Strindberg went back to bed to sleep off his hangover. The next morning he realized that he was in fact in Dagny's room and he had been too drunk to remember. Dagny saw the humorous side of this incident and seems to have accepted her treatment as a fair price to pay for an evening of fun.

The guilt that Strindberg felt at betraying Frida with another woman was heightened when he received a letter from her assuring him that she did love him after all. He decided that he had to stop seeing Dagny before Frida returned to Berlin. Fortunately for him, his friend Bengt Lidforss arrived from Sweden just in time to take Dagny off his hands. Lidforss and Dagny became lovers and he remained 'a friend of the house' even after her marriage to Przybyszewski, who wrote about this *ménage à trois* in his semi-autobiographical novel *Overboard*.

Przybyszewski was fifteen years younger than Strindberg and had been one of his most devoted followers, addressing him as 'Maestro' and kissing his hand when they met. After his affair with Dagny had finished Strindberg had visions of Przybyszewski taking revenge and coming to kill him. As it happened, Przybyszewski never did him any harm. Strindberg perhaps did not appreciate the fact that, as is evident from the way he writes in *Overboard*, Przybyszewski enjoyed seeing his lovers flaunting themselves with other men, and even encouraged them, while suffering masochistic feelings of jealousy as a consequence. He had once undressed Dagny in front of another man in order to show off her beautiful body and had further demonstrated his 'generosity' by bequeathing Martha to his friends at the 'Ferkel'.

Frida returned to Berlin on 1 April 1893 and she and Strindberg resumed their relationship. The prospect of devoting his life to this comparatively sane and innocent young woman must have seemed like a cosy dream in contrast to the wild excesses he had experienced with Dagny but still he hesitated. It was not long before Frida heard rumours about his brief liaison and when she tackled him about it he told her everything. She was reasonably sanguine about it and her description of Dagny in *Marriage With Genius* is presented with a light and humorous touch. One can detect a slight hint of jealousy disguised as irony in her tone but there is also a genuine note of fascination, admiration even, for this woman who had seduced her future husband. And she does not blame either Strindberg or Dagny for following their instincts. As she herself was later to earn a similar reputation for wild promiscuity, maybe 'Aspasia' served as an early role model:

> How comical that he was called a woman-hater. He could not live without a woman, he was so much a man that even his thoughts matured better if, when transformed into words, they fell on womanly, receptive soil.
> Munch had, after a long hesitation, finally brought his Norwegian friend to the Ferkel. She was brilliant as far as the piano-playing and men's souls were concerned, but above all she knew the art of listening. She hankered after adventures and Strindberg's life had interested her for a long time. She was all over him in no time, dropped Munch, forgot the others, or seemed to forget them, she was Galathea and Strindberg became Pygmalion.
> 'The pleasure in being allowed to talk about you draws me there,' he wrote to me in Munich.
> Even that pleasure had been granted by Aspasia. That is how it had started. He had talked about me with her, the other woman. He had talked about me for hours.
> 'Deeply moved,' I laughed. 'But how did it end?'
> 'Like false stories of friendship with women like that – in bed.' [. . .]
> 'And what about poor Aspasia?' I stuttered, overwhelmed at the comic aspect, incapable of seeing anything but the grotesque side of the story. 'What happened to her, in the cold, in that outfit, in a respectable Berlin boarding house?'
> 'I don't know how she got out of it, nor whether the boarding house was that respectable, but it has not harmed her, she was not angry with me. She would not dare, because then she would have had to accept defeat, and her vanity would not allow that. On the contrary, she found the situation original and novel . . .'

Strindberg spent the next few weeks working on the final draft of his manuscript of *A Madman's Defence,* having secured a publisher in both France and Germany. 'I've gone through the history of my marriage again,' he said to Adolf Paul. 'It was a constant fight lasting fifteen years. But at least I have lived.'

— Chapter 14 —

Not So Happily Married

> We are afraid of losing ourselves through the assimilating power of love and that is why we sometimes have to break out in order to make sure that I am not you.
>
> *The Cloister*

At the same time that he was preparing *A Madman's Defence* for publication Strindberg learned that both *Lady Julie* and *Creditors* were going to be staged in Paris. He was beginning to feel more optimistic about his future as a writer again. In the meantime, now that his affair with Frida had become public knowledge, she was anxious to secure his commitment. 'Do you want to get married now?' she asked. 'Of course I do,' he replied.

Frida's version of the way he proposed to her in the end emphasizes the comic overtone but also shows her tendency to self-dramatization:

> 'I ask you, do you want me for your husband? I am not showing you any disrespect by this question. If you say 'no', then at least you have had the honour of being asked by August Strindberg if you want to be his wife, and one day in the future you can say: Strindberg wanted me, but I refused him. That should ensure you of a place in the History of Literature.' [. . .]
>
> 'You'll never be bored with me,' he added thoughtfully.
>
> *Marriage With Genius*

Just as Siri had done, Frida warned Strindberg that she would never be a conventional housewife:

> 'I'm not marrying you to get a woman who can keep a clean and tidy house for me. We can get a maid to do that.'
>
> 'I have not got the slightest talent for looking after children.'
>
> 'That's because you haven't had any children of your own. We'll employ a nurse.'
>
> 'I can't cook.'
>
> 'We'll employ a kitchen maid; there are plenty of kitchen maids around, but only one wife like you.'
>
> 'But servants cost money . . . I haven't got any money . . . only debts.'
>
> 'Me too!'
>
> Then the laughter got the better of us again. What do we care about everyday life?
>
> *Marriage With Genius*

Frida had no illusions about Strindberg and there was definitely a healthy open line of communication from the beginning between the two of them:

> They soon got onto the subject of his prospects. He dictated and she wrote. 'So and so many plays accepted for production . . . One thousand.'
> 'Minus thirty percent for miscalculation,' she added.
> 'Thirty! I always allow ninety percent for miscalculation, sometimes a hundred . . .'
> 'Be sensible, please, this is serious . . .'
> And then they laughed.
> What divine levity! To look upon the horrible seriousness of life as if it were something one could blow away; to have the poet's carefree way of treating money matters as if they were unreal.
> 'How could we put up with the misery of life if we didn't treat it as unreal? If I were to take it seriously I would weep all day, and I have no desire to do that.'
>
> *The Cloister*

Once again Strindberg would be marrying for love with little regard for the practicalities of domestic life.

The complications surrounding their forthcoming wedding did not end with the Dagny Juel affair. Strindberg still had Frida's parents to cope with. Friedrich Uhl's response when he finally received Strindberg's letter asking for permission to marry Frida was that he would rather give the author of *The Father* a literary prize than his daughter's hand. Frida's mother advised her to send her father a copy of Strindberg's *The People of Hemsö* in order to demonstrate that a man who could write such a great popular novel was not such a poor prospect after all.

In spite of his caustic remarks Friedrich Uhl duly gave his consent to the marriage and Frida and Strindberg exchanged rings on 11 April to make their engagement official. Two days later Frida returned her ring to Strindberg with a terse note. The consummation of their relationship had, it transpired, proved a disappointment to them both. Strindberg was convinced that Frida had not been a virgin and had confronted her with his suspicions. Frida was mortified and protested her innocence. In the end her sister, Marie, came to Berlin and managed to sort things out between them.

Marie's first impressions of Strindberg were not very favourable and she reported to her parents that she was not particularly impressed with her sister's choice of husband. After a week or so she was won over by his charm and revised her opinion. She was prepared to accept him as 'a warm and kind man, even if he did have some strange ideas'.

Plans for the wedding were resumed and Frida and Strindberg decided to delay no further. There remained one or two more obstacles to overcome: Strindberg was divorced, with an ex-wife still living; he was also a Protestant while Frida was a Catholic, which meant that the Church would not allow them to marry in either Austria or Germany. The solution lay in Heligoland, a small island in the North Sea near the estuary of the River Elbe. This colony had only recently been handed back to Germany and was still under British jurisdiction.

Strindberg was also desperately short of cash. He asked Adolf Paul, who was acting as his unofficial agent, to try and get some money out of the theatre producer who was planning a production of *Playing With Fire* at the Lessingtheater in Berlin and had also expressed an interest in doing *The Companions* and *The Bond* later in the year. Strindberg told Paul that he would promise the producer a new play, one on a German subject, so he needed a big advance – '500 Marks, or 300, or 200 at least.' He got his 500 Marks and was able to pack his trunk.

Their last day in Berlin, 27 April, did not start well. When he went to fetch the train tickets Strindberg bumped into Siri's first husband, Carl Gustaf Wrangel, who was travelling with Sofia In de Bétou. The couple were now married. 'A bad omen!' wailed Strindberg, especially as Carl Gustaf had wished him all the best – again. 'It won't work out,' he confided in Paul. 'It will be a failure, like the first time.'

Adolf Paul and Bengt Lidforss saw Frida and Strindberg off at the railway station. Strindberg had given them some money to buy flowers for his bride-to-be and they turned up with bouquets like real gentlemen. Frida was delighted. None of their friends was able to afford to go to Heligoland and Paul wrote in his diary that after Strindberg had left Berlin the life went out of the 'Ferkel'.

Frida's parents did not attend the wedding. They still disapproved of the match though they were relieved to see their headstrong daughter getting married rather than living with Strindberg. Her sister was the only member of the family to make the trip to Heligoland. When they got there they had to wait for several days for confirmation of Strindberg's divorce from Siri, proving that he was free to marry again. Marie needed to return home and Frida told Strindberg that she intended to leave with her and the whole thing was almost called off. Fortunately the vital telegram arrived at the eleventh hour and the marriage took place on 2 May, first in a civil ceremony at the town hall and later, in the evening, at Pastor Schröder's parsonage, with four sea-pilots straight from the harbour who had been hired as official witnesses.

The newly-weds stayed on in Heligoland after the wedding until Frida suggested that they should go to England. She had heard that there were

Frida and Strindberg's wedding ceremony on 2 May 1893 almost turned into a farce and set the tone for a most bizarre marriage. When he later came to write The Cloister *Strindberg managed to distance himself enough from the emotional situation to volunteer the following account:*

When they were exchanging their vows the bride burst into hysterical laughter, which threatened to invalidate the whole ceremony, since her earnest husband had no idea what to make of such a lunatic scene. It was not a particularly grand wedding party that assembled in the parsonage later that evening. Apart from the bride's sister there were four pilots, who acted as witnesses when they pledged their vows of fidelity 'before God'.

In Marriage With Genius *Frida added a coda to this episode, which, understandably, Strindberg omitted from his version:*

The slightest upset – happy or painful – always produces an animosity towards the German language in August Strindberg; he simply can't find the words, or he mixes them up; his accent suddenly changes from German to Swedish. So he repeated what the good Pastor said and got it more and more wrong, with a stronger and stronger foreign accent.

I couldn't help it. I burst into laughter . . . and I burst! Heaven help me! I laughed so much, even though decency and good tradition demand that one should cry rather than laugh on such an occasion. I laughed . . . I couldn't do anything else. The good Pastor's last question was so terribly indiscreet, it was:

Do you swear that you are not carrying any other person's child?

In his distracted state he also directed this question to August Strindberg. [. . .]

With indescribable dignity August Strindberg answered the question – which, after all, could only refer to me – with one hand on the Bible and the other raised to swear on oath, solemnly and sincerely in grammatically incorrect German:

'I swear that I do not carry a child by any other person under my heart.'

The solemn words . . . and the even more solemn expression . . . at that very moment --.

Defying all laws of decency I burst into uncontrollable laughter.

some people in London who might be worth cultivating – the Irish critic Justin Huntley MacCarthy had written an article about *The Father* in the *Fortnightly Review*, the publisher William Heinemann had expressed an interest in Strindberg's poetry and the Dutch producer J T Grein was keen to do one of the plays at the Independent Theatre. Strindberg did not particularly want to go to England but was persuaded by Frida's enthusiasm for the trip and the fact that she spoke good English, having spent some time at a convent school in north London as a child.

Frida and Strindberg left Heligoland on 20 May and travelled to Hamburg where they boarded a ship for Gravesend. The crossing took over forty-eight hours because the sea was so rough. Frida suffered terrible sea-sickness so they stayed in Gravesend for a few days so that she could recover before continuing the journey. While they were there, advance copies of *A Madman's Defence* arrived from Strindberg's German publisher. Frida had promised Strindberg that she would not read the book but once she saw a copy she could not resist the temptation. Strindberg describes her reaction to it in *The Cloister*:

> He saw by the unusual expression on her face that something ominous had come into their life.
> 'What are you reading?'
> 'Your last book!' she answered, putting a curious emphasis on the words.
> 'So it has arrived! Don't read that book. It will poison you.'
> It was the ruthless description of his first marriage, written in self-defence, and as a last testament, for he had intended to take his own life when he had finished writing it. For two years the sealed manuscript had been deposited with a relative, and he had never intended it for publication. But in the spring of that year, under the pressure of circumstances, and because people had been trying so unfairly to annihilate him, both face to face and in the press, he had sold the book to a publisher.
> Now it had fallen into the very hands into which it should never have fallen. At first he wanted to snatch the book from her, but he was restrained by the thought: 'It has happened, therefore it was meant to happen!' and with a deadly calm, as if he had witnessed his own execution, which nothing could have prevented, he left the room.

Frida regretted reading *A Madman's Defence*, as she admitted in *Marriage With Genius*, because she saw for the first time exactly how ruthlessly Strindberg could expose someone he had loved so deeply as Siri:

> He was right, I should not have read it. He was haunted by his past, and I was haunted too, it struck me now – after it had become common property. – I have lived through his love for his companion in the early years of his manhood, and his hatred. I saw him kiss her and saw him sully her in the view of the whole world. From having been his wife, I had become one of a thousand strangers, someone to

whom he revealed this woman, to whom he revealed the most secret corners of her soul. Like the rest of the world I could see him in the other woman's arms and hear his raging love cry . . . I got lost in the distant past . . . I was no longer myself, only the other one, only her!

But then I was suddenly overwhelmed – by another frightening image. It was not Siri von Essen any more who was sacrificed to the curious public, but me. Myself . . . yes, yes, soon it would be my turn. What had my father said when we got engaged? First Miss Julchen and then Miss Uhlchen. [. . .]

For the first time Art seemed like an enemy and a destroyer to me.

Frida and Strindberg arrived in London on 8 June after a miserable delay in Gravesend. J T Grein invited them to stay with him at his flat in Pimlico and he wrote an article about them that was published in a Dutch newspaper shortly afterwards. Frida was clearly the driving force during their visit and Grein was charmed from the first moment he saw her: 'A pretty young lady stood before me,' he wrote, 'stylishly dressed after the latest Viennese fashion, a petite, full-figured, lively brunette with eyes which were sparkling with life.' His portrait of Strindberg is more awestruck: 'His speech was as powerful as his person. Short sentences, strangely constructed, without decorative word-mongering, but striking the right word in the right place just like in his books, which, for that reason, are so difficult to translate.'

At the time that the Strindbergs met Grein he was working for an export company. His real passion was the theatre and he had been running the Independent since 1891 when he had chosen Ibsen's *Ghosts* for the opening production. Now he was hoping to put on a production of *The Father*, though nothing came of these plans in the end.

Strindberg couldn't settle down in London. He complained about the weather, which was hot and stifling, and declared that he was unable to write. He was also worried about Siri and the children and had asked Adolf Paul, who was making a trip to Finland, to find out what he could. 'If you read anything about Fru von Essen in the Finnish newspapers, for instance about her theatre plans, please let me know,' he urged. 'I knew she was going to Finland.'

It was while they were in London that Strindberg first showed Frida the photograph of Siri that he used always to carry with him. 'She is beautiful,' he announced proudly. Frida, who was almost twenty years younger than Siri, records that she found it odd that anyone could find a middle-aged woman who looked so thin and worn-out beautiful. She suspected that Strindberg was still in love with Siri and wondered whether he had married again so soon after his divorce in order to make his first wife jealous.

Frida handled Strindberg's relationship with Siri with remarkable maturity and it was she who first mooted the idea that she should look after Siri's three children. Strindberg then suggested that Karin, his eldest daughter, who was thirteen at the time, could teach Frida Swedish. In return Frida would instruct Karin in German. Frida wrote a passionate plea in French to the children's guardian, Strindberg's brother Oscar, explaining how much Strindberg loved his children and how much he missed them. 'I could be a mother to them,' she said, and told Oscar how she kept looking at their portraits and how she loved them too as if they were her own. When she was told about this plan Siri was appalled at the suggestion that she should part with any of her children to be cared for by someone she had never met. The matter was dropped but a year later Strindberg, once again using Oscar as a go-between, suggested that Karin should come and live with him and Frida.

> My daughter Karin is now practically grown up and if economically necessary she has to leave home. If she and her mother so wish, my home is open to her and Karin will not be treated as a stepdaughter but as my wife's teacher in the Swedish language. There will be no question of a mother-daughter relationship, and between a twenty-two-year-old young wife and a fifteen-year-old girl there is bound to be friendship; they will call each other 'du' and my wife will not make any attempts at any so-called upbringing. As I live in a small house Karin will have a room of her own and 200 francs in pocket money, apart from clothes and whatever else she needs. Of course it is an advantage to her to learn a foreign language and if it is German first, it can always be French next year when we go to France . . . .

Oscar thought that this would be a good idea but when he suggested to Siri that they should try it, at least for one summer, Karin was so upset that she responded personally. 'There is no question of me leaving Mother,' she wrote, concluding that 'I would be the most ungrateful, nastiest child in the world if I left my mother and nothing could make me do that.' She also wondered, rather pointedly, how Strindberg could promise to give her pocket money when he so often failed to support them. Her letter effectively put an end to Strindberg's plans for a live-in tutor for Frida and the subject was never raised again.

1. August Strindberg, 1875, the year that he first met Siri von Essen [photo: G W Brunstedt]

2. Siri von Essen, c. 1881

3. Siri as the heroine in Louis Leroy's play *Camille* at Dramaten, 1877
[Photo: Gösta Florman]

4. Siri as Margit in *Sir Bengt's Wife* at Dramaten, 1882

5. Siri, Gersau, Switzerland, 1886
[Photo: August Strindberg]

6. Strindberg and Siri playing backgammon, Gersau, Switzerland, 1886 [Photo: August Strindberg]

7. Siri, 1891

8. Strindberg, Gersau, Switzerland, 1886
[Photo: Siri von Essen]

9. Strindberg with his daughters Greta and Karin, Gersau, Switzerland, 1886 [Photo: August Strindberg]

10. Karin, Hans and Greta Strindberg, Helsingfors, some time in the mid-1890s

11. Frida Uhl, Vienna, 1892 [Photo: V Türk]

12. Frida, London, 1890

13. Kerstin Strindberg, c. 1905
[Photo: M Schmidmayr]

14. Strindberg, Värmdö in the Stockholm archipelago, 1891, the year before his divorce from Siri
[Photo: John Lundgren]

15. Harriet Bosse as Puck in *A Midsummer Night's Dream* at Dramaten, 1900

16. Harriet as Eleonora in *Easter* at Dramaten, 1901

17. Harriet as the Lady in *To Damascus* at Dramaten, 1900
[Photo: Herman Hamnqvist]

18. Harriet as Indra's Daughter in *A Dream Play* at the Svenska Teatern, Stockholm, 1907 [Photo: Atelier Jaeger]

19. Anne-Marie Strindberg, 1904

20. Fanny Falkner as Judith in *The Dance of Death* (*Part II*) at Intiman, 1909
[Photo: Atelier Jaeger]

21. Fanny (left) as Judith and Anna Flygare as Alice in *The Dance of Death* (*Part II*) at Intiman, 1909 [Photo: Atelier Jaeger]

22. Fanny with Johan Ljungkvist in *Swanwhite* at Intiman, 1908

23. Fanny, 1909

24. Fanny [undated]

25. Greta Strindberg as Kersti in *The Crown Bride*, 1909–10

26. Strindberg, Furusund in the Stockholm archipelago, 1907
[Photo: Otto Johansson]

27. Strindberg in the Blue Tower, 1908
[Photo: Herman Anderson]

28. Strindberg, Stockholm, 9 April 1912
[Photo: Magnus Wester]

29. Strindberg's funeral cortège, Stockholm, 19 May 1912

— Chapter 15 —

Separation and Pregnancy

I have read your last beautiful letter again and again. You are sad, my dearest child, you as well, and now that I can see no way of meeting you I am in despair. You love me, I think, and I love you and yet we are separated.
Letter to Frida Uhl, 22 July 1893

After ten days in London Frida could see that Strindberg was unhappy so she suggested that he should return to Germany while she stayed behind in order to try and find someone who would stage his plays or publish his books. They certainly needed to earn some money somehow. Frida pawned her fur coat, some lace and jewellery – including her wedding ring – and while this raised only £5 it was enough for Strindberg's travelling expenses. He planned to go to Rügen, an island off the Baltic coast, where Adolf Paul and some other friends were staying for the summer. Grein generously invited Frida to stay on as his guest in London.

During the months of June and July Frida and Strindberg kept up a lively correspondence. They wrote to each other almost every day, sometimes in German and sometimes in French:

Rügen 25th June 1893
At last on Rügen! Where I dive into the sea, head first to drown my dark thoughts, only with partial success, I am afraid.

And today, Sunday evening 25th June, I received your letters, full of love for me, and tears! It broke my heart to learn how torn by anguish you are for me, old wretch, who eats, sleeps and drifts about without being able to muster enough strength to work seriously in order to keep myself alive. You see, what depresses me is the thought that I may have overestimated myself when I married you, and that I will leave you in misery sooner or later. I lack hope and a suffocating apathy is hanging over my soul, which is subsiding into sleep. Maybe I am worn out by overwork, suffering and penury. My springtime love 'seconda primavera' – shook me awake for a moment. But the past keeps popping up sowing seeds of dissent in my life.

Worries about the future torment me and I don't have any strength left to stretch out my hand for the fruits which, after so many years of struggle, must hang there ripe for the picking.

> At the moment I am occupied with the natural sciences and can't deal with fiction any more, nor my theatrical ventures.
>
> Everything is quiet here, the sea, the forest, the people (even the women), but not me. What are you up to? What do you want? How are you? Mrs Kainz died the other day. Alas. Happy she. Schleich has become a bit crazy, says Paul. Mad, happy man.
>
> We'll see each other again. But when?
> Your August
> Sellin on Rügen

Frida tried to keep Strindberg's spirits up and whenever she wanted to emphasize her love for him and her belief in him as a writer she wrote in French:

> July 1893
> Tu a donné le meilleur de ce que ce siècle a produit en Europe. Et tu n'est pas content – Hm! Je ne suis pas si ambitieux [sic] que toi.

At this point in her letter Strindberg added a note in the margin: 'Bravo, you spoke the truth there.'

Frida ends with a declaration of her love for him: 'Tu m'a donné le bonheur – le seul bonheur possible pour moi sur cette terre.'

With growing debts and bleak prospects ahead, nothing could assuage the anxiety that Strindberg was feeling for his future with Frida. He was also feeling guilty about Siri and the children, who did not have enough money to live on. Frida responded by sending letters to everyone she could think of in Austria and Germany, begging them to put on his plays or commission new ones. She had the audacity to ask one producer to announce the production of a Strindberg play – even if he had no intention of going ahead – simply to generate some publicity.

Strindberg was in despair. Not only had he given up writing, he had also stopped painting. His seascapes, which fetch several millions today, excited little interest. He had given one painting to Frida as an engagement present and had managed to sell one to an art collector in Finland, a Mr Dalberg, who had refused to pay for it because it was unsigned.

The heat on Rügen was oppressive and Strindberg grew more and more agitated. Friends were subsidizing him but not enough to allow him to leave because he had run up a huge bill at the hotel where he was staying. With his creativity blocked, he turned his attention to alchemy, conducting experiments with foul-smelling substances. He was not successful in turning base metals into gold, of course, but some of his chemical formulas were taken seriously enough to be accepted for publication in the scientific journals.

When all other attempts to raise funds had failed Strindberg steeled himself to write to Frida's sister, Marie:

> Sellin, Rügen, 22nd July 1893
> . . . forgive us our youth and our craziness and help us. If you can. I feel horribly ashamed, but the situation is untenable. Release me from this prison and let me set off in search of my lost little lamb. If you have 500 Marks at your disposal, then please send them, dearest sister, and I swear never to believe in castles in the air again.
> I agree that we are both a bit mad, but we are sincere, we love each other and our future is secure.
> I kiss your hand and beg you to embrace your parents. Don't say a word about this to Frida. That word would cost me my happiness.
> Your brother in spite of everything.
> August

Marie sent him some money and Frau Uhl invited him to Mondsee. 'Come and stay as long as you like,' she wrote. When Frida discovered that Strindberg had told her family about their financial difficulties she was very angry, though she thought he should go to Austria to see them if he wanted to. By the end of July a note of deep melancholy is evident in Strindberg's letters to her:

> 24 July 1893
> You have felt compassion for me, and between contempt and compassion there is only a small step for a woman in love. Disharmony came out of that. I am extra irritable because of mental overstrain, problems and sadness. And your absence depresses and pains me. When I get out of this hell and when we have found each other again I shall think of these five weeks as the most awful ones I have ever experienced.
> I sent a telegram to you yesterday 'I am coming' but I had forgotten the number of the house where you are staying so the telegram was returned from London. [. . .]
> Do you still believe that we are happy and that we will be able to put up a fight against poverty? Believe me, I can hardly carry on . . .

Strindberg departed for Mondsee a few days later and was made welcome by Frida's mother and sister though her father remained aloof. Marie left after a few days and on 8 August she sent an affectionate letter to Strindberg. It is clear that her new brother-in-law had completely won her over in spite of his reputation. 'My husband sends his greetings and I embrace you from all my heart,' she wrote. 'You know full well, you great magician, that you enchant all women, you – their enemy . . .'

In *The Cloister* Strindberg writes about what it felt like to be the new son-in-law in Frida's family:

> From being a father and a husband he would once more become a child, be grafted on to a family, and get a new father and mother in place of those he had lost many

years previously. A factor which would help to increase the confusion was that both his father-in-law and mother-in-law had been separated for seven years, but now, on account of their daughter's marriage, they were to meet again. He had thus become a sort of hyphen, but since the daughter – now his wife – had also been on bad terms with her father, it seemed likely that this family reunion would turn out to be a feast of multiple reconciliations. [. . .]

As he approached the place of the rendezvous he grew nervous, but, as usual, he finally succeeded in getting back his courage by looking at the matter from the writer's point of view: 'If I don't come out of this with honour, at least I can get a chapter for my novel!'

The ability to distance himself just enough to be able to record a painful experience in an artistic way was a life-saving device for Strindberg on many occasions. The writer in him came to the rescue like a *deus ex machina* and alleviated the pain of reality by sublimating it into art.

Frau Uhl was to turn into a mother figure for Strindberg and she undoubtedly offered him more comfort and consolation in his depressed state than Frida was capable of. At the beginning of August he wrote to Frida, who was still in London, asking her to join him straight away:

> You are afraid of coming to Mondsee, because you are the daughter of the house here and afraid of being treated like a child. But don't you think that my presence and your new situation as a young wife will change your position? Your mother is so good towards me, and I think that she, for your sake, and for mine will not treat you like a schoolgirl any more.

A couple of days later he wrote to her again:

> Your father is not angry yet, but he might be, and to his question: Where is my daughter? I have no answer.
>
> Drop your fixed idea to create wealth in a year. Let Grein and Heinemann look after the theatre on their own. They will probably let us use it anyway . . .
>
> Your father said: 'Order your wife to come here.' I told him: 'I don't give my wife any orders.' Then he said: 'In that case I shall order her.'

Friedrich Uhl was worried about his daughter's reputation and thought that it was most irregular for a newly married young woman to be away from her husband for so long. For two people who had professed themselves to be so deeply in love it is indeed puzzling. Nothing appeared to be forcing Frida to stay in London and the prolonged separation had already given rise to gossip and speculation. 'You must know that Mitzi [Marie] thinks you are pregnant and people here say that you are trying to hide something strange during your stay in London,' Strindberg told Frida on 5 August. 'If that is so why do you conceal it from me? Four or five months does not make any difference.' There is no evidence that Frida was expecting a baby at this time (she became pregnant later on in the year) and nothing to suggest that she was having an affair with J T Grein, as some rumours had claimed.

While Strindberg was at Mondsee he read some of the articles on literature and theatre that Frida had written for the *Wiener Zeitung*. He was impressed and he realized how little he had encouraged her. In a letter that he wrote to her on 7 August he apologizes for not having taken more interest in her work:

> In quiet moments I reproach myself for not having taken you and your career seriously enough, that I have suppressed you. But I did not know the extent of your talent since I had never read a word written by you. Now that I have read some of your articles, which are full of colour and style I am convinced that you are quite clever and that I have made fun of you unfairly.

Strindberg had been staying with the Uhls for over a week and still Frida did not come. This was probably deliberate: she did not like the idea of Strindberg getting closely involved with her family and she resented her father issuing orders. They finally got word that she was on her way but due to a misunderstanding about the dates she arrived at Mondsee the day after Strindberg had left for Berlin. After his visit Strindberg wrote a remorseful letter to Frida's mother asking her to forgive him for being the cause of so many worries and problems.

Frida stayed with her family for a few days and she and Strindberg were finally reunited in Berlin on 15 August. Their marriage had certainly got off to a very shaky start and Frida seems to have been very nervous and irrational during this period. Not long after she returned to Berlin she wrote Strindberg a fierce letter, addressing him as 'vous', and suggesting that divorce was the only way out, a step that Strindberg cautioned against in the strongest possible terms. 'Have you thought of the consequences of divorce?' he warned her. 'Revenge. Nothing but ruin. Irrevocable! If you try and piece it together it will fall apart again. One prostitutes oneself, plays out a drama for the audience, who prepare themselves for a new Madman's Defence.'

As soon as they were together again Frida and Strindberg fell back into the pattern that had started before they were married – on the verge of separating one moment and devoted to each other the next. Whatever her faults, and whatever problems she might have had, Frida was never one to dwell on things for too long. Once a quarrel was over she would not bring the subject up again. In many ways her chameleon-like character suited Strindberg, who had a tendency to brood. He reflected on the nature of their love in *The Cloister* and concluded that no one could explain what causes dissent between the partners in a marriage. How could one be happy and in love one day and then . . .

> . . . a wisp of cloud appears, no one knows from where, all virtues turn into vices, beauty becomes ugly, they face each other like hissing serpents. They wish each other far, far away, regardless of the fact that they know that if they are separated for a moment they will begin to suffer the pangs of loss, which is a greater misery than any other that life has to offer. [. . .]
>
> So it is that a man and wife who love each other may sit for an eternity wondering why they hate each other, that is to say they flee from each other even though they seek each other. [. . .]
>
> Love has all the symptoms of insanity; hallucinations, or seeing beauty where none exists [. . .] attacks of persecution mania, during which they suspect the other partner of spying on them, of setting traps for them, or pursuing them, why, even of seeking to take their life, often by means of poison.

When Frida announced that she was pregnant in mid-October, Strindberg, who was always at his most loving and reverential when his wives were expecting, was thrilled, whereas she could only see problems ahead. She had little faith in his alchemical experiments and did not see how he could possibly earn a living as a scientist. In a somewhat anxious state she went to stay with Marie in Vienna, where she planned to have an abortion. She then changed her mind about the baby but wrote to Strindberg saying once again that she thought they ought to get a divorce and offering to take the blame for the marriage breakdown if necessary on condition that he did not claim any rights over their child. If he was not prepared to act quickly and sue her for 'wilful desertion' within one month, she said, she would sue him for physical abuse. Strindberg does not appear to have taken Frida's threats very seriously. While she was in Vienna he spent five days in Lund consulting his solicitors about a pirated version of *A Madman's Defence* that had appeared in a Swedish magazine, and before long Marie had yet again acted as peacemaker and effected a reconciliation between them.

Strindberg travelled to Austria and met up with Frida at a *pension* in Brünn on 25 October. He would have been happy to stay there, conducting his scientific experiments and writing his book *Antibarbarus*, but Frida complained that the smell of the sulphur that he used made her morning sickness worse and in the end she managed to get him to agree to go to her grandparents' house in Dornach. It was a decision she made for the sake of the baby but in *Marriage With Genius* she makes it clear it was not what she really wanted to do:

> There is only one place for the two of us where food and drink won't dry up. Where we don't have to work first in order to get something to eat – my grandparents'

home in Dornach by the Danube. We call Dornach 'Faeaker country'. I grew up with an aversion to it. Father never sets foot there, it is too distasteful for him. My sister despises it, because in all its gluttony it is the body's scorning of the soul. She is also afraid of it, because mother and grandmother are both crazy about children and want to keep Mitzi's [Marie's] little son at any price –. On the whole, Dornach is, to a great extent, a terribly hostile environment towards men, from which no marital ship returns undamaged. [. . .]

. . . to me it has always been like a denial of love. It is the last place I would choose of my own free will. But I have no choice.

Frida and Strindberg arrived in Dornach at the end of November and stayed there for the next nine months. Apart from the ever-present financial problems, this period seems to have been a reasonably harmonious time for them both, though Frida was right about the antipathy towards men that the household engendered. It was a matriarchal set-up where the women were clearly in command and at first Strindberg thrived on the atmosphere there and got on remarkably well with Frida's rich female relatives. Not surprisingly, this all eventually found its way into *The Cloister* in one guise or another:

In the house there was a surplus of the good things of this world and, after their period of semi-starvation in Moravia, at this place the situation was the reverse. Here it was a question of avoiding gormandizing without hurting anyone's feelings. Pheasants, hares, venison were everyday food, and became like a punishment in the end. [. . .]

. . . the servants were as numerous as those they served. The old people, who had grown away from all enterprises, all opinions, and all passions, were easy to live with, and the young couple, who had their own apartment, were only required to appear at mealtimes.

Strindberg enjoyed the garden and, inspired by the River Danube and the beautiful surrounding countryside, he started to paint again and did some new landscapes, hoping to be able to sell them in Paris. He did find buyers for his work there later in the year but in the meantime he kept them so that the baby would have some colourful pictures to look at.

Frida wanted her child to be fair-skinned and have blond hair like Strindberg's son, Hans, and he teased her about this. She and Marie were dark-haired yet everyone in her family aspired to the Aryan ideal. Friedrich Uhl was openly anti-Semitic and even though one of Frida's great-grandmothers on her mother's side had been Jewish the word 'Jew' was used as a term of abuse in the Uhl household. When Strindberg pointed this out to Frida she said sternly: 'You mustn't joke about it. Only we are allowed to do that.'

Notwithstanding the differences between them, Strindberg found himself turning increasingly to Frida's mother for serious discussions on religion and mysticism, which were beginning to absorb him more and more. Frau Uhl had studied Swedenborg and Buddhism and was also interested in the occult.

By this time Strindberg's ten-year period of atheism had just about come to an end and with Frau Uhl's encouragement he seriously considered converting to Catholicism. However, after a great deal of studying and agonizing, his Protestant upbringing proved too strong an influence and he could not bring himself to do it. He identified too much with the sufferings of Job and Jeremiah and he could not help favouring the stern God of the Old Testament. What had drawn him to the Catholic faith in the first place was its mysticism; on the other hand he was also fascinated by Swedenborg's vision of Heaven and Hell. His autobiographical novel *Inferno*, which he completed in Paris after he had separated from Frida, deals with this period of religious conflict in his life. Written in much the same vein as *A Madman's Defence,* and heavily informed by the books on psychology and religion that he had been reading, *Inferno* is a powerful and penetrating book about a man's journey into madness and his search for a return to sanity, painfully observed at every turn. In the end the man is led back to the faith of his childhood, embracing his own personal brand of Protestantism.

Strindberg remained attracted to Buddhism though, especially since he felt that Buddha, unlike Christ, rejected the world of worldly and sensual pleasures; he explored these ideas in his later plays, especially in *The Ghost Sonata* and *A Dream Play*.

In *The Cloister* Strindberg reproduces a conversation in which the mother-in-law figure talks to her daughter's husband about his search for God:

> Your opinions about women are correct, and your godlessness isn't your fault, for He has not wanted to know you, but soon He will come to you. You'll see. You've married a worldling, but you won't put up with her for long when you realize that she'll drag you down among the banalities of life. Once you are alone you'll find the first vocation of your youth again.

Frida was becoming increasingly uneasy about the close bond that was developing between her mother and Strindberg, feeling that they were conspiring to undermine her own position as a wife and future mother. The critic Friedrich Buchmayr claims that Frau Uhl was partly responsible for destroying her daughter's marriage; she was certainly not slow to condemn the way Frida conducted herself and, as the above passage from *The Cloister* suggests, she told Strindberg that he would be better off without her. (Frida's jealousy and insecurity about Strindberg's relationship with her mother was to prove well-founded. He maintained contact with Frau Uhl well into the late 1890s, long after he and Frida had parted for good. He spent three months in Mondsee in 1896 and Frida never knew that he had been there and had been asking about her until many years later when she came across some of the letters that Strindberg had written to her mother.)

On 26 May 1894 Frida had her daughter Kerstin. It was a long labour and Strindberg was present throughout the birth. He held Frida's hand, kissed her forehead and smoothed her pillow, supporting her in every way possible:

> An angel from heaven could not have been a more perfect Samaritan than he.
>
> But then something suddenly happened, so unexpectedly that I could not understand it. After an especially wild scream which the most horrible pain wrenched from me, I lay completely exhausted. And at that moment he bent over me and said calmly and earnestly and in so quiet a voice that no one could hear, but insistent all the same: Stop play-acting, child, I know that giving birth is not painful, but a pleasure for women.
>
> The effect of these words was magical. For a fraction of a second it was as if he was right. My mouth which had opened to let out a new scream, became silent, I lay still, did not actually feel anything, stared at Strindberg without being able to think. But no sooner was the word uttered than I thought I might have dreamt it; he who had said it held me like before in his arms, helped me despite his own poor aching limbs, made me more comfortable among the cushions, dried the sweat from my forehead and smiled in a friendly and encouraging way to me like before.
>
> *Marriage With Genius*

Inevitably, after the baby was born, things changed. Frida was unable to breast-feed and the infant cried a lot and Strindberg found it difficult to work with so much domestic disturbance going on around him. He spent his time writing articles for the French press on both science and the arts and a selection of them – 'Moi', 'L'Homme à venir', 'D'où nous sommes venus', 'Des Arts nouveaux!' and 'Qu'est-ce-que le moderne?' – were published in *L'Echo de Paris*. Some of these pieces and others that he had written earlier, most notably 'A la zoologie de femme', were later incorporated into his collection of essays entitled *Vivisections*.

He was growing restless, frustrated that he had no proper role to play in this house full of women:

> He felt how he was being pulled down in this environment where everything circled around material things, and where the animal side of things dominated: food and excrement. And where wet-nurses were treated like milch-cows, and kitchen maids and rotting vegetables were the order of the day.
>
> *The Cloister*

His lack of power and status within the Uhl family was emphasized when they came to make arrangements for the baby's christening. Frau Uhl wanted the child to be baptized in the Catholic faith and she duly pressed Strindberg for his formal consent. Strindberg was offended, not so much by the family's desire to keep his daughter within their faith as by the fact that they had not bothered to consult him at all on the matter. Frida, caught in the middle, stayed out of the argument, partly because she was so exhausted after the birth but also because her feelings about the issue were relatively neutral.

After this Strindberg felt that his position in the household was no longer tenable, though he was not yet in a position to escape and could certainly not afford to take his wife and daughter anywhere else to live. He missed the cosmopolitan life and was feeling cut off from the artistic centres of Europe. His play *Creditors* had just opened at the Théâtre de l'Oeuvre in Paris and was reportedly a great success but he had been unable to go and see it for himself.

Feeling increasingly trapped, Strindberg turned his thoughts to establishing a retreat – he called it a 'monastery' – that would function as a kind of non-confessional home for intellectuals:

> The aim of this monastery was to train 'supermen' (in the Nietzschean sense) by means of asceticism, meditation and the practice of science, literature and art. Religion was not mentioned, since he did not know what religion there would be, or whether there would be any religion at all.
>
> *The Cloister*

It was a project that he had been brooding over for some time and he sketched out plans for the building and drew up the rules for how the community would function. He favoured simple food and drink and advocated celibacy as something that was conducive to the creative process. He had written two of his strongest dramatic works, he claimed – *Lady Julie* and *Creditors* – during periods of enforced celibacy.

Strindberg poured out his ideas that summer in series of letters, thirty-five in all, to an old college friend, Leopold Littmansson:

> Have you heard of Nietzsche? No! Oh . . .
>   The riddle of life : the will to power: over the spirit.
>   Happiness: to grow and rule.
>   Misfortune: not to be allowed to grow and to be overruled.
>   That is happiness, this feeling of power, to sit in a cottage by the Danube among six women who think I am a bit of an idiot and know that at this moment in Paris, in the headquarters of the spirits, 500 people are sitting dead quiet and are stupid enough to subject their brains to my ideas. Some rebel, but many leave the place

with my mouldy semen in their grey substances: they go home, pregnant with the sperm from my spirit and then they spawn my offspring. [. . .]

I am always ready to move on when I notice that people are touching my wings. And I am always ready to pull up the tent poles when it gets stuffy around me. And it is now.
July 1894

Littmansson was a Swedish Jew who had married a rich Frenchwoman and was now living in a large luxury villa in Versailles. He was very enthusiastic about the idea of a new community and he invited Strindberg to come and stay with him to discuss the proposal. Strindberg needed no prompting. With some money in his pocket from Littmansson, he made his escape to Paris on 15 August, leaving Frida and the baby behind.

— Chapter 16 —

The Beautiful Jail-Keeper

> I thought that you had banished me from your heart five years ago. Consequently I felt rejected, hated, lost, lost. When I realize that you have loved me and asked for forgiveness and reconciliation and that I have not known about it, I only just found out. What torment!
>
> *Letter from Frida Uhl to Strindberg, Christmas Eve, 1902*

It was only about eighteen months since their wedding and once again Strindberg and Frida were separated, unable, for lack of money, to settle down and establish a proper home for themselves and their child. Ideally, Frida wanted to live with Strindberg in Paris and resume her work as a journalist. Strindberg was not too keen on this proposal though he was careful not to dismiss the idea of an occupation for her altogether, suggesting that when she joined him she should work from home, reviewing books or even writing a novel of her own. The letter he wrote to her on 2 September 1894 is quite diplomatically worded:

> My financial situation is improving, but without the housewife's watchful eye everything will run away. That does not mean that you should be my maid and stay at home when I go out, nor does it mean that I stay at home when you go out.

Almost immediately Strindberg began to feel lonely in Paris and declared himself willing to return to Dornach if Frida wanted him to:

> 4 September 1894
> Once again, do you want me to come back? If one has money one can get books, journals, newspapers, all the little 'divertissements' which make life bearable. Just think! Tiled stoves, beautiful lamps, draperies, rugs, and, above all a wet nurse. A glass of wine in the evening, lovely evenings with just the two of us. Here [in Paris] you have to stay at home, have terrible maids, be exploited endlessly. An expensive and fast disappearing illusion. [. . .]
> Admit that lack of money is the greatest cause of our domestic troubles.

This is hardly the tone of a truly doting husband but like all the letters that Strindberg wrote during this time there is a tenderness mingled with a streak of sadness, as if he sensed that their relationship was coming to a premature end.

> 6th September 1894
>
> Telegraph me if you want me to return to Dornach or I could go somewhere near Dornach where we can meet.
>
> I have everything I could wish for but I want to leave everything just to be with you and lead a cat and dog life with you. Remember what I told you once: a bad marriage is better than none at all. It is too quiet here. Nobody bothers or harasses me. I miss a really good honest quarrel, where you remain master of the situation, without being contradicted.
>
> Just call me, beloved master, and I'll come like a donkey laden with gold.

Frida, meanwhile, was finding the atmosphere at home very claustrophobic. She had agreed to allow Kerstin to be baptized as a Catholic and a date was set for the christening – 12 September. Strindberg's signature was conspicuously missing from the baptismal papers and he did not attend the ceremony.

A few days later Frida made plans to leave for Paris, a trip that was made possible thanks to a gift of money from her grandfather that was just enough to pay for her train ticket. (Strindberg also sent her 200 francs after selling a couple of his paintings to the Danish artist Willy Gretor, but the money does not seem to have arrived before her departure.) Leaving Kerstin behind with her family and a wet-nurse, Frida set off for Paris with high hopes. She was planning a series of articles on the arts for the *Wiener Zeitung* and the *Wiener Abendpost* and she certainly did not envisage herself as a full-time housewife.

Strindberg had moved by now into a large and elegant apartment in the quiet residential district of Passy that belonged to Rosa Pfaeffinger, who was the richest of Willy Gretor's many mistresses. The first few weeks that he and Frida spent together in Paris were happy and busy. Frida was in love with Strindberg and in love with Paris:

> The last autumn days are enchanting, mysteriously beautiful. Once again dreams of love build castles in the air on sunny red clouds over the old canopy of trees. Once again the slim white limbs of the birches bend like ballerinas.
>
> *Marriage With Genius*

In the middle of October they moved to the Hôtel des Américains, a small family *pension* in the Latin Quarter. It was around this time that Strindberg met two Norwegian actors, Alma Fahlström, who was Harriet Bosse's sister, and her husband Johan, who offered to try and sell some of his pictures back in Kristiania where they ran a theatre company.

Frida wasted no time in working her old magic and making useful contacts among the publishers, writers and artists of the city, and after the dull domesticity of her life in Austria she found the experience exhilarating. One of the influential people that she met was a handsome young German called Albert Langen. He ran a Paris-based publishing company with Willy Gretor and they had accepted Strindberg's *A Madman's Defence* for publication. Langen engaged Frida as a translator and also asked her to help out with some of the secretarial work in his office. This was how she first met the precocious young playwright Frank Wedekind, who was working as Langen's personal secretary at the time.

Langen, Gretor and Wedekind: Frida was attracted to them all and flirted with them each in turn. They were fashionable and amusing and, perhaps more importantly, closer to her own age than the forty-five-year-old Strindberg, whom they treated with respect and deference. Gretor was by far the most outrageous of the three: he maintained a simultaneous ménage with two different women, each of whom had a child by him, and then finally married a third, the wealthy Rosa Pfaeffinger, who ended up financing the whole entourage. It was Wedekind, however, who eventually became Frida's lover.

The Swedish writer Jan Myrdal suggests that Frida was probably not unfaithful to Strindberg during this period, at least not in the strictly technical sense, though there is no doubt that her behaviour humiliated him. 'I was no saint, no martyr, no philosopher, no sage – not even a calm, wise or good human being,' she says in *Marriage With Genius* and in the letter that she wrote to him in April 1895, six months after they had parted for good, her tone is no less remorseful:

> As far as I am concerned – August, when I think about the past, bad memories keep recurring again and again. Yes, I have done you harm, often. When I think about it ... I have hurt your genius and your heart. How mean, stupid ... small I was!!

In any event, the fun didn't last for long. News came from Dornach that Kerstin was ill and that the wet-nurse was leaving for a better-paid job. Frida returned to Austria alone. On the day that she left Paris, Strindberg had a dinner appointment and was unable to accompany her to the Gare du Nord to catch the train so they parted in the middle of a busy street outside the Printemps department store, waving and blowing kisses. They were not to know then that they would never see each other again.

Back home in Austria, Frida was under a lot of pressure. She would be a rich woman in her own right one day and her relatives – especially her maternal grandmother – were worried that Strindberg might start making claims on the family's wealth now that she was legally married to him. They issued an ultimatum: if Frida wanted their continued support then she would have to divorce him. Frida caved in and went to Vienna to consult a lawyer, who sent a preliminary letter to Strindberg on her instructions. Frida also wrote to him. 'Let us part,' she said, 'but not as enemies.'

There followed yet another period of anguished letter-writing. At first the tone between them is friendly and loving, but this soon gives way, on Strindberg's part at least, to one of doubt and suspicion. By November he was heading towards a period of serious depression. He could not afford to stay in the two-roomed suite that he was renting in the Hôtel des Américains so he moved down to the ground floor, where he occupied a small back room with a window facing a row of outside toilets. Although Langen had paid him 600 francs for *A Madman's Defence*, and the Théâtre de l'Oeuvre had given him 357 francs for their production of *The Father*, which was due to open on 13 December, it was not enough.

There did not appear to be any solution to his financial difficulties. He had no new novels or plays to sell and his scientific work was of no commercial value. It was under these straitened circumstances that he wrote a letter to Frida on 8 November that was to have very serious consequences for them both:

> I don't know what is happening to me, but I fear for our future. I have allowed myself to be deceived, in my gullible state, but there are limits which you can't transgress without facing consequences. And if I were not listening to my inner voice of self-preservation I would go under one of these days. You always wrestle, always [wrestle] with me and I defend myself; but it does not amuse me any more to do battle with you. You arrived in Paris and told me that you didn't want to see the man who had made a declaration of love to your sister and yet . . .
>
> You want to use a pimp's furniture. I cancel the furniture and you ask for it back.
>
> You finally realize, after disputes, that M. Langen has outraged me with his late visits. You tell me that you have put him off and I know that you have in fact invited him one evening to read manuscripts until midnight, for four whole hours from eight o'clock. And that happened the very day when you assured me that this would not happen any more. You offer yourself as his secretary and you make yourself available to go and see him every morning.
>
> This whole web of lies and deception is going to end with a bang; rather sooner than later. At this moment I only have one feeling, one single, last feeling and that is to defend my honour and to avenge myself and to rid myself of that which is debasing me.
>
> Do you act intentionally and consciously or is it your dishonest nature which drives you? In London your reputation was further damaged since you dined in public with an unmarried man, you yourself a young married woman; in Berlin you are known, in Vienna too, and in Paris you have started well.
>
> And everywhere I introduce you you spoil my business and exploit my contacts for your own benefit and against my interests.

Why play this comedy of love when we hate each other? You hate me as the superior one who has never done you any harm and I hate you because you act as an enemy.

If I am to continue this battle with you I'll have to adopt your corrupt morals, which I do not want to do. I leave the field, never mind where I go.

And you'll see: the moment you are alone, and no longer have any interest in humiliating me you won't have the same energy as before. To do evil is your strength but you always have to have a victim, and one who loves to play the naive one. I don't want to play this role any more. Find yourself another man!
Farewell!
August S.

The phrase 'pimp's furniture' is a reference to Frida's relationship with Willy Gretor. Much later Frida admitted to Gretor's daughter that she had indeed pursued him, so Strindberg's suspicions were not completely unfounded:

> I was quite fascinated by Willy Gretor that autumn and did everything to gain his friendship, like suggesting that I should come to his studio to take lessons – but I was met by a constant and demonstrative coldness, so I struck up a close friendship with Frank Wedekind instead, in order to make Gretor jealous. But even that failed.

By now Strindberg knew that his relationship with Frida could not be salvaged. 'Seized by a furious desire to inflict wounds on myself, I commit suicide,' he was to write in his novel *Inferno*, 'in that I send off a heinous, unforgivable letter where I say goodbye to my wife and child, hinting at a new relationship.' The next day he wrote to Frida again, though it was by no means a conciliatory letter. He accused her once more of not being a virgin when they first met. 'Why did I marry you?' he asks himself. 'I loved you.'

In his relationships with all three of his wives Strindberg always played the role of the seduced rather than the seducer. He never had to fight that hard to win them over but he never fully appreciated just how much they loved him. His jealousy always got in the way.

Frida did not proceed with the divorce, having discovered that, as a Catholic, she could apply for an annulment instead because she had married Strindberg in a civil ceremony. For the time being she did nothing about this and Strindberg waited in vain for her to return to him in Paris.

As 1894 drew to a close Strindberg found himself struggling to make ends meet. He was eating too little and drinking too much (he had gone back to taking absinthe) and was suffering from psoriasis. He was still pursuing his interest in alchemy and during one of his experiments he spilt chemicals on his hands. His friends raised enough money through the Swedish Church in Paris to send him to the St Louis Hospital for treatment. It was the first time that he had ever stayed in hospital and the nuns who looked after him gave him the peace and care that he needed to withdraw from the world for a while.

He had accepted by now that he and Frida would never be together again. 'I don't know much about my marriage,' he confided to a friend. 'I did not take it very seriously as you probably noticed in Berlin, and it will probably be dissolved – but I am not sure. At times it was great fun, and good, but language, race, ideas about right and wrong, bad habits made it hard sometimes.' He wrote to Frida while he was in hospital, anxious for news about her and Kerstin:

> 7th January 1895
> ... I now have a feeling that I won't see you again, the same feeling as when we parted on the traffic island, in the dark amidst the noise of carts and carriages.
>
> Whether it is true or not: please write a few lines about yourself and your child! Why part as enemies? Let us be modern! Treat me as a sacked lover, who is always more harmless than a husband, and believe that I am noble enough to hand over the role of victor to my lady.
>
> In other words: Let me talk to you by post because I really am too bloody unhappy.

When he left hospital on 31 January Strindberg moved to a small family *pension* on the rue de la Grande Chaumière near the Luxembourg Gardens in Montparnasse. Over the course of the following year he made many friends there within the artistic community, including Gauguin and Delius. He was able to pay his way with the help of some money that Torsten Hedlund had raised on his behalf back in Sweden. Hedlund was the proprietor of the Gothenburg newspaper *Handelstidningen* and he and Strindberg shared an interest in theosophy.

As Strindberg's situation began to improve slightly he was able to send some money to his children – including Kerstin, whose grandparents regarded the gift as an insult. And he was still writing to Frida, nurturing the hope that she would come back to him:

> February 1895
> A lover can allow himself to be poor, but a husband can't. There are moments when I think that your presence would restore my interest in life. [. . .]
>
> I am not happy. The two months after your departure have aged me and the bitter experiences have robbed me of my courage. It is not much fun here. A kind of prison.

In April Strindberg was granted permission to use a laboratory at the Sorbonne and he spent most of his time conducting experiments in chemistry and discussing his theories with eminent French scientists, who treated him seriously and with respect.

He wrote again to Frida, hinting that he would like to visit her in Austria. Frida replied at the end of April in a friendly but non-committal way, reporting that Kerstin was now walking and talking. She blamed herself for the failure of their marriage and apologized for being stupid and petty:

> I played with life until it smashed me to the ground. I ask your forgiveness for the wrong I have done you. Forget it. Forget me. Our marriage was a mistake. But believe this much at least: for your own sake, not mine: I have never committed the really serious sin that you accuse me of. I have sinned because of pride, stupidity and lack of love for my neighbour, in other words I have treated you badly but I have not deceived you. [. . .]
>
> Rather die than be your wife again. We are too unequal as fighters. [. . .]
>
> We will be the end of each other! So let's finish! Finish everything. For good. It is sad that love should end like this. Sad like the autumn which makes the trees into naked beggars and kills the heart. Have you ever loved me? I often ask myself that. And I know the answer: no. That is probably the one thing I cannot forgive you. The rest, why not? The past only seems like a dream now. One cannot have a grudge against illusions.
>
> So – live well – you whom I thought I loved. Whom I tried to forget. And who does not live for me any more. Live well and without bad feeling. We shall never see each other again in this world.

She did not want Strindberg to visit her and she told him that she intended to go ahead with the annulment of their marriage.

Frida moved to Vienna at the end of April and on 10 May she wrote a warm letter to Strindberg telling him that Kerstin was being well looked after by her family and that they did not need any money:

> You have a devoted friend in me. Marriage is a struggle of egotism. [. . .]
>
> And now, August, if you will allow me, I press your hand like a good friend. The wife is gone. Believe me, it is better that way. You will find someone else one day who will make you happy. Forgive me for not succeeding in that myself.
>
> Frida Strindberg

There was no further correspondence between them for almost a year after this. In February 1896 Strindberg moved to the Hôtel Orfila, a cheap lodging-house in rue d'Assas. He had spent two years in Paris living on the breadline and had achieved very little, save for the sale of one or two of his paintings. It was around this time that he began to suffer from bouts of persecution mania and started to write his *Occult Diary*, a journal in which he recorded his dreams and his ideas about telepathy and the supernatural world. In his letters to Torsten Hedlund in Gothenburg he describes the symptoms of his disturbed mental state: palpitations and a feeling of electrical currents passing through him.

In the spring of that year Frida invited Strindberg to come and stay with her and Kerstin in Bavaria. The offer came too late; he told her that he wanted to see his child but not her mother. By this time Frida had fallen in love with Frank Wedekind and she had decided to move to Munich in order to be with him. She struggled to make a living as a translator and journalist and, as she had done for Strindberg, set about helping Wedekind to establish himself as a dramatist. Wedekind always acknowledged her support and attributed a great deal of his commercial success to her social and organizational skills.

In June Strindberg met up again with Edvard Munch, who had come to Paris to plan a major exhibition of his paintings. It was he who told Strindberg that Stanislaw Przybyszewski had been arrested in Berlin on suspicion of killing Martha Foerder. Strindberg was convinced that Przybyszewski was a murderer and was going to kill him too because of his affair with Dagny Juel. Day after day he heard the same piece of piano music – Schumann's 'Aufschwung' – something that Przybyszewski himself had often played – and his terror that the man had come to Paris to get him intensified. He was not convinced even when he was told that Martha's death had subsequently been recorded as suicide.

The description of Munch that Strindberg gives in an article that he wrote for the *Revue Blanche* could equally well have applied to himself at the time:

> Thirty-two-year-old Edvard Munch, the esoteric painter of love, jealousy, death and sorrow, has often been the victim of deliberate misunderstandings on the part of the hangman-critics who exercise their craft unfeelingly like executioners at the rate of so much per head. He came to Paris to seek the sympathy of the connoisseurs, without fear of that scorn which destroys cowards and weaklings but makes the shield of the brave shine like the sun.

Munch had a nervous breakdown in 1908 and spent eight months in a mental hospital where he had electric shock treatment. Years of overwork combined with alcohol abuse (especially absinthe) had taken their toll. He recovered and never drank again after that. It is surprising that Strindberg, who had led a very similar sort of life as Munch since their days together at the 'Ferkel' in Berlin, did not suffer from such severe side-effects.

In July 1896 Strindberg went to Ystad, a small town in southern Sweden, to stay with Anders Eliasson, a friend of his who was a doctor.

Eliasson had treated him the previous year and on this visit he diagnosed 'a neurosis' and prescribed some drugs that Strindberg found too potent, and a regime of cold showers. After a month or so Strindberg felt well enough to travel and he accepted an invitation from Frau Uhl to visit Kerstin. He had hoped to see Frida as well but by this time (though unknown to him) she had moved to Munich to live with Wedekind.

Strindberg stayed with the Uhl family for about three months. Frida's mother was genuinely welcoming and they resumed the genial relationship that they had enjoyed before, but the grandmother was hostile, viewing him, as ever, as a mere fortune-hunter. His greatest delight was Kerstin, now two and a half years old. Slowly he started to emerge from the creative wilderness and, in what was to turn out to be a significant journey into the soul, he began simultaneously to plan five new works: the novels *Inferno* (in which he would weave his daughter Kerstin into the character of Beatrice), *Legends* and *The Cloister*, and two new plays, *To Damascus* and *Advent*.

He returned to Dr Eliasson's in Ystad on 1 December and two months later started to write *Inferno*, where he turned the scenery around Dornach into a mythological landscape. He wrote in French, as he had done with *A Madman's Defence*, but whereas Siri had figured prominently in the earlier work, Frida played a very small part in the new one. In fact, she has already departed by the time the action begins:

> It was with a feeling of joy that I returned from Gare du Nord in Paris after having deposited my little wife who was going to see our child who had fallen ill in a foreign country. The sacrifice of my heart was made!
>
> Our parting words: when shall we meet again? – Soon! Still resounded like non-lies, since something told me that it was forever.
>
> And this farewell which we exchanged in the month of November 1894 also became the last, because up to this moment, in May 1897, I have not seen my beloved wife again.
>
> When I reached Café de la Regence I sat down at the table where I had recently been with my wife, my beautiful jail-keeper who spied on my soul day and night, guessed my secret thoughts, watched the way my ideas wandered, jealously observed my striving towards the unknown . . .

The annulment of Strindberg's marriage to Frida was made official in February 1897. What he did not know at this time was that Frida was expecting a child by Wedekind and this was what had prompted her to take action to get the process completed.

There had been no real acrimony in her parting from Strindberg and their union was dissolved without any big drama, almost like a dream coming to a painless end — except that for him the dreams he used to have about her continued to haunt him for some time. He went on corresponding with her mother — affectionate letters, continuing their philosophical debates, and always seeking news of Frida and Kerstin. On 25 July, with a curious sense of premonition, he wrote to her from Lund:

> My dearest mother-in-law
> Your letter frightened me at first. 'I wish I were as happy as you and ignorant of the facts.' So something terrible must have happened to Frida, but what?
>   What is this terrible thing?
>   1. Is she dead?
>   2. Insane?
>   3. Ill?
>   4. Has she started a new (old) relationship?
>   I beg you to tell me because I am about to go to Berlin and Munich with my new book. You see, if No. 4 is true I must avoid Germany altogether. My dreams and premonitions told me a long time ago: she is a deserted mother with a child. Is that so? And does she live alone? Unhappily?

The next day Strindberg wrote to her again, urging her to tell him the truth:

> Lund 26th July 1897
> My dear good mother-in-law
>   Let me tell you what makes me so worried about Frida! One night between the 31st January and 1st February I saw Frida in mourning. Frida in white with a black headscarf, like a nun; when the scarf was lifted her face was transformed into that of an old gentleman.
>   On 10th May I saw Frida in a white shroud, anointed after having been killed in a fire.
>   On 29th May I dreamt that my first wife and I went to visit Frida who came running straight up to me to greet me in a friendly way. When she saw the other woman I introduced her as my stepmother. And then Frida and the other one went for a walk, arms linked. Frida was dressed in brown and looked as if she had cried a lot.
>   On 3rd June I saw Frida, her face ashen white but the yellow and brown shone through. On the same day I saw two white pigeons and a big canary in my room.
>   On 10th July I saw Frida here in the street in broad daylight: dressed in brown — but suddenly she was gone.
>   Finally: if she is alone and unhappy I'll write a few words of comfort to her.
>   If she is 'happy' and not alone, I only need to know where she is living so I can avoid any duels and avoid the place.
> Yours August
> P.S. Last night (between Sunday 25th and Monday 26th) I was woken up by someone screaming: Thérèse!

Frida's baby was born in Munich on 21 August and she named him Friedrich after her father and gave him the surname Strindberg. Her mother agreed to care for the child alongside Kerstin, who was now three years old. Wedekind took no interest whatsoever in his son – only once did he send him birthday greetings and then he got the date wrong. He did not stay with Frida for long and when their relationship ended she turned her attention to his brother Donald for a while and moved to Paris with him.

Strindberg did keep in touch with his daughter Kerstin for a few years, mainly, it must be said, because he wanted to continue to communicate with Frida's mother. He finally got to know about Frida's son some time in 1900 and this effectively put an end to his visits to Austria as he had no wish to risk bumping into her. In August of that year he drew a line under his relationship with the Uhl family when he sent them a cheque for 2000 Gulden with a note that detailed what he considered to be his outstanding debts:

> Travel money received from:
> Maria Weyr, for a journey from Rügen to Mondsee in 1893
> Friedrich Uhl, for a journey between Mondsee and Berlin, 1893
> Maria Reischl, for a journey from Dornach to Paris, 1894 and Klam-Lund 1896
> Payment to Frida Uhl (for the squandered trousseau)

When he wrote to Kerstin in 1901 Strindberg was just three weeks away from getting married for the third time:

> 20 April 1901
> My dear, dear child
> Forgive me, but I was ill with a fever when your last dear portrait arrived. Do you think that I can forget you who led me through Inferno as my Beatrice, through nights of anguish and days of unease? Oh no, I am not like that and never will be.
>
> There are scene changes in all dramas, and new characters appear, but in the last act everyone will turn up again and the author must not forget a single one. That is the eternal law of drama and life, and shame on the person who forgets that! Now you know. God bless you and everyone who loves you.
> Your father.

Of all his five children Kerstin was the one Strindberg saw the least of and she was not part of the inner circle of his family during the last five years of his life.

On Christmas Eve in 1902 Frida wrote him a rather sad but loving letter. She congratulated him on his marriage to Harriet Bosse and wished him all the best for the future. What had prompted her to contact him, however, was the fact that she had been visiting her mother and Kerstin (after a prolonged absence) and had come across the cache of letters that he had written to them over the years:

> I thought you had banished me from your heart five years ago. Consequently I felt rejected, hated, lost, lost. When I realize that you have loved me and asked for forgiveness and a reconciliation and that I have not known about it, I have only just found out. What torment! What poor comfort!
>
> August I thank you, I thank you on my knees. You will never hear from me again. These will be my last words. Bless you for being the only great and noble person I have encountered in my unhappy life. Bless you for being the father of my child. I thank you for the past and for the future. There is no one else in this world whom I can thank for one single hour of pure joy. And I ask your forgiveness, I who will never forgive myself, never! [. . .]
>
> I don't deserve any compassion, because I have made a big mistake, I have been aware of all the faults, all the contempt . . . in thought and deed . . .
>
> August, death would be sweet for me, if I could wipe out my life. But I was never common. I did not desert you in order to sell myself as she [her mother] said. No, no! I have given, and I have given more than I was entitled to give. I was not cheap, oh no, not that at least. [. . .]
>
> Tell your wife that I bless her if she makes you happy! And tell her – how I have suffered. [. . .]
>
> Goodbye, August, goodbye forever!
>
> But not as enemies, not in pain. Farewell and above all from my side:
>
> Forgive me!
>
> Forgive the one you have forgotten.
>
> Frida.

She was to write him two more letters, one dated 2 July 1904 and the other, undated, in 1907. 'Your daughter Kersti adores you without knowing you,' she said. Strindberg did not respond to Frida but he did write to her mother, explaining why he had not been in touch with Kerstin:

> Stockholm, 2 March 1907
>
> My dear mother,
>
> My life has become so complicated through three marriages . . . and now I live in a free liaison with my (legally) divorced third wife, mainly for the sake of our daughter. The little girl, Anne-Marie, is now five. Her sister Greta, who was born in the first marriage, is now twenty-two and lives and works here as an actress, but I can't introduce her to Anne-Marie and Miss Bosse. They don't love each other. So there is disharmony.
>
> I have been thinking about Kerstin's destiny for a long time. It is so tied up with that of her mother's and since I always believed that she would have a stepfather I did not want to get involved in these awkward situations.
>
> So I said to myself; Kerstin does not need me. In a few years' time she will be grown up and step into life as a person in her own right. What good is a nominal father to her? Why tear the girl apart with feelings? No, I can't crawl back into this

net. Through Kerstin I would enter into direct contact with her mother. I don't want that. I must not do that. She has a brother who does not belong to me, that much Kerstin knows. [. . .]

I don't know whether Frida is alive, whether she is married, etc. I could risk meeting her and in that case I am sure that Kerstin would probably try to reconcile us in her childish way. It would not work. Why stage tragedies? This is enough.

In three years Kerstin will be grown up, maybe engaged to be married, she will have her own friends, relations . . . and then she will not need me. You know how children are.

Another time I'll write more.

Yours (soon) sixty-year-old August Strindberg.

Kerstin wrote to Strindberg in 1909 and told him that she had seen Frida in Vienna. 'She must be very unhappy,' she said. 'She was so pale, with tired eyes, my mother. But who can help her? Only she herself.' A few days later Strindberg replied:

5th September 1909
My child,
I have not had any letters from Dornach. And I have become so estranged from everything to do with Austria – more than estranged. It seems like an old fairy tale, unbelievable, but it was true once, after all.

Is the rich old great-grandmother still alive? Was she not rich? Is Auntie Melanie still alive? I know nothing and am not eager to know anything as it all seems so strange to me.

I am sixty years old and live in a boarding house . . .

But I still write and to me life is only material for dramas, mainly tragedies . . .

Live well! And think of me only as a souvenir!

Your father.

The phrase 'think of me only as a souvenir' was not the most appropriate one that Strindberg could have selected for a fifteen-year-old daughter who desperately craved affection, even if it was true that they had not seen each other for thirteen years. She had been sent off to boarding school and there had been long periods during her early childhood when she had not seen Frida very much either. So both parents had failed her in many respects. And while she had never felt very close to Frida, Strindberg had always been a distant glamorous figure to her.

Kerstin married a German journalist and publisher, Ernst Sulzbach, in 1917 and they had a son in 1924. They separated soon after and when Hitler came to power Kerstin applied for Swedish citizenship and moved to Sweden, where she was actively involved in the anti-Nazi movement. Towards the end of her life she became something of a recluse in Stockholm. She died in 1956 and lies buried in the same grave as her father.

She was never to see a great deal of her mother, who moved around Europe a lot before the First World War, mixing in bohemian circles in Berlin, Munich and Vienna. In 1908 Frida fled to England, having scandalized Viennese society when she fired a gun at a party where Prince Fugger-Babenhausen was a guest. She started a nightclub in London, called the Cave of the Golden Calf in Heddon Street, just off Regent Street, which opened on 26 June 1912. Here she presided over all the famous artists and writers of the time, including Katherine Mansfield, Ezra Pound, Wyndham Lewis, Augustus John and Ford Madox Ford. Richard Cork's description of her brings to mind the excesses of the 'Ferkel' in Berlin and the infamous Dagny Juel:

> Maddening, sexually ravenous, unreliable, yet magnificently fearless, she issued an outspoken manifesto trumpeting her bold and emancipated aims: 'We want a place given up to gaiety, to a gaiety that does not have to count with midnight.'
>
> Ford Madox Ford recalled the glory of the Cave: '. . . there would be a dinner, a theatre or a party, a dance. Usually a breakfast at four after that. Or Ezra and his gang carried me off to their nightclub which was kept by Madame Strindberg, decorated by Epstein and situated underground. London was adorable then at four in the morning after a good dance. You walked along the south side of the park in the lovely pearl-grey coolness of the dawn . . . Those who cannot remember London then do not know what life could hold.'
>
> Ezra Pound also remembers how Frida would wave a customer away from her table, saying as she did so that sleep with him she would, but talk to him, never: One must draw the line somewhere.

The Times, 31 December 1998

When the Golden Calf had to close because it was losing money, a few months before the outbreak of war, Frida went to America, where she gave lectures and generally promoted Strindberg's work. She got involved in the newly developing film industry, writing screenplays. On meeting a well-known Danish actress, Asta Nielsen, in New York, she tried to persuade her to take part in a movie version of *Crimes and Crimes* that she had written. Nielsen accepted at first but then pulled out when she saw how chaotic the conditions in the studios were. The director Ernst Lubitsch later used Nielsen in another adaptation of *Crimes and Crimes*, which was released in Germany under the title of *Rausch* [*Intoxication*].

In the 1920s Frida returned to Europe. The Danish writer Vagn Börge recalls meeting her in Stockholm, where she was researching material for her autobiography, *Marriage With Genius*:

> She seemed self-confident, intelligent, considerate and wise. Undoubtedly, she must have looked stunning in her youth when Strindberg met her. She was still very

careful about her appearance. [. . .] I didn't doubt for a moment that she, like Siri von Essen, was an exceptional person. Like her she has an artistic nature and obviously she was an upper-class girl who, as an artist and a bohemian, had rebelled against the bourgeois ideas of her own class early on in life.

Frida never married again and she hung on to the name Strindberg for the rest of her life. Throughout her 'stormy journey with many shipwrecks' she never forgot him and she always kept track of what he was doing. 'Through him my insignificant existence was raised to a higher sphere,' she said. 'And when one has experienced the ecstasy of flying once, it becomes an indispensable habit.' When she heard that Strindberg was ill in 1911 she wanted to go to Stockholm to see him but he told her to stay away. She ended her days at her family's summer residence in Mondsee, where she died in 1943 at the age of seventy-one.

Strindberg's friend Georg Brandes once asked Frida if she would still marry Strindberg if she had her time again. 'Oh yes, she replied, 'I would marry him again, without a moment's thought or doubt. At any price.'

Strindberg's Works: 1893–97

Strindberg wrote comparatively little while he was married to Frida Uhl, though he did many paintings and developed his interest in photography. He completed the following works during this period.

The Bond [*Bandet*] play, 1893
Antibarbarus essays, 1894
Inferno novel, 1897
Legends [*Legender*] essays, 1897

Part I of his play To Damascus [Till Damaskus]*, though not written until 1898, was directly inspired by Frida.*

Part 3
Harriet Bosse (1878–1961)

— Chapter 17 —

Waiting in the Wings

> In the belief that we finished our journey To Damascus today I ordered some roses – with thorns, of course – there are no others to be had! and I send them with a simple thank you: Now see to it that you become the actress of the new century here!
>
> *Letter to Harriet Bosse, 5 December 1900*

The Norwegian-born actress Harriet Bosse was twenty-two when she first met Strindberg in 1900. She was beautiful and full of life and, like Siri and Frida before her, there was something both hypnotic and ethereal about her that created an immediate impact. 'One feels giddy when she enters a room,' said the Swedish writer Hjalmar Söderberg, 'in fact a little unsure of who is standing before one.'

The first thing people noticed about Harriet was her exotic looks. Strindberg used to fantasize that she was from Indonesia because her features appeared Asiatic to him. Just five feet three inches tall and with dark eyes, prominent eyebrows and black hair, she was the opposite of the Nordic stereotype. 'When I saw Harriet's beauty, which sometimes could be "otherworldly", I shuddered,' he wrote in his *Occult Diary* in September 1901, and wondered 'how can light come from darkness?' Sometimes she seemed to him like an angel and sometimes he saw her as a demon. She certainly had a character strong enough to match Strindberg's own and in a letter that she wrote to him in the same year she describes herself as 'the most evil woman born'.

Many theatre directors are said to have found Harriet difficult to work with, for though she was a sensitive and conscientious actress she was something of a perfectionist and could be temperamental. When Strindberg first met her she shared with Siri and Frida that ideal mix of youth, beauty, talent, spirit and vulnerability that he always found irresistible. She inspired him to write for the theatre and played an active part in the whole creative process. Harriet was such a perfect muse that during the year 1900–1901 alone he completed six new plays with her in mind as the heroine: *Easter, The Dance of Death (Part II), The Crown Bride,*

Swanwhite, *Kristina* and *A Dream Play*. There is often something wistful and mysterious, altogether more nuanced, about his female characters from this time onwards. They frequently display a rawness, a hypersensitivity, with a touch of melancholia.

Harriet proved herself to be a finer and much more successful actress than Siri, with a career that lasted for almost fifty years; and as a sterner critic of Strindberg's work she reaped the reward of a substantial body of beautifully crafted tailor-made roles. She inspired a long and fruitful period of artistic cross-fertilization that not only continued for several years after their marriage was formally dissolved in 1904 but went on until Strindberg died. Altogether she acted in fourteen of his plays.

Harriet's social background was much closer to Strindberg's own than that of his first two wives. Her father, Johann Bosse, was German, and made a living as a publisher and bookseller. He and his Danish wife, Anne-Marie Lehman, had fourteen children of whom only seven survived into adulthood. By the time Harriet, the thirteenth child, was born in the Norwegian capital, Kristiania, on 19 February 1878, one of her sisters, Alma, had just made her debut at the Kristiania Theater at the age of fifteen.

The Bosse family moved around a lot while Harriet was growing up and she attended schools in Norway and Sweden, feeling equally at home in both countries. Her parents encouraged their children to be independent and Harriet remembers travelling alone by train from Kristiania to Stockholm when she was only six years old. It was an artistic household and music played an important part. Johann sang in a famous choir with King Oscar II in Stockholm when they were living in Sweden, and all the children took piano lessons from an early age. Harriet's sister Dagmar, who was twelve years older, became a concert and opera singer, praised for her clear diction and natural, unsentimental delivery. She established an international name in Germany and France and was a popular performer all over Scandinavia. Her reputation was endorsed by Grieg, who admired her enough to dedicate one of his song-cycles to her.

When Harriet was sixteen she enrolled at the Conservatoire in Stockholm – the same institution that Siri had attended some twenty-four years earlier – which had now become part of the Royal College of Music. She studied there for three years, where she specialized in solo singing and continued with the piano. Her father was hoping that she would become a respectable music teacher but it looked as though she was all set to follow Dagmar's lead and become a professional singer.

Dagmar and Alma both come across as very positive role models who demonstrated that it was possible for a woman to break with middle-class conventions and have a career outside the home. And her sister Inez, who was fifteen years older and had been a widow since 1890, supported herself by running a glove shop in Stockholm, so Harriet was fortunate to have three sisters who were able to offer practical support and advice, for she was only fifteen when their mother died. Dagmar offered Harriet a home and helped to support her while she continued with her studies. In the meantime Alma had started her own theatre company with her husband, Johan Fahlström, having worked as an actress at the Kristiania Theater for fifteen years.

In the summer of 1896 Alma wrote to Dagmar asking her to send Harriet to Kristiania straight away because she wanted to put her on the stage. The role that she had in mind was Juliet in an abridged version of *Romeo and Juliet* that she and her husband planned to produce for one week at the Tivoliteatret in Kristiania, followed by a five-week tour of the provinces. It was a gamble to give a leading role in a classical play to someone with no theatrical experience whatsoever but Alma felt that Harriet, who had at least been trained to sing and project her voice, would be ideal.

Directed by Alma, the play was a triumph and Harriet became an overnight sensation. On 18 August she wrote to Inez in Stockholm about the excitement of the opening night:

> You can't possibly imagine what a wonderful evening it was!!!!!! I walked around there the whole evening as if in a dream and was not awake enough to be really scared! After my big scene with the poison, I was called back by the audience three times, but I still have no idea how I got on or off, just a dim recollection that Alma pushed me . . . and that I stood there and took my bow like a fool.

The sudden adulation was sweet. Harriet kept a journal when the company went on tour and recorded everything she was learning about the craft of acting from Alma and the small ensemble of actors, who all impressed on her the need for teamwork and loyalty if a production was to work successfully. She reveals the dare-devil side to her character when she writes in her journal about how she went to the top of the cathedral tower in Trondheim, an old city of pilgrimage in northern Norway. When she had climbed as high as she could go she stepped onto two rafters that stretched from one side of the tower to the other, with a sheer drop to the ground below. 'It was great fun standing there,' she wrote, bringing to mind Hilde Wangel in *The Master Builder,* who challenges Solness to climb to the top of the roof of the house that he is building.

Ibsen's play had first been produced in 1893 and while Harriet had probably not seen it or even read it, it is likely that she knew about it. By this time Ibsen's reputation was well established and Harriet had seen a production of *Peer Gynt* that Alma had acted in. The young heroine, Hilde, in *The Master Builder* was a perfect role for Harriet but she did not get the chance to play her until 1919 when Intiman (under new management and in a new location) put it on in Stockholm.

In November 1896, two months after Harriet had returned to Stockholm to resume her studies at the Conservatoire, Johann Bosse died, leaving each of his children a small legacy. Alma decided to use her 3000 kronor inheritance to lease and refurbish the Alhambrateatret in Kristiania. For her opening production, in August 1897, she chose to direct *Once Upon a Time* by Holger Drachmann. He was a Danish writer who had been one of Strindberg's friends and drinking companions at the 'Ferkel' in Berlin. Alma decided to take the small comic role of the maid herself in *Once Upon a Time*, and she cast her husband as the Prince. She then sent a telegram to Harriet in Stockholm asking her if she would come and play opposite him as the beautiful young Princess. Harriet duly obliged and spent the next year with Alma's company, appearing in about a dozen different productions, including *Facing Death*, one of Strindberg's one-act plays.

The close relationship that had developed between the two sisters came to a painful end when Alma saw a portrait of Harriet that her husband had painted for the Annual Salon Exhibition in Paris. It emerged that he and Harriet had been having an affair. Alma's immediate reaction was to tell Harriet to leave and she always blamed her for the subsequent break-up of the company at the Alhambrateatret. She eventually donated the portrait to the Nordiska Museet in Stockholm, where it is still hanging today.

Alma and Johann's marriage survived and Alma continued with her career as an actor-manager, becoming a well-established and much sought-after director in Norway. After Harriet left Kristiania she never visited her sister and brother-in-law again and when, many years later, she returned to Norway as a famous actress, she was not invited to their home. And this episode in their lives explains why, in the end, Sweden gained and Norway lost one of Scandinavia's major acting talents of the age.

Having garnered a good deal of experience and some measure of success as a straight actress, Harriet abandoned her plans to become a singer and so gave up her place at the Conservatoire, deciding instead to go to France to study theatre. Arriving in Paris in November 1898, she quickly fell in with the large colony of Scandinavian artists who had gravitated there, just as Strindberg himself had done some four years earlier. She knew that Strindberg had in fact met Alma and Johan in 1894 when they had all been staying at the Hôtel des Américains. Alma and Johan had managed to sell a couple of his paintings in Norway and he had given them a landscape entitled 'Snöstorm över havet' ['Snowstorm over the Sea'] by way of commission.

Harriet went to the theatre a great deal in Paris and during her six-month stay there she took full advantage of André Antoine's offer of a free seat in a box at his experimental Théâtre Libre, where she saw her first production of *Lady Julie*. She also enjoyed free tickets at the Théâtre de l'Oeuvre, courtesy of the director Aurélien Lugné-Poë, and saw exciting new productions of plays by Ibsen and Bjørnson. She admired the natural acting style of both theatres and as a direct result of what she had seen she was later to be responsible for introducing Swedish audiences to a form of dramatic presentation on stage that was realistic and unaffected.

In the spring of 1899 Harriet was offered contracts at two theatres in Kristiania, one at the prestigious Nationalteatret and the other with a new theatre that the actor-director Rudolf Rasmussen had taken over. Either offer would have been useful for her career, and she had worked with Rasmussen before, but the problem was that Alma and Johan were still living and working in Kristiania and she had no wish to go back and face them again. She returned instead to Stockholm, where her sisters Dagmar and Inez and her brother Ewald were living. She reckoned, as Siri had done, that the cosmopolitan Swedish capital would offer plenty of opportunities for a keen young actress.

It is strange that Strindberg, who was one of the greatest stylists of the Swedish language, should three times have chosen to marry women who were not native Swedes. Siri and Harriet had both grown up speaking Swedish but each had a strong accent. With a lot of training and dedication Siri had managed to improve her pronunciation sufficiently to act convincingly in Swedish and when Harriet started looking for work in Stockholm she was advised to do the same. 'If you can learn to speak like a normal person, we shall employ you at Dramaten,' said Nils Personne, the theatre's artistic director, who saw Harriet's audition – a piece from a fairy tale by Hans Christian Andersen. In August he offered her a one-year contract on condition that she undergo a period of intense voice coaching.

The first role that Harriet played at Dramaten was Loyse in *Gringoire* by Théodore Faullain de Banville and her first major part was as Puck in

A Midsummer Night's Dream in February 1900. By this time she had acted in one of Strindberg's plays, *Facing Death*, and had seen three others – *Gustav Vasa*, *Crimes and Crimes* and the French production of *Lady Julie*. The historical play *Gustav Vasa*, which had opened at the Svenska Teatern on 18 October 1899, was the work that excited her most and she began to read all of Strindberg's published work and resolved to find out as much as she could about him.

On New Year's Eve 1899, as the old century gave way to the new, she went with her brother Ewald to Strindberg's ground-floor apartment at 31 Banérgatan. Pressing their faces against the darkened window they whispered 'Happy New Year' to the unseen genius.

During the run of *A Midsummer Night's Dream* at Dramaten Strindberg went along to one of the performances with the actor August Palme, who had been cast in the role of the Unknown One in the forthcoming production of *To Damascus (Part I)*. Palme thought that they might spot an actress in the company who would be suitable to play opposite him as the Lady. Strindberg did not select any of the three women that Palme had in mind but picked out Harriet immediately. She got the part 'because of her pretty legs', he said jokingly afterwards. His choice was based on the fact that Harriet was dark and looked mysterious, like Frida on whom the character of the Lady is based.

Some weeks later August Palme told Harriet that Strindberg wished to see her to discuss the role. Could she visit him at his apartment on Banérgatan on 31 May? When the day came she had nothing that she considered suitable to wear so she borrowed a suit from Dagmar, which was so loose on her that she had to take it in with safety pins. Nervously she approached Strindberg's front door and paused for a long time before ringing the bell. Once inside, she began to relax.

> Strindberg opened the door with a bright sunny smile. I was invited into a room where the table was laid with wine, flowers and fruit. No one could charm people like Strindberg, when he wanted to, and I was completely under his spell. We sat at his beautifully laid table and talked about everything under the sun. But he did not mention his writing.
>
> *Strindberg's Letters to Harriet Bosse*

Just before she left, Strindberg asked Harriet for a feather from her hat, saying that he wanted to have it as a souvenir of their meeting and use it for a quill pen. She readily agreed and the quill became one of his most treasured mementoes of her.

Soon after this meeting Strindberg went to Furusund to join his sister Anna and her family. They entertained friends as usual, including the feminist socialist Kata Dalström, who had visited Strindberg on the island the year before. She paints a picture of him as a congenial host and a stimulating conversationalist, though she mocks him gently for his fastidiousness in matters of propriety and dress, recalling one occasion when he refused to pose for a photograph in his shirtsleeves and with a glass of whisky in his hand. 'During the two summers and winters that we socialized,' she wrote, 'I never saw an ugly or unfriendly aspect of him.' She had fierce arguments with him about feminism and 'the woman question' and tackled him on his reputation as a misogynist:

> 'I'm sorry but even though you dislike women you'll have to put up with me sitting here.' 'Me dislike women? I have been married twice. I don't dislike them when they are unaffected and natural. Read the foreword to Sir Bengt's Wife, dear Kata; when you have read that you may understand better why people say that I am a "woman-hater". It is the artificial and false aspect of womanhood that I cannot endure,' he answered passionately.
>
> That was the first and only time I heard Strindberg speak directly about the woman question.
>
> *Vecko-Journalen, 1915*

Unfortunately, Strindberg's relationship with his brother-in-law Hugo became somewhat strained during their time on Furusund in the summer of 1900 and by the end of June he had returned to Stockholm alone. According to Anna and Hugo's daughter, Märtha Fröding, Strindberg had been trying to persuade his sister to leave her husband because she was unhappy in her marriage. She had been tempted by his offer of somewhere to stay but decided against walking out in the end. Hugo felt undermined by what he perceived to be Strindberg's unwarranted interference and was further humiliated when he later saw elements of his life and marriage hijacked as the subject-matter for a play. This caused a rift within Strindberg's family for some time.

It is generally acknowledged that Alice and Edgar in *The Dance of Death* are based on Anna and Hugo, though there are certain elements in the characters that suggest other role models, most notably Strindberg's friend Gustaf af Geijerstam and his wife. Alice and Edgar have been married for twenty-five years and are locked into a passionate but destructive relationship. They resemble Laura and the Captain in *The Father*, some ten years on, and Strindberg was drawing on events that he witnessed that summer.

On 5 July Harriet saw Strindberg again at his apartment. 'Visit by Miss Bosse for the second time,' he wrote in his *Occult Diary*. 'She accepted the role in *To Damascus*. Her sister waited outside in a cab.' It is significant that not long after this meeting Strindberg wrote to Frau Uhl asking her to send him the papers to prove that his marriage to Frida had been dissolved. In fact the marriage had been formally annulled in 1897 and Strindberg duly received the certificates he had asked for. He did not see Harriet again until rehearsals for *To Damascus* began at Dramaten in the autumn.

Strindberg describes the dress rehearsal of *To Damascus* on 15 November in his *Occult Diary*:

> After the first act, I got up onto the stage and thanked Bosse. Made a comment about the last scene where the kiss should take place with the veil down. As we stood there in the middle of the stage surrounded by several people and with me speaking seriously about the kiss, Bosse's little face was transformed, grew bigger and assumed a supernatural beauty, it seemed to come close to mine and her eyes absorbed me with black fire. Then she suddenly ran away for no reason and I stood there awkwardly with the feeling that a miracle had taken place and that I had been given a kiss which had intoxicated me. After that Bosse haunted me for three days and I was aware of her presence in my room.

The scene with the kiss had actually happened, of course, with Frida, and it was that seductive gesture with the veil that had triggered Strindberg's infatuation with her.

> THE LADY: What have you done with me . . . when I was in the chapel just now I could not pray; a candle went out on the altar and a cold wind brushed my face when I heard you calling me.
>
> THE UNKNOWN ONE: I didn't call you. I was only longing for you . . .
>
> THE LADY: You are not the fragile child that you make out, your powers are immense and you frighten me . . .
>
> THE UNKNOWN ONE: When I'm on my own I'm as weak as an invalid but as soon as I meet someone else I become strong. Now I want to be strong. That is why I follow you!
>
> THE LADY: You're welcome. Maybe you can save me from the werewolf!
>
> THE UNKNOWN ONE: Is there a werewolf?
>
> THE LADY: I call him that . . .
>
> THE UNKNOWN ONE: Then I shall fight against trolls, rescue princesses and kill werewolves. That is to live!
>
> THE LADY: Come, my protector! (*She pulls down the veil over her face, kisses him quickly on the mouth and leaves hurriedly.*)
>
> *The* UNKNOWN ONE *remains standing, surprised and rooted to the spot. A loud accord of women's voices can be heard. It sounds like screams coming from inside the church. The illuminated rose window becomes dark at once: the tree above the bench moves: the funeral*

> *guests get up from their places and look towards the sky as if they were witnessing something unusual and frightening.*
>
> The UNKNOWN ONE *rushes after the* LADY.
>
> To Damascus (Part I), Act I

Having woven his love for his second wife into fictional drama, Strindberg was about to weave it back into real life with someone new. Frida was gone and Harriet stood, literally, in the wings, ready to take her place.

Strindberg did not attend the première of *To Damascus* but he wrote to Harriet on the same day, 19 November, thanking her for her magnificent portrayal of the Lady but urging her to put a little more mischief – a little more of Puck – into the character. It would appear that he had decided not to act upon his attraction to her as swiftly as he had done with Frida for he ends the letter in a friendly, avuncular way. 'And so – good luck on your journey that is strewn with thorns and rocks,' he says. 'Such is the road. I shall just put down a few flowers along the way.' To emphasize the point he sent her a bouquet of roses – 'with thorns, of course' – on 5 December, the last night of *To Damascus*.

The end of the first year of the twentieth century saw him in a reflective mood. 'Alone at home,' he recorded in his diary on Christmas Eve. 'Read my correspondence with Siri Wrangel and found a lot of strange things during the years 1875–76.' And on 23 January 1901, the day after his fifty-second birthday, he is still taking stock of his life:

> Is it possible that all the horrible things I have experienced were staged for me in order that I should become a playwright and depict all the states of the soul and all kinds of situations. I was a playwright already at the age of twenty. But if my life had passed quietly and peacefully I would not have had anything to write about.

He had just completed *The Crown Bride* (also known as *The Virgin Bride*), very much with Harriet in mind, when he started having erotic dreams about her, which he recorded in graphic though encoded detail in his diary.

At around this time Strindberg started to send Harriet the manuscripts of all the plays that he was working on and from February onwards she began to visit him on a regular basis. On reading *The Dance of Death (Part II)* she told him that while she acknowledged that it was an extremely powerful play she did not feel that it was suitable for her as she was nervous about taking on anything that was too challenging before she had had a chance to establish herself.

Strindberg's intention with *The Dance of Death (Part II)* was to create a lighter, more optimistic version of the earlier play – it has a summer setting, unlike *Part I*, which takes place in late autumn. Edgar and Alice are still quarrelling, though, and Edgar turns against their friend Kurt, whose son Allan has fallen in love with their daughter Judith. The young couple get caught up in the atmosphere of passion and intrigue (Edgar wants Judith to marry a sixty-year-old army captain) and by the end of the play their future together is by no means certain. It is more likely that Strindberg had his daughter Greta in mind for Judith rather than Harriet, though in the end it was Fanny Falkner who took the role when the play was first produced in 1909. Harriet appeared as Judith in a later production, in 1921.

Harriet also expressed doubts about the part of Eleonora in *Easter*, which Strindberg had completed shortly before *The Dance of Death* (*Part II*). Eleonora is a young woman who has run away from a psychiatric hospital, and she represents Christ in a self-sacrificing way. She is a woman with a vision, a religious mystic, and a forerunner of Indra's Daughter in *A Dream Play*:

> ELEONORA: I don't know of any time or space . . . I'm everywhere, any time. I'm in my father's prison and in my brother's classroom. I'm in my mother's kitchen and in my sister's shop on the other side of the Atlantic. When things are going well for my sister and she's selling well I can feel her happiness and if things go wrong I suffer, but I suffer most when she's doing something wrong.

The character of Eleonora is based in part on Strindberg's sister Elisabeth, who had suffered prolonged periods of mental illness, and he told Harriet that she was perfectly capable of tackling the role. The secret was not to worry about it, not to analyse it too much and above all not to portray Eleonora as a stereotypical madwoman.

Strindberg could not resist the temptation to lecture Harriet on art and literature and the theatre and to explain to her his theories on drama and acting. He was the experienced artist and Harriet was his willing, impressionable protégée, intelligent and eager to learn. As he had done with Siri and, to a lesser extent Frida, he began, in a Pygmalion-like fashion, to educate her by giving her books to read. She struggled with novels in French and German and devised a timetable of several hours' study a day in the subjects she felt weakest in. She was to draw on this experience of self-improvement when she became Scandinavia's first actress to play Shaw's Eliza Doolittle in April 1914.

The pattern of Strindberg's relationship with Harriet was developing along the familiar lines of attraction, obsession, denial, realization and panic that he had experienced when he fell in love with Siri and Frida. By the beginning of March 1901 he is no longer denying his feelings for

Harriet but before he has even declared himself he has already rationalized the outcome should things go wrong:

> I have bought new clothes as if I expected engagement visits. What if it is all fiction and remains fiction, the whole thing? Well? Then I'll write it down and make it beautiful. And the pain of loss will be transformed into poetry. Dante never won his Beatrice, that is why he remained faithful to her despite the fact that she was married to someone else.
>
> <div align="right">1 March, <i>The Occult Diary</i></div>

When he finally found the courage to ask her, Strindberg's proposal of marriage to Harriet was made in a roundabout way, demonstrating that he was unsure both about his own motives as well as her possible response. He approached the subject by consulting her about the plot of *To Damascus (Part III)*. Did she think that the Unknown One should enter a monastery or should he go back into the world and live amongst people again? They discussed the matter and then, in a letter that Harriet wrote on 4 March but did not send for three weeks, she put her thoughts into words:

> If you think the woman whom you have created for the Unknown One has the power to tie him to life by taking his hand and showing him all the bright and good things which also exist in the world, then it is not right for him to enter a monastery. But what if she cannot do it! How disappointed he will be if it transpires that she simply was not as talented, as gifted and wise as he had imagined? [. . .]
>
> I can well imagine the little woman's jubilant joy if – despite all her doubts – the Unknown One only takes her hand quietly and walks away with her towards the goal.
>
> And forgets about the monastery!
> Yours Harriet Bosse

It was a clever and diplomatic reply. She had hinted that her response would be positive but she had also left Strindberg with a dignified escape route if he felt he needed to back out. She had gauged his mood perfectly and his actual proposal, when the moment came a few days later, was by no means a straightforward 'Will you marry me?':

> I had been asked to call on him about Eleonora; I went up to Strindberg determined to ask him to give the role to a more experienced actress. Even this time the table was laid with flowers and fruit. Strindberg was just as charming and kind. He asked me not to worry about Eleonora's part – it would be fine. He told me how hard and difficult life had been for him, how he longed for a ray of sunshine, a woman who could reconcile him with mankind and womanhood. And then he put his hands on my shoulders, looked me deeply in the eyes and asked with great tenderness: 'Would you like to have a little child by me, Miss Bosse?' I curtseyed and answered, quite hypnotized: 'Yes, please,' and then we were engaged.

> After the engagement I started to reflect on what I had done. I felt a great responsibility. How could I give this man anything of value – how could I, a mere nobody, reconcile him with mankind and womanhood. What pleasure could he have in exchanging thoughts with me – who knew nothing about anything. I was afraid of the impending marriage, but was unable to tell him what I thought of our union. It was only towards the end of our engagement that I plucked up courage and wrote to him about my doubts.
>
> Strindberg's Letters to Harriet Bosse

Harriet and Strindberg exchanged rings on 6 March and the following day they made their engagement official with an announcement in the newspaper. The wedding date was set for 6 May.

— Chapter 18 —

The Immortal Beloved

> Miss Bosse, You must have a little more patience with me and my correspondence, whose ultimate aim is: Eleonora. That is also the purpose of all the books I send you. You say that the part is so sensitive that it hardly bears touching. Yes, that is why I don't want to analyse it or take it apart, or philosophize about it. But, on the other hand, I didn't want you to fall into the traditional way of playing a mentally ill person. But I am sure you will not do that, because you seem to be born with all the ideas of the new century.
>
> *Letter to Harriet Bosse, 25 February 1901*

On 23 March 1901 Strindberg wrote to the director Emil Grandison about his play *Swanwhite*:

> I am now writing my *Swanwhite* for Dramaten, the ideal piece of pure beauty, the apotheosis of love, with one set. The most beautiful theme based on Swedish folk songs – and the part of Swanwhite as a wedding gift for my bride – of course!

In the meantime his play *Easter* was in rehearsal at Dramaten. It opened, appropriately, just before Easter, on 4 April, with Harriet as Eleonora. There were just six performances that spring and only two the following autumn. The critic Tor Hedberg dismissed the play as naive and silly; other reviewers were less negative but were not particularly enthusiastic about the piece. Harriet played the lead again in a revival in 1905 in Gothenburg that met with more or less the same lukewarm response.

That month Strindberg and Harriet were thinking seriously about their engagement. Only eleven of Harriet's letters written in 1901 have survived but judging by those that Strindberg wrote to her between 28 April and 2 May she was apprehensive about their future together. She was all too aware of his awesome reputation – indeed, Anna Branting (the wife of Strindberg's friend Hjalmar Branting) emphasized that very fact in the letter that she sent to Harriet congratulating her on her wedding: '. . . being August Strindberg's wife means having a high position in society,' she wrote, 'it is almost like wearing a queen's crown.' Was it all just a romantic dream? Here was a man, already twice divorced, and thirty years older than she was. She respected him but what could she possibly have to offer him? Strindberg's letter of 28 April provides the answer:

> Beloved,
> You ask me if you can offer me anything good and beautiful in life, and yet – look what you have given me already!
> When you, my beloved, good friend, came into my home three months ago, I was sad, old, ugly, almost evil and feeling hopeless.
> And then you came.
> What happened?
> At first you made me almost good.
> Then you gave me back my youth.
> And after that you nurtured my hopes for something better.
> Then you taught me beauty in life – in moderation – and beauty in literature – Swanwhite.
> I was sad, you made me happy.
> What do you fear from me?
> You – young, beautiful, talented, and above all, good – how much you can teach me! And you dare tell me that you want to increase your knowledge.
> You have taught me to speak in pure and beautiful words, you have taught me to think beautiful and great thoughts, you have taught me to forgive my enemies, you have taught me to respect other human destinies, apart from my own.
> Beloved! Who can separate us if Providence does not wish it?
> If Providence wants it – well, then we shall part as friends for life; and you will become 'die ferne unsterbliche Geliebte'. I, your servant, Ariel, who guards you from a distance. I warm you with my love and my tender thoughts, I will protect you with my prayers.
> Let us now wait until 6 May and see if Providence wants to separate that which he has united.

And on 2 May, in the last letter that Strindberg wrote to Harriet before the wedding, he is still trying to allay her fears:

> He loves her and she loves him. What more do you want? What is the world – and the people in it – afraid of? The past? But that is gone like the hour that went and does not exist any more. Look ahead! Only the present and the future are real.
> Let us embrace reality, and say: tomorrow.
> Tomorrow!
> My Empress, are you – who are equipped with the weapons of youth, beauty and talent – afraid of entering your home with your friend, your premier servant, your loved one?

At the age of fifty-two, after many years of living abroad without a permanent home, he was ready to settle down to a bourgeois existence in the city of his birth. He had created a substantial body of work and of the eight plays that he had written since 1898 at least five – *Gustav Vasa, Erik XIV, Crimes and Crimes, To Damascus* and *The Saga of the Folkungs* – had been produced in Stockholm either by Dramaten or the Nya Teatern, which the actor-director Albert Ranft had acquired in 1898 and renamed the Svenska Teatern to reflect the new interest in Swedish drama. All of this had yielded a decent income for Strindberg and he was able at last to send some money to Siri and the children in Finland, though he was clearly finding his daughters' continuing dependence on him irksome. 'If you beg when you are able to work and get paid for your work, which I have not always been,' he wrote in a letter to Karin and Greta on 25 April, 'you ought to know that there are such things as workhouses and welfare – which some people seem to be ignorant of!' By this time, Karin was twenty-one, just two years younger than Harriet, who, it must be remembered, had been earning her own living since the age of sixteen, and Greta was twenty and had already embarked on her career as an actress in Helsingfors.

With enough money to maintain a moderately comfortable standard of living and with a beautiful and talented young actress to inspire him, Strindberg was poised to start a new phase in his life. He had found a spacious five-room flat in a newly built apartment block at 40 Karlavägen in Östermalm, an area that was fast developing into one of the most fashionable districts of the capital. (Östermalm is still regarded as the Mayfair of Stockholm.) He bought new furniture and installed a telephone and told Harriet, who was then living with her sister Inez, that he would provide everything that they needed for their married life together, including a piano.

The wedding took place as planned on 6 May with Strindberg's brother Axel and Harriet's brother-in-law Carl Möller (who was married to Dagmar) as witnesses. Together with a few friends and relatives, the couple celebrated with a wedding breakfast at Hasselbacken, a smart restaurant in the Djurgården, the park where Strindberg took his morning walks. Strindberg's entry in his diary for that day is one of joy and contentment:

> Got married for the third time. After an engagement full of lovely moments and beautiful battles against ugliness. The homecoming when the drawing-room was full of flowers and the whole apartment illuminated, was like a fairy tale.

And the day after he noted, simply: 'Harmony'.

Strindberg and Harriet had lived separately during their short engagement and do not appear to have had a full sexual relationship before getting married. And there are hints that their wedding night was a disappointment to them both although Strindberg noted in his diary that they had intercourse twice.

Though Harriet was not working in May or June they did not have a honeymoon straight away; Strindberg had suggested a trip to Germany and Switzerland later in the summer. Harriet went to stay with Inez for a few days at a rented cottage in the country and returned on 25 June happy and refreshed. Strindberg was later to resent Harriet's close relationship with her sisters as he knew she had a tendency to confide in them about everything that was going on in her life. Like Siri and Frida she was gregarious and loved parties and going to restaurants while Strindberg by this time preferred to stay at home in the evenings.

Harriet was looking forward to her delayed honeymoon but on the morning of their departure, seven weeks after the wedding, she had her first real taste of what living with Strindberg would entail. With the travel tickets booked, hotel reservations made, and their trunks packed, he announced without warning that the trip was off. 'We can't go – ' he said, 'the powers don't want us to.' It is possible that he had been disturbed by the news of Dagny Juel's horrible death, which had been reported in the *Svenska Dagbladet* on 20 June. Harriet was naturally very upset:

> I had to cancel the tickets and the hotel bookings. There was nothing for it but to stay at home and swallow the tears.
>
> To cheer me up Strindberg laid the table with fruit and German wine, placed the table in front of the window with a view across the sunlit Gärdet and he told me how much more beautiful it was to see the sun illuminating something rather than having the sun in one's face, how much better it was to have people at a distance rather than being right amongst them and then he gave me Baedeker to read about travel! – which would save me from all the real troubles associated with travelling.

In response to the disappointment of her cancelled honeymoon, Harriet took matters into her own hands. On 26 June she left home without telling Strindberg where she was going. He spent an anxious few days worrying about where she was and then received a letter from her. She had found a cottage for rent in Hornbaek in Denmark and explained that she had booked it provisionally, convinced that he would want to join her there. It was a shrewd hunch. Strindberg arrived a few days later.

The holiday lasted for about a month and so Harriet was able to enjoy a honeymoon with her new husband after all. It ended on a sour note, unfortunately. A newspaper photographer took a picture of her while she was bathing in the sea and Strindberg, incensed at this invasion of their privacy, attacked the man and beat him about the head with his walking stick.

After this incident Strindberg decided to go to Berlin. Harriet was delighted and was curious to see this exciting city where her husband had once lived and worked. To her dismay, she found that he had booked a room in a suburban *pension* in Charlottenburg, the district where his German translator, Emil Schering, had a house, which was well away from the bohemian bars and cafés that she had heard so much about. In vain she begged him to take her to a nightclub called the Café Bauer but he refused, claiming that a 'whore's café' was no place for a respectable woman. He then called Harriet a whore herself for wanting to go to such a place. She was hurt by the vehemence of his reaction to what was to her a perfectly reasonable and innocent request and their quarrel about the matter was to rankle with her for a long time afterwards. She was miserable and to complicate things even further she did not feel well. It did not occur to her that the reason for this was that she was almost certainly pregnant and it was Strindberg who explained the symptoms to her. He was thrilled at the prospect of becoming a father again.

They returned to Stockholm in the middle of August as Harriet was due to appear in *Easter* and *Karl XII*. She was still brooding about Strindberg's behaviour towards her in Berlin as well as trying to sort out her feelings about having a baby. She was further unsettled when the theatre notified her that they had cancelled the production of *Karl XII*, which left her with very little to take her mind off her anxieties. One day she said in jest that she did not understand how she had fallen pregnant and Strindberg took her comments personally as a slur on his virility. Harriet found her life with him intolerable and after yet more rows – including one when she told him that she intended to give her baby the surname Bosse – she walked out on her husband of three months. It was another 'crash' as Strindberg called it, and on 23 August, the day after she left, he fell into a deep depression. 'Alone. Sad. Cried a lot,' he wrote in his diary. 'Thought life was a cruel spectacle, especially as regards our best feelings. Life is humbug.'

For the next few days he shut himself away, still alone and still weeping. He re-read all his letters to Harriet and the entries that he had made in his diary since they had first met. He saw the beauty in their relationship and the happiness that she had brought him and on 27 August he wrote to her at her sister Dagmar's where he thought she had gone, asking her to come back to him:

> Just say one word! About your intentions, as soon as you are clear about them yourself.
>
> I can't think of a way to make you come back, because I don't know why you left. But if, on the other hand, you are waiting for a word from me, I don't need to say: your home is waiting for you, as pure as when you left it.

Harriet was in fact staying in a small boarding house in Östermalm but Strindberg's letter reached her and she replied by return of post:

> 27 August 1901
>
> Can you not understand why I left? I left in order to save the last remnant of female pride and self-respect.
>
> What you said to me that memorable day in Berlin has rung in my ears, the accusations you expressed then have soiled me so that the most loving words from you can never wash them away or conceal them. [. . .]
>
> I blame myself for being too cowardly to leave you in Berlin – my excuse was that I was not feeling well. [. . .]
>
> I haven't been very happy these last few days, as you can imagine, because you are the father of my little child, after all. But rather than put up with a horrible future full of unfair accusations and pain for us both, I'll leave while I still have all the beautiful things you have given me fresh in my mind.
>
> Do you remember that I always said: I'll do anything you wish as long as you are kind to me!?
>
> Harriet

Altogether Harriet stayed away for six weeks, during which time she and Strindberg saw each other occasionally and corresponded almost every day. On 29 August he wrote her a long, reflective letter. It is largely a declaration of love though he also accuses her of being dishonest:

> This – our marriage is the most inexplicable thing I have ever experienced, the most beautiful and the ugliest. Sometimes only the beauty is apparent – and then I cry, I cry myself to sleep in order to forget the ugliness.
>
> And at moments like that I take all the blame, all the guilt upon me. And when I saw you sad and in despair in May and June, in your green room, mourning your lost youth, which I have 'ravaged' then I accuse myself, then I cry in pain at all the hurtful and unfair things I have done to you, I kiss the sleeve of your dress where your little hand appears, asking you to forgive me for all the grief I have caused you. [. . .]
>
> Can we not step down a little in our demands as far as personal illusions are concerned and team up in areas where we have common interests only, like parenthood, friendship and our art, which we share.

Harriet's letters show her trying to find a way to stay in touch with him, not least for the baby's sake, without surrendering her independence. She suggests that it might be better for them both if they lived apart but continued to work together as they had done before they got married. Maybe that would make it easier to retain their respect for each other and to forget the difficulties in their relationship. If they kept a physical distance between them perhaps that would strengthen their spiritual bond. On 3 September she wrote with a note of finality:

You have given me so much that is beautiful, Gusten! I thank you for that! It has been a joy for me to be trusted with act after act in your work, an honour I was proud of.

Our little child will be good and kind. I shall always speak kindly of you to it. Of course I'll call it Strindberg if you like. If it is possible I think you should stay in [the apartment on] Karlavägen. You have a home there which you ought not to break up.

Feeling that he was never going to be able to persuade her to return to him with rational argument (and no doubt mindful of what had happened with Frida in the first few months of their married life), Strindberg used all the eloquence he could muster to appeal to Harriet's maternal instincts. In a romantic letter that he wrote the next day he addresses his thoughts to the child in her womb:

> 4th September 1901
> To my child! (The unborn Little One)
> My child! Our child! --- Our Midsummer child! Your parents were walking about in their home waiting for something and since all waiting seems long and maybe boring, they thought that they were boring.
> They waited for something to arrive, they did not know that it had arrived, in a quiet, scented room under white veils, with yellow walls, yellow like the sun and like gold!
> Then your mother was seized by a longing to see her native country, a wonderful longing which pulled her away from home and hearth with a bleeding heart.
> In the shimmering, green beech forest by the blue sea you were carried, you child of the South and the North!
> And your beautiful mother rocked you in the blue waves in the sea which washes three kingdoms --- and in the evenings when the sun was about to set – she'd sit in the garden and look the sun in the eyes in order to give you light to drink.
> Child of the sea and the sun, you slept your first sleep in a little red ivy-covered house in a white room where the words of hatred had never even been whispered, and where nothing impure had been contemplated even!
> After that you made a dark journey, a pilgrimage to the city of Sins, where your father cried and your mother learnt from his tears where that path might lead . . .
> After that you came home to the golden room where the sun shines night and day, and where affection awaited you, but then you were taken away! . . .
> (The End.)

Harriet did not address the points that Strindberg had made though her brief acknowledgement – 'My child thanks you for the kind and beautiful greeting' – offers a hint that she had not been unaffected by his words. In an undated letter (probably written on 5 September) he wrote to her again:

Harriet, let me see you again! I promise not to talk about anything but our artistic interests, and to show you that I am glad from the heart to see you. I am writing 'The Growing Castle' [*A Dream Play*]. It is about you of course! Agnes – who will release the Prisoner from the castle...

May I talk to you about it?

How is the little one? (the unborn child)

On 8 September Harriet asked him to come and see her at Dagmar's apartment. She had been ill for a couple of days and the doctor had been called twice. Strindberg went immediately but found her affected and false. 'You are a stranger to me,' he told her and left after only ten minutes. Harriet visited him in turn at Karlavägen a few days later, and she too left after just a short while.

In spite of this failure to effect a reconciliation Strindberg did not give up. He decided that the best way to win Harriet back would be to tempt her with the promise of a challenging role so he told her about his play *Kristina* and said that he had been talking to Dramaten about various other projects that he had in mind. As a peace offering he sent over a couple of paintings for her dressing room at the theatre. One of them was called 'The Child's First Cradle' and it showed a sunset by the sea in Denmark where they had spent their delayed honeymoon and where their baby had probably been conceived. Harriet wrote and thanked him and said that she was very excited about the prospect of playing Queen Kristina. She had swallowed the bait.

— Chapter 19 —

A Mother and an Artist

> What is it that you want to experience? Surely you, as a mother and an artist, need not live through my bachelor experiences.
> *Letter to Harriet Bosse, September 1901*

At the beginning of September 1901 Strindberg had sent the grand piano back to the shop, thinking that his marriage to Harriet was definitely over. 'She was the last sunray in my life,' he wrote in his diary a few days later. 'I thank her for that. I have loved her so much that I must be punished for it.' He had sent her some roses and she had written a note of thanks but still she stayed away.

Contemplating suicide, he begged his brother Axel to come and visit him. 'I shall not go through with this!' he wrote on 16 September, and added a separate note with instructions about his funeral:

> No autopsy, a simple burial, no speeches, a regular Lutheran ritual without any frills. A black coffin, a black crucifix with the inscription: 'O crux ave spes unica.'

He did not carry out his threat and gradually the black cloud of his depression lifted. The letters between him and Harriet continued and their disagreements were temporarily set aside in favour of their common professional interests. Strindberg was still keen to involve her in his work and on 21 September he further outlined his plans to her:

> Now I am working on the fourth act. I do miss a table where we can sit and talk about *Kristina*; especially the ending, which is the most important thing.
> I shall send the manuscript of *Swanwhite*, the original, and ask you to keep it as a souvenir of our union that started so beautifully. You know that you can play the part whenever you like.

Harriet replied the next day, explaining why she could not come back: 'Sometimes a mad desire may come over me, a desire to laugh, to be happy, to embrace everything and everybody in sheer joy – and you will not be able to understand this. But if I deny myself this I shall wither away and die.' However, that same evening she turned up unexpectedly at the apartment, though she stayed only a short while, which plunged Strindberg further into despair, as he recorded in his *Occult Diary*:

> 22nd September, Sunday
> Day of horror. Suicide mania. Harriet came in the evening to stay. But left again. (She later told me that she thought she was on the verge of madness. Left me and went down to the Munkbridge without knowing why. She sat there the whole night long on her bench – until morning.)

His entry for the following day indicates what a rollercoaster of emotions he was on:

> 23rd September, Monday
> Went with Harriet to Lindigö Bridge and had lunch together.
> Most extraordinary day! – C'est la vie! complete harmony, everything light!

And then he was inviting her to come and discuss his work again:

> 24th September 1901
> Come and sit here at our uncluttered dining-room table and talk about *Kristina*.
> I had a terrible feeling this morning that you disliked the play, that I had overestimated it and that you were angry with me.

They continued on this restless, seemingly aimless round of meetings and partings until the end of the month. In an attempt to get away Strindberg even left the apartment on Karlavägen and rented a room on Brahegatan. Within a day he was back. Both of them seemed to thrive on the drama and tumult they created for themselves

As far as Strindberg was concerned, the image that he had always had of Harriet as a childlike creature was now becoming something of an *idée fixe*. In his attempts to reconcile himself to the fact that he had lost her as a potentially equal marriage partner he turned her into an icon and an object of worship. He enlarged a photograph of her as Puck – the role she had been playing when he had first become so attracted to her – and kept the picture where he could see it while he worked. Thus she turned permanently into a captivating mythical spirit, forever charming and ethereal – and forever juvenile. He was fully aware of this and on 28 September he wrote and told her what he had done:

> To me you were not a human being, but an apparition ... your fair little good spirit brightened up my darkness and when I now see the picture of Puck here above the 'troll' flowers I see a kind child who wants to play 'troll' and be horrible but cannot.
> When I saw your regal beauty – on the beach – I trembled at my arrogance at having dared desire you, and I feared that the world, the whole world must have envied me. It was too much for me ... I was ashamed and became scared.
> How could I be so stupid as to believe that you loved me? It was my 'hubris' and I was punished by the most horrible visions.

A few days later Harriet agreed to return to Karlavägen. She and Strindberg celebrated by going out to dinner and his entry in his diary for 5 October tells the story: 'Harriet back in again --- light. God be praised!' He immediately went out and purchased another piano for her (significantly a small upright rather than a grand) and she showed her appreciation by playing the music of his favourite composers – Grieg, Beethoven, Schumann, Mendelssohn and Peterson-Berger.

As Strindberg had always hoped, Harriet's return was perhaps in part prompted by the prospect of the role of Kristina, the powerful seventeenth-century Swedish Queen in the play that he had just completed, and that of Indra's Daughter in *A Dream Play*, the drama that he was currently working on. And there was also her own *Swanwhite* still waiting to be done. To be pregnant and yet to have such tantalizingly wonderful roles dangled in front of her was frustrating for Harriet but whenever she grew irritable Strindberg kept her spirits up by promising her that Indra's Daughter would be the role of a lifetime. And so it proved, though not until 1907, by which time he and Harriet were divorced.

During her pregnancy, Harriet and Strindberg amused themselves at home, playing chess and entertaining friends. All was well for a while. At Strindberg's suggestion Harriet took up modelling in clay as a way of passing the time. She protested that she had no talent but Strindberg bought her all the necessary materials and urged her to make a small statue of herself as Puck, which she did. When it was finished he was so pleased with it that he had eight copies of the figure cast in bronze and presented them as gifts to friends.

He also encouraged her to read the classics of European literature and to study languages, just as he had done with Siri. Harriet acknowledged that she was indebted to him for the development of her literary tastes:

> I read among others Balzac, Maeterlinck (Strindberg was so keen on Maeterlinck that he amused himself by translating one chapter from *Le trésor des humbles*, and dedicated it to me), Zola, Gorky, Emerson, Kipling, Kielland. Bjørnson's *Fortaellinger* [*Stories*] I already knew and loved! [. . .]
>
> With endless patience he watched over my languages – it was his plan that I should not stay in Sweden as an actress – I was to get out, preferably learn German in order to get into a German environment. Strindberg's letters to Schering also demonstrate that he made an effort in trying to place me in a German theatre company. However, I liked it at Dramaten, I was offered parts that I enjoyed there and I had nothing to complain about. [. . .]
>
> While I was expecting little Anne-Marie, Strindberg was kind and considerate towards me all the time.
>
> *Strindberg's Letters to Harriet Bosse*

Throughout the autumn and winter the couple achieved a certain degree of harmony. When Strindberg noticed that the smell of tobacco made

Strindberg started to write a long poem dedicated to Harriet and called 'Trefaldighetsnatten' ['On the Eve of Trinity Sunday'] shortly after he married her in 1901. He reworked it over the following year and then sent her the first completed version at Midsummer in 1902, not long after their daughter, Anne-Marie, was born. After that he revised it again and translated it into German. He always compared the poem to a Beethoven sonata, and it charts his relationship with Harriet, from radiant bride to hissing Gorgon. 'Trefaldighetsnatten' incorporates the famous poem 'Chrysaëtos', in which he describes his despair when Harriet left him after their honeymoon (the title 'Chrysaëtos' – 'Golden Eagle' in Greek – is a reference to the quill-feather that Harriet plucked from her hat and gave to Strindberg at the beginning of their relationship) and 'I Dreamt . . .' completes the picture of disillusionment.

I Dreamt . . .

I dreamt that
I looked at the wretched clothes
On my body – and my crutches . . .
Like a wounded crow I seemed . . .
With my legs dangling under the wing.
I was so ashamed, I cried . . . a door opened
And from the drawing-room a woman entered;
It was the woman from the stairs . . .
But dressed as a bride, radiant with youth,
Beauty, goodness, childish charm.
She offered me her hand, telling me with her eyes:
Now you are mine and I am yours.
I knelt and realized for a moment
How wretched, how helplessly wretched I was.
Unworthy of a woman's love.
She smiled and asked me to rise.
I rose and – there I was, young and healthy,
A cripple no more!
[. . .]

I sat at table with my bride.
Everything was pleasing, and we made up words
And thoughts together and passed them on.
I found myself sparkling with wit,
At times we rose on wings of thought.
Sometimes we sought the depths, the essence of matter;
The world and nature, obscure human destinies
We grasped as from an open book . . .
It was a marriage of two souls.
However, I mentioned that she was perfect
In manners and style, not least in dress.
And yet – in all her beauty there was a tastelessness
Which always annoyed me.
There was a piece of ribbon on her right shoulder,
I restrained myself for a long time
But suddenly, in the course of a conversation,
I could not steer my hand any longer
I seized the ribbon without thinking,
Without malice . . .
But then, at once, my bride was transformed,
Her face as cruel as the Gorgon's,
Where every line became a little serpent,
Was revealed when she was demasked.
And in a voice, hoarse from keeping late hours
She hissed:
I see, you're pedantic
And find faults where you ought to adore.
No, I answered, but I want you perfect
And if I see a stain I want to take it out.
And she: You stain remover, you
Go home. If I don't please you
I can find others.

Harriet feel ill, for example, he stopped smoking for several weeks and thereafter always kept his cigarettes locked away in the 'poison cupboard' in the hall. Their tastes and opinions on everything except the theatre were seldom compatible but somehow they managed to reach a compromise for a while. Strindberg had bought a lot of new furniture for the apartment, which Harriet dismissed as old-fashioned. However, they did have separate bedrooms (just as Strindberg and Siri had done) and Harriet was able to express her own taste more personally in hers, which was decorated in yellow and green. Strindberg often referred to it as 'the yellow room'.

During this time Strindberg began painting again, something that he had not done since he left Paris in 1896. Rather like Siri (though definitely unlike Frida, who always had an eye for the avant-garde in art), Harriet never showed any true appreciation of Strindberg's pictures. Even later, when she was much older and came to write the commentary to the published letters, she describes them in a somewhat dismissive way. Neither did she fully appreciate his interest in Eastern religions, which was beginning to filter more and more into his dramatic writings. *A Dream Play* incorporates elements of Buddhism, which he had begun to study many years before and which had continued to interest him during the time that he was in contact with Frida's mother. On 18 November he had noted in his diary:

> Am reading about Indian religions.
> The whole world is just an illusion (=Nonsense or comparable insignificance). The divine primordial power (Maham-Atma, Tad, Aum, Brahma) allowed himself to be seduced by Maya or the productive power. Hereby this divinity sinned against itself (love is a sin: that is why the agonies of love is the greatest hell there is). So the world only exists because of a sin, if it exists at all, that is – because it is only a dream picture. (That is why my Dreamplay is a picture of life), a phantom which it is the task of asceticism to annihilate. But this task clashes with the love instinct, and the end result is a constant wavering between lust and penitence: This seems to be the answer to the riddle of life!

On 25 March 1902, Annunciation Day, their baby daughter was born; she was named Anne-Marie after Harriet's mother. Harriet's sisters Inez and Dagmar were in attendance at what proved to be a long labour. When Strindberg repeated his assertion that childbirth was a naturally pleasurable experience for a woman, Inez and Dagmar made sure that he could hear Harriet crying and screaming, and whenever he closed the bedroom door they opened it again. The power of suggestion might have worked with his second wife but it definitely had no effect on his third.

It did not take long for Harriet to feel totally trapped. She was not prepared for the responsibilities of motherhood and although Strindberg never explicitly said that he wanted her to stay at home she sensed an underlying pressure to do so. He was proud of her talent as an actress and always actively helped and encouraged her to develop a career and yet he wanted a model wife and mother too.

It was the same contradictory message that he sent out to all of his wives: they should be both seductive and maternal, part devil and part angel – in a mixture that suited him. Siri and Frida had these elements in abundance and so did Harriet. The trouble was: how could they ever get the balance right? His first two wives had not cared to master the skills of homemaking while they were married to Strindberg and Harriet was the same; the difference with his third marriage was that he had reached a stage in his life where he had developed daily routines for his work and had no interest in socializing for the sake of it and chasing after new experiences. His bohemian days were over. 'It was mainly the great difference in age that separated us,' Harriet acknowledged years later. 'The fact that Strindberg had lived his life, was finished with a great deal of things that I had not even started.' With hindsight she admitted that if she had been less impetuous and less stubborn about her own desire for independence the marriage might have worked. At the time, however, she was not prepared to consider such compromises.

At the beginning of July Harriet moved out of the apartment and took Anne-Marie to Räfsnäs near Mariefred on Lake Mälaren. Strindberg missed her and the baby and did not know when, if ever, they were going to return to him. He kept in touch by letter:

> 4th July 1902:
> At first it was calm like after an earthquake with thunderbolts --- but then it became too calm, and I missed the tripping steps of your little soul on the floors, and I missed the doors that were left open, and most of all perhaps the little cries from the nursery. [. . .]
> What did we fight about? About retaining our separate personalities when it seemed as if we were going to blend into one. You had the upper hand, because you had friends – I was completely alone, enchanted by you and the Little One.

Strindberg's letters kept arriving at Räfsnäs throughout the summer, sometimes with romantic poems enclosed, all of them dedicated to Harriet. She was no doubt wary of this kind of sentimental flattery for she could not possibly have lived up to his portrayal of her as the ideal woman. An astute reader will also pick up on the fact that some of his descriptions could equally well have referred to Siri or Frida as well as Harriet.

Strindberg's poem 'The Dutchman' is part of a play fragment (published posthumously) called The Flying Dutchman, *based on the legend of the sea captain who is doomed to sail around the world in eternity. Every seven years he is allowed ashore to seek redemption through the love of a woman. In this poem the Dutchman, who has been rescued after being shipwrecked, meets his mother. He tells her about his bitter experiences with women and how he has been married six times without finding true love. When he sees Lilith he praises her beauty in a 'Hymn to Womanhood'. Strindberg sent this to Harriet in July 1902.*

The Dutchman
At the Sight of Lilith

What is it? Who is it?
A human child in white veils,
A chorus of harmonious lines
Which can be glimpsed under the veil.
A whole universal system in miniature,
A picture of the Great Cosmos!
Look at the large parabola of the hip. Like a comet's orbit,
Which leads into imagined solar systems, not yet known . . .
She turns round and at once I notice
The same lines, changed into half-ellipses,
As those which form the earth's orbit round the sun,
And together they create the egg,
From whose focal point the womb's radius emanates.
From the shoulders to the groin is inscribed
The holy hexagram,
The marvellous Orion in the universe
Where the Belt is marked through the navel . . .
[. . .]
Thus you were created by heavenly light, Woman,
– an image of the Creator in his Creation –
Of fragments borrowed from the Universe,
That is why you are everything!

> All-giver,
> Without whom I am nothing!
> But, child of heaven! From the earth,
> From all the kingdoms in nature
> The fine stuff was made,
> For your spirit to dwell in.
> [. . .]
> Oh, even I have rested in the shade of curls
> At a mother's breast and a wife's bosom
> Once – they were fair, light
> Like the tender shoots of a spring birch;
> Once – they were black like cypresses;
> Like scourges plaited by slender snakes
> They hit me in the eyes;
> And were woven into a hair shirt
> Which I had to wear while I starved!
> Oh, kindly scourge . . . .

By the end of the summer Harriet was ready to return to Stockholm and take up where she had left off a year before at Dramaten. She acted in nine productions over the next eight months. Once she was working again she was able to push the difficulties in her marriage to the back of her mind and was much happier. She appeared in *Karl XII* from 21 August, followed by Jerome K Jerome's *Miss Hobbs* in September, Strindberg's *Samum* in October and *Much Ado About Nothing* in November. Between January and April 1903 she was in *War in Peace* (a comedy by Gustav von Moser and Franz von Schönthan), Ibsen's *The Wild Duck*, Goethe's *Egmont* and a comedy by Giacosa.

While Harriet was at the theatre, Strindberg spent his evenings at home, occasionally inviting friends over for the musical soirées that he always enjoyed. With nine plays still waiting for a production, and after the two extremely successful years of 1899–1901, he felt his waning popularity with the theatre producers very keenly. He resumed his correspondence with Leopold Littmansson, whose wife had just died. 'When real life betrays you,' he wrote in his letter of condolence, 'you can always make a new existence, like I have done when I got fed up with myself.' He also tried to rekindle Littmansson's interest in the idea of the artists' retreat. 'When shall we build our Fridhem ['Home of Peace'] and cultivate the soil and philosophize (non-denominational) in the evenings?'

Harriet took a break in May 1903 and she and Anne-Marie spent two and a half months in a rented a cottage on Blidö in the Stockholm archipelago. Apart from a brief visit to see them, Strindberg stayed at home. Harriet returned to the city in August and she formalized their separation by taking a furnished apartment on Biblioteksgatan. Strindberg was not far away and they continued to see each other regularly, especially on Sundays, when they would have a family dinner together. Harriet employed a nanny, and Anne-Marie would also stay with her Aunt Inez (now a widow with a twelve-year-old son) or with Strindberg, who was never without a maid during these years. It was an arrangement that suited Harriet well. She had her independence and did not have to ask her husband's permission to go out. Strindberg was less comfortable with this compromise and he often complained of loneliness, but at least he had the pleasure of watching his daughter growing up, something that had been denied him with Kerstin.

The visits continued throughout the winter. On Strindberg's birthday in January 1904 Harriet turned up with a bouquet of red roses for him. The next day they quarrelled. And so it went on. For Harriet as well as for Strindberg, divorce seemed the only possible solution to the emotional scenes of the past three years that had exhausted them both. However, they continued to make love and the fear of another pregnancy seems to have added to their anxieties, as Strindberg noted more than once in his diary.

— Chapter 20 —

Strindberg as Childminder

> When I saw Harriet's beauty which sometimes could be sublime I trembled. When Harriet was in our apartment it was literally light; when she left it became dark, literally, not figuratively speaking.
>
> *The Occult Diary*

In May 1904 Harriet had a mental breakdown. In need of a rest, away from the theatre and her family, she spent three weeks in a sanatorium outside Stockholm, during which time the preliminary divorce papers were signed. Strindberg acknowledged her restlessness and in an undated letter from this period he tried to warn her against the folly of chasing after happiness:

> You have been seeking happiness, away from me. Have you found it? Do you think happiness exists unalloyed, or do you think it has a price? It is bought with suffering and sacrifices but can be so intense that one can live on the memory of it for several years. The memory of one Sunday morning still keeps me alive.

On 1 June Harriet travelled on her own to Paris, leaving two-year-old Anne-Marie in Strindberg's care. While she was away, she reflected on their decision to get divorced. 'I loved Strindberg,' she wrote later, 'but I stuck to my freedom.' She was no longer prepared to 'live in a cage'. Strindberg meanwhile took Anne-Marie to a house called Isola Bella on Furusund, where, with the help of his two maids, Ellen and Sigrid, he slipped easily into the role of the devoted father.

He looked after Anne-Marie for most of that summer and consequently father and daughter developed a close bond. They went on walks together by the sea and had long conversations. Strindberg indulged the child's every smallest wish except for one: he was afraid of dogs and he refused to let her have a puppy. His letters to Harriet are full of news of their daily doings and his own delight in Anne-Marie's company:

> 8 June
> She is kind, never cries, is affectionate and cuddly. When life is hard she smiles and has conversations with me; and her warm little hand guides me across the stones, the way forward. She seems to have come to terms with life and does not fear the awful

people. She makes friends herself, preferably with grown-ups. The pharmacist is her good friend, and she introduced herself to a German the other day. Sigrid cannot explain which language they were speaking to each other.

Strindberg was not even prepared to disrupt his routine in order to welcome Harriet back to Stockholm some three weeks later, as he explained in a letter to her:

> 18th June 1904
>
> It was my intention to meet you in town but I didn't want to abandon my post at Baby's side. She is so used to me now that she hates being with the maids. I shall dismiss Ellen whenever you want me to. Or as soon as she is rude to you.
> I have warned her.
> Our lilac trees are waiting for you and for Midsummer! [. . .]
> The Little One has had a tummy ache but Sigrid helped her by giving her some massage, and it worked immediately. Now she is well and we have changed our diet

Harriet joined them on Furusund for a few weeks in July before going to Finland on tour. Moved by Strindberg's caring attitude, she was able to relax and enjoy her daughter too and forget about the forthcoming divorce. It was another idyllic summer vacation, like so many that Strindberg had enjoyed in the archipelago, and Harriet later described this as the most peaceful period of her marriage.

The letter that Strindberg wrote on 7 July to his friend, the painter Richard Bergh, shows him in a carefree mood;

> Here I am at Isola Bella with wife and child, sailing boat, bath-house, pike fishing, perch rods, opera terrace and sunshine, just like in the fairest of summer days that I have experienced. C'est la vie, quoi, as long as it lasts. I know nothing about tomorrow, even less about the autumn. I take one day at a time (carpe diem) like the almanac.

As he had always done when away for the summer, Strindberg entertained family and friends and there were boat trips, parties and musical evenings. He had patched up his quarrel with Anna and Hugo by this time and they had joined him for a while on the island, staying in a rented property nearby. When he wrote to Bergh again a month later his tone is just as upbeat and betrays no hint of the discord between him and Harriet that led to him leaving Furusund on his own and without warning the very next day:

> 8 August
> The summer is coming to a close. Everything is repeated and recurs again. Last Saturday my wife and I were entertaining the whole family Philp for supper. The atmosphere was brilliant. Philp made a speech and was very youthful. Not one

disharmonious note. What do you think of that? Music, flowers, wine, speeches, young people, beauty . . . and then it was over. But before then we had had some evenings on the terrace with Carmen music, one dinner and one supper at the Philps' and an unforgettable game of bowls, which ended with a race at night (I held the record).

C'est la vie, quoi? It is possible that this too will be repeated before summer is over. Que sais-je?

The reason for his abrupt departure is not clear and unusually for him he has left no clues in *The Occult Diary*, nor in any of his letters from this period. There is just a hint, as the critic Barbro Ståhle-Sjönell has pointed out, in an outline that Strindberg wrote for his next novel, *The Roofing Party*:

Bang – and they are enemies. Philp makes a speech for Harriet and me. Bang – we part – and Henry is her knight in shining armour. Bang – and he is her enemy --- I and Harriet part, but we get together again. Ellen returns. Philp and Anna and Märtha are reconciled.

Ståhle-Sjönell's theory is that Harriet and Strindberg quarrelled because she had accused him of having an affair with Ellen, the maid; and, although he had denied this, Harriet decided to pay him back by allowing not only Anna and Hugo's son, Henry, to flirt with her, but their daughter Märtha's fiancé, Hugo Fröding, as well.

Once the holiday was over, so was the marriage, finally and irrevocably, as far as Strindberg was concerned, as he explained in a letter to Bergh on 14 September:

Quite so; it came to an end. It was only magic lantern pictures that I gave you from Furusund. Changing pictures, dissolving views. But isn't the whole of life like that? Two minutes of bliss for thirty days of torture. That is the price.

The impending divorce did not stop Strindberg from writing to Harriet while she was away in Finland. Once again his letters are full of reports on Anne-Marie's progress and he describes the everyday events in her life with obvious warmth and pride. He records her likes and dislikes, every tummy ache and minor upset. 'She is not happy,' he wrote in one letter. 'She probably misses you, but doesn't say anything, is only thoughtful. In the afternoons she is down at the large sandpit; in the mornings she is with Auntie Inez.'

Harriet's tour abroad was a great success; she was fast becoming a major celebrity, guaranteed to bring the audiences in. She was thoroughly professional and had a reputation for hard work and total reliability that had earned her the respect of her fellow actors as well as the theatre management. By this time she had negotiated an exceptionally high salary of 6000 kronor a year (plus a 1000 kronor clothes allowance) at a time when the standard wage for a factory worker was about 800 kronor a year and the average annual income for unmarried women was around 330 kronor.

The director of the Svenska Teatern in Helsingfors at that time was Corny Wetzer. He was an exacting man, who insisted that all his actors use 'rikssvenska' – the received pronunciation for Swedish – rather than the lilting accent that most Swedes in Finland spoke. Harriet got on very well with him and they developed a good working relationship that lasted until 1916 when he left the Svenska Teatern.

Wetzer often selected the same plays that Harriet had done in Stockholm the previous season and in 1904 he chose to open with *War in Peace* on 1 September, followed by *A Venetian Comedy* by Per Hallström, *The Wild Duck*, *To Damascus* (Part I) and *Romeo and Juliet*. Her leading man was a popular young actor called Gunnar Wingård but there was another Gunnar – Gunnar Castrén – who became her close friend and confidant (and some say her lover) while she was in Finland. Castrén was an academic and literary critic and he reviewed several of the plays that Harriet appeared in at the Svenska Teatern. He praised her graceful gestures and fine voice from the beginning and he was a great help to her in her career.

It was during this trip to Finland that Harriet first acted with Strindberg's daughter Greta, who had been working at the Svenska Teatern for four years. There is no record of how they got on and it is not known either whether Siri went to the theatre to see the plays that they appeared in together.

In *The Occult Diary* Strindberg refers to a letter that he received from Harriet while she was away, in which she said that she was willing to give up the theatre and stay with him – a sacrifice that he had in fact never asked her to make. This letter has not survived and it seems uncharacteristic of her, unless it was a desperate last-minute offer to save the marriage. It was in any case too late, for Strindberg had already instructed his lawyers to press on with the divorce, which finally came through on 27 October.

Back in Stockholm, Harriet reverted to the old routine again with her daughter and ex-husband almost as though the divorce had never happened. Strindberg's sister Anna moved in with him for a month or so after a serious row with her husband and Harriet took a new apartment on Stureparken, about a mile away from Karlavägen. Her relationship with Strindberg was friendly and relaxed. They saw each other regularly and they remained lovers. Harriet still took Anne-Marie to see him for

Sunday dinner and after the meal she would play the piano for him and they would discuss their work. He was, as always, willing to use his influence in order to help her professionally and wrote to all his friends in the theatre, telling them what a good actress she was and seeking out openings for her. And he continued to urge her to polish up her German so that she would be ready to work abroad if the opportunity arose.

On the surface they had organized an amicable and civilized way of life for themselves. Each was busy working and their daughter was a source of pride and pleasure to them both. On the other hand, it is clear that they still needed each other to help them through the bouts of melancholia that they were both prone to. They still cared about each other and the bond remained strong.

Strindberg's sister Elisabeth died in the mental hospital in Uppsala on 10 December that year. 'She was like my twin, and when she died we thought it was for the best,' he wrote to Harriet. 'I just wanted to show you "the Easter girl" who suffered for others, but took other people's misfortunes upon her so that she could not be really good.' He sent Harriet a photograph of Elisabeth with the letter.

Strindberg's *Occult Diary* is full of the dreams and fantasies that he was still having about Harriet. He was convinced of the power of telepathy between them and on 19 December he wrote to her:

> I sense in my daytime thoughts and my dreams at night that you are not happy, as if the world and the people in it torment you; and you often seek me. Is that so? If I can advise and comfort you, you know that you can have my company whenever you want to; for I am just as close to you as before, you and the Little One. No one has managed to prise you out, any of you, both of whom I have the most beautiful memories of from your home at Biblioteksgatan.
>
> Can you not feel that I am with you and wish you well? I wish you all the best . . . even though you deserted me.

He spent Christmas Eve (the most important night of the festive season in Sweden) with her and Anne-Marie, together with her sister Inez and nephew Alf; and on 1 January he wrote a letter thanking her, addressing her as 'Beloved'.

In the spring of 1905 Strindberg negotiated a contract with a new publisher, Henrik Koppel of Ljus förlag, for both volumes of *Getting Married* to be issued in a cheap edition priced at just 1 krona a copy. He was paid 1200 kronor for the first printing of 10,000 copies and this title was the first of several to be published in this format over the next five years; because the books were so inexpensive, Strindberg's plays and novels now reached a wider readership than ever before.

Harriet and Strindberg spent their fourth wedding anniversary on 6 May together but neither of them records the significance of the date. They were still arguing, often about trivial things, as Strindberg had noted in *The Occult Diary* a few months before (on 1 February): 'Went to see Harriet in the evening. A big quarrel about a *dinner service*!'

On 24 June Strindberg wrote once more to Emil Schering to ask him whether he could find anything suitable for Harriet:

> She speaks German perfectly, in a way I could never learn; I mean the pronunciation; her grammar is flawed, but it is just a question of a part. No wonder, since her father was German! But she had the fixed idea that she could not, because like all Scandinavians she preferred French until she visited Paris last year! There she discovered the misery!
>
> Now she has been taking regular lessons in pronunciation the whole winter and reads novels and plays in German.

The summer was a lonely period for them both. Harriet decided to take Anne-Marie to Hornbaek in Denmark where she and Strindberg had stayed shortly after they were married. Strindberg opted for Täckholmen on Furusund in the archipelago. It is significant that he regarded Furusund as his 'honeymoon island' and he urged Harriet to come and join him:

> 7th July 1905
> Harriet
> If I am wrong about my feelings yet again, I will still risk it!
>
> Where are you? Are you happy? Have you forgotten? Are you unhappy? Shall I help you?
>
> I am sitting on our honeymoon island, the most beautiful, purest, calmest place I have seen. Like a nest for seagulls where one can hide.
>
> No shortage of money or comfort, but it is joyless. I am not such an egoist as they say because I can't enjoy myself without company.
>
> Alone, everything in abundance, but maybe you are short of money. But I cannot share from a distance.
>
> If you want to get away from people then this is the hiding place. You have the sea, houses, people but no one can see you.
>
> Send a word by telegraph if you want to come northwards. Täckholmen is big, like a big hug and friendly!

Nine days later he wrote again, nostalgic for the good times they had had together and telling her that he could only remember the beautiful things about her, even 'those loving words' that she had uttered when they had parted at the beginning of the summer.

Strindberg did not spend his time on Furusund in complete solitude, however. The letter that he wrote to Harriet on 30 July seems to have made her jealous because he describes a lively evening he had spent in the company of some friends who worked in the theatre:

> Last Thursday I was invited to the Svennbergs. I had not expected such a cosy home with a 'Japanese' garden behind the house.
>
> Mrs S. is beautiful with a soulful transparent face – she was gentle and gracious.
>
> The sister-in-law Mrs Olga (H-m) was there. They did not have any servants; the husband and wife took turns in the kitchen; it was peaceful and charming until dawn; we parted at half past six.
>
> Mrs Olga is not beautiful; the sister so much more so. Mrs O was sad, looked as if she had been through a lot, not bitter, but suffering, but she tried to conceal it.
>
> Last Saturday they came to me in the evening; I value (as you know) the ladies' company, because it neutralizes masculine coarseness and forces one to suppress – yes we call it that – our bad sides. One seeks out the best in oneself and dresses up as if for a party. The mood is familiar, educated, watchful. In other words pleasant!

In his letter of 4 August Strindberg is quick to allay Harriet's fears that he was attracted to either of these women, pointing out in an almost fatherly way the absurdity of her reaction. He was merely describing a lively social occasion that he had enjoyed:

> The invisible ones, the absent friends, for whom one usually raises a toast, were sitting at the table; we sensed their presence and the party was, seemingly, for them.
>
> But we did not express any longing to meet up again. And will probably never meet again, they and I. That was all! [. . .]
>
> We are quarrelling by post like an old married couple. And surely you don't demand that I live absolutely alone, since you don't.
>
> It is lovely here, rainy and cold!

Harriet stayed away from Furusund that summer and when it was time to return to work she decided not to go back to Dramaten. She was disappointed with the roles they were proposing and after her previous success in Finland she thought that she could do better by going freelance. Accepting an offer from the director Victor Castegren at the Stora Teatern in Gothenburg, she left Stockholm in September, leaving Anne-Marie once again in Strindberg's care. When she arrived, however, she discovered that the roles that Castegren had in mind were no more challenging than the ones she had turned down at Dramaten. Feeling depressed, she turned to Strindberg for advice. He told her to leave the company and return to Stockholm if she wanted to and suggested that maybe she should take a year off and recuperate at a health spa. If she decided to stay, she should let him know if she needed any money; he also recommended a certain doctor in Gothenburg who might help her to calm her nerves and warned her against another one who was 'on the brink himself and able to make a sane person insane'. Harriet decided to stick it out for a little longer and Strindberg tried to cheer her up by writing to her about Anne-Marie, who was happy to spend all day painting pictures like her father:

> 17th September 1905
> My dear friend
> Anne-Marie is asleep, the Unknown One on the ground floor is playing E minor; Rosa is left behind on my sofa with her eyes open and a scarlet dress on. (Rosa was introduced to Henning Berger yesterday when he came here for a whisky hour.) The house is quiet, both Ebba and Sarah are quiet people . . .
>
> But outside the window I can see the moon above the Gustav Adolf church, Venus under the Pleiades across Lidingön and Capella (that is your star, remember). The whole day I have been living in a kind of blissful rapture as if an unknown happiness has hit me. I am released from the coal mines of Swedish History, feel that I have arrived at the present hour again which is the best of all times, because all past is the trough in which the present should grow.
>
> What is going to happen now? Wonderful time present, I answer.
>
> If I had a pension I would write idylls and pastoral poems. If you were here I would write monologues for you. Or adapt *Macbeth* and Schiller's *Maria Stuart* etc. into monologues.

Harriet stayed on in Gothenburg and one day, towards the end of September, she received a letter from Strindberg outlining his plans to start a small theatre company that would tour around Scandinavia. He had spent the previous night talking until six in the morning with a group of enthusiastic young writers and they had encouraged him in his idea of taking charge of his own destiny since he had been unable to find a producer in Sweden willing to put on any of his plays since February 1902, when Dramaten had done *Karl XII*.

Strindberg wanted Harriet to come back to Stockholm straight away and help him with the project. She, of course, would be the company's leading player and they would do Shakespeare and Schiller and pieces that he would write specially for her. All they needed were two more actors and some starting capital. Strindberg had been through all this before, of course, and it is ironic that he should try to woo Harriet back with exciting schemes of working together with their own company when their marriage was over – just as he had done in similar circumstances with Siri.

Harriet does not appear to have taken Strindberg's plans seriously and by this time she was beginning to enjoy herself, having won over the Gothenburg audiences – and the critics. 'She came, she saw and she conquered,' wrote one enthusiastic reviewer in the city's leading newspaper, *Handelstidningen*, of her performance in Gustav Wied's *The First Violin*.

She was not ready to return to Stockholm just yet, as is evident from Strindberg's letter to her of 1 October:

> Anne-Marie is now a big girl, she teaches me how to speak Swedish.
>
> Daddy must not say yees, but yes. She has also informed me that my hair is green.
>
> She longs for her mummy to come and play with her and hold her hand at night.
>
> At the moment she is invited by the kind Gustaf Jansson to play with his two little boys whom she has been introduced to on the stairs.
>
> She has also made the acquaintance of a little Hervor, the three-year-old daughter of a Captain Lindström at 1, Svea Träng, here at Karlavägen.
>
> Your daughter is kind and obedient, I never hear any screams from the corridor. But she does not love porridge, and since she is healthy and must eat, she is given other food, but not smörgåsbord.
>
> *The Dance of Death* is playing in Germany and is, reportedly, a success. Is now touring from Cologne to Leipzig and Berlin etc. [. . .]
>
> How long will you be staying in Gothenburg?
> Your friend
> August Sg

Harriet told him that she was thinking about going straight to Germany and Austria to look for work, which did not please him at all. He made sure that she knew how much Anne-Marie was looking forward to seeing her again and what effect her absence was having on them:

> 29th October
> The Little One and I have waited for you since last Saturday. She is counting on her fingers five, seven, ten, eight days. And she has already composed the menu: flower buds with butter (artichokes), big crayfish (lobster) – and mummy shall sit on her big chair which no one has been allowed to sit on since she went away.
>
> Today the Little One has been invited out to dinner; 'elle dine en ville' (at Mrs M.). She is very interested in Daddy's portrait and Uncle B misses her little tripping steps across the drawing room when she is away. She always stops so politely in the green room and asks from there: 'May I come in?' She never rushes straight in.

One of the additional reasons for Strindberg's impatience was the difficulty he was having with the childcare arrangements for Anne-Marie. In the middle of September he had sacked Ellen, the nanny who had been with them for a couple of years, because he thought she did not play enough with the child and did not wash her and comb her hair properly. He then employed a new nanny, Sarah, to be followed after a few weeks by Elin. He clearly found the whole business of hiring and firing servants distasteful.

Harriet finally came home on 6 November, though she did not stay for long. After two weeks she left for Berlin with Strindberg's blessing. The fact that she was already contracted to the Svenska Teatern in Stockholm did not deter her. Her reputation was such that she was in a good bargaining position and she reckoned that she could negotiate better terms on her salary, clothing allowance, share of box-office receipts and choice of repertoire abroad.

In the meantime Strindberg had decided that he would give up the apartment on Karlavägen because it was too big and too expensive for him on his own. While he made the arrangements to move out, Anne-Marie went to stay with Inez.

Harriet returned just before Christmas and a few months later she received an offer of a five-year contract from the Hebbel Theater in Berlin. To her dismay, however, Albert Ranft at the Svenska Teatern would not release her and so she had no option but to stay in Sweden. It was probably just as well for having struggled to perfect her Swedish accent she was not yet that proficient in German and, as it turned out, the director of the Hebbel Theater who had hired her, died a few months later, which would have made her position in the company even more insecure. Furthermore, Ranft was paying her a salary of 10,000 kronor a year, which was a huge sum at that time. In spite of the setback, Strindberg still urged her to seek work in Germany and suggested that he should rent an apartment there for her and Anne-Marie, with servants to take care of them, and so live together as a family again.

Although Harriet maintained a separate apartment for herself and Anne-Marie she and Strindberg did in effect still function as a married couple. They continued to see each other regularly, Strindberg bought her flowers and champagne and they still made love. To the outsider it would have seemed like the ideal relationship and yet they were divorced. Over Christmas and the New Year Harriet made preparations for another tour of Finland and she remembers this period as a time of tranquillity and harmony:

> Before I went to Helsingfors in the spring of 1906 Strindberg had told me that the royalties for those of his plays which were going to be produced during my guest tour should be handed over to the children by his first marriage who were then living in Finland. I am sure he suffered many times at not being able to help them more generously with money. When circumstances became a bit more tolerable he was the first to help his children.
>
> Strindberg had struggled with financial difficulties practically all his life. It was only just before he died that things looked up. When we got married he thought he

was wealthy – he had just received 6000 kronor from his publisher for one book. He thought this money would never come to an end. If I needed money he was always helpful, and many times when money was short he sold some of his paintings through some friend.

Strindberg very rarely talked about his previous marriages. He did mention Siri von Essen with kindness and affection, though.

Strindberg made me promise never to read *A Madman's Defence* or play Lady Julie, a promise which I have kept.

Strindberg's brother-in-law Hugo von Philp died in January 1906. The two men had not been getting on particularly well for the past five years or so but after his death Strindberg began to revise his opinion somewhat. In his play *The Pelican*, which he wrote a year later, the absent father is more a character to be pitied while the wife, based to a certain extent on his sister Anna, is a demonic mother-figure.

Harriet went back to Finland in March for a six-week tour. By now her box-office appeal meant that she was in a better position to dictate her own terms and conditions and she had started to suggest to Conny Wetzer the classical roles that she wanted to do. Her list of plays at this time included *A Midsummer Night's Dream*, von Hofmannsthal's *Elektra*, Hermann Sudermann's *Johannes*, Oscar Wilde's *Salome*, and *Pelléas and Mélisande* by Maeterlinck. She also made sure that Strindberg was not forgotten and pressed for productions of *To Damascus*, *Swanwhite* and *Kristina*.

Wetzer started her off with *Pelléas and Mélisande* and a revival of *Romeo and Juliet*. She was modest enough to turn down the role of Ellida in Ibsen's *The Lady from the Sea*, claiming that she would need another twenty years before she could do it justice, but she did agree to play Hilde in *The Master Builder*. In addition, Wetzer chose two of Strindberg's plays – *Easter* and the first ever production of *The Crown Bride*. Harriet's leading man in *The Crown Bride* was Gunnar Wingård. It was a huge success with the Finnish audiences and, in a reversal of the usual pattern, Albert Ranft decided to take the play into the repertoire at the Svenska Teatern in Stockholm the following season, with Harriet and Gunnar once again playing the lead.

Strindberg sets the action of *The Crown Bride* in Dalarna, a province in central Sweden that has strong folklore traditions. A young woman from a poor background, Kersti, falls in love with Mats, a rich miller's son. When she becomes pregnant the couple run away to live in the forest. The prospect of an inheritance lures them back to the village where Mats persuades his family to accept Kersti as his bride, though he does not tell them that they now have a baby. However, in order to get married in church she knows she will have to wear a bridal crown as a sign of chastity, so in an act of desperation she kills her child. Filled with remorse, Kersti confesses her crime on her wedding day and is sent to prison, where she later finds peace through Christianity. She is allowed out of prison to go to church and one Easter Sunday she falls through the ice and drowns while crossing a frozen lake. Her death brings redemption and the two families are eventually reconciled.

The Crown Bride comes across today as a rather melodramatic play and Strindberg's use of regional dialect and folk music, and the references to old-fashioned rural practices, limits its appeal to modern audiences. But in 1906 it was something of a triumph and Harriet appeared in several revivals after that, as did Greta Strindberg, for whom the role of Kersti was probably the most important of her career.

Harriet returned to Stockholm from Finland at the beginning of May, having secured a promise from Sibelius that he would compose the music for *Swanwhite*, which had yet to find a producer. She now had romantic links with three men who were all very important to her, both personally and professionally: the actor Gunnar Wingård, the critic Gunnar Castrén and the playwright August Strindberg. And the rumours were beginning to fly.

After a summer holiday with Anne-Marie in Denmark, Harriet returned to work at the Svenska Teatern in Stockholm. Strindberg had started on what were to be his two last major prose works: *The Roofing Party* and *The Scapegoat*. He and Harriet continued to see each other but less regularly than before:

> 5 November 1906
> Have not seen Harriet since 6 October when I withdrew because she was expecting her suitor Dr Castrén and I did not want to be placed on the reserve. Whether he has arrived I do not know.
>
> *The Occult Diary*

Strindberg was in high spirits as the year came to an end. Greta had moved to Stockholm that summer and had been working for the Rönnblad Provincial Touring Company since the autumn. After the many difficulties that she and her father had experienced while she was growing up in Finland, they were now getting on well. She shocked him somewhat when she announced her engagement to her cousin Henry von Philp on 21 December but he quickly came to terms with the idea and gave the couple his blessing. And after what had seemed to him like an eternity cast out into the wilderness, the theatres were once again endorsing him as a dramatist.

By far the most important theatrical contact that Strindberg made in 1906 was with a talented young actor-manager called August Falck, who had put on a powerful production of *Lady Julie* in Lund and Malmö that September. Though the play had been produced in many other countries around Europe, this was the first time that Swedish audiences had had a proper chance to see it.

The energetic twenty-four-year-old Falck gave Strindberg just the impetus he needed to get his plans for a new company of his own off the ground and together the two Augusts set about creating a revolutionary 'intimate theatre'.

— Chapter 21 —

After the Fire

> People and life tried to separate us, in a way, but I think that we shall meet anyway, one day, somewhere else . . .
>
> *Letter to Harriet Bosse, 12 May 1907*

In his entry in *The Occult Diary* for 20 January 1907 Strindberg mentions that Harriet came to see him; in the margin he added later that they went to the yellow room 'for the last time'. From then on he made a conscious effort to rid himself of his obsessive feelings about her. For a start, there were to be no more shared summer holidays. Harriet usually took Anne-Marie to the seaside in Denmark and then on to the country in northern Sweden, where she believed the mountain air was beneficial to the vocal cords, while Strindberg stuck to the familiar places in the Stockholm archipelago. His letters to her continue to show a deep concern for their daughter:

> 19th October 1907
> Harriet,
> Don't let the child stay indoors because of a cough because then she'll be so delicate that she will have to stay indoors the whole winter.
>   I reproach myself every time I 'feel' that she is alone and sad and that is quite often . . .

Three things helped Strindberg to make the final break from Harriet: his own writing, his developing plans for a new theatre and her relationships with other men, most notably Gunnar Castrén and Gunnar Wingård. By way of exorcism he began working on *Thunder in the Air* (also known as *Storm*), the first of his five chamber plays, all of which convey a feeling of disillusionment and resignation. With *Thunder in the Air* especially he wanted, as he later wrote to Harriet, 'to write you and our child out of my heart'. It is the story of a husband, who is called simply the Man, and his ex-wife, Gerda. They have a child, who now lives with Gerda and her second husband. One day Gerda and the child meet the Man unexpectedly. It transpires that she has recently moved into the same apartment block. This encounter brings back painful memories for them both and they rake over the old territory of past disappointments:

> GERDA: Why did you marry me in the first place?
>
> THE MAN: Surely you know why a man wants to get married? You also know that I didn't exactly have to beg for your love. And don't you remember how we both smiled at those busybodies who advised against our union? But why did you tempt me? I've never understood that. Soon after the wedding you didn't even look at me. And even at the reception you behaved as if you were attending someone else's wedding. I thought you might have conspired with my enemies to kill me.

Gerda, like Harriet, is young and spirited and in *Thunder in the Air* Strindberg uses the character to issue a string of reprimands against women as dangerous seducers of men. This play is one of the few works where Strindberg hints at Harriet's infidelities, though he never accused her openly as he had done with Siri in *A Madman's Defence*. Maybe this quiet admission says more about his hurt pride than the exaggerated account he gave of his first marriage:

> THE MAN: I have been dishonoured, you mean?
>
> THE BROTHER: Didn't you know?
>
> THE MAN: What do you mean?
>
> THE BROTHER: Yes, she dishonoured you, when she left . . .
>
> THE MAN: So for the last five years my reputation has been sullied, without my knowing it?
>
> THE BROTHER: Surely you knew?
>
> THE MAN: No, I didn't. When I remarried a young girl, thirty years my junior, I realized that the age difference might become an obstacle one day so, although she consented happily to the marriage, I promised her that I would set her free as soon as my age were to prove a serious problem. Well, our child was born within a decent passage of time and we didn't want any more children.

In an undated letter to Harriet from this period Strindberg makes a final plea for the heartache to end:

> Don't let us meet, it is too painful. This is the seventh year of these eternal goodbyes, have I not suffered enough?
> And I have broken with the world that you are living in, once and for all.
> Let it be finished. Keep to your friends, who are my enemies, but don't come into contact with my destiny any more, I am not taking revenge, but I am shielded as long as I act in the right way.
> Enjoy your freedom which you have desired for so long, I don't want to tie you or be your jail-keeper whom people feel they have a right to kill.
> Farewell!

It was a step in the right direction emotionally, although he stayed in touch because of Anne-Marie and also because Harriet continued to act in some of the plays that he had written specifically for her. Not that he went to the theatre very often any more, even when such legendary actresses as Sarah Bernhardt and Eleonora Duse played in Stockholm. He seldom attended rehearsals of his own productions and, terrified of the critics' response and hypersensitive to the audiences' reaction, he would stand in agony by the telephone at home on opening nights, waiting for someone from the theatre to call and tell him how it was going.

As soon as he had finished *Thunder in the Air* he started work on his second chamber play, *After the Fire*. In February and March he wrote *The Ghost Sonata*, considered by many to be one of his best plays. He was clearly fired up by the prospect of having his own theatre and being in control of how his work was produced:

> If you ask me what does an intimate theatre want, and what is meant by chamber plays, I'll answer like this: In drama we're looking for the meaningful theme but with certain limitations. In the treatment of it we avoid all ostentation and all calculated effects. – The author should not be tied to any specific form because the theme determines the form – so freedom in execution, only restricted by the unity of concept and the feeling of style.
> *Memorandum to the Members of the Intimate Theatre from the Director*

After completing *The Ghost Sonata* Strindberg paused nervously while three other major works came under the scrutinizing eye of the public and the critics: *A Dream Play, Playing With Fire* and his novel *Black Banners*.

Dramaten presented *A Dream Play* – 'my most beloved drama, the child of my greatest pain' as Strindberg described it – on 17 April, with Harriet playing the heroine, Indra's Daughter. They had met sporadically during the rehearsals but Strindberg stayed away on the opening night. It played to mixed reviews, with at least some of the critics acknowledging it as a masterpiece.

Playing With Fire followed on 3 May, achieving its Swedish première some fifteen years after Strindberg had written it. It was presented as an evening's entertainment at the National Restaurant in Stockholm and the Lover was played by Mauritz Stiller, who later gained notoriety for his relationship with Greta Garbo.

As a chamber piece, *Playing With Fire* is intentionally a far less serious play than *A Dream Play* but it added to Strindberg's reputation as a provocative writer and softened the blow when his viciously satirical novel *Black Banners* was published on 29 May by Björck & Börjesson to equally vicious reviews. He had waited three years to find a company brave enough to take the risk of bringing out a book that attacked the establishment of the day in a style worthy of Dickens – and the establishment was not pleased with his cruel caricatures of its most eminent literary figures.

At the beginning of the 1907 autumn season Harriet and Gunnar Wingård recreated the roles of Kersti and Mats in a revival of *The Crown Bride* at the Svenska Teatern in Stockholm. The critics were divided: some thought that it was poorly staged and created an embarrassing atmosphere of affectation and false psychology, while others were full of praise. Bo Bergman, for example, wrote that it contained 'strong and beautiful poetry' and declared it one of Strindberg's finest plays.

Strindberg and Falck were hoping to open their new intimate theatre in September, having signed a rental agreement with the landlord in June. However, they were having trouble getting the financial backing they needed, and the refurbishment was taking longer than planned. Strindberg personally raised about a third of the 60,000 kronor required for the first year's rental by persuading Bonnier's to advance him the money, lodging his manuscript of *The Occult Diary* with them as surety.

By the time Intiman finally opened on 26 November, with Prince Eugen (the son of King Oscar II) in attendance, Strindberg had completed two more chamber plays: *The Pelican* and *The Black Glove*. *The Pelican* is an expressionistic piece about a middle-aged widow with two children. The son, Fredrik, is a student and an alcoholic, and the daughter, Gerda, who has just got married, is frail and neurotic. Gerda's husband starts an affair with the mother, in the mistaken belief that she has inherited some money, and Gerda and Fredrik find a letter that reveals that their mother had also betrayed their father. Fredrik accidentally sets fire to their apartment one day and their mother falls to her death after jumping off the balcony while he and Gerda decide to perish together in the flames. *The Pelican* was chosen for the inaugural production at Intiman and was a sell-out, although the critics were baffled by it; after the row over *Black Banners*, they were naturally inclined to be hostile. They went on to murder all of Strindberg's chamber plays and in desperation he and Falck decided to revive *Lady Julie*. It was a shrewd move and the audiences loved it. Thus emboldened, they added a few of Strindberg's plays from the 1880s to the repertoire, reckoning that after twenty years or so these works would prove to be a little more in tune with public taste than they had been originally.

At the beginning of 1908 they put on *Sir Bengt's Wife*, the play that Strindberg had written with Siri in mind and with which she had had her first real success on stage. After this it was thanks to the Danish critic Otto Borchsensius that the work of Intiman began to be taken seriously. He was in Stockholm to review a production of *Master Olof* at Dramaten and he decided also to go and see Falck's production of *The Bond,* starring Anna Flygare. 'During the course of the evening I forgot completely that I was there to review it,' he wrote, 'and I surrendered to the magic of Strindberg's genius.'

Intiman's first season was further strengthened by the first-ever production of *Kristina* in March, with Manda Björling in the lead. Harriet missed her chance to play this role that Strindberg had promised her because she was still under contract to Albert Ranft at the Svenska Teatern.

On 4 April Harriet announced her engagement to Gunnar Wingård. The news came as a surprise to Strindberg, and to most of her friends as well, for they had expected her to marry Gunnar Castrén. Strindberg responded with good grace and dignity but there is still a great deal of pain and reproach expressed in the letter of congratulation that he wrote to her:

> 8th April 1908
> When you told me last Saturday that you were engaged, I almost knew. But I could not wish you happiness because I don't believe in it, since it doesn't exist. I didn't worry about the child because I believe in God.
>
> I had wanted to say goodbye to you and thank you – in spite of everything – for everything, for the spring months seven years ago, when I, after twenty years of misery, got some sunshine back into my life. But I could not bring myself to write; I had feelings which made me hesitate. Sunday passed, Monday too, in work and quiet resignation. You noticed that I stopped visiting you exactly a year ago for reasons you know. [. . .]
>
> I wish you all the best and I am as ever, despite everything, your friend and your child's friend. [. . .]
>
> Just one thing! Let me have the Little One when you marry! Or do you want me to go far away? Bumping into each other here in the streets would be painful and impure. And the child needs to be protected!
>
> Shall I go away? I think I am a disturbing influence here and from this apartment there are invisible threads which transmit inaudible airwaves which still connect . . .
>
> Our bond is not broken, but it must be cut off . . . or we shall be sullied . . .
>
> You remember our first days, when the auras of other souls disturbed us in their wickedness, destroyed things for us just by thinking of us!
>
> Tell me what you want! But make sure it does not drag us down into obscure abysses before which I tremble. . .
>
> Now the telegram has arrived about your Swanwhite! After all!
>
> Why did you not want to be the one I created for you? I did not pull you down as you said! I don't think so!
>
> One more word, just one. Do not go under! Harriet! If you do I'll cry again at

the transitoriness of everything that is beautiful. . .
Your Swanwhite which you gave to me and I gave to you!

On 10 April, in acknowledgement that their relationship was now formally over, he returned all the letters that Harriet had written to him:

> . . . when you start a new relationship it is customary to return your letters, or burn them. I have read ours and I have had a few solemn hours. These letters contain what is best in us, our souls dressed for Holy days the way our life seldom is. It is not fiction; it is truth; it is not posing; it is not illusions; and if by illusions we mean something unreal, then this is true reality.
>
> This is how it was, not how it appeared to be. Shall I burn this? As a sample I send you some of mine. I have a couple of hundred letters from you, all beautiful, like mine. Not one ugly word, not one ugly thought. You see, my child, in your letters you live and show yourself as the Great Woman I knew you were. If everyday life does not correspond to this self it is because life itself is so ugly and provides such ugly situations.
>
> One's words and one's tongue are so unclean that they cannot express the sublime; what is written on paper is purer. Burning your letters would be like burning you and I can't do that. Tell me what you want me to do with them.

Apparently Harriet did not reply so Strindberg then wrote a second letter, on 3 May, saying that since Albert Ranft had gone away without reaching a decision about doing *Swanwhite* at the Svenska Teatern he had offered it to Falck instead:

> Falck will do it. Ranft knows that; and with a young child of seventeen who looks like you, can smile like you but who is of a melancholy disposition. She is well educated, of good family. Couldn't you, if necessary, adopt her as your pupil, your spiritual child since you do not want to have any mortal children? In that way you could still act the part, but through her.

The seventeen-year-old in question was an aspiring actress called Fanny Falkner and how Harriet responded to this somewhat audacious request from her ex-husband is not known. She was just three weeks away from her wedding to Gunnar Wingård and still Strindberg could not get her out of his soul. He had 'visitations' and vivid erotic dreams about her, which he describes in his *Occult Diary*, and he kept a copy of the letter that he sent to her on 13 May:

> My dear beloved darling friend!
> Your little heart was beating the whole day!
> You are unhappy and seem to be calling out for me!
> Say one word! Only one! I shall answer beautifully. I shall help you out of this! I want to do anything for you, for both of you.
> Just say one word!
> August Sg.

This time Harriet replied straight away:

> 13 May 1908
> You were not going to write – Yes, my heart is beating – all day long – but it is probably just nerves – I have worked too hard this year.
> The banns have already been read twice for me.
> Wish me happiness – I believe in happiness.
> Harriet

Two days later Strindberg sent her a card, telling her that there was an apartment available on the fourth floor at 40 Karlavägen. 'Four rooms and a kitchen etc.' he wrote. 'The rent does not have to be paid.'

After this Strindberg began to suffer from severe stomach pains. He was convinced that Harriet was seeking him in spirit and he wrote desperate entries in his *Occult Diary* about her almost daily 'visitations'. On 21 May he recorded that he had bought a revolver. On Harriet's wedding day, 24 May, he was inconsolable:

> Cried most of the time. Axel came; Nils Andersson came. I accompanied him in a cab to the train. When I got back at half past seven I cried for the Little One, who, I sensed, was missing me. After that Harriet came to me in love; and I showed her with gestures that I have not deserted her; she answered with roses in the mouth! – Fell asleep. Was woken up at midnight and embraced her in infinite love xxx. By then she was married.
>
> *The Occult Diary*

Axel visited Strindberg almost every day after that until things were calmer. On 30 May Strindberg contacted Fanny Falkner and a couple of weeks later she came to the apartment and played some Mendelssohn on the piano for him. Music always had a soothing effect on him and with Fanny's gentle support he gradually managed to regain his sanity. But he could never forget Harriet, who remained for him the goddess of love, his last and most durable muse.

In his book *Fem år med Strindberg* [*Five Years With Strindberg*] August Falck recalls that while they were working together between 1906 and 1911 Strindberg always wanted to know what Harriet was doing and talked about her constantly. He also remembers seeing a portrait of Harriet as Puck hidden behind a curtain in Strindberg's apartment. This secret place was set up like a shrine, where her youthful image acquired the status of a religious icon.

Harriet was pregnant when she married Gunnar Wingård. The couple spent their honeymoon in England and they returned to live in an apartment near the Djurgården. Strindberg gave up taking his daily walks in the park after this as he did not want to risk bumping into her. He went on writing love letters to her, however, and he only stopped doing so when Gunnar threatened to shoot him.

Though Harriet and Gunnar made an attractive couple their marriage seemed ill-fated from the start. Gunnar had financial problems and was reputedly unfaithful to her. They were also professional rivals, both of them ambitious and used to adulation from the public. They appeared in several plays together at the Svenska Teatern and in 1909 they went on tour in Finland. 'Mr Wingård was unaffected, restrained and – in the big scenes – manly and forceful,' wrote one enthusiastic reviewer of their performances in Henry Bernstein's *The Thief*. 'Miss Bosse was gentle and supple, passionately and ruthlessly in love and the demanding second act was very effective thanks to their artistry.'

Even though Harriet was the undisputed prima donna of the Svenska Teatern, she was becoming increasingly dissatisfied with the roles that they offered her, which she considered to be too lightweight. Meanwhile, Dramaten had moved to a new location at Nybroplan and Tor Hedberg, a respected critic and director, had been appointed artistic director there. He announced a repertoire that included Shakespeare, Ibsen and Schiller, and Harriet saw her chance. In the autumn of 1911 she rejoined her old theatre and stayed there for the next seven seasons.

By this time her marriage to Gunnar had broken down. Their son, Bo, born on 9 January 1909, was not yet three years old when Harriet went to Denmark to seek a quick divorce – just as Siri had done when she separated from Carl Gustav Wrangel. The divorce was made absolute in January 1912 and some nine months later Gunnar committed suicide by shooting himself through the heart. Anne-Marie was called home from school and found her mother in bed, shocked and distressed.

Gunnar's funeral on 10 October was an occasion of great public mourning in Stockholm. Extra trams were laid on to get people into the city centre and an enormous crowd – mainly women – followed the cortège to the Northern cemetery. It was a tremendous ordeal for Harriet, particularly as Gunnar's devotees were blaming her for his death. After the burial she waited until the crowd had dispersed and then she placed two pink dahlias on the grave. She no longer had Strindberg to turn to for comfort and advice – he had died in May that year. Each of her children had lost a father and she herself had in effect been twice widowed in the space of a few months.

At the time of Gunnar's death Harriet was in the middle of rehearsals of Hugo von Hofmannsthal's tragedy *Elektra*. On stage almost continuously for two hours, she delivered a performance that drew unanimous praise for its controlled intensity. One critic declared himself 'completely spellbound' and another said her voice sounded 'like silver bells'. And von Hofmannsthal acknowledged that she was one of the best interpreters of the role that he had even seen. The director Olof Molander published a book about Harriet in 1920 and claimed that with Elektra she reached the pinnacle of her career:

> Her eyes are shiny, her voice sounds remote when she beckons to the others to join her in the dance. Again she raises her knee, swings the torch above her head and makes her victory dance in wide circles around the grave. Suddenly, while the wild rhythm is beating, Elektra falls to the ground, consumed with jubilant fervour and dies without a sound, like the ashes from an enormous bonfire.
>
> Harriet, en skiss

According to Adolf Paul, Harriet was 'small, elegant and lovely-looking' and when he visited her at her apartment in Stockholm in 1919 the first thing he noticed on being shown into her drawing room was a portrait of Strindberg hanging on the wall.

Harriet's career and reputation continued to grow until the end of the 1920s, after which time she had to fight off the competition from younger actresses and to accept less money than she had been used to in order to keep working. She was deprived of the security of a regular contract at Dramaten in 1918 and over the next ten years or so was only invited back to make a handful of guest appearances there. Even so, she was able to support her two children and she sent Bo to boarding school from an early age while her sister Inez looked after Anne-Marie when she was working away from home. There were still plenty of producers eager to hire her, though she had to work hard, often doing up to twenty-six performances a month, much of it on tour across the country.

After studying English at a school in Oxford for a year, Anne-Marie got married in 1926 and a year later so did Harriet. Her third husband was the Swedish actor Edvin Adolphson, who was fifteen years her junior. They had first acted together in *Nju* by Osip Dymov at the new Intiman in 1921 and after they married they continued to play opposite one another until Edvin moved into film. Harriet had already appeared in one or two films herself, including an adaptation of Strindberg's play *The Companions* that Adolf Paul had written and produced in Berlin in 1919, but it was a medium that she never really took to. She always found the studio environment too chaotic and noisy and as filming in Sweden was invariably scheduled for the summer months she was reluctant to sacrifice her holidays by the sea and in the mountains.

Harriet had made her first trip to London on her honeymoon in 1908 and after that she went to England regularly. During one of these visits the Swedish Ambassador introduced her to the actor Robert Loraine, who had played the Captain in the first English production of Strindberg's play *The Father* in 1927. He and Harriet discussed doing either *A Dream Play* or *Easter* together but when Loraine was offered work in America the project was abandoned. Harriet never acted in Britain though the Arts Theatre in London offered her the part of Indra's Daughter in 1931. She turned it down because she thought the theatre was too small and they were unable to offer enough rehearsal time.

However, she did play the part of Eleonora in Berlin in November 1930, when the Skandinavisches Theater invited her and her ensemble to give a special one-night performance of *Easter*. The evening was a sell-out and it was a glittering occasion. They played in front of an audience that was mostly made up of representatives from Berlin's diplomatic corps including Anne-Marie's husband, who had travelled from Paris where he worked for the Norwegian Foreign Office.

Harriet's third marriage lasted only a little longer than her first two and one of the problems was the way that the memory of Strindberg and her loyalty to their shared past was still an important feature of her life. She had kept Strindberg's letters but had no intention of ever showing them to anyone and was adamant that they should not be published in her lifetime. Unfortunately, she made the mistake of hinting to Edvin about what was in the letters, saying that people would revise their opinion of Strindberg as a vindictive egotist if only they knew how tenderly he had treated her. Edvin's curiosity was aroused and one day when he was at the bank he opened the safe where the letters were kept. He returned home and started to question Harriet about Strindberg. Did she realize the commercial value of the letters? At this point she became suspicious and Edvin admitted that he had read some of them. Harriet's response to this act of betrayal was to smash a mirror over her husband's head. The couple separated in 1931 and the marriage was dissolved in 1932, the year that Harriet agreed to the publication of the Strindberg letters.

There are two main reasons why Harriet finally decided to allow the letters to be published during her lifetime rather than after her death as she had originally intended. Primarily, it must be said, she needed the money as her earning power was diminishing and she was worried that she would not have enough to live on in her old age. Secondly, she allowed herself to be convinced by various people – friends as well as scholars — that she had a moral obligation to release the letters, not only in the interest of academic research but also to shed new light on Strindberg's character and to present a more balanced view of his reputation as a misogynist. One of the most persuasive of these people was Harriet's close friend Jenny Bergqvist-Hansson, who argued that the general public had a right to know what the real Strindberg was like. She was married to the director of the publishing house Natur & Kultur and this was the company that Harriet chose.

In *Strindberg's Letters to Harriet Bosse* Harriet adds a commentary, which fills in the background to the correspondence. In the foreword to the book she said:

> Why write all these books about a great man? Why not just stick to his writing or at least to the writer, rather than unearth the innermost secrets in a human being?
>
> Whatever the answer, the fact remains: the general public believe that they have a right to research and also judge a person. So I think it is the duty of someone who has been close to a great man — a duty which one has no right to shy away from — to add one's contribution, in order to ensure that the picture the public receives of him is as little distorted as possible.
>
> Strindberg had numerous facets to his character. This book is about how I saw him and how he appeared to me. Others may have perceived him in a completely different way.
>
> It is not my intention to write a detailed account of our relationship, nor a psychological analysis of Strindberg. I have only wanted to offer my contribution towards a greater understanding of this remarkable man, and I am happy to be able to present the lightest and best of Strindberg — his letters to me. I have, consequently, used Strindberg's letters as a basis for the book and I have let him speak through these. I myself have no literary pretensions. I have only wanted to connect the letters, build around them and fill out with necessary comments. [. . .]
>
> How I wanted my Strindberg book to teach people to be a little less egotistical — like Strindberg showed himself to me — to be merciful like him, great in love like he was! His letters have so much to tell people these days. The older I get the more I understand Strindberg --- If Strindberg had received more love, encouragement and understanding from his fellow countrymen, I am sure his books would have been of lighter hue. But nobody bothered to understand him, even less help him.

Harriet's publisher seems to have allowed her to present the material in the way that she wanted and she chose to include all but three of the two hundred or so letters that Strindberg had written to her between 1900 and 1908. (The three that she omitted contained disparaging comments about one of her sisters, Gunnar Wingård and Frida Uhl.)

By 1932, when she was in her mid-fifties, Harriet's acting career was definitely in decline. She still wanted to play the great character roles but had already discovered that the fashionable directors now had new favourites to cast. In 1928 she had asked the artistic director of Dramaten, Tore Svennberg, for a long-term contract. He turned her down so she appealed to Crown Prince Gustav Adolf to intervene on her behalf, which he did, but without success. When Svennberg resigned she telephoned his successor, Erik Wettergren, and begged him to take her on. She followed this up with a letter to him, on 11 May 1932, pleading her case:

> I would like to point out that I have belonged to Swedish theatre for thirty years and during that time I have spent twenty years at Dramaten. [. . .]
>
> I have no pension at my disposal, I have no assets and I am economically dependent on my work.

A year later she finally got her contract. She stayed loyal to the theatre and its directors for the next ten years though they ignored her considerable talent and rewarded her with fewer parts for progressively less and less money. Eventually her roles became so insignificant that the critics began to ignore her too. In the ten years to 1943 she appeared in only fifteen productions. In 1935 she suffered the humiliation of being put on a beginner's salary, which was 1000 kronor less than she had been able to command thirty years earlier. 'If I am to keep the standard that my traditional position demands, 5000 kronor is not enough,' she protested to Olof Molander, who had become the artistic director at Dramaten the year before. Molander, her one-time champion, was no longer interested in promoting her. He was busy carving a reputation for himself as an important interpreter of Strindberg's work and Harriet was of no use to him now. He was a demonic *régisseur*, who dictated every gesture, every move and every intonation of his actors.

Harriet was gracious enough to congratulate Molander on his production of *To Damascus* (*Part I*) in 1937, even though she had not been given a role herself. She enclosed with her letter a short handwritten poem by Strindberg entitled 'A Mongolian Song':

> Olof Molander!
> I so wanted to give you visible proof of my gratitude for *Damascus* – an unforgettable performance.
>
> Please receive this little manuscript by Strindberg. It is as if he himself were to ask me to thank you.
> Harriet Bosse

Having had enough of the intrigues and backbiting of the theatre, Harriet retired from the stage altogether in 1943. 'I have been dead for a long time now – almost twenty years,' she said in a letter to the critic Oscar

Wieselgren in 1949. 'It was Olof Molander who killed me. I hope he won't forget to tell his confessor that – and ask for forgiveness.'

Molander went on attacking her reputation, even after her death. In 1965 he wrote to Torsten Eklund, the scholar who had edited the first published volumes of Strindberg's letters:

> Strindberg knew about her 'past' but denies it even to himself, until the break-up is a fact and he can vent his spleen in *A Blue Book*. How strange these fabrications of myth and how unbelievably difficult to obliterate! Bosse was certainly no innocent, not in any respect. --- But anyway: I don't blame her for having lovers, but her charming mendacity which let one incredibility after another slip through her sensuous lower lip, that I have *great experience* of, both in and outside of our work. [. . .]
>
> At the same time we all know that Strindberg suspected even his brother Axel and Richard Bergh of coveting the Daughter of Indra and that she had been the mistress of Palme and probably slept with Personne and others.

After her retirement Harriet became a very private person, finding comfort in the Christian Science movement for a while. In 1955 she went to live in Norway to be near her children but it never seemed like home. 'I can't get used to liking it here – the Norwegian temperament is different,' she wrote to a friend in 1958. 'And they want to make me into a Norwegian native – wrong, my mother was Danish, my father was German, I may have been born in Oslo, but I could just as well have been born on the Atlantic, I don't have one drop of Norwegian blood in me.'

She always maintained an interest in Strindberg's work and on one occasion she took one of her grandsons to see Olof Molander's production of *Easter* at the Nye Teatret in Oslo. She was so appalled at the actress's interpretation of the role of Eleonora that she could not help crying out 'Oh no! Oh no!' throughout the entire performance.

Having survived all of her brothers and sisters, Harriet died in Oslo on 2 November 1961 at the age of eighty-three. She had always been discreet about her past and she had never spoken of Strindberg with anything but tenderness and affection. (Her second and third husbands she mentioned hardly at all.) In the eyes of the public she was forever the pure and innocent girl who had captured the heart of Sweden's greatest dramatist and this was the legend she preferred to perpetuate.

— Chapter 22 —

Harriet's Legacy

During her long career on the stage Harriet Bosse appeared in fourteen of Strindberg's plays, six or maybe seven of which he wrote specially for her. He responded to two contradictory sides of her character: the saintly, Christ-like woman, as in *Easter* and *A Dream Play*, for example, and the manipulative seductress, as in *Thunder in the Air* and *Kristina*.

The intensity of feeling that inspired Strindberg to write Harriet into his plays, especially *Kristina* and *A Dream Play*, was a direct consequence of her decision to leave him as soon as they had returned from their trip to Berlin in August 1901. He was shocked into submission and after she had returned to him in the autumn she always had the upper hand in their relationship. This was to prove to be the secret of her success as his muse: she remained forever elusive and unpredictable and he could never be certain of her commitment to him.

In 1908, just before she married Gunnar Wingård, Strindberg wrote to her telling her that he had always known her true nature and that he had revealed it in his play *Kristina*. It is not altogether a flattering portrait. Strindberg's queen is flirtatious, capricious and dangerous. It was a role that suited Harriet extremely well. In an interview in the *Nya Dagligt Allehanda* on 6 October 1928 she claimed that of all Strindberg's heroines Kristina was the one that she enjoyed playing most of all. She had had to wait until 1926 for her first opportunity, when she produced a beautifully judged, mature performance. 'She delivered all the demonic femininity with an almost confusing cheerfulness – and with superb technical mastery,' noted one critic.

Kristina

Strindberg's title for his play *Kristina*, without the epithet of 'Queen', neatly sums up his republican outlook. The action starts with a flourish: the young virgin queen, the only daughter of Gustaf Adolf (Gustavus Adolphus), who died fighting for the Protestant cause during the Thirty Years War in 1632, is secretly planning to convert to Catholicism. She is

Harriet Bosse's roles in Strindberg's Plays

1898: Therese in *Before Death* (Centralteatret, Kristiania)

1900: The Lady in *To Damascus, Part I* (Dramaten, Stockholm)

1901: Eleonora in *Easter* (Dramaten, Stockholm)

1902: Emerentia Polhem in *Karl XII* and Biskra in *Samum* (Dramaten, Stockholm)

1904: The Lady in *To Damascus, Part I* (Svenska Teatern, Helsingfors)

1906: Kersti in *The Crown Bride* (Svenska Teatern, Helsingfors) and Eleonora in *Easter* (Svenska Teatern, Helsingfors)

1907: Indra's Daughter in *A Dream Play* and Kersti in *The Crown Bride* (Svenska Teatern, Stockholm)

1916: Henriette in *Crimes and Crimes* (Dramaten, Stockholm)

1917: Kersti in *The Crown Bride* (Lorensbergsteatern, Gothenburg)

1918: Kersti in *The Crown Bride* (Dramaten, Stockholm)

1919: Bertha in *The Companions* (film adaptation by Adolf Paul)

1921: Judith in *The Dance of Death, Part I* (Alan Ryding Touring Company) and Henriette in *Crimes and Crimes* (Dagmarteatret, Copenhagen)

1924: Henriette in *Crimes and Crimes* (Dramaten, Stockholm)

1925: Henriette in *Crimes and Crimes* (Dagmarteatret, Copenhagen)

1926: Kristina in *Kristina* (Lorensbergsteatern, Gothenburg) and the Lady in *To Damascus, Part III* (Konserthusteatern, Stockholm)

1928: Kristina in *Kristina* (Konserthusteatern, Stockholm) and Margit in *Sir Bengt's Wife* (Alan Ryding Touring Company)

1933: Gerda in *Thunder in the Air* (Dramaten, Stockholm)

1936: Henriette in *Crimes and Crimes* (Dramaten and Riksteatern, Stockholm) spending vast sums of money on the arts and making gifts of titles and land to her favourites, a strategy that alarms her cautious old Chancellor, Axel Oxenstierna. She is surrounded by sycophants, including her dull cousin Karl Gustav, who is prepared to do anything to become king and wants to marry her, and other admirers, such as her favourite, Claes Tott (a character who bears some resemblance to Strindberg himself), and a discarded lover, Magnus De La Gardie.

The play is written in four acts and the action is continuous within each act.

Act III

Claes Tott and Magnus De La Gardie are talking about Kristina before she appears. Tott is unaware of de la Gardie's earlier involvement with her.

TOTT: --- Can't the philosophers explain why heartache hurts more than anything else! --- I have seen Johan Baner fall in love -- the hero turned into a child; he drenched six handkerchiefs with tears in one day! . . . But the cruellest thing of all is that people laugh at that kind of pain! ---- Another thing, Magnus! Do you think she is playing with me?

DE LA GARDIE: Playing? Can a woman do anything else? Love surely is but a game!

TOTT: Playing with heaven and hell is a dangerous game!

DE LA GARDIE: Some people die in the process.

TOTT: I love her with all my youth, I worship her as a higher being, and I call her my first love!

DE LA GARDIE: A higher being?

TOTT: Yes, that's right! Can't you see how she soars above life, how everything is insignificant to her. The crown which kings put on their heads she tramples underfoot. I am almost sure that one day she'll throw it away!

DE LA GARDIE: (*pays attention*) Do you think so?

TOTT: Yes, she is an eagle, born in the air of air, that is why she finds it hard to breathe down here! --- If only I could follow her in flight!

DE LA GARDIE: But she never stays with anything, neither actions nor decisions.

TOTT: Because she doesn't want to tie herself down; that is what's so great about her!

DE LA GARDIE: She has no opinions!

TOTT: What does she need opinions for? All opinions are vindicated. But she is forever young, forever new.

DE LA GARDIE: God, how you love her!

TOTT: Yes, I do.

DE LA GARDIE: Has she no faults then?

TOTT: No, because you can't list her qualities under the bourgeois concepts of 'merits and demerits'.

A little later Kristina turns up and dismisses Tott at once. She asks De La Gardie to sell her his country mansion, Ekolsund, so that she can give it to her new lover, Tott.

DE LA GARDIE: I don't want to sell it!

KRISTINA (*angry, speaks in a loud deep voice*) Not to your King?

DE LA GARDIE: Says the Queen!

KRISTINA (*raises her rapier*) Are you reminding me that I am a woman?

DE LA GARDIE: Is that something to be ashamed of?

KRISTINA: For me, yes --- And do you know, one day I would like to meet you on the field with weapons and then you'll see that I am in no way inferior to you.

DE LA GARDIE: You mean you want to give me satisfaction?...

KRISTINA (*looks at him, wondering whether there is a hidden meaning, then smiles and changes her tone*) Will seventy thousand do for Ekolsund?

DE LA GARDIE: It depends – on the successor! Maybe it is *the* successor?

KRISTINA (*humiliated, ashamed swallows the insult*)

DE LA GARDIE: I am sorry; but you asked for it.

KRISTINA: Do you enjoy hitting out at me?

DE LA GARDIE: Hitting idols gives me pleasure, but hitting a woman one has loved — oh, it hurts, – oh, but that pain alleviates the other pain.

KRISTINA: You always talk about the pain of separation . . . I don't feel anything like that. I only enjoy being free again!

DE LA GARDIE: Again! --- Wait, one day you'll feel . . . yes, you will, you, like everyone else who plays with that elemental force, that creative power that springs from the roots of the tree of life . . .

KRISTINA: (*scornful*) What could that be?

DE LA GARDIE: Love! But you don't know what that is!

After dismissing De La Gardie and her cousin Karl Gustav, Kristina calls for Tott, who is unaware of the plots and scheming going on around him. Having been accused of squandering large sums of money, she is now desperate to recover some of it, and she has blackmailed Karl Gustav into parting with some cash in return for keeping quiet about his illegitimate child with the daughter of a merchant.

Kristina relaxes in Tott's company and begins to feel sorry for him. It is not difficult to identify a lovesick Strindberg in the dialogue that he gives to Tott here.

KRISTINA: You're so handsome today, Claes!

TOTT: If I seem less ugly than earlier it is because you have entered my spirit.

KRISTINA: Are you still gambling?

TOTT: I'm not gambling, not drinking, hardly eating and not one foul word has passed my lips!

KRISTINA: Have you seen any friends?

TOTT: I only see you!

KRISTINA: You're sad, my dear!

TOTT: I can't tell sadness from happiness any more; I'm alive but I am dead! Our evening yesterday was like . . . Kristina, now you've got my soul in your little hand; you open the hand and my soul flies out – and I am no more! I can see my image in your eyes; you close your eyelid and the image is gone and so am I!

KRISTINA: Claes, you're too high up. I can't see you – Come down!

TOTT: When you've taken my soul there's only my lifeless body left . . .

KRISTINA: You know the paper kite . . . as long as the string ties it to the earth it will rise, but if you let go of the string it comes down!

TOTT: (*ecstatically*) It's I who tie you to the earth, but you are going to lift me up . . .

KRISTINA: (*with real emotion*) Claes, you make me unhappy . . . I'm not the person you think I am, dearest.

TOTT: You don't know who you are and where you come from any more than the child knows; any more than you can remember all the dreams from the night before. When the gods sent you, their daughter, down here, they extinguished your memory . . .

KRISTINA: Your love is the greatest and the first that I have encountered and you are the noblest spirit I have ever met!

TOTT: No, I'm not, I'm a small slate that you write on; I was nothing before I saw you. Now I'm everything through you!

A Dream Play

A Dream Play was first produced at the Svenska Teatern in Stockholm on 17 April 1907 and it is Strindberg's first Expressionist drama. (Some critics claim that it is both Symbolist and Expressionist and most agree that it is certainly his most metaphysical work.) He adopted the same loose structure that he had chosen for *Lucky Per's Journey* and *To Damascus*, seeing each of these dramas as a review of life. For *A Dream Play* he stipulated that the scenery should be painted in a stylized way to convey the symbolism of dreams as he wanted to emphasize the dualism of existence – that nothing is what it appears to be. He originally wanted to use a magic lantern in order to create a series of dissolving images to represent the distorted fluidity of dreams but the stage crew could not master the technology involved at the time.

Strindberg also aimed to show that a universal analogy exists between the various realms of creation: the physical world being symbolic of the spiritual world and this, in turn, being symbolic of God. And apart from the clear influences from Buddhism, Hinduism and the writings of Swedenborg, he was also echoing Kierkegaard's belief in 'repetition' – the idea that it is God's punishment to make us go back and do things over and over again.

The heroine, Indra's Daughter, who assumes the name of Agnes when she descends to earth to find out about humankind and to solve the riddle of life, is an idealized portrait of woman. This 'lamb of God' is a Christ-like creature but, unlike Eleonora in *Easter*, she plays a full part in human affairs. She discovers that things have improved on earth since her brother last came on a similar errand. She lives first as the wife of a lawyer, when she experiences the hardships of married life without money, and then she takes over the Concièrge's role, listening to people's problems, symbolically gathering them up into her shawl.

Among the other people that she meets are the Officer, who waits in vain at the stage door of the Opera House with a bouquet of roses for his fiancée, and the Poet, who, because he has understood the riddle of life better than anyone else, feels great sadness and pity for the human race. Indra's Daughter also feels great compassion for mankind and her recurring cry is: 'Det är synd om människorna.' This is difficult to translate into English. Literally it means 'It is sad about the human beings (or 'mankind' or 'humankind') and it has been rendered variously as 'Mankind is to be pitied,' or 'Men are to be pitied,' or, more colloquially, 'I feel sorry for mankind,' or 'It's a shame about people.' In the original Swedish, however, the phrase comes across as more emotional and has more resonance, partly because the word for 'man' in the sense of 'human being'- 'människa' – is a feminine noun, the plural forms being 'människor' ('human beings') and 'människorna' ('the human beings' or 'mankind' or 'humankind').

The structure of the play is deliberately fluid and the continuous action weaves itself through various social settings without any sharp divisions, the characters being presented together at pivotal points in the drama, where their hopes and dreams are highlighted. The oppressed coal-carriers, for example, who work hard at a physically demanding job, appear alongside the gentry, who undergo torturous treatment to keep themselves fit and slim before sitting down to eat. In another scene the Schoolteacher challenges the Officer to recite his two times table but the poor man, who is about to receive an honorary doctorate, cannot say what two times two is. Ingmar Bergman uses this scene almost verbatim (and drew many other images from *A Dream Play*) in his film *Wild Strawberries*.

In his foreword to *A Dream Play* Strindberg writes:

> Time and space do not exist; from an insignificant background of reality imagination spins and weaves new patterns: a mixture of memories, experiences, fancies, paradoxes and improvisations. – The characters split, double, multiply, evaporate, solidify, spread, and come together. But one consciousness reigns above them all, that of the dreamer; because there are no secrets, no inconsistencies, no scruples, no laws. He does not judge, does not acquit, he only relates facts; and since the dream is mostly painful, less often happy, a note of melancholy and compassion with all living things runs right through the meandering narrative.

In the following extract Indra's Daughter becomes acquainted with the Officer, who is engaged to Victoria, an opera singer.

DAUGHTER: You're imprisoned in your rooms; I have come to liberate you!

OFFICER: I have waited for this, Agnes, but I was not sure that you'd want to.

DAUGHTER: The castle is strong, it has seven walls, but it will work . . . Do you want to or not?

OFFICER: To be honest, I don't know, because, whatever happens, it will hurt. Every joy in life has to be paid for in double measure with sorrow. From my present position it is difficult, but if I am to buy sweet liberty then I must suffer threefold. Agnes, I'd rather put up with it, as long as I can see you!

DAUGHTER: What do you see in me?

OFFICER: The beauty that is the harmony in the universe. There are lines in your body which can only be found in the orbits of solar systems, in the beautifully sounding string, in the vibrations of light. You are a child of heaven . . .

DAUGHTER: So are you!

OFFICER: Why then should I look after horses? Manage stables and have straw delivered?

DAUGHTER: So that you should long to get away from here.

OFFICER: I do, but it is so hard to escape!

DAUGHTER: But it is one's duty to seek freedom in the light!

OFFICER: Duty? Life has never admitted any duties for me.

DAUGHTER: You feel wronged by life?

OFFICER: Yes! It has been unfair . . .

Indra's Daughter meets up with the Officer again while talking to the Concièrge outside the Opera House. He is waiting for Victoria at the stage door.

OFFICER: (*singing*) Victoria!

CONCIÈRGE: She'll be here soon!

OFFICER: Good! The carriage is waiting, the table is laid, the champagne is on ice . . . May I embrace you, my dear ladies. (*embraces the* DAUGHTER *and the* CONCIÈRGE, *singing*) Victoria!

VICTORIA: (*singing, from above*) I am here!

OFFICER: (*starts walking*) I am waiting!

DAUGHTER: Do you know me?

OFFICER: No, I only know one woman . . . Victoria! For seven years I have walked around here waiting for her . . . at noon when the sun reached the chimneys and in the evenings when dusk was falling . . . Look here at the asphalt, can you see the traces of the faithful lover! Hurrah! She is mine! (*singing*) Victoria! Well, she must be changing now. [. . .]

OFFICER: For seven years I've been coming here! Seven times three hundred and sixty-five make two thousand five hundred and fifty-five! And I have looked at this door with the four-leafed clover two thousand five hundred and fifty-five times, without knowing where it leads to. And that four-leafed clover that is supposed to let in the light . . . for whom should it let in the light? Is there anyone inside? Is anyone living there?

CONCIÈRGE: I don't know! I have never seen the door being opened! . . .

(*They decide to have the door opened but first they need to find a locksmith.*)

Indra's Daughter wants to find out what it is like to be married and have children. She marries the Lawyer and learns that love cannot survive the trivialities of everyday life.

DAUGHTER: --- Let us in God's name avoid the pitfalls, now that we know them so well!

LAWYER: Yes, let us. We are humane and enlightened people; we can forgive and forget.

DAUGHTER: We can smile at trivialities.

LAWYER: We, only we can do that! Do you know, today I read in the Morning News . . . by the way . . . where is the paper?

DAUGHTER: (*embarrassed*) Which paper?

LAWYER: Do I have more than one paper?

DAUGHTER: Please smile and don't use such harsh words . . . I have used your paper to make the fire.

LAWYER: Damnation!

DAUGHTER: Please smile . . .

Indra's Daughter continues her odyssey on earth and becomes increasingly disillusioned, but the Lawyer tells her that the worst is still to come.

LAWYER: --- Now you've seen most things but you haven't tried the worst.

DAUGHTER: What could that be?

LAWYER: Repetition . . . retakes . . . go back to zero. Do your homework again! . . . Come!

DAUGHTER: Where to?

LAWYER: To your duties!

DAUGHTER: What are they?

LAWYER: That is all the things you detest. All the things you don't want to do but have to do. Abstaining, forsaking, putting up with, leaving . . . everything that is unpleasant, repulsive, painful . . .

DAUGHTER: Are there no pleasant duties?

LAWYER: They become pleasant when they are completed.

DAUGHTER: When they do not exist any more. So duty is something unpleasant. What are the pleasant things in life then?

LAWYER: Sinning is pleasant.

DAUGHTER: Sinning?

LAWYER: Which must be punished, yes. If I have had a pleasant day and evening, then I suffer anxiety and have terrible remorse the day after.

DAUGHTER: How strange!

LAWYER: Yes, I wake up in the morning with a headache; and then the repetition begins, the perverse repetition. In the way that everything which was beautiful, pleasant, witty yesterday appears ugly, horrible and silly in recollection this morning. Pleasure sort of rots and happiness falls apart.

In the last section of the play Indra's Daughter meets the Poet, who 'knows best how to live'.

> DAUGHTER: --- Victoria, the growing castle and the Officer . . . was something I dreamt . . .
>
> POET: Something I wrote once.
>
> DAUGHTER: Then you know what fiction is . . .
>
> POET: Then I know what dreams are . . . What is fiction?
>
> DAUGHTER: Not real, but more than real . . . not a dream, but waking dreams . . .
>
> POET: And human beings think that we poets are just playing . . . making up and inventing!
>
> DAUGHTER: That is lucky, my friend, because otherwise the world would be desolate for lack of encouragement. Everyone would be on their backs looking at the sky; no one would get a grip on the plough or the spade, the plane or the pickaxe.

At the end, Indra's Daughter says farewell to the Poet and enters the burning castle. An enormous chrysanthemum appears on the roof.

> DAUGHTER: Our departure is imminent and the end is near.
> Farewell, you mortal being, you dreamer,
> You Poet who knows best how to live.

In Sweden the role of Indra's Daughter has become a major challenge for classical actresses – a kind of female Hamlet – but more importantly the work is now seen very much as a director's play. Mauritz Stiller created a memorable production at the Lorensbergsteatern in Gothenburg, with music specially composed by Stenhammar in 1916, and five years later Max Reinhardt was invited to do it at Dramaten in Stockholm. Olof Molander tackled the play at least seven times and was in the middle of preparing an eighth production when he died in 1966. Ingmar Bergman has directed it at least four times and Robert Wilson gave a sensational interpretation at the Stadsteatern in Stockholm in 1998.

Strindberg's Works: 1900–08

Strindberg wrote the following works during the period when he was closely associated with Harriet Bosse.

Midsummer [*Midsommar*] play, 1900
Easter [*Påsk*] play, 1900
The Dance of Death [*Dödsdansen*] play, 1900
The Crown Bride [*Kronbruden*] play, 1900
Swanwhite [*Svanevit*] play, 1901
A Dream Play [*Ett drömspel*] play, 1901
Charles XII [*Karl XII*] play, 1901
Engelbrekt play, 1901
Kristina play, 1901
Gustav III play, 1902
Faircreek and Foulbay [*Fagervik och Skamsund*]
   short stories and poetry, 1902
The Nightingale in Wittenberg [*Näktergalen i Wittenberg*] play, 1903
Through Deserts to the Promised Land [*Genom öknar till arvland*]
   play, 1903
Hellas play, 1903
The Lamb and the Beast [*Lammet och vilddjuret*] play, 1903
Alone [*Ensam*] novel, 1903
Fairy Tales [*Sagor*] short stories, 1903
The Gothic Rooms [*Götiska rummen*] novel, 1904
Black Banners [*Svarta fanor*] novel, 1904
Historical Miniatures [*Historiska miniatyrer*] essays, 1905
New Swedish Destinies [*Nya svenska öden och äventyr*]
   short stories, 1906
The Roofing Party [*Taklagsöl*] novella, 1906
The Scapegoat [*Syndabocken*] novella, 1906
Thunder in the Air [*Oväder*] play, 1907
After the Fire [*Brända tomten*] play, 1907
The Ghost Sonata [*Spöksonaten*] play, 1907
The Pelican [*Pelikanen*] play, 1907
A Blue Book, Part I [*En blå bok*] diary, 1907
Abu Casem's Slippers [*Abu Casems tofflor*] play, 1908
The Black Glove [*Svarta handsken*] play, 1908
A New Blue Book [*En ny blå bok*] diary, 1908

Part 4
Fanny Falkner (1890–1962)

— Chapter 23 —

The Last Romantic Attachment

> I am determined to make you into a great actress; but you must take it seriously and work hard because it is not child's play!
>
> *Letter to Fanny Falkner, 30 May 1908*

By the time Strindberg met Fanny Falkner he had already produced his best work for the theatre. Siri and Harriet, and to a lesser extent Frida, were fortunate enough to meet and fall in love with him when he had the energy and the will to seek new forms of dramatic expression. Fanny, unfortunately, failed to ignite him in quite the same way, mainly because of his failing health, but also perhaps because she lacked the inspirational talent and flair for acting that had fired him before. At the beginning of their relationship, of course, Strindberg saw Fanny as a new and exciting muse — yet another actress who could feed his creativity.

A few months after Harriet married Gunnar Wingård, Strindberg moved into a new apartment in what was to be his last home, on Drottninggatan, the street where he had first encountered Siri. His landlords were Fanny's parents.

Fanny Falkner's mother and father, Meta and Frans Nilsson, were originally professional singers with a choral quartet that toured around Scandinavia giving recitals. Meta was Danish and Frans was Swedish and they changed their name to Falkner some time in the mid-1890s. It was then — and still is — quite common for people in Sweden to change a surname ending in '-son' to indicate a move up the social ladder. Two of Frans Nilsson's brothers opted for the name Falkner at around the same time.

When Fanny was born, on 9 June 1890, the third eldest of six children, her parents were living in Karlshamn, a small town in southeastern Sweden. Strindberg had met the family — including the one-year-old Fanny — when he had stayed at a boarding house kept by Fanny's uncle in Skurup, about fifty miles from Karlshamn.

Fanny's parents stopped touring in the early 1890s when a growing family made it impractical and after that Frans went into the textile business with one of his brothers in Stockholm for a while. They were not successful and the company lost a lot of money after they entered into a series of risky deals. When she looked back on her childhood the two dominating elements that Fanny remembered were the constant financial problems that the family faced and her father's alcoholism. Like Strindberg, she knew what it was like to fear the bailiffs knocking at the door demanding money and threatening eviction. It was Fanny's mother who was responsible for their financial recovery; she became a boarding-house landlady, sub-letting furnished apartments and single rooms to her tenants.

In spite of their relative poverty, Fanny was well educated, and she and her sisters gained subsidized places at the French School in Stockholm, which had been set up for the children of diplomats. Fanny proved to have an exceptional talent for art and in 1904 she transferred to a technical school to start training to be an art teacher. Here she studied, among other things, geometry, technical drawing, life drawing, landscape painting and calligraphy. On graduating three years later she went to stay with her mother's sisters, who ran a boarding house in Copenhagen, and became a private pupil of the Danish painter Eduard Saltoft.

Copenhagen at that time had a thriving artistic community and many artists, including women, came from all over Scandinavia to work and study there. Fanny had not been there for long, however, before her parents called her back to Stockholm, having regretted their decision to allow her to leave home so young. They were afraid that she was mixing with unsuitable company and would turn into a decadent bohemian. What they could not have foreseen was the effect that a visit to the theatre that autumn would have on their daughter's destiny. In September Fanny took the ferry from Copenhagen to Malmö and went to a production of *Lady Julie,* directed by August Falck, with Manda Björling in the title role. It was the first Strindberg play that she had ever seen.

On her return to Stockholm a few weeks later Fanny bumped into Manda by chance and the two women became friends. Falck, who went on to marry Manda in 1909, had engaged her to work for him at Intiman. When she and Fanny met she was busy preparing for her role in Strindberg's play *The Pelican*. Intiman was conveniently situated just a couple of blocks away from where Fanny lived and she suggested that Manda should rent one of her mother's apartments, which she did. She quickly became an adopted member of the Falkner household and joined them for meals, when she would tell them what was going on at Strindberg's new theatre. Fanny had had no ambitions to be an actress herself before this but Manda's amusing stories about life on stage whetted her interest and she was in the audience on the night that Intiman first opened its doors to the public on 26 November 1907. When Manda told her that Falck was looking for bit-part players and walk-ons Fanny decided to go for an audition and was duly hired.

Fanny made her acting debut at Intiman on 21 January 1908 in a non-speaking role in Strindberg's play *The Ghost Sonata*. The critics neither understood the piece nor appreciated it and it ran for just twelve performances before being dropped from the repertoire. Strindberg never saw *The Ghost Sonata* on stage again in his lifetime and it was left to the German director Max Reinhardt to show the Swedes what a masterpiece it was with his bold experimental production in Stockholm in 1917.

Strindberg's next production at Intiman was a revival of *Sir Bengt's Wife*, which opened on 25 February and ran for forty-eight performances. Manda played Margit, the role that he had created for Siri, and Fanny was cast as her page-boy. It was during the dress rehearsal that Strindberg noticed Fanny for the first time. 'There she is,' he told Falck. 'There is our *Easter* girl, alive and well. She must play the girl in *Easter*.' Here was yet another ingenue, ready to be groomed for stardom and a place in Strindberg's heart.

In her book *August Strindberg i Blå Tornet* [*August Strindberg in the Blue Tower*] Fanny recalls the first time she met Strindberg:

> Strindberg came up from the auditorium, on his way back to Falck's room. Just inside the door he stopped and looked at me. And then he walked on without saying a word, serious and handsome. Not a word was spoken.

Falck thought that Strindberg was mad to think about casting Fanny in a leading role when she had had no training and no experience of speaking on stage. He already had in mind another actress, Anna Flygare, to play the part of Eleonora in *Easter*. Without consulting Falck, Strindberg invited Fanny to his apartment on Karlavägen to rehearse the role under his direction with the actor Alrik Kjellgren, who was to play Benjamin. For Fanny these rehearsals were a baptism of fire and Strindberg's emotional energy was unlike anything she had ever experienced before:

> Strindberg himself was completely moved, tears ran down his cheeks, he was enormously inspiring for us both. I could hear him sob, it got worse, he burst into tears, his face was completely tear-stained and red. I felt terribly sorry for him.
>
> He then turned to Kjellgren and said the following words – which he still remembers – What do you think, she is a born artist. Her expressions, her eyes, her hair – her hair!

August Strindberg i Blå Tornet

When Strindberg learned of Falck's decision to cast Anna Flygare rather than Fanny as Eleonora in his play Easter *he was furious. Falck argued that Fanny's voice was weak and her movements clumsy. Strindberg lost the battle with Falck on this occasion but he did not give up on Fanny. He arranged for her to have professional coaching and, just as he had done for Siri, he drew up a list of the basic principles of speaking on stage. In a letter that he wrote to Fanny on 30 May 1908 he gave her the following advice:*

1. Speak slowly, legato, all words in the sentence strung together; the commas and full stops must not produce a staccato, but glide across with a little extra sound which I shall teach you.
2. Speak naturally but do not 'talk'.
3. A broad register in the beginning, a little affected; imagine making a speech or preaching, but without shouting.
4. Begin to speak grammatically correctly, and get used to a slightly pedantic speech on a daily basis, as if you were reading aloud or giving a lecture. Stop talking or chatting when you are speaking normally. In other words: don't be careless but speak slowly.
5. Watch your consonants especially your R's. The vowels are easier to hear.
6. If you make a habit of speaking carefully every day you won't need to read so much.
7. Speak, articulate, 'phrase' like a singer. Listen to your own voice and enjoy it when it sounds good.
8. Flygare speaks carefully as a rule, listen to her, imitate her.
It should sound a little exaggerated, important!
And the whole secret about speech is: slowly, drawn out, legato. Beginners prattle but do not speak. They deliver in staccato, which is the worst of all.
Walk in nature; speak to yourself there, read poetry; that strengthens your voice.
And learn to breathe through the nose, when you speak, then you get the best delivery. [. . .]
I am determined to make you into a great actress; but take it seriously and work at it because it is not child's play.

Fanny was not to know at this point, of course, of the strength of Strindberg's feelings for Harriet, who had first brought the character of Eleonora to life on stage and made it her own at the première some seven years earlier, nor of his sorrow at the death of his sister Elisabeth.

Falck and Strindberg were both powerful personalities and they often clashed during their time at Intiman. Like many successful actor-managers, Falck was possessed of a deadly combination of charm and ruthlessness. Most of those who worked for him respected him as a director, though he was not considered to be a particularly good actor. He flirted openly with all the pretty young actresses who came within his orbit – including Fanny. Strindberg seems to have known about this because he asked Falck discreetly to leave Fanny alone. Apparently, Falck obliged.

Easter opened at Intiman on 16 April with Anna Flygare playing Eleonora. Strindberg was enormously impressed with her interpretation of the role. 'Every evening I can sense both how much you enjoy being in the limelight and how you take on my Eleonora's suffering, just because I have written this play,' he told her in a letter that he sent to her on 25 April. The next day he wrote to her again: 'Now please give me all the photographs of your Easter-girl as a souvenir of this *Easter* which I shall never forget!' He in turn presented her with a portrait of himself, which she always treasured. The play was a great success and ran for 182 performances.

By the early summer of 1908 Fanny had developed something of an infatuation for Strindberg and on Midsummer's Eve she went alone to his apartment. When the maid answered the door she lost her nerve and handed over a bunch of wild flowers that she had picked specially for him without enquiring whether he was at home to visitors. A few days later he responded with an invitation for her to call on him again. And so their real friendship began.

Fanny began to see him regularly after that and one day he asked her whether her parents had any spare rooms to let as he had decided to move. The Falkners offered him a furnished apartment consisting of three living rooms, one of which had a balcony facing the street, plus a modern shower room and a lavatory. The accommodation was basic and not very spacious but the apartment block was modern, with central heating, electricity, a telephone system and a lift. Strindberg thought it would suit him very well and so he took it. He arranged to employ a maid to do the cleaning and as there was no kitchen it was agreed that Fanny's mother would prepare his meals and have them sent down to him.

Strindberg moved in in July and brought with him just his clothes, some books, photographs and paintings – and a coffee-making machine. Having sold off some of the furniture that he had bought when he was married to Harriet, and having put the rest in storage, he thus symbolically marked the end of his relationship with her.

He brightened up his new rooms with vases of flowers placed in front of mirrors and settled down to a regular routine. He would rise each morning at seven and go for a walk, returning for breakfast followed by three hours of intensive writing before lunch. In the afternoons he rested and whenever he had friends over in the evenings Meta Falkner would serve a late supper with wine. Fanny's younger sisters – Eva and Ada, who were twins, and Stella – were usually to be found sitting on the stairs outside Strindberg's door on these occasions, listening to the lively chatter and the music.

Strindberg grew especially fond of Fanny's sister Stella, who was four years old at the time and reminded him of his daughter Anne-Marie. She would come down to his apartment and once, when he asked her what she wanted for Christmas, she told him that she would like a box of paints. It so happened that he had just bought some so he fetched them and gave them to her. It was like magic and Stella thought that Strindberg was a conjuror and Santa Claus rolled into one. In her book Fanny describes his natural way with children when she recalls a doll dressed in Sami costume that Strindberg had bought for Stella:

> It was charming to see him kneeling in front of the little girl, he took her hand and kissed it and handed over the doll in a chivalrous fashion saying:
> Its name is Swanwhite after your sister . . . You don't need to be careful with it. If it breaks I'll just buy a new head for it.
> It was a lovely sight, those two – the affectionate poet on his knees in front of the little child.

On another occasion Strindberg organized a party for Anne-Marie and invited the youngest three Falkner girls together with Manda's daughter Renée. He decorated the table with place cards and little boxes of chocolate in the shape of musical instruments – harps, drums and trumpets – wrapped in white and gold paper. After the children had eaten he entertained them with board games.

The Falkners became a surrogate family for Strindberg and from this point of view his involvement with Fanny to begin with was more like that of a father with a favourite daughter. It is a measure of his generosity that he offered Fanny the sum of 60 kronor a month (which effectively more than doubled the income that she was getting as an apprentice actress at Intiman) to act as his part-time assistant. This had the effect of boosting the family's finances generally and Fanny was pleased to help him in any way that she could. She was flattered when he asked her to design the cover for his play *Abu Casem's Slippers* and she produced a beautiful drawing, using elegant Arabic lettering. She also painted a watercolour landscape for him, which he hung in the entrance hall to his apartment. He was still urging her to develop her acting career, so he went on paying for her drama lessons and voice coaching and also arranged for her to have professional photographs taken. It is evident that Fanny had a strong interest in the theatre but she was not passionately in love with the idea of being an actress as Siri had been, nor was she a naturally gifted performer like Harriet. Her motivation seems to have come from her admiration of Strindberg and his work and an overriding desire to please him.

The first play scheduled for the autumn season at Intiman that began on 4 September 1908 was a revival of *The Father*. Karin Alexandersson was cast as Laura and Fanny was given the part of her daughter, Bertha. Fanny's breakthrough came when Strindberg and Falck decided to recast the production of *Easter*. She was to take over the role of Eleonora in Stockholm while Anna Flygare and Alrik Kjellgren took the play on tour. And so after the initial disagreement with Falck, Strindberg finally got his way and Fanny made her debut in the leading role that he had earmarked for her. It has to be said, however, that Falck's original judgement was vindicated for in the end it was Anna Flygare who made the role her own. Overall, the audiences and critics favoured her, and Strindberg was gracious enough to acknowledge the fact when he told her: 'Your Easter-girl stands out like a milestone in Swedish Art.'

Easter became a popular favourite all over Sweden and was revived many times. Fanny appeared in a production in 1912 at the Folkets Hus Teatern in Stockholm, by which time she had become a much better actress, as the critic Anna Branting observed, saying that 'she combined the purest nature with this strangely unreal appearance which is often associated with holy madmen in old legends'. Harriet Bosse played Eleonora again for the third and final time in her career when the play was done with Alan Ryding's Touring Company in 1920-22 and at the new Intiman in 1921; by this time she was considered rather too old for the part and Anna Flygare's reputation remained intact.

When Anna Flygare was interviewed in 1948 by the *Svenska Dagbladet* in connection with the centenary of Strindberg's birth, she said that playing Eleonora had changed her life:

> I, who have – or at least had – a foul temper and was, fundamentally, quite an unpleasant person – *and* yet people thought I was Eleonora! That is why people have trusted me so much and shown me affection and given me their confidence. People have [always] wanted to protect and look after me. It is all thanks to him, I always think, when I look at this portrait which Strindberg gave me after the première of *Easter*.

While Fanny was playing Eleonora in the recast production of *Easter* at Intiman she was also rehearsing the part that she is perhaps best known for: Swanwhite, in the play of the same name. This is the work that Strindberg had written specially for Harriet – the embodiment of spring in his midwinter days – and dedicated to her when they became engaged in 1901.

Strindberg and Falck disagreed once again about casting Fanny rather than Anna Flygare in a leading role and again they compromised by mounting two separate productions. This time it was Fanny who went on tour while Anna stayed in Stockholm. With this system of duplicated casting, the company managed to put on 150 performances during the 1908-09 season. The critic Sven Söderman declared it to be one of Strindberg's most delightful plays and praised Fanny, who 'with her fragile virginal appearance gave an indescribably charming interpretation of the fairy tale Swanwhite'.

According to Gunnar Ollen, who has written extensively about Strindberg's entire dramatic output, *Swanwhite* owes something to the work of Maeterlinck, who was one of Harriet's favourite writers. Strindberg also drew on traditional Nordic folksongs and ballads, which were enjoying something of a popular revival in Scandinavia at the time; and there is more than a hint of a pre-Raphaelite fascination with medieval mythology, which adds a touch of danger to an otherwise exaggeratedly romantic story. The resulting drama is no mere pastiche, as he was careful to explain in his *Open Letters to the Intimate Theatre*:

> I put everything into the separator, including maids and the Green Gardener and the Young King, and then I threw the cream away and that is why it is mine! – But it is mine for another reason too, because I have lived that fairy tale in my imagination! A spring in midwinter!

On 26 November, the first anniversary of the opening of Intiman, Strindberg organized a dinner at his apartment before the performance of *Swanwhite* and threw a party at the theatre after the curtain. Fanny, August Falck and Alrik Kjellgren have all described this evening in detail. Strindberg sat and watched while the others danced and when someone started creating lighting effects with various coloured spotlights (accounts

Swanwhite

Swanwhite *tells the story of a beautiful young princess, ill-treated by her stepmother while her father is away at war, and betrothed at the age of fifteen to a king she has never seen. The king sends a messenger in the shape of a handsome young prince and the young couple fall in love. What begins as forbidden love ends as love of the purest kind, strong enough to conquer even death, for when the prince drowns, Swanwhite is able to resuscitate him.*

The following extract is from the first act, just after Swanwhite's first meeting with the prince. 'Your playful gestures are original, graceful and your very own,' Strindberg wrote to Fanny after he had watched her rehearse this scene in October 1908. 'They will be successful and be imitated for years, although they are inimitable. Keep them and invent other gestures like those.'

SWANWHITE: (*dancing on the floor*) I know his name, the most beautiful name in all the world!

THE PRINCE: (*rises, catches her and puts his hand over her mouth*)

SWANWHITE: (*throws her head back*) Oh, oh! Look, there is a hole in the ceiling and I can see the sky, a little bit of the sky, a window-pane, and behind the window-pane, a face. Is it the face of an angel? No, but look, look! It is your face!

THE PRINCE: Angels are little girls, not boys!

SWANWHITE: But it's you!

THE PRINCE: (*looks at the ceiling*) It's a mirror!

SWANWHITE: Oh, poor us! It's my stepmother's bewitching mirror. She has seen everything!

THE PRINCE: And in the mirror I can see the fireplace, and from the fireplace hangs a pumpkin!

SWANWHITE: (*produces a strangely shaped, multi-coloured pumpkin from the fireplace*) What's this? It looks like an ear! The witch has even heard what we've been saying. Oh dear! (*throws the pumpkin into the chimney, runs across the floor towards the bed, stops suddenly and lifts her foot up*) Alas, she has put needles all over the floor. (*sits down and rubs her foot*)

(*The* PRINCE *kneels in front of* SWANWHITE *in order to help her.*)

SWANWHITE: No, you must not touch my foot! You must not!

THE PRINCE: My dear sweet one, we must get your stocking off if I'm going to be able to help you.

SWANWHITE: (*sobbing*) You must not, you must not see my foot!

vary as to whether it was Falck or Kjellgren who was responsible for this) he was ecstatic and shouted 'More, more!' while giving instructions about the colour changes he wanted. Anna Flygare, dressed in purple velvet, and Fanny, dressed in green velvet, performed an Isadora Duncan-inspired dance in front of the red velvet curtains. The party went on until four in the morning and as Strindberg got up to leave he declaimed: 'Long live youth!' When he raised his hat in salutation it touched an electric light bulb suspended from the ceiling above his head and he stood there for a long while, as if in a trance, haloed, before making his exit.

— Chapter 24 —

At the Last Gate

> Don't be impatient! Ships can make port in a gentle breeze.
> *Letter to Fanny Falkner, 7 September 1909*

At the beginning of 1909 rumours got back to Strindberg about him and Fanny – people thought they were having an affair. He had certainly given her money on several occasions – after the première of *Swanwhite* he had handed her an envelope containing a 100 kronor note – and their special relationship had not gone unnoticed. One incident in particular may have fuelled the gossip: when Fanny was on tour with *Swanwhite* she wrote to Strindberg and mentioned that the weather was very cold; his immediate response was to go out and buy her a fur coat. Was this purely an avuncular gesture or did it have a more romantic significance? The letter that he wrote to Fanny around this time is fierce in its denial that she should read anything into his behaviour:

> Do I have to write this letter? Eight days ago it came to my notice that people were talking about me getting married again to a young girl.
> I found it so incredible and so crazy that I, an old and sick person should try and tie a young person to my heavy destiny, which soon ought to be at an end, according to the laws of nature. That your name was implicated is something I cannot be blamed for. When they took my last child away from me I lost interest in life and I was only trying to help in an unselfish way. That was all!
> Don't answer this letter, just go on showing me the same confidence as before; and people will stop talking.
> I am no company for a young girl. Go into the countryside and meet some young people. Go with Mr. Falck today. Tell me before you leave and I'll give you some money. But if you part with a single öre I'll regard it as a fraud.
> Also, I want to be alone, and I have a right to be, but you who are young, must get out among people. Go and enjoy yourself now and meet some new people. And be happy to leave behind your present life.

In spite of his instruction that she should go out and enjoy herself without him, Strindberg was undoubtedly becoming more and more dependent on Fanny's company by this time. He was deliberately pushing her away in an attempt to prevent himself from falling too deeply in love with her.

Whenever she did follow his advice, of course, they missed each other terribly and Strindberg waited impatiently for her letters, scolding her when she did not reply to him immediately.

In an interview that she gave on Swedish Radio in 1949 Fanny talked about how Strindberg had expressed an interest in every aspect of her life, especially her clothes. He told her not to wear grey, for example, as it wiped out the contours of the body. And on one occasion, she remembered, he looked at a black jacket that she was wearing and told her that it was too loose in the waist. When she said that she could not afford to have it altered he said, 'Just bring me a needle and some thread and I'll take it in for you.'

Strindberg knew that a relationship with Fanny would not really work and there is no evidence that he felt the sexual tension and the deep, passionate love for her that he had experienced with his three wives. For her part, Fanny was always aware that she was in the presence of a great man when she was with him, even though he never behaved or spoke to her in a superior way. She always felt secure and safe with him. 'When he rang on the internal telephone,' she said, 'I flew down the stairs.'

He enjoyed planning treats and in the summer of 1909 he sent her younger sisters to a large country estate where his brother Olle was working as head gardener. He paid for the whole holiday.

Fanny was following his advice and was on holiday in Dalarna in central Sweden when Strindberg wrote to her telling her that Baron Theodor Adelsvärd wanted to stage a single open-air performance of *Swanwhite* at his country mansion for the entertainment of his guests. The Baron wished her to play the lead, which she happily agreed to do. After this she travelled to Dalarö (the place where Strindberg had taken refuge in the autumn of 1875 after he had fallen in love with Siri) and got to know the Bonnier family and others from Strindberg's artistic circle.

While she was away Fanny met a young artist called Yngve Berg. She modelled for him and he fell in love with her but she turned him down as she had spurned the advances of another artist a few months previously. Strindberg was the only man that she was interested in. Back in Stockholm after her summer break, she called on him at his invitation to take tea on his balcony. He complimented her on the white dress she was wearing and laughingly said that she was made of air. 'Only now, at the age of sixty,' he said, 'do I realize that it is women who are the main attraction.'

He continued to offer her advice on how she should conduct herself and in a letter dated 7 September he warned her against behaving indiscreetly in public:

> Ma mouche, don't go to operettas; you'll develop bad taste and young gentlemen will only want to destroy my attempts at improving your taste.
> And they will only want to gloat in your company and afterwards they'll boast about it in the bars and that will not be good for your reputation.
> I don't stand in very high esteem myself but I find joy in seeing you being held in high regard. Don't step down.
> Don't be impatient! Ships can make port in a gentle breeze.

A few days later he wrote her a note asking her to help him out of the Blue Tower:

> Tired of sitting in the tower and growing grey. I long for my Djurgården which I have not seen since 10 July last year. But while the bridge is being watched from number 57 I cannot bring myself to go. What I need to know is: if the separation has started, that is if my beloved child is still in someone else's hands. You who helped me leave Karlavägen, please help me to leave the tower to which you brought me.
> Use the telephone, if necessary!
> ? is: Has the separation begun? That is, do they live apart?

Fanny did not understand quite what he meant by this – she thought that it might have been a veiled proposal – and when she asked him to explain he merely replied, 'Go, my dear child, go away.' What was on his mind, however, were the rumours going round that Harriet and Gunnar Wingård were having problems in their marriage. They were living at 57 Strandvägen, in an apartment that overlooked the park, and Strindberg had stopped taking his regular walks there because he thought they might be spying on him. If they were having difficulties then he saw this as a chance to claim access to Anne-Marie whom he had not seen since April 1908.

During the summer he had been working on what was to be his last play, *The Great Highway*. Divided into seven loosely connected episodes, it is an odd mixture of serious drama and bizarre comedy. In the sixth scene, called 'At the Last Gate', the main character, the Hunter, recalls the joy that his daughter had brought him. The tone of his speech is gentle and melancholy: 'Happiness does exist, but it is brief like lightning, like sunshine, like the convolvulus which flowers for one day and then no more!'

Some critics have seen *The Great Highway* as a metaphor for Strindberg's life, in which he tries to record the passion, the love and disillusionment that he has known and his appreciation of God and the beauty of nature.

It is not hard to see Fanny in the character of the Girl, and the Hunter as Strindberg himself:

> GIRL: So you care about me?
>
> HUNTER: I care about you . . . I'm full of care . . . for you . . . goodbye.
> A flower seen through the garden fence
> Which gives a moment's pleasure to the passer-by,
> Is loveliest when unbroken, when spreading its scent
> With the wind . . . one brief moment and then it's gone.
> Now onwards!
>
> GIRL: Goodbye! Onwards!

Strindberg wanted Fanny to play the part of the Girl and yet again he had to fight August Falck to get his way. Falck was slimming down the ensemble of actors at Intiman to save money and by this time he wanted Fanny out of the company as he was fed up with the gossip about her and Strindberg.

One evening in September Strindberg invited Fanny to his apartment and took her onto the balcony to look at Saturn through a telescope that he had recently acquired. She complained of a headache and he offered her a glass of wine, saying, 'Do you want me to hypnotize you?' She replied that she did not mind, thinking that he was offering to cure her headache, but he put his hand on hers and said, 'Why don't we get engaged, you and I?'

He asked her whether she had been aware of anything odd recently. She thought not but he insisted that there had been something in the air. Fanny did not share his belief in 'the powers' or the mysteries of Fate and she was confused. 'But, Mr Strindberg . . .' she protested. He said that she should call him by his first name or any other name that she cared to choose. They kissed when she left the apartment. As the door closed behind her Fanny came to her senses. She could not believe that he had just proposed to her and she burst into tears in panic.

The next day Strindberg gave Fanny a ring set with a large pearl. 'This one is for you to wear until you get the wedding rings,' he said. Then he opened another box and gave her a second ring with a sapphire. He placed it on her little finger, saying that it was a special gift of thanks for her portrayal of Swanwhite. He made her promise to keep their engagement secret for two weeks, after which time he would put on his tailcoat and ask her parents formally for her hand in marriage. 'What do you think your old man will say?' he asked her, knowing that Fanny's father was younger than him.

The prospect of marriage seemed to rejuvenate Strindberg. Just as he had been with Siri and Harriet, he was full of plans for new writing projects that this beautiful and saintly creature, his muse, had inspired. He showed Fanny photographs of country houses where they might live and urged her to go out and buy a white dress to wear at their official engagement party. Fanny could not deny the sincerity of his ardour but it frightened her:

> I was very fond of him and wished only to give him some happiness – but I could not forget that he was so much older than I. I liked touching his hair, stroking his cheeks, but I could not love him like I wanted to. That is why it was so fragile. [. . .]
>
> I wanted to be able to give him my whole life, I did not want to marry anyone else, ever, for as long as he was alive – as long as I did not have to marry him. It was not because I thought of his complicated past or because I was afraid that this relationship too would end in a catastrophe. On the contrary, I held back because of my own feelings of inadequacy, a fear of not being able to live up to his dream. I told him that.
>
> *August Strindberg i Blå Tornet*

Fanny tried to extricate herself from the situation. She told Strindberg that she was not the person he imagined she was, that she was too young, that she was not as intelligent as he thought she was. Strindberg brushed her misgivings aside and reassured her that he was not proposing marriage simply to have someone to nurse him if he should fall ill. 'I won't live for very long,' he said. 'And afterwards you can always marry a baron – or whoever you please. You can have anyone, you just have to stretch out your hand. What if a real prince meets Swanwhite . . .'

After five days Fanny told him that she would not marry him, to which Strindberg replied, 'My dear child, I can wait. I am not going to pester you, you can come when you like . . . and when you have thought it over.'

For the time being they let the matter rest. The gossip about them persisted, unfortunately, and many of Strindberg's influential friends in the theatre misinterpreted the situation and ostracized her. She was eventually barred from Intiman, and in February 1910, when she went there to discuss *The Great Highway*, she found herself locked out. Strindberg tried to intervene on her behalf but without success so he advised her to resign, which, to Falck's relief, she did.

After this her acting career was more or less finished. Only one producer – Albert Ranft at the Svenska Teatern – offered her any work and then only after a lengthy interrogation about her friendship with Strindberg. He especially wanted to know what Strindberg had written about him in *A Blue Book*. This four-volume work, written between 1906 and 1908, is dedicated to Swedenborg and is a collection of short essays, meditations, character profiles and aphorisms about science, philosophy and religion. Strindberg also included a number of caricatured pen-portraits of people he knew. Fanny told Ranft that as far as she was aware he did not feature in *A Blue Book*. He agreed to hire her for the autumn but she was given just two minor roles for the entire 1910–11 season.

With the prospect of future work in the theatre drying up completely, Fanny decided to go back to painting and she turned one of the rooms on the floor above Strindberg's apartment into a studio. Strindberg encouraged her and took a keen interest in her work and one morning when she went to her studio she found a scribbled note beside a portrait that she had done of her sister Stella. 'Bravo,' he had written. He commissioned her to paint his portrait, which was subsequently exhibited in the Hallin Gallery on Drottninggatan. Strindberg was very pleased with the result and paid her 200 kronor for it but he did not want the picture himself after the exhibition was over so Fanny kept it.

Marriage was still very much on Strindberg's mind in the spring of 1910, though he had not pressed Fanny for an answer. 'What would the audience say about a marriage where the husband is over sixty and the woman is eighteen, nineteen?' he asked the journalist Fredrik Ström. 'Answer me honestly.' Ström assumed Strindberg was talking about the theme for a play and said, 'That would be like bestiality.' He picked the same word ('tidelag' in Swedish) that Jean uses to describe Lady Julie's sexual appetite. Strindberg was apparently shaken by this response and said no more about the subject.

On Fanny's twentieth birthday in June Strindberg wrote to the actor Alrik Kjellgren at Intiman telling him how much she missed her old friends and begging him to send her a card from the whole company. He himself sent her a bouquet of twenty pink roses. She was touched by this gesture but by this time she knew that marriage to him was not what she wanted. 'I could not marry him because he was August Strindberg – but I could sacrifice my whole life for him if necessary,' she wrote. 'I worshipped him in my own way.'

Fanny stayed in touch with Strindberg and visited him several times in 1911, though the daily contact they had previously enjoyed was broken because by this time she and her parents had moved away from Drottninggatan, having finally given up trying to make a living from renting rooms after three years of hard struggle. Harriet Bosse had found the family an apartment in the building where she was now living with Gunnar and the children, on Valhallavägen. Strindberg stayed on in the Blue Tower. His new landlady provided meals to begin with then after a while he started ordering his food from the restaurant that had opened up on the ground floor of the apartment block.

One of the last things that Fanny did for Strindberg before he died was to give him one of her paintings. It was a self-portrait and he had commissioned it, stipulating in very precise terms what he wanted. He had asked her to pose wearing a blue hat with a blue veil because, he said, he had once met a woman on Drottninggatan dressed like that. This woman, he told her, 'was like a princess, tall, slim and fair'. He had spoken to Fanny about Siri, who in his imagination by now had no flaws and shone again like a jewel in his mind.

The last time Fanny saw Strindberg was in July 1911. She had moved with her family yet again, to Huddinge, then a village outside Stockholm, so she had not been able to see him very often though they had maintained almost daily contact by phone. His maid Mina, who had previously worked for the Falkners, had also kept her informed about him. There was nothing particularly special about what was to be Fanny's final conversation with Strindberg. She remembers that it was a hot day and she was anxious to get out of the city. 'Yes, my dear child, you go to the country, you go,' were his last words to her. He showed her to the door and she curtseyed to him and left.

Fanny continued to live with her family after Strindberg's death, which affected her deeply for many years. In the words of her sister Stella, 'Her protector was gone but not her need of protection.' She had a love affair with an army officer, which ended tragically when they made a suicide pact: the young man shot himself and died, and Fanny took poison but survived. This incident, which both families sought to cover up, marked the beginning for Fanny of a series of mental crises and near-breakdowns. She had handed over all her letters and memorabilia relating to Strindberg – including the portrait she had painted of him – to Professor Vilhelm Carlheim-Gyllensköld, who paid her a fee of 1000 kronor and gave her mother a further 300 to help her with the rent. Biographers and scholars had wasted no time in dissecting every aspect of Strindberg's life and there were many people who wanted to talk to her about her relationship with Sweden's greatest dramatist. Everywhere she turned she seemed to see his name in print.

In 1920 Fanny was approached by a writer called Algot Ruhe, who offered to help her put together a book about her years with Strindberg.

She agreed, though in the end he was not altogether true to the material and did not show the final manuscript to her before it went to the printers. *August Strindberg i Blå Tornet* was published in 1921 and the first edition sold well. Strindberg's friend Emil Schering later translated the book into German.

When she finally emerged from a prolonged period of grief and depression, Fanny started painting again. She became well known for her delicately executed miniature portraits, and built up enough of a reputation to attract the attention of the Danish royal family, who gave her several commissions. In 1922 she moved to Copenhagen, where she earned her living as a porcelain painter. She returned to Stockholm a few years later and on Christmas Eve 1928 she married Axel Christiansen Lund, a Danish businessman. She was pregnant at the time and soon after the birth of their daughter Suzanne in 1929 the couple were divorced.

Fanny spent the next ten years on her own, bringing up her daughter in a series of rented rooms in Sweden and Denmark. In 1939 she moved into a large apartment in Copenhagen that she shared with a friend who was a nurse. Suzanne was able to have her own bedroom for the first time and in the living room Fanny created a corner dedicated to Strindberg's memory, with a photograph of him and a laurel wreath that had been presented to her at Intiman.

It was thirty years since she had appeared on stage but in 1940 Olof Molander approached her to offer her the role of Indra's Daughter in a production of *A Dream Play* that he was putting on at Dramaten. Fanny turned him down. He must have known that Harriet Bosse would not have hesitated to seize the opportunity to play for the second time in her career the heroine that Strindberg had created for her but he chose to give the part to another actress.

Like his wives before her, Fanny never forgot about Strindberg and never stopped talking about him. 'He is a person you'll never be free from. He is always present,' she said when she visited Stockholm in 1957 to celebrate the fiftieth anniversary of the opening of Intiman.

In May 1962, fifty years after Strindberg's death, the material that Fanny had handed over to Vilhelm Carlheim-Gyllensköld was made available to the general public. Scholars and writers had already enjoyed privileged access to the letters (including August Falck and Alrik Kjellgren, who had both quoted from them in their memoirs), while Fanny had had to rely on her memory alone when writing her book. When she re-read Strindberg's letters to her she decided she would write a new book about her relationship with him and she made an appointment with the

Swedish publishers Norstedts to discuss her plans. It proved to be too daunting a task and she later dropped the idea. By now her daughter was married with a son and was living in Italy and Fanny applied for an artist's bursary that would allow her to go and paint in Capri. She was turned down. Aged seventy-three, and feeling lonely and depressed, she committed suicide in her apartment in Copenhagen on 6 October 1963.

Conclusion

— Chapter 25 —

1912: The Final Curtain

To own nothing, to wish for nothing, that is to make oneself unattainable for the worst blows of destiny.

Alone, 1904

In December 1911 Strindberg caught a chill that developed into pneumonia. He spent Christmas Eve with his daughter Greta and her husband, Henry von Philp, but was too ill to leave his apartment on Christmas Day.

Early in the New Year he paid all his debts and went to his lawyer to draw up a will. He left an equal share of his estate to each of his children, with the exception of Kerstin, who remained outside the inner family circle. She was still living with Frida's mother in Austria and as she was an heiress in her own right he saw no need to make provision for her.

It was a comfort to him that he was at last able fully to assume the role of the caring father. He had paid for Karin's honeymoon in Lindau on Lake Constance (where the family had stayed in 1887 when he was married to Siri) and had given gifts of money to Greta and Anne-Marie – and Hans, his twenty-seven-year-old son, who had visited him in Stockholm the previous summer. It was the first time that they had seen each other for eighteen years.

Though no longer entertaining thoughts of marrying Fanny Falkner and living in a grand house in the country, Strindberg kept in close touch with her. He was still interested in what she was doing and anxious to help her in any way he could. He had tried to persuade her to start auditioning for the stage again and when she rejected this idea he organized several portrait commissions for her so that she could start supporting herself as a painter.

In spite of his deteriorating health, Strindberg still managed to find the energy to write about the things that mattered to him and he went on attacking the Swedish establishment in all its manifestations. Since completing *The Great Highway* in 1909, paragraph after paragraph of passionate journalism had flowed from his pen, arguing in favour of egalitarianism, the decentralization of state power, disarmament and the abolition of private schools. He praised Zola and Tolstoy and criticized the class system, the monarchy and sycophantic poets. Anything that smacked of cant was severely censured and he emerged as a stronger republican and pacifist than ever before. A series of fifty-four newspaper articles that he wrote during an intense seven-month period in 1910–11 caused such a stir in the country that the press dubbed the ensuing controversy the 'Strindberg Feud'.

As he approached his sixty-third birthday in 1912 his public profile was as high as ever. Theatres all over Sweden were planning new productions of his plays, and news reached him that some form of personal honour was in the offing. Characteristically, he used an article published in the *Aftontidningen* on 15 January to remind his readers that the Liberals, who were now in power after five years of Conservative rule, faced some important issues and had a lot of difficult decisions to take, especially on the question of universal suffrage and defence spending. His date of birth, 22 January, he wrote, should be commemorated for an event that was much more significant: it was the anniversary of the signing of the Declaration of Rights in the English Parliament in 1689.

His protestations were discreetly ignored – it was clear that Stockholm, and indeed the whole nation, had no intention of letting his birthday pass without some form of public celebration. On 17 January he wrote to Richard Bergh:

> Please tell Branting that since I obviously have to greet the people: I will come out onto the balcony, but tell them not to stay, no speeches, no singing because then I might feel obliged to take my life out of sheer politeness. You see, I am still ill, although I pretend to myself that I am well. Have not been out.
>
> In order for the people to recognize my balcony I'll put my most beautiful electric lamp outside, the one with the red eye, towards Tegnérlunden!
>
> If I am really unwell I'll telephone the Folkets Hus; but will put lights on in the window as a sign of greeting and as a thank you; maybe I'll stand by the drawing room window.
>
> I don't dare invite anyone but my daughter, son-in-law and Axel for dinner, for fear of misusing my strength.
>
> Please tell Branting this.
> With the very best wishes.
> August Strindberg.

It was all to no avail. Bouquets of flowers were delivered to his apartment on his birthday and tributes poured in from all over the world, including a telegram from Chicago, where four thousand Swedes had gathered for a celebration in his honour. In the afternoon a small family group – just Anne-Marie, Greta and Henry, and his brother Axel – arrived for dinner as arranged. It was not long before another party of guests knocked on the door and in walked Hjalmar Branting, Richard Bergh, Karl Nordström and Vilhelm Carlheim-Gyllensköld. They told him that they had come to present him with the 'Anti-Nobel Prize for Literature' and handed him an official-looking award that Fanny had designed and written out for him.

Over the previous ten years the Swedish Academy had awarded the official Nobel Prize for Literature to many people whose work Strindberg knew well, including Bjørnstjerne Bjørnson, Henryk Sienkiewitz and Selma Lagerlöf. In 1911 the honour had gone to Harriet Bosse's favourite author, Maurice Maeterlinck. It seemed that the judges were determined to overlook Strindberg's reputation – just as they had failed to acknowledge Tolstoy, Chekhov and Ibsen (all of whom had died since the inception of the prize in 1901) – and his friends and admirers were determined to rectify this.

The money for Strindberg's 'Anti-Nobel Prize' came from all quarters of Swedish society – workers, students, artists, actors, academics, publishers and politicians – and by the beginning of March, when he actually received the cheque for 45,000 kronor, more than 20,000 people had made a donation.

Far from having a quiet evening at home on his birthday as he had wished, Strindberg found himself at the centre of a huge public rally. At 7.30 a drumroll signalled the start of a torchlight procession that made its way along Drottninggatan and soon the whole area around the Blue Tower was lit up. It is estimated that there were about ten thousand people on the streets in the city centre that night.

Strindberg went out onto his balcony with Anne-Marie and saw the banners of the Workers' Union and the Socialist Party, who had organized the event. People were cheering and singing revolutionary anthems. Strindberg waved and they cheered all the more. Prompted by Anne-Marie, he started throwing roses down into the street and the crowd went wild. This was proof indeed that the ordinary people of Stockholm appreciated him even if the members of the Swedish Academy did not.

Later that night a gala dinner was held at Berns' restaurant (the setting for his first successful novel, *The Red Room*) and 1500 people raised their glasses to him. Strindberg did not feel well enough to attend but Fanny was there, sharing a table with his friends Christian Eriksson, Richard Bergh, Karl Nordström and Vilhelm Carlheim-Gyllensköld. 'It was a long programme with endless tributes,' she later wrote. 'I had sent him a bunch of Italian anemones. The next day I received a note from him: "Thank you for the flowers, they won (as always) the first prize."'

The birthday celebrations seem to have invigorated Strindberg and for the next few weeks he returned to his normal working pattern and he started up his musical soirées at home again. He donated his 'Anti-Nobel Prize' money to various charities in Sweden – to the registered unemployed, child victims of polio and the Young Socialists, and his thoughts turned to the help he himself had received when he had been penniless in Paris. He decided to contact Nathan Söderblom, who had been rector of the Swedish Church there in the 1890s:

> 18 March 1912
> Herr Professor
> I could tell you a great deal about all kinds of things but I am old and ill and I have to put my house in order and settle my accounts. Around 1892 (?) I happened to hit upon bad times in Paris and received a couple of hundred francs in a roundabout way from the Swedish Church Relief Fund. I have tried to comfort myself with the fact that I have given to others since, during the last ten good years, and donated quite large sums. But that does not help; this must be dealt with separately. Therefore I send this money to you and since I don't know the address in Paris I must ask you to please hand over these 1000 kronor to the Relief Fund for countrymen in need. It should be considered as a repayment, not a charitable act, obviously not!
>   There is one little word missing in this short letter, the little word which is so difficult to say: Thank you! for helping me on that occasion and thank you for kindly taking the trouble this time.
> Yours
> August Strindberg

Nathan Söderblom replied on 29 March. 'There were a few words that my heart spoke at once,' he wrote. 'Now I must put them down on paper: "God bless you!"'

By this time Strindberg was seriously ill with stomach cancer. He was in a lot of pain and could only take fluids. He went on his last early morning walk on 9 April – it was a cold day, with snow falling. There were frequent bulletins in the press but he, like everyone else, still hoped for a recovery. As always his head was still full of plans; when he heard about the coal miners' strike in England, for example, he thought that it would make a good subject for a play.

On 15 April he heard the news that the *Titanic* had struck an iceberg and sunk the previous day. Harriet Bosse's nephew Arne (the son of her sister Alma) was one of the passengers who drowned. Strindberg got out of his sickbed and dressed himself in his black frock coat and white necktie as a mark of respect.

The next day Gunnar Nyström, a surgeon from Uppsala, called on him to drain the peritoneal cavity, and other distinguished doctors continued to treat him at home. On 18 April he wrote a farewell letter to his friend the composer and violinist Tor Aulin in Gothenburg:

> My dear Tor Aulin,
> Yesterday your flowers; from where? Where are you? Here or there? I am absent, but all over the place when my soul is out of its cage, which is derelict, and will soon collapse.

'If music can give you some relief from the pain, then call me;' Aulin replied, 'if it is humanly possible I shall come.'

Strindberg wrote to Anne-Marie on 19 April, telling her not to worry about him:

> My dear little daughter!
> Thank you for your flowers! but you must not come and see me. There are so many medicine bottles, doctors and noise; it is not pleasant.
> Enjoy yourself while you're young, in the company of the young and don't mourn the old man who only wishes to die.
> Father

When Siri died in Helsingfors on 22 April, Karin wrote to Strindberg from Finland with the news. Greta read her letter out loud to him and he struggled to sit up in bed, weeping while she spoke. With a great effort he got up and put on the black frock coat again. He told Greta to send a wreath of white lilies and laurel leaves for the funeral and when she asked him what inscription he wanted on the white ribbons he said: 'None. She will understand.'

Karin arrived in Stockholm for the burial of Siri's ashes in the family vault on 25 April, and Hans, recovering from rheumatic fever, came a week later. From then on he and his two sisters did not leave their father's side. Strindberg was now very weak and receiving regular morphine injections.

Harriet had flowers delivered every day though she did not contact Strindberg personally, and Frida Uhl, who was living in London, sent several telegrams begging to be allowed to see him but he did not reply to any of them. Fanny Falkner was also anxious about him:

> One day when I rang the bell to Strindberg's flat his daughter Greta opened the door. She was warm towards me, hugged me and cried, but did not think I ought to see him when he was suffering so much, but wait instead until he lay among the flowers, all handsome...
> The following day Mina had said that I could come in. But when I reached the door Philp turned up, took my arm and pushed me away saying that I had no business there. I had to leave.

> The next time I went there I cried and begged Mina to let me in. I promised to be quiet and not disturb him. She went in and came back with this strange message:
> 'He said that you should not be sad, Miss Fanny, because he has been thinking about you.'
> I answered that I did not care whether he had been thinking of me as long as I could see him. Then she went inside again and came back with an even stranger message:
> 'Mr Strindberg says that if you cry, Miss, he'll cut you out.'
>
> *August Strindberg i Blå Tornet*

On 1 May, Labour Day, the miners in southern Sweden and the workers in northern Sweden sent telegrams and Strindberg acknowledged them both. A week or so later he instructed Mina to take a large suitcase to Harriet:

> The only thing in it was a letter to his daughter Anne-Marie and 1500 kronor in paper notes. Strindberg wrote to our daughter that he remembered giving me a grand piano when we got married, but that he had made me sad later by exchanging the grand for an upright.
> 'Maybe mother wants to buy a new grand piano with these 1500 kronor now?'
> It was as if Strindberg needed to make his peace before he died, mend what he felt had broken.
> After Strindberg's death I was sent a Chinese box containing all my letters to him, and a few small souvenirs plus my little withered bridal crown of myrtle.
>
> *Strindberg's Letters to Harriet Bosse*

Strindberg died on 14 May and the funeral took place five days later. He had left instructions that he should be buried in a simple coffin, early in the morning; the burial plot should be in the main part of the cemetery rather than the section reserved for rich people. He further specified that there should be no speeches, no funeral address – no fuss – only that Fanny's father should sing Orpheus's song from Shakespeare's *Henry VIII*. A plain wooden cross with his name and dates and the inscription *Ave crux, spes unica* was the only memorial he wanted.

The funeral cortège left the Blue Tower shortly before 8 am. Crowds had been gathering along the two-mile route to the Northern cemetery for two or three hours beforehand and around four thousand people joined in the procession that followed the hearse, including Prince Eugen, who was a talented painter and numbered many artists among his friends. Karin, Greta, Hans and Anne-Marie led the group of family mourners at the head of the procession, and Fanny walked with the actors she had worked with at Intiman. Harriet stayed away, preferring to sit alone, on a bench in the Djurgården, where Strindberg had taken his daily walks for many years.

In accordance with his wishes, there were no speeches or addresses but Nathan Söderblom, who conducted the burial service, read from the Bible, selecting a passage from Matthew, Chapter 3 as his main text: 'Blessed are those who hunger and thirst for righteousness, for they shall be satisfied.'

Among the many floral tributes was one from King Gustav V and one from the *Riksdag*. But the Swedish Academy ignored him in death as they had done in his lifetime: they sent no wreath and no official representative to pay their respects to Sweden's finest writer.

Notes

General

Punctuation: Strindberg tended to use punctuation a bit like a musical score. He frequently inserted exclamation marks or question marks in the middle of his sentences for extra emphasis and used multiple dots and dashes to indicate a pause or change of subject. His punctuation has been retained in the quoted material in this book. Three dots within square brackets [. . .] indicate that text has been omitted from the original for editorial purposes.

Swedish Currency: In 1880 an unskilled worker in Sweden earned about 650 kronor a year. This had risen to about 950 by 1900 and 1250 by 1910. According to a report in the magazine *Idun*, a family of four with an income of 1500 kronor a year in 1890 would typically spend it as follows:

    250 kronor on housing (rent or mortgage)
    100 kronor in taxes
    150 kronor on clothes
    600 kronor on food
     75 kronor on fuel
     50 kronor for a maidservant
     75 kronor on health-care
    200 kronor on miscellaneous expenses

When Siri and Strindberg decided to divorce in 1892 she wanted 2500 kronor a year to support herself and the children. Harriet Bosse was earning around 6000 kronor a year in the early 1900s.

French Currency: When Strindberg was living in France in the 1890s he paid 260 francs a month for a room at the Hôtel des Américains. Dinner with coffee at Madame Charlotte's cost 1.50 francs. In 1894 he told Frida Uhl that two furnished rooms would cost 50 francs a month to rent.

Dramaten: The Royal Dramatic Theatre [Kungliga Dramatiska Teatern] was founded in 1788 by King Gustav III. The building was destroyed by fire in 1825 and the company moved to the Royal Opera House, where it functioned as the Royal Theatre [Kungliga Teatern] for the next thirty-eight years. King Karl XV purchased a new building at Kungsträdgården (about 300 metres from the theatre's present site at Nybroplan) in 1863 and the company once again became 'Royal'– until 1888, when the King and the state withdrew most of its financial support. Under the new name of the Dramatic Theatre [Dramatiska Teatern – popularly shortened to 'Dramaten'] the theatre was then run by an association of actors, with the King and the state contributing part of the rent, until 1903. From 1903–07 the theatre was under the sole management of the actor Gunnar Fredriksson. In 1908 new premises were found at Nybroplan, and though officially run by a limited company, who reverted to the theatre's original eighteenth-century name – the Kungliga Dramatiska Teatern – the theatre has been supported by state subsidy ever since.

Introduction

page 15: The English edition of Frida's book *Marriage With Genius* (originally written in German) was first published in London in 1937. All extracts quoted here were translated by the author into English from the Swedish edition. (*See* Bibliography.)

Chapter 2

page 36: Bonnier's edition of *He and She,* eventually published in 1919, retains the fictitious names that Strindberg originally used for himself, Siri, Carl Gustaf and Sofia. In the National Edition, published by Norstedts förlag in 1996, their real names have been reinstated.

page 38: Bo Bennich-Björkman, Professor Emeritus at Uppsala University, has managed to unravel the complicated story of Siri's finances at the time of her divorce from Carl Gustaf Wrangel. (For full details see Bibliography.)

NOTES

Chapter 6

page 73: 'Spada' was the nickname of the journalist John Janzon, who was the foreign correspondent for the *Stockholm Dagblad* at that time.

page 75: 'Second Night' is a long poem of some twenty-two stanzas. The extract reproduced here is from stanzas 1, 2 and 3.

Chapter 7

page 81: 'Högstedt's Piccadon and Lennström's wafers of maize': these refer to the holy communion wine and host. Högstedt and Lennström were the shopkeepers who provided them.

page 90: Chevillon's (the Hôtel Chevillon) was one of the two main hotels in Grèz-sur-Loing and it was a popular venue for dancing.

Chapter 8

page 102: Holenberg (or Hohlenberg) was the Strindbergs' landlord.

Chapter 9

page 105: Putte was the Strindbergs' pet name for their son, Hans.

Chapter 12

page 139: Franz Lenbach: German painter, best known for his portraits of Bismarck.

page 141: 'our own little Ferkel far off in the West' – the western part of Berlin.

page 141: 'The money has arrived . . .' – Strindberg had received an advance of DM1000 from the German publisher of *A Madman's Defence*.

page 141: 'Tomorrow we shall celebrate the first anniversary, maybe together.' Frida is referring here to her love affair with Hermann Sudermann.

Chapter 13

page 147: Julius Meier-Graefe's description of Dagny Juel is quoted in J P Hodin's biography of Edvard Munch. (*See* Bibliography.)

page 149: After Dagny Juel's death Stanislaw Przybyszewski married one of his mistresses. He never achieved the literary fame that he aspired to and he died, relatively unknown, in 1927.

page 150: Bengt Lidforss wrote an obituary in the *Dagens Nyheter* on 19 June 1901. He kept Dagny Juel's memory sacred until he died of syphilis in 1913.

Chapter 15

page 162: Mrs Kainz was the wife of Strindberg's friend Joseph Kainz, a famous German actor.

page 162: Carl Ludwig Schleich was a doctor and a regular visitor at the 'Ferkel'. He was a fellow-admirer of Dagny Juel.

page 162: Tu a donné le meilleur de ce que ce siècle a produit en Europe. Et tu n'est pas content – Hm! Je ne suis pas si ambitieux [ambitieuse] que toi. – You have given the best that this century has produced in Europe. And you are not happy – Hm! I am not so ambitious as you.

page 162: 'Tu m'a donné le bonheur – le seul bonheur possible pour moi sur cette terre.' – You have given me happiness – the only possible happiness for me on this earth.

page 167: 'Faeaker country' – the land of the Phaeacians in the *Odyssey*.

Chapter 16

page 176: There is no evidence to suggest that Strindberg ever made a declaration of love to Frida's sister Marie.

page 177: Frida's comments about Willy Gretor are quoted in Göran Söderström's book *Strindberg och bildkonsten*. (*See* Bibliography.)

page 181: Café de la Regence: Strindberg omits the acute accent [Régence].

page 182: The new book that Strindberg refers to is his novel *Inferno*.

page 183: Frida's mother, maternal grandmother and sister were all called Marie. Her sister's married name was Weyr (her husband was the sculptor Rudolf Weyr) and her grandmother's surname was Reischl. Strindberg generally uses the name Maria rather than Marie for all of them.

Chapter 17

page 194: Intiman is the popular name for Intima Teatern [the Intimate Theatre] established by Strindberg and August Falck in Stockholm in 1907.

page 195: In common with Norwegian, but unlike all other European languages, Swedish is a so-called 'musical' or 'tone' language. A distinctive feature of Swedish is that all the vowels, nine in all, are 'pure' (there are no diphthongs) and these are not modified even when they occur in unstressed syllables or at the end of a word.

page 196: Strindberg wrote *To Damascus* in three parts and Part I is the play that is most often performed. Modern directors generally feel that Parts II and III are too philosophical in tone and lacking in dramatic structure to be staged successfully.

Chapter 18

page 204: 'die ferne unsterbliche Geliebte' ['the immortal beloved far away'] is a reference to Beethoven's song cycle of that name (Opus 98).

page 206: The Gärdet, in the northeastern part of central Stockholm, was an area of common land that had previously been used by the military for training, and Strindberg's apartment on Karlavägen overlooked this. It is still largely an open green space today.

page 208: 'Your green room' refers to Harriet's bedroom in the apartment on Karlavägen, which had a green rug on the floor. Strindberg usually refers to this as 'the yellow room'.

page 209: Harriet apparently found it hard to pronounce 'August' and so she called Strindberg 'Gusten'.

Chapter 19

page 211: 'O crux ave spes unica.' : 'Hail the cross, my only hope.'

page 213: Although Harriet's father was German and she had learned the language as a child, she did not feel confident of her pronunciation or her knowledge of grammar. Strindberg wrote to Emil Schering, his German translator, on several occasions between 1901 and 1905 in an attempt to find work for Harriet in Germany.

Chapter 20

page 225: By 1905 Strindberg had placed his books with several different publishers in Sweden. Bonnier's tended to concentrate on the novels and short story collections (with the notable exception of the explosive *Black Banners*, which they rejected for fear of libel action), while Geber's published the plays. In 1911, after lengthy negotiations, Strindberg agreed to grant exclusive rights to Bonnier's to re-issue virtually everything he had ever written, for which he negotiated the sum of 200,000 kronor, to be paid in four annual instalments. The works excluded from this agreement were *He and She*, all the other letters, his diaries, and various unpublished manuscripts.

page 227: The Svennbergs: the actors Tore Svennberg and his wife, Karin Wiberg.

page 228: Rosa was Anne-Marie's doll. Ebba was Strindberg's housemaid and Sarah was the nanny who was hired after he had dismissed Ellen.

page 233: August Falck's production of *Lady Julie* in 1906 had just two performances – one at Akademiska Föreningen at Lund University on 18 September and the other in Malmö the following evening. The only other production of the play to date in Sweden had been a private performance at Gillessalen [the Guildhall] in Uppsala in the autumn of 1904.

Chapter 21

page 235: Harriet did not play Gerda in *Thunder in the Air* until 1933.

page 238: *The Occult Diary* was not published in Strindberg's lifetime. Bonnier's first brought out an edition of extracts in 1963 and the full text did not appear in print until 1977.

page 238: Strindberg had stopped visiting Harriet because of her relationship with Gunnar Castrén.

page 241: Nils Andersson was a lawyer who shared Strindberg's interest in the occult. They had first met in Lund in 1898.

page 241: Strindberg uses 'x' in his *Occult Diary* as a code for sexual intercourse. Three crosses, 'xxx', signify that he made love to Harriet three times, though in this instance he was dreaming and referring to what he describes as her telepathic 'visitations'.

page 245: A further forty letters from Strindberg to Harriet and nine from her to him were discovered amongst the papers of one of his friends, Carlheim-Gyllensköld, in 1934. They were published by Bonnier's in a separate volume, edited by Åke Runnquist and Torsten Eklund, in 1955. Only twenty-two of the letters that Harriet wrote to Strindberg have survived; she had destroyed the rest soon after he died.

Chapter 23

page 264: Tekniska Skolan, which Fanny Falkner went to in 1904, was Stockholm's main state art college at the time and a very prestigious place. Originally established as Slöjdskolan [the Arts and Crafts College] in 1860, it had been re-organized and renamed in 1878. Today it is known as Konstfackskolan [the Art College].

page 265: The 'Blue Tower' was Strindberg's ironic name for the apartment block on Drottninggatan where he lived for the last four years of his life. This was probably a reference to the Blue Tower in Copenhagen, a prison in which several members of the Danish royal family had been incarcerated in the Middle Ages, and where, in the seventeenth century, King Christian IV's daughter Leonora Christina spent twenty-two years on charges of treason. There was a kind of turret on the corner of Strindberg's building – though the roof was green rather than blue – and it is still known as the 'Blue Tower'. His old apartment currently houses the Strindberg Museum.

Chapter 24

page 273: 'Ships can make port in a gentle breeze.' – this is a line from a short poem (since lost) that Fanny had written for Strindberg.

page 275: Strindberg's warning to Fanny not to go to the operetta was in response to her telling him that she had received an invitation from Åke Bonnier (and possibly his brother Tor as well) and Yngve Berg. She heeded his advice.

page 276: It is customary in Sweden for a married woman to wear two plain gold rings – one for the engagement and one for the marriage – on the fourth finger of the left hand. She would wear other rings, set with precious stones, on the right hand or on other fingers of the left hand.

A man would wear one gold ring from the time of his engagement but would not add a second on marriage like his wife.

Chapter 25

page 286: The journalist and critic Hjalmar Branting, who had been a friend of Strindberg's since the 1880s, was now the Leader of the Social Democratic Party. He became Prime Minister for the first time in 1920.

page 286: Tegnérlunden – the Blue Tower is situated on the corner of Drottninggatan and this square.

page 286: The Folkets Hus: the headquarters of the Socialist Party.

page 288: Nathan Söderblom (1866–1931) was Professor of Theology at the University of Uppsala from 1901 until 1914, when he became the Archbishop of Sweden. A Member of the Swedish Academy from 1921, he won the Nobel Peace Prize in 1930.

page 288: Around 1892 (?): The bracketed question mark appears in Strindberg's original letter. He in fact received money from the Swedish Church Relief Fund in 1895.

page 289: Mina was Strindberg's maid.

page 290: 'he'll cut you out': this is an ambiguous phrase – the Swedish word 'stryka' means cut out, cancel or delete – and Strindberg probably intended it as a joke, implying that if Fanny were a character in one his plays he would write her out and so deprive her of a chance to perform and take a curtain call at the end.

page 290: When Strindberg died his friends E Walter Hülphers and Wilhelm Peterson-Berger wrote a valedictory hymn but in respect for his wishes it was not sung at the funeral. Instead, on 4 June, several working men's choirs came together in Stockholm to sing the hymn at the beginning of a performance of Strindberg's play *Gustav Adolf* at the Cirkusteatern.

Select Bibliography

Works by August Strindberg

The books listed here are in the original Swedish and, unless otherwise stated, are from the Swedish National Edition of Strindberg's Collected Works, published by Norstedts förlag in Stockholm from 1984.

Återfunna (De) breven (Bonniers förlag, Stockholm, 1955)
Brev till min dotter Kerstin (Bonniers förlag, Stockholm, 1961)
Brott och brott (Samlade skrifter, Bonniers förlag, Stockholm, 1987)
Dåres (En) försvarstal (Bonniers förlag, Stockholm, 1920)
Dikter i urval (av Ingemar Lindahl) (Wahlström & Widstrand, Stockholm, 1966, 1993)
Dödsdansen (1988)
Drömspel (Ett) (Bonniers förlag, Stockholm, 1974)
Ensam (1994)
Erik XIV (1992)
Fadren, (1984)
Folkungasagan (1992)
Fordringsägare (1984)
Från fjärdingen till Blå Tornet, Ett brevurval 1870–1912 (Bonniers förlag, Stockholm, 1946)
Fröken Julie (1984)
Giftas, vol. I och II (Bonniers förlag, Stockholm, 1957)
Gustav III (1988)
Gustav Vasa (1992)
Han och hon (1996)
Hemsöborna (Bonniers Förlag, Stockholm, 1950)
Inferno (1994)
'Jag är en djävla man', Citat valda och kommenterade av Per-Anders Hellqvist (En bok för alla, Stockholm, 1994)
Kammarspel (1991)
Kamraterna (1988)
Klostret (1994)
Kristina (1988)
Kronbruden (1990)

Legender (including *Jacob brottas*) (Gernandts förlag, Stockholm, 1898)
Lycko-Pers resa (Bonniers förlag, Stockholm, 1962)
Marodörer (1988)
Mäster Olof (Bonniers förlag, Stockholm, 1962)
Nio enaktare (1888–1892, 1984)
Ny (En) blå bok (Björck & Börjesson, Stockholm, 1908)
Nya (Det) riket (Bonniers förlag, Stockholm, 1957)
Ordalek och småkonst och annan 1900–talslyrik (1989)
Påsk (Bonniers förlag, Stockholm, 1959)
Röda rummet (Folket i Bilds förlag, Stockholm, 1962)
Sagor (1994)
Sömngångarnätter (Bonniers förlag, Stockholm, 1884)
Stora landsvägen (Bonniers förlag, Stockholm, 1909)
Stridsskrifter (Askelin & Hägglund, Stockholm, 1981)
Strindbergs brev, vols. I–XV ed. Torsten Eklund, vols. XVI–XX ed. Björn Meidal (Bonniers förlag, Stockholm, 1948–96)
Strindbergs brev till Harriet Bosse (Natur och Kultur, Stockholm, 1932)
Svanevit (1990)
Svarta fanor (Björck & Börjesson, Stockholm, 1907)
Svenska folket (Gidlunds förlag, Stockholm, 1974)
Svenska öden och äventyr (Bonniers förlag, Stockholm, 1957)
Tidiga 80–talsdramer: Gillets hemlighet, Herr Bengts hustru, Lycko-Pers resa (Bonniers förlag, Stockholm, 1919)
Till Damaskus (1991)
Tjänstekvinnans son I–II (Wihlke & Son, Oslo, 1973)
Ur ockulta dagboken (Bonniers förlag, Stockholm, 1963)

Biographies and Critical Works

Adolfson, Edvin *Edvin Adolfson berättar om sitt liv med fru Thalia fru Filmia och andra fruar* (Bonniers förlag, Stockholm, 1972)
Bing, Erik Henriques *Min kunst passer ikke for vor tid* (Forlaget Tågaliden, Copenhagen, 1994)
Boethius, Ulf *Strindberg och kvinnofrågan t.o.m. Giftas 1* (Prisma, Stockholm, 1969)
Börge, Vagn *Kvinden i Strindbergs liv og digtning* (Levin & Munksgaard, Copenhagen, 1936)
Brandell, Gunnar *Strindberg – ett författarliv, I–IV* (Alba, Stockholm, 1985–89)

Buchmayr, Friedrich *Wenn nein, nein! August Strindberg und Frida Uhl, Briefwechsel 1893–1902* (Bibliothek der Provinz, Weitra, 1993)
Buchmayr, Friedrich, *Die andere Welt – August Strindberg in Oberösterreich* (Litteratur im Stifterhaus, Linz, 1994)
Cullberg, Johan, *Skaparkriser* (Natur & Kultur, Stockholm, 1992)
Dahlbäck, Maj *Siri von Essen i verkligheten* (Natur & Kultur, Stockholm, 1989)
Engström, Albert, *August Strindberg och jag* (Bonniers förlag, Stockholm, 1923)
Falck, August: *Fem år med Strindberg* (Wahlström & Widstrand, Stockholm,1935)
Falkner, Fanny *August Strindberg i Blå Tornet* (Norstedt & Söners förlag, Stockholm, 1921)
Falkner-Söderberg, Stella *Fanny Falkner och August Strindberg* (Rabén & Sjögren, Stockholm, 1970)
Grein, J T *Ett möte med Strindberg* (Strindbergiana 3, Atlantis, Stockholm, 1988)
Hedén, Erik *Strindberg* (Tidens förlag, Stockholm, 1926)
Hellström, Victor *Strindberg och musiken* (Norstedts & Söners förlag, Stockholm, 1917)
Hildeman, Karl-Ivar *Strindberg, hans släktinger och Pelikanen* (Strindbergiana 9, Atlantis, Stockholm, 1994)
Hodin, J P *Edvard Munch* (Thames & Hudson, London, 1972)
Jacobsen, Harry: *Strindberg och hans första hustru* (Bonniers förlag, Stockholm, 1946)
Kossak, Ewa K, transl. from Polish *(Dagny Przybyszewska, zblakana gwiazda)* by Christina Wollin *Irrande stjärna, berättelsen om den legendariska Dagny Juel* (Bonniers förlag, Stockholm, 1978)
Lagercrantz, Olof: *August Strindberg* (Wahlström & Widstrand, Stockholm, 1979)
Lamm, Martin *August Strindberg* (Hammarström & Åberg, Stockholm, 1948)
Larsson, Carl *Jag* (Bonniers förlag, Stockholm, 1931)
Lind Af-Hageby, L *August Strindberg* (Stanley Paul & Co., London, 1913)
Linder, Sten *Ibsen, Strindberg och andra* (Bonniers förlag, Stockholm, 1936)
Lundegård, Axel *Några Strindbergsminnen knutna till en handfull brev* (Tidens förlag, Stockholm, 1920)
Meyer, Michael *Strindberg* (Oxford University Press, Oxford, 1985)
Molander, Olof, *Harriet Bosse, en skiss* (Norstedts förlag, Stockholm,1920)

Myrdal, Jan *Om August Strindbergs jagromaner och fallet Frida* (Strindbergiana 14 Atlantis, Stockholm, 1999)
Ohlander, Ann-Sofi och Strömberg, Ulla-Britt *Tusen svenska kvinnoöden* (Rabén Prisma, Stockholm, 1996)
Ollén, Gunnar *Strindbergs dramatik* (Sveriges Radios förlag, Stockholm, 1932)
Paul, Adolf *Min Strindbergsbok* (Norstedts & Söners förlag, Stockholm, 1930)
Philp, Anna och Hartzell, Nora *Strindbergs systrar berättar om barndomshemmet och om bror August Strindberg* (Norstedts förlag, Stockholm, 1926)
Selander, Nils och Selander, Edvard *Carl XVs glada dagar* (Norstedts förlag, Stockholm, 1927)
Schildknecht-Wahlgren, Maria *Minnesbilder* (Bergendahls boktryckeri, Göteborg, 1959)
Smirnoff, Karin *Så var det i verkligheten* (Bonniers förlag, Stockholm, 1956)
Smirnoff, Karin *Strindbergs första hustru* (Forum, Stockholm, 1925, 1977)
Söderström, Göran: *Strindberg och bildkonsten* (Forum, Stockholm, 1972)
Strauss, Monica, *Cruel Banquet, The Life and Loves of Frida Strindberg* (Harcourt, Orlando, 2000)
Strindberg, Frida, transl. from German (*Lieb', Leid und Zeit*) by Karin Boye *Strindberg och hans andra hustru* (Bonniers förlag, Stockholm, 1933–34)
Uddgren, Gustaf *Boken om Strindberg* (Åhlén & Åkerlund, Göteborg, 1909)
Vallgren, Ville *Ville Vallgrens ABC bok med bilder* (Söderströms, Helsingfors, 1916)
Waal, Carla, transl. from English (*Strindberg's Muse and Interpreter*) by Rebecca Alsberg *Harriet Bosse, 'Det nya seklets skådespelerska'* (Natur och Kultur, Stockholm, 1993)
Wirmark, Margareta *Den kluvna scenen* (Gidlunds förlag, Stockholm, 1988)

Journals and Pamphlets

Acta Universitatis Umensis *Teater i Stockholm 1910–1970* (Almquist & Wiksell, Stockholm, 1982)
ADAM Centenary Issue (Adam International Review, London, 1949)
Bonniers Månadshäften (Stockholm, June 1912)
Monié Karin *Kvinnosyn i dikt och verklighet* (Kulturhuset, Stockholm, 1981)

Articles in Newspapers and Journals

Bennich-Björkman, Bo 'Strindbergs försvarstal låg nära sanningen' Under strecket (*Svenska Dagbladet*, 23 August 1997)
Berendsohn, Walter 'August Strindberg och hans syster Elisabeth' (*Ord och Bild*, 62, 1953)
Bianchini, Lisa 'August Strindberg på Sandhamn' (*Idun*, 8 February 1925)
Cork, Richard 'London's Bold Cave Woman' (*The Times*, 31 December 1998)
Essen, Siri von 'Artistkolonin i Grèz par Nemours' (*Ny Illustrerad Tidning*, 2 February 1884)
Ekenvall, Asta 'Myten om det manliga och det kvinnliga. Om Strindbergs kvinnohat' (*Meddelanden från Strindbergssällskapet*, 26, Dramaten 75/76, 1960)
Eklund, Torsten 'Strindbergs tredje äktenskap i ny belysning' (*Meddelanden från Strindbergssällskapet*, 19, Dramaten, 1956)
Fröding, Märta 'August Strindberg sådan jag minnes honom' (*Idun*, 26 July 1925)
Strindberg, August och Essen, Siri von 'En okänd historia av August och Siri' (*Moderna Tider*, July 1996)
Welinder, Hélène 'Strindberg i Schweiz' (*Ord och Bild*, 1912)

Interviews

Dalström, Kata *Vecko-Journalen* (1915)
Falkner, Fanny *Sveriges Radio* (1949)
Flygare, Anna *Svenska Dagbladet* (1948)
Philp, Anna von *Idun* (1925)
Strindberg, August *Gil Blas* (1895)
Strindberg, Greta *Göteborgs Handels- och Sjöfarts-Tidning* (22 January 1912)
Uhl, Frida *Dagens Nyheter* (31 May 1926)

Unpublished Letters

Bosse, Harriet: Letters to Olof Molander (Handskriftsavdelningen, Kungliga biblioteket, Stockholm)
Molander, Olof: Letters to Torsten Eklund – 19 September and 18 February 1965 (Handskriftsavdelningen Kungliga biblioteket, Stockholm)
Uhl, Frida: Letters to Strindberg (Handskriftsavdelningen Kungliga biblioteket, Stockholm)

English Translations by Eivor Martinus of Strindberg's plays

The First Warning, Pariah, Motherly Love (Amber Lane Press, Oxford, 1986)
The Great Highway (Absolute Press, Bath, 1990)
Chamber Plays: Thunder in the Air, After the Fire, Ghost Sonata, The Pelican, The Black Glove (Absolute Press, Bath, 1991)
The Father, Lady Julie, Playing With Fire (Amber Lane Press, Oxford, 1998)

Index

ABC (Vallgren) 71
Åberg, Gurli 56
Abu Casem's Slippers (Strindberg) 269
Academy of Music, Stockholm 27, 47
Adelsvärd, Baron Theodor 274
Adlersparre, Sophie 84, 85
Adolphson, Edvin 243–44
Advent (Strindberg) 181
After the Fire (Strindberg) 237
Aftontidningen 286
'Against Payment' (Strindberg) 88
Ahlqvist, Inez (née Bosse) 193, 195, 206, 216, 220, 223, 225, 230, 243, 244
'A la zoologie de femme' (Strindberg) 169
Alexandersson, Karin 269
Alhambrateatret, Kristiania 194
Andersen, Hans Christian 195
Andersson, Nils 241
Antibarbarus (Strindberg) 145, 166
Antoine, André 103, 195
Aristotle 84
'Artists' Colony in Grèz par Nemours, The' (Essen) 71–72
Arts Theatre, London 244
'Aufschwung' (Schumann) 180
August Strindberg i Blå Tornet [*August Strindberg in the Blue Tower*] (Falkner) 16, 265, 277, 280, 289–90
Aulin, Tor 289
'Autumn' (Strindberg) 89

Balzac, Honoré de 213
Banville, Théodore Faullain de 195
Beck, Julia 56
Beethoven, Ludwig van 213, 214
Before Death (Strindberg) 250
Benedictsson, Victoria 76, 84–86, 98, 103
Bennich-Björkman, Bo 69
Berg, Yngve 274

Bergh, Richard 222, 223, 247, 286–87
Bergman, Bo 238
Bergman, Ingmar 255, 258
Bergqvist-Hansson, Jenny 245
Bernadotte, Jean 81–82
Bernhardt, Sarah 237
Berns' Restaurant, Stockholm 54, 287
Bernstein, Henry 242
Birch-Pfeiffer, Charlotte 50
Björck & Börjesson 237
Björksten, Emilie 79
Björling, Manda 239, 264–65
Björling, Renée 268
Bjørnson, Bjørnstjerne 60, 74, 76, 82, 195, 213, 287
Black Banners (Strindberg) 237, 238
Black Glove, The (Strindberg) 238
Blue Book, A (Strindberg) 247, 278
Bolin, Wilhelm 63
Bond, The (Strindberg) 155, 239
Bonnier, Albert 36, 54, 74, 82, 94, 96–97, 98, 102, 110
Bonnier, Isidor 85
Bonnier, Karl Otto 82
Bonniers förlag 81, 97, 238
Borchsensius, Otto 239
Börge, Vagn 186
Bosse, Alma – *see* Fahlström, Alma
Bosse, Anne-Marie – *see* Lehman, Anne-Marie
Bosse, Dagmar – *see* Möller, Dagmar
Bosse, Ewald 195, 196
Bosse, Harriet 12–13, 15–16, 58, 67, 79, 104, 110, 113, 174, 183, 184, 263, 267, 268, 269, 270, 275, 277, 278, 280, 287, 288, 289, 290
– early life 192–93
– debut as an actress, Kristiania (1896) 193

– debut at Dramaten (1899) 195
– first meeting with Strindberg (1900) 196
– plays the Lady in *To Damascus* at Dramaten (1900) 198–99
– engagement to Strindberg (1901) 201–02
– plays Eleonora in *Easter* at Dramaten (1901) 203
– marriage to Strindberg (1901) 205
– development of her career at Dramaten (1901–03) 207–19
– first separation from Strindberg (1901) 208–12
– birth of her daughter, Anne–Marie (1902) 216
– second separation from Strindberg (1902) 217–20
– first tour of Finland (1904) 222–24
– divorce from Strindberg (1904) 224
– second tour of Finland (1906) 230–32
– plays Kersti in *The Crown Bride*, Helsingfors and Stockholm (1906) 231–32
– plays Indra's Daughter in *A Dream Play*, Stockholm (1907) 237
– marriage to Gunnar Wingård (1908) 241
– birth of her son, Bo (1909) 242
– divorce from Gunnar Wingård (1912) 242
– reaction to Strindberg's death (1912) 290
– marriage to Edvin Adolphson (1927) 243
– divorce from Edvin Adolphson (1932) 244
– publication of the Strindberg letters (1932) 244
– retirement from the stage (1943) 246
– later life (1943–61) 247
– death (1961) 247
Bosse, Inez – *see* Ahlqvist, Inez
Bosse, Johann 192, 194
Brandes, Edvard 112

Brandes, Georg 90, 103, 187
Branting, Anna 203, 269
Branting, Hjalmar 69, 83, 94, 203, 286–87
Brzozowski, Wincent 149
Buchmayr, Friedrich 168
Buckle, Henry Thomas 56
Buddhism 168, 216, 254
By the Open Sea (Strindberg) 105

Cadell, Pauline 11
Carlheim-Gyllensköld, Vilhelm 279–80, 287
Carl XVs glada dagar [*The Merry Days of Carl XV*] (Selander) 68
Casinoteatret, Copenhagen 98, 287
Castegren, Victor 227, 235
Castrén, Gunnar 224, 232, 235, 239
Catholicism 90, 168, 249
Centralteatret, Kristiania 250
Chekhov, Anton 287
'Chrysaëtos' (Strindberg) 214
Cloister, The (Strindberg) 16, 129, 135, 138–42, 153, 154, 156–57, 163–64, 165, 167–70, 181
Companions, The [also known as *Comrades*] (Strindberg) 93–95, 155, 243, 250
Conservatoire, Stockholm, 192, 194
Cork, Richard 186
Creditors (Strindberg) 11, 13–14, 103, 104, 106, 131, 153, 170
Crimes and Crimes (Strindberg) 52, 186, 196, 204, 250
Crown Bride, The [also known as *The Virgin Bride*] (Strindberg) 110, 191, 199, 231–32, 238, 250

Dagens Nyheter 23, 31, 50, 60, 83
Dagmarteatret, Copenhagen 103, 250
Dahlström, Erik 102–03
Dalström, Kata 197
Dance of Death, The (Strindberg) 191, 197, 199–200, 229, 250
David, Marie 14, 90–91, 107–09
Dehmel, Richard 131

Delius, Frederick 178
'Des arts nouveaux!' (Strindberg) 169
Dickens, Charles 238
Doll's House, A (Ibsen) 30, 64–65, 79, 85
'Doll's House, A' (Strindberg) 85
'D'où nous sommes venus' (Strindberg) 169
Drachmann, Holger 131, 194
Dramaten, Stockholm 22, 23, 49, 50, 51, 54, 55, 56, 58, 60, 61, 64, 94, 97, 106, 195, 196, 198, 203, 205, 210, 213, 219, 227, 228, 237, 239, 242, 243, 246, 250, 258, 280
Dream Play, A (Strindberg) 14, 61, 168, 192, 200, 210, 213, 216, 237, 244, 249, 250, 253–58, 280
Duncan, Isadora 272
Duse, Eleonora 237
'Dutchman, The' (Strindberg) 218–19
Dymov, Osip 243

Easter (Strindberg) 14, 191, 200, 203, 207, 231, 244, 247, 249, 250, 254, 265–67, 269–70
Echo de Paris, L' 169
Egmont (Goethe) 219
Ehrnrooth, Adelaide 110
Ekelund, Waldemar 110
Eklund, Torsten 247
Elektra (Hofmannsthal) 231, 242–43
Eliasson, Anders 180–81
Emerson, Ralph Waldo 213
Emeryk, Wladyslaw 148–49
Epstein, Jacob 186
Erik XIV (Strindberg) 204
Eriksson, Christian 287
Essen, Baron Carl Reinhold von 24–28
Essen, Betty von – *see* In de Bétou, Elisabeth ('Betty') Charlotta
Essen, Siri von 12–15, 16, 129, 130, 134, 137, 138, 145, 153, 155, 157, 158–59, 162, 181, 187, 191, 192, 195, 199, 200, 205, 206, 213, 216, 217, 224, 228, 231, 236, 238, 242, 263, 265, 266, 269, 274, 277, 279, 285, 289
– early life 24–28
– marriage to Carl Gustaf Wrangel (1872) 28
– birth of her daughter Sigrid (1873) 28
– first meeting with Strindberg (1875) 22
– development of her relationship with Strindberg (1875–76) 33–51
– divorce from Carl Gustaf Wrangel (1876) 42
– death of her daughter Sigrid (1877) 50
– debut as an actress at Dramaten (1877) 49–50
– death of her mother (1877) 50
– first contract with Dramaten (1877) 50
– marriage to Strindberg (1877) 51
– birth and death of her daughter Kerstin (1878) 52
– birth of her daughter Karin (1880) 55
– termination of her contract with Dramaten (1881) 56
– birth of her daughter Greta (1881) 58
– on tour in Finland (1882) 63
– plays Margit in *Sir Bengt's Wife* at Dramaten (1882) 67
– first visit to Grèz-sur-Loing (1883) 71–73
– birth of her son, Hans (1884) 76
– reaction to *Getting Married Vol. II* (1885) 84
– first meeting with Marie David (1885) 90
– portrayal as the Baroness/Maria in *A Madman's Defence* (1887–88) 21–22, 45, 49, 97–98, 108
– considers divorce from Strindberg (1888) 102
– stars in the première of *Lady Julie*, Copenhagen (1889) 104
– separation from Strindberg (1889–92) 106–08
– renewal of friendship with Marie David (1891) 107–09

- divorce from Strindberg (1892) 108
- returns to Finland (1893) 108
- later life (1893–1912) 109–13
- death (1912) 113

Eugen, Prince 238, 290

Facing Death (Strindberg) 194, 196
Fahlstedt, Amalia 76
Fahlström, Alma (née Bosse) 174, 192–95, 288
Fahlström, Johan 174, 193–95
Falck, August 233, 238, 239, 240, 264–67, 269–72, 273, 276–77, 280
Falkner, Ada 268
Falkner, Eva 268
Falkner, Fanny 12–13, 15, 16, 200, 240–41, 285, 289–90
- early life 263–65
- debut at Intiman (1908) 265
- first meeting with Strindberg (1908) 265
- development of her relationship with Strindberg (1908–12) 266–69
- plays Eleonora in *Easter* at Intiman (1908) 269
- plays Swanwhite at Intiman (1908–09) 270
- reaction to Strindberg's proposal of marriage (1909) 276–77
- reaction to Strindberg's death (1912) 279, 290
- later life (1912–63) 279–81
- suicide attempt (c. 1913) 279
- publishes *August Strindberg i Blå Tornet* (1921) 279–80
- marriage to Axel Christiansen Lund (1928) 280
- birth of her daughter Suzanne (1929) 280
- divorce from Axel Christiansen Lund (1929) 280
- death by suicide (1963) 281

Falkner, Frans 263–64, 290
Falkner, Meta 263–64, 267–68
Falkner, Stella 268, 278, 279
Father, The (Strindberg) 13–14, 77, 88, 93– 94, 97, 98–99, 106, 115–21, 130, 154, 157, 158, 176, 197, 244, 269

Fem år med Strindberg [*Five Years With Strindberg*] (Falck) 241
Finsk Tidskrift 63
First Violin, The (Wied) 229
First Warning, The (Strindberg) 12, 39, 99–100
Flygare, Anna 239, 265–72
Flying Dutchman, The (Strindberg) 218
Foerder, Martha 148, 150, 180
Folketeatret, Copenhagen 94
Folkets Hus Teatern, Stockholm 269
Forstén, Ina 22, 24, 28–32, 51, 79
Fortaellinger [*Stories*] (Bjørnson) 213
Fortnightly Review 157
Franz Josef, Emperor 133
Fredrika Bremer Association 84
Freie Bühne, Berlin 130
French School, Stockholm 264
Fröding, Hugo 223
Fröding, Märtha (née Philp) 197, 223
Fröhlich, Caroline 90
Fröhlich, Edma 90
Fröhlich, Lorenz 27
Fru Marianne (Benedictsson) 103
Fugger-Babenhausen, Prince 186

Garbo, Greta 237
Gardie, Sophia De La 57
Gate Theatre, London 11–12
Gauguin, Paul 178
Gauntlet, A (Bjørnson) 76
Gazetten 43
Geijerstam, Gustaf af 83, 92, 98, 197
Getting Married (Strindberg) 13, 65, 76–81, 84–90, 94, 102, 225
Ghost Sonata, The (Strindberg) 14, 168, 237, 265
Ghosts (Ibsen) 158
Giacosa, Guiseppe 219
Goethe, Johann Wolfgang von 219
Gorky, Maxim 213
Grandison, Emil 203
Great Highway, The (Strindberg) 12, 61, 275–77, 285

Grein, J T 157–58, 161, 165
Gretor, Willy 174–75, 177
Grieg, Edvard 192, 213
Gringoire (Banville) 195
'Growing Castle, The' [*A Dream Play*] (Strindberg) 210
Guillemot and Weilandt 38, 48, 53
Gustav III, King 57, 81
Gustav IV, King 81
Gustav V, King 291
Gustav Adolf, Crown Prince 246
Gustav Vasa (Strindberg) 196, 204
Gustav Vasa, King 58

Hallin Gallery, Stockholm 278
Hallström, Per 224
Handelstidningen 178, 229
Hansson, Ola 103, 130
Harriet, en skiss [*Harriet, a Sketch*] (Molander) 243
He and She (Strindberg) 15, 30–31, 33–37, 96
Hebbel Theater, Berlin 230
Hedberg, Frans 23, 54
Hedberg, Tor 203, 242
Hedda Gabler (Ibsen) 88
Hedén, Erik 30
Hedlund, Torsten 178, 179
Hedman, Märtha 109
Heidenstam, Verner von 90, 91, 99
Heimat (Sudermann) 131–33
Heinemann, William 157
Henry VII (Shakespeare) 290
Hillberg, Emil 93
Hinduism 254
Hitler, Adolf 185
Hofmannsthal, Hugo von 231, 242–43
Holstein-Gottorp dynasty 81
Holten, Sophie 90–91, 108
'Homme à venir, L'' (Strindberg) 169
Hugo, Victor 52
Huysmans, Joris-Karl 148

Ibsen, Henrik 30, 51, 54, 55, 60, 61, 64–65, 67, 85, 88–89, 99, 116, 131, 158, 194, 195, 219, 231, 242, 287

Ibsen, Suzannah 131
Ibsen, Sigurd 131
In de Bétou, Elisabeth ('Betty') Charlotta 26–28, 37–38, 40–43, 50
In de Bétou, Mathilde 27, 50, 54
In de Bétou, Rosa Amalia 51
In de Bétou, Sofia 33–40, 49, 155
Independent Theatre, London 157, 158
Inferno (Strindberg) 16, 112, 168, 177, 181
In Rome (Strindberg) 23
Intiman (Intimate Theatre), Stockholm 194, 238–39, 243, 264–72, 276–77, 278, 290
Inutiles, Les – see *Useless Ones, The*
'Island of the Blissfully Happy, The' (Strindberg) 79
'It Is Not Enough' (Strindberg) 85–87

Jacobsen, Harry 39, 68
Jacobsen, J. P. 88
Jane Eyre (Charlotte Brontë, adapt. Birch-Pfeiffer) 50, 63
Janzon, Pelle 56, 68
'Jealousy' (Munch) 147
Jerome, Jerome K 219
Johannes (Sudermann) 231
John, Augustus 186
Josephson, Ludvig 56, 58, 61, 74, 79, 82, 94
Juel, Dagny 146–51, 154, 180, 186, 206

Karl XII (Strindberg) 207, 219, 228, 250
Karl XIV Johan, King 82
Karl XV, King 23
Karolinska Institutet, Stockholm 93, 98
Keys of Heaven, The (Strindberg) 61
Kielland, Alexander 56, 213
Kierkegaard, Søren 254
Kipling, Rudyard 213
Kjellberg, Frithiof 68
Kjellberg, Isidor 74
Kjellgren, Alrik 265, 269, 270–72, 278, 280
Konserthusteatern, Stockholm 250
Koppel, Henrik 225
Kossak, Ewa 147

Kristiania Theater 192, 193
Kristina (Strindberg) 192, 210, 211, 212, 213, 231, 239, 249–53
Krogh, Christian 88, 131
Lady from the Sea, The (Ibsen) 231
Lady Julie (Strindberg) 13–14, 93, 103–04, 121–23, 130, 153, 170, 195, 196, 233, 238, 264
Lagercrantz, Olof 24
Lagerlöf, Selma, 287
Lange, Algot 24, 30, 32, 51
Langen, Albert 175–76
Larsen, Nathalie 103–04
Larsson, Carl 55–56, 71, 73
Larsson, Karin 73
Leffler-Edgren, Anne Charlotte 76
Legends (Strindberg) 181
Lehman, Anne-Marie 192
Lenbach, Franz 139
Leroy, Louis 49
Lessingtheater, Berlin 155
Leväinen, Olga 111
Lewis, Wyndham 186
Lidforss, Bengt 150, 155
Lie, Jonas 13, 74
Lindberg, August 54
Linder, Sten 88
Littmansson, Leopold 170–71, 219–20
Ljus förlag 225
Looström, Claes 73
Loraine, Robert 244
Lorensbergsteatern, Gothenburg 250, 258
Lubitsch, Ernst 186
Lucky Per's Journey (Strindberg) 14, 61–62, 74, 82, 110, 254
Lugné-Poë, Aurélien 195
Lund, Axel Christiansen 280
Lund, Suzanne 280
Lundegård, Axel 85
Lundgren, Ernst 53
Luther, Martin 58

Macbeth (Shakespeare) 228
MacCarthy, Justin Huntley 157

Madame Bovary (Flaubert) 30
Madman's Defence, A (Strindberg) 16, 21–22, 31, 33, 36, 45, 49, 53, 71, 91, 97–98, 102, 105, 108, 112–13, 151, 153, 157, 166, 168, 175, 176, 181, 231, 236
Madox Ford, Ford 186
Maeterlinck, Maurice 213, 231, 270, 287
Manet, Édouard 43
Mansfield, Katherine 186
Marauders (Strindberg) 93
Marholm, Laura 130
Maria Stuart, (Schiller) 228
Marriage With Genius (Uhl) 15, 129, 132, 139, 140, 150–51, 153, 156, 157, 166, 169, 174, 175
Master Builder, The (Ibsen) 55, 193–94, 231
Master Olof (Strindberg) 14, 29, 42, 56, 58–60, 65, 67, 93, 96, 98, 106, 239
Maupassant, Guy de 21
Meier-Graefe, Julius 147
Mellin, Constance 30, 79, 105
Mendelssohn, Felix 213, 241
Midsummer Night's Dream, A (Shakespeare) 196, 231
Min Strindbergsbok [*My Book About Strindberg*] (Paul) 16, 129, 133–34, 138, 145, 147
Miss Hobbs (Jerome) 219
'Moi' (Strindberg) 169
Molander, Olof 243, 246–47, 258
Möller, Augusta 41
Möller, Carl 205
Möller, Dagmar (née Bosse) 192–93, 195, 196, 205, 207, 210, 216, 280
Monde poétique, Le 74
Monet, Claude 43
'Mongolian Song, A' (Strindberg) 246
Morgenbladet 56
Moser, Gustav von 219
Motherly Love (Strindberg) 12
Much Ado About Nothing (Shakespeare) 219
Munch, Edvard 131, 132, 146–48, 151, 180
Musset, Alfred de 21
Myrdal, Jan 175

Napoleon 82
National Restaurant, Stockholm 237
Nationalteatret, Kristiania 195
Natur & Kultur 245
Neuman-Hofer, Otto 135
New Blue Book, A (Strindberg) 11, 17
New Kingdom, The (Strindberg) 67, 81
Nielsen, Asta 186
Nietzsche, Friedrich Wilhelm 97, 170
Nju (Dymov) 243
Nordiska Museet, Stockholm 194
Nordström, Karl 91, 287
Norstedts förlag 281
Norwegian Women's Association 89
Nya Dagligt Allehanda 249
Nya Teatern, Helsingfors 63, 102
Nya Teatern, Stockholm 56, 58, 60, 61, 82, 93, 94, 106, 205
Nyblom, Helena 76
Nye Teatret, Det, Oslo 247
Ny Illustrerad Tidning 60, 71
Nyström, Gunnar 289

Occult Diary, The (Strindberg) 16, 179, 191, 197–98, 201, 211, 221, 223, 224–26, 232, 235, 238, 240–41
Ollen, Gunnar 270
Olsson, Ida Charlotta 24
Once Upon a Time (Drachmann) 194
Open Letters to the Intimate Theatre (Strindberg) 270
Ord & Bild 80
Oscar II, King 28, 67, 81, 192, 238
Österling, Hans 99
Outlaw, The (Strindberg) 23
Overboard (Przybyszewski) 150

Palme, August 196, 247
Pan 148
Pariah (Strindberg) 12, 103, 104
Paul, Adolf 16, 129, 131, 133–34, 138, 142, 145, 147, 151, 155, 158, 161, 243
Peer Gynt (Ibsen) 61, 194
Pelican, The (Strindberg) 231, 238, 264
Pelléas and Mélisande (Maeterlinck) 231

People of Hemsö, The (Strindberg) 97–98, 154
Personne, John 97
Personne, Nils 195, 247
Peterson-Berger, Wilhelm 213
Pettersson, Emilia 46
Pfaeffinger, Rosa 174, 175
Philp, Anna von – *see* Strindberg, Anna
Philp, Henry von 110, 223, 232, 285, 289
Philp, Hugo von 51, 197, 220, 223, 231
Philp, Märtha von – *see* Fröding, Märtha
Pillars of Society, The (Ibsen) 51
Playing With Fire (Strindberg) 39, 99, 101, 155, 237
Politiken 90
Pound, Ezra 186
Protestantism 168
Przybyszewski, Stanislaw ('Staczu') 131, 147–50, 180

'Qu'est-ce-que le moderne?' (Strindberg) 169

Ranft, Albert 110, 205, 230, 231, 239, 240, 277–78
Rasmussen, Rudolf 195
Red Room, The (Strindberg) 23, 52, 54, 60, 80, 88, 98, 287
Reinhardt, Max 258, 265
Reischl, Marie 183
Residenztheater, Berlin 131
Revue Blanche 180
'Reward of Virtue, The' (Strindberg) 81
Riksteatern, Stockholm 250
Romeo and Juliet (Shakespeare) 193, 224, 231
Rönnblad Provincial Touring Company 110, 232
Roofing Party, The (Strindberg) 223, 232
Rops, Félicien 148
Rousseau, Jean-Jacques 84
Royal College of Music, Stockholm 192
Royal Dramatic Theatre, Stockholm – *see* Dramaten
Royal Library, Stockholm 22–24, 40, 42, 48, 50, 54, 95

Royal Opera House, Stockholm 24, 47
Royal Palace, Copenhagen 32
Ruhe, Algot 279
Ryding, Alan 250, 269

Saga of the Folkungs, The (Strindberg) 204
'Sailing' (Strindberg) 25
St Birgitta 56
St Louis Hospital, Paris 178
Salome (Wilde) 231
Saltoft, Eduard 264
Samum (Strindberg) 103, 106, 219, 250
Sardou, Victorien 51
Scapegoat, The (Strindberg) 232
Schering, Emil 207, 213, 226, 280
Schiller, Friedrich von 228, 242
Schleich, Carl Ludwig 162
Schlittgen, Hermann 132
Schönthan, Franz von 219
Schopenhauer, Arthur 84
Schumann, Robert 180, 213
'Second Night' (Strindberg) 73, 75
Secret of the Guild, The (Strindberg) 55, 60
Selander, Nils 68
Seligmann, Joseph 54
Shakespeare, William 228, 242, 290
Shaw, George Bernard 61, 200
Sibelius, Jean 232
Sienkiewitz, Henryk 287
Sir Bengt's Wife (Strindberg) 14, 64–67, 93, 238, 250, 265
Sisley, Alfred 43
Skandinavisches Theater, Berlin 244
Sleepless Nights on Waking Days (Strindberg) 75
Smirnoff, Vladimir 111
'Snöstorm över havet' ['Snowstorm over the Sea'] (Strindberg) 195
Social-Demokraten 30, 104
Söderberg, Hjalmar 191
Söderblom, Nathan 288, 291
Söderman, Sven 270
Sofia, Queen 13, 81, 84
Son of a Servant, The (Strindberg) 24, 46, 93, 94, 96
Sons of the Earth, The (Przybyszewski) 148

Sorbonne 178
Spencer, Herbert 84
Sphinx, La (Dumas) 54
Staaff, Pehr 71, 83
Stadsteatern, Stockholm 258
Ståhle-Sjönell, Barbro 223
Stenhammar, Wilhelm 258
Stiller, Mauritz 237, 258
Stockholms Aftonpost 23
Stora Teatern, Gothenburg 227
Storm – see *Thunder in the Air*
Strindberg, Anna 37, 42, 46–48, 51, 68, 110, 196, 220, 224, 231
Strindberg, Anne-Marie 184, 213, 214, 216, 217, 220, 221–30, 235, 237, 242–43, 268, 275, 287, 289, 290
Strindberg, August
 – early life 22–24, 46–48
 – first meeting with Siri von Essen (1875) 22
 – development of his relationship with Siri von Essen (1875–76) 33–51
 – marriage to Siri von Essen (1877) 51
 – birth and death of his daughter Kerstin (1878) 52
 – bankruptcy (1879) 53–54
 – birth of his daughter Karin (1880) 55
 – birth of his daughter Greta (1881) 58
 – first visit to Grèz-sur-Loing (1883) 71–73
 – birth of his son, Hans (1884) 76
 – on trial for blasphemy (1884) 81–83
 – divorce from Siri von Essen (1892) 108
 – first meeting with Frida Uhl (1893) 131–32
 – affair with Dagny Juel (1893) 146–51
 – marriage to Frida Uhl (1893) 155–56
 – first separation from Frida Uhl 161–65
 – birth of his daughter Kerstin (1894) 169

– second separation from Frida Uhl 171–74
– annulment of marriage to Frida Uhl (1897) 181
– first meeting with Harriet Bosse (1900) 196
– proposal of marriage and engagement to Harriet Bosse (1901) 201–02
– marriage to Harriet Bosse (1901) 205
– first separation from Harriet Bosse (1901) 208–12
– birth of his daughter Anne-Marie (1902) 216
– second separation from Harriet Bosse (1902) 217–20
– divorce from Harriet Bosse (1904) 224
– develops plans with August Falck for an 'intimate theatre' (1906–07) 233, 235
– opening of Intiman (1907) 238
– reaction to Harriet Bosse's marriage to Gunnar Wingård (1908) 239–42
– first meeting with Fanny Falkner (1908) 265
– proposal of marriage to Fanny Falkner (1909) 276
– reaction to Siri von Essen's death (1912) 289
– death (1912) 290
– reputation as a misogynist 11, 30, 84, 97, 121, 134, 135, 139, 151, 197, 245

Strindberg, Axel 46, 47, 76, 90, 93, 96, 98, 205, 211, 241, 247, 286–87
Strindberg, Carl Oscar 46–48
Strindberg, Elisabeth 46, 47, 67, 200, 225, 267
Strindberg, Erik 112
Strindberg, Friedrich 183
Strindberg, Greta 58, 61, 63, 67, 94, 97, 105, 106, 110–13, 184, 200, 205, 224, 232, 285, 287, 289, 290
Strindberg, Hans ('Putte') 76, 79, 82, 91, 105, 111–12, 167, 285, 289, 290

Strindberg, Karin 55, 78, 94–96, 97, 98, 105, 106, 107–08, 110–13, 159, 205, 285, 289, 290
Strindberg, Kerstin (b. 1878) 52, 111
Strindberg, Kerstin (b. 1894) 169, 174, 175, 178–85, 220, 285
Strindberg, Ludvig 47
Strindberg, Nora 46, 51, 68
Strindberg, Oscar 46, 47–48, 110, 159
Strindberg, Olle 46, 274
Strindberg, Ulrika Eleonora 46
Strindberg och hans första hustru [*Strindberg and His First Wife*] (Jacobsen) 68
Strindberg's Letters to Harriet Bosse 196, 202, 213, 245, 290
Strindbergs systrar berättar om barndomshemmet och om bror August Strindberg [*Strindberg's Sisters Reminiscing*] (Philp & Hartzell) 51, 68
Ström, Fredrik 278
Stronger, The (Strindberg) 11, 103, 104
Sudermann, Hermann 131–33, 231
Sulzbach, Ernst 185
Sunday Times 12
SVEA 71
Svennberg, Tore 246
Svenska Dagbladet 149, 206, 269
Svenska Teatern, Helsingfors 24, 56, 94, 106, 110, 224, 250
Svenska Teatern, Stockholm 196, 205, 230, 231–32, 238, 239, 240, 242, 250, 253, 277
Swanwhite (Strindberg) 192, 203, 213, 231, 232, 240, 270–71, 273–74
Swedenborg, Emanuel 168, 254, 278
Swedish Academy 287, 291
Swedish Church, Paris 178, 288
Swedish Destinies and Adventures (Strindberg) 67, 73, 79
Swedish Life Guards [Svea Liv Garde] 28, 35
Swedish National Museum 131
Swedish People, The (Strindberg) 56–57

Taine, Hippolyte, 56
Tavaststjerna, Karl August 131

Théâtre de l'Oeuvre, Paris 170, 176, 195
Théâtre Libre, Paris 103, 195
theosophy 178
Thief, The (Bernstein) 242
Thunder in the Air (Strindberg) 12, 235–37, 249, 250
Tiden 69, 83
Time Out 12
Titanic, SS 288
Tivoliteatret, Kristiania 193
To Damascus (Strindberg) 61, 129, 181, 196–99, 210, 204, 209, 224, 231, 246, 250, 254
Tolstoy, Leo 286, 287
'Trefaldighetsnatten' ['On the Eve of Trinity Sunday'] (Strindberg) 214–15
Trésor des humbles, Le (Maeterlinck) 213
Türke, Gustav 130–31

Uhl, Friedrich 109, 133, 142, 154, 163, 164, 167
Uhl, Frida 12–13, 15, 16, 58, 108, 113, 191, 196, 198, 199, 200, 206, 209, 216, 217, 245, 263, 289
 – early life 133
 – first meeting with Strindberg (1893) 131–32
 – reaction to Strindberg's proposal of marriage (1893) 141–42
 – marriage to Strindberg (1893) 155–56
 – reaction to reading *A Madman's Defence* 157-58
 – birth of her daughter, Kerstin (1894) 169
 – first meeting with Frank Wedekind (1894) 175
 – annulment of her marriage to Strindberg (1897) 181
 – birth of her son, Friedrich (1897) 183
 – autobiography, *Marriage With Genius* 15, 129, 132, 140, 150–51, 153, 157–58, 169, 174, 175, 186
 – later life (1897–1943) 181–87
 – death (1943) 187

Uhl, Marie (Frida's mother) 129, 154, 163, 164, 165, 167–70, 181, 182, 198, 199, 216, 285
Uhl, Marie (Frida's sister) – *see* Weyr, Marie
Uppsala University 22, 23
Useless Ones, The [*Les Inutiles*] (Cadol) 54

Vallgren, Ville 71
Vasateatern, Stockholm 110
Vecko-Journalen 197
Venetian Comedy, A (Hallström) 224
Virgin Bride, The see *Crown Bride, The*
Vivisections (Strindberg) 169

Wall, Rudolf 31, 83
War in Peace (Moser & Schönthan) 219, 224
Warburg, Karl 64
Wedekind, Donald 183
Wedekind, Frank 175, 180, 181, 183
Welinder, Hélène 79–80, 83
Wettergren, Erik 246
Wetzer, Conny 224, 231
Weyr, Marie (née Uhl) 133, 154, 155, 163, 164, 166, 167
Whitlock, Anna 76
Wied, Gustav 229
Wiener Abendpost 133, 174
Wiener Zeitung 133, 165, 174
Wieselgren, Oscar 246–47
Wild Duck, The (Ibsen) 88, 219, 224
Wild Strawberries (Bergman) 255
Wilde, Oscar 231
Wilson, Robert 258
Wingård, Bo 242–43
Wingård, Gunnar 224, 231, 232, 235, 238–42, 245, 249, 263, 275, 279
'Woman's Rights' (Strindberg) 77–79
Wrangel, Baron Carl Gustaf 15, 28–43, 45, 49, 50–51, 53, 79, 155, 242
Wrangel, Sigrid 28, 30, 39, 42–43, 45, 50, 53, 79

Zola, Émile 213, 286